SHADOW OF DEATH

To Tom

SHADOW OF DEATH
A NOVEL

PATRICIA GUSSIN

Best Wishes!!
Pat Gussin

Oceanview Publishing

IPSWICH, MASSACHUSETTS

ISBN 1-933515-00-7

Published in the United States by Oceanview Publishing,
Ipswich, Massachusetts
Visit our Web site at www.oceanviewpub.com
Distributed by Midpoint Trade Books
www.midpointtrade.com

10 9 8 7 6 5 4 3 2 1

PRINTED IN THE UNITED STATES OF AMERICA

This book is for Bob

ACKNOWLEDGMENTS

There are many to thank for their support and encouragement as this book progressed, revision through revision, to reality. In the beginning, my friend, Philip Spitzer, gave me that critical spark of hope, and he introduced me to Stacey Donovan, my earliest editor. Along the way, I was privileged to have author Barbara Parker provide guidance and critical advice. Thank you Philip, Stacey, and Barbara.

I am also greatly indebted to my reading group who made such crucial suggestions: Nancy Ashley, Mary Ann Bedics, Mary Bole, Scott Bole, Grace Gillaspy, Pat Matone, and Mike Rohovsky. Thanks to Diana, Joel, and Jessica Katz, who took the time to reacquaint me with Detroit; to Susan Hayes, who turned a manuscript into a book; to Susan Kendrick of Write to Your Market for her expertise and enthusiasm; to Debra Stowell of Circle Books, St. Armands Circle, for her overall support; and an ultra special thanks to Sue Greger, President of Oceanview Publishing, who made it all happen.

Mostly thanks to my fabulous husband Bob Gussin, medical scientist, fellow writer, and reviewer extraordinaire. From first to last draft, he provided inspiration and motivation. Simply said, he kept me going and for that and everything else, I thank my lucky stars.

AUTHOR'S NOTE

At 3:30 on a muggy Sunday morning, July 23, 1967, Detroit erupted into the worst outbreak of urban rebellion in U.S. history as gangs swarmed into the streets at Twelfth and Clairmont, to loot and burn. By 9:00 Sunday morning, anarchy reigned. Armed police stood by and let the destruction spread completely out of control.

The fifth largest city in America was on fire. Governor Romney declared a state of emergency, but the inferno was not contained until President Johnson called out the Army. Three thousand armed men converged on the West side; hundreds of Vietnam-trained paratroopers on the East side; city and state police and National guardsmen patrolled in military tanks.

After five days the city came under tentative control. Forty-three dead; hundreds wounded; thousands arrested; thousands homeless; millions of dollars of property destroyed.

The cover of *Life* magazine screamed, "Negroes Revolt," but the riots were less about race than the vicious cycle of poverty and hopelessness. Color television sets became more significant than skin pigmentation as looters burned and thieved in integrated bands.

During the five days of the riots, Detroit General Hospital treated more than eighty percent of the victims. At a time rife with incriminations, the medical staff and the faculty of Wayne State Medical School received nothing but accolades. Hundreds of physicians and professors remained in service around the clock in the face of danger and tension and received unanimous praise from the public, including those wounded and angry as they passed through the hospital doors.

Yea, though I walk through the valley

of the shadow of death . . .

—Psalm 23

PROLOGUE

DETROIT, JUNE 1971

Emotionally drained, too numb for more tears, the young woman sagged in the battered lawn chair, the lone piece of furniture except for the crib positioned diagonally across the room. The lingering dusk of early June threw darkening shadows, but the woman made no move to turn on the bare overhead light. Cradling her head in her hands, she sat slumped, still wearing the black crepe dress that she'd worn to the services. She'd known it was too short, the scooped neck cut too low for a funeral, but there had been no time to shop for bereavement apparel.

The woman was alone, but for the baby sound asleep in the portable crib. Through the open screen door, the lone voice of a mother calling her children intruded into the silence as she faced her reality: death, a death she'd never be able to reconcile as long as she lived. The cloying scent of the flowers, banks of them, arranged in a sweeping semi-circle around the coffin still permeated her nostrils, making every breath a sickening throb. No matter how tightly she squeezed her eyes shut, she could see him lying in front of her, close enough to touch. If only his chest were to rise up and down with each respiration as in peaceful sleep. Eyes closed quite naturally. Hair combed just so. Navy blue pin-stripe suit, cut and pressed to perfection. White shirt, midnight blue patterned tie. But the plastic sheen on his face and lips pressed too close together, penetrated through her grief, forcing her to face reality.

How had it come to this, she asked herself over and over? Cowardice and selfish deceptions? Now it was too late. Tomorrow she would leave this place forever.

The baby whimpered, and the woman slowly lifted her head. With a heavy heart, she rose to go to her child. Please, God, protect this innocent child. Don't let my baby pay the price for my mistakes.

PART ONE

CHAPTER ONE

SEPTEMBER 1967, FOUR YEARS EARLIER, DETROIT

Laura Nelson let out a long breath, clutched her black bag, and headed toward the men's surgical ward. She didn't know that walking into that room would impact her life forever.

"I'm so nervous," she whispered to her fellow med student, Susan Reynolds.

"They are why we're here. Right? Real live patients." With a thumbs up, Susan crossed the hall to her assigned ward.

Laura and Susan were first year students at University Medical School and best friends. So far all their courses had been in the classroom or labs: anatomy, physiology, biochemistry, histology. But today they were in City Hospital to do a history and physical examination on their very first patient.

Laura was apprehensive, but also very excited. Until today, she had stepped inside a hospital only twice, for the birth of her two children — cheery semi-private rooms, happy memories. Now she stared into the men's ward at City Hospital, aghast at the medieval scene. Narrow cots lined all four walls and patients were crammed so close together they practically touched. A disinfectant odor mixed with foul human smells twisted her stomach. Groans, droning equipment, clanking bed rails, made her wonder how she'd be able to concentrate on her list of questions.

Squinting to locate her patient among a sea of mostly black faces, she realized that all eyes were on her as one of the patients let out a whistle. She blushed self-consciously. Ignore them, she said to herself. Holding her head high, Laura moved to the foot of bed 5 where her eyes settled on an emaciated young male with grayish dark skin. Distracted by a hissing noise coming from a machine connected to a hole in the boy's neck, she stood for a moment, gaping at it. The respirator synchronized the rise and fall of the chest with the wheezy sound. Other than that, her patient's body was perfectly still. Was he unconscious or just sleeping?

Unzipping her instrument bag, she considered how she'd proceed if her patient was unconscious. Her instructions were to take a complete medical history, to examine the patient, and report back for a de-brief session in one hour. As she reached to awaken the boy, a plump woman, slumped in the metal chair by the head of the bed, stirred.

"Excuse me, Ma'am."

The woman jerked awake, her rough hands flying to straighten her navy polyester skirt. She looked up at Laura, one hand covering her throat.

"I'm Laura Nelson, one of the student doctors here." Laura reached for the notes in the pocket of her white coat. "Are you with this patient? Anthony Diggs?"

"Yes. He's my baby."

"What is his medical problem?" Laura asked, staring at a bulky dressing on the left side of the boy's head.

"They shot him. In the head. The police. The riots. They say he was looting, but there's no way he would do that." The woman's voice dwindled. "Look what they did to him." The mother leaned over and placed a worn hand gently on her son's cheek.

Laura hesitated a moment and swallowed. "What happened then?"

"Your people tried to take out the bullet," the mother responded, shaking her head back and forth. "Brain surgery. Major brain surgery. Isn't that on his chart?"

Laura glanced at the chart at the end of the bed, four inches of nearly illegible notes bulging out of the cardboard binder. She was only here to practice taking a history and to do a physical examination. She wasn't supposed to read the chart. "Of course," she improvised, rather than trying to explain that she was a mere first year student, that she hadn't yet touched her first patient.

"Anthony is a good boy," the woman whispered, rocking forward. "He's going off to college next month, Michigan State University."

Laura had to lean forward to hear the woman over the din of the other patients. As she did, she felt a tug at the hem of her white coat. Turning, she gasped as a scrawny man in the next bed looked her up and down with beady, lecherous eyes and a grin exposing broken teeth. Both of his legs and one arm were shackled to the bed. A prisoner! "Come work on me, pretty lady," he sneered.

Not knowing what to do, Laura ignored him, turning back to her patient's mother. "I'm sorry, Mrs. Diggs," she said. "What were you saying?"

"Diggs was my maiden name. I'm Lucy Jones," the woman corrected. "Anthony graduated from Cass Prep with a scholarship. Now they say he will never wake up." The woman looked at her with pleading brown eyes. "Can't you help him?"

Laura, forgetting that she should act like a doctor, stood at the patient's side and stroked the woman's rough hand, not daring to think of anything this horrible ever happening to her boys. Then she glanced across to the other two medical students assigned to the ward. Both male, both looking very competent, strategically moving stethoscopes across their patients' chests. Regaining her composure, she reached into her black bag and pulled out her instruments.

"Why does his throat get clogged up?" Lucy asked softly. "The nurses are always trying to fix it."

"I don't really know, I'm only a medical student," Laura said. "I have to ask you more questions, then examine your son."

On her way from the medical school to the hospital, Laura had imagined a "normal" patient, whatever that was. Not the thin chest, the bony ribs, the gurgling sounds that filled her stethoscope as she tried to hear the heartbeat. No way could she have imagined so many tubes coming out of one body: one connecting the crusted hole in his throat to the respirator; one in his nose draining greenish stomach juices; an intravenous line in his left wrist; another tube dripping amber liquid into his right arm. Laura gawked at the tube coming out of his penis, draining rusty-orange urine. According to her notes, she was supposed to check the whole body, but she decided against turning the body over. However, she did notice beet-red sores invading his dark brown skin, oozing pus onto the loose gauze dressing on his buttocks. That must be the putrid smell that almost made her gag. Get used to it, she thought, as she performed the series of tests she'd scribbled on a cheat sheet she'd stuffed into her lab coat pocket.

When she was done, she hastily covered Anthony's body with the white sheet and light blanket. It was after five o'clock. She was due back in the surgical conference room. After packing up her otoscope, stethoscope, reflex hammer, and jotting down a few notes, she opened the curtain and turned to the boy's mother.

"Thank you Mrs. Jones," she said, impulsively leaning over to give the poor woman a parting hug, murmuring words she hoped were reassuring.

"But Doctor, tell me—"

Laura left the bedside without further comment, unable to offer any hope, mentally rehearsing what she'd report about this patient.

Chief Complaint: Gunshot wound to the head.

History of Present Illness: She had nothing more from the mother, but the patient was obviously in a coma; that's all she could tell without reading the chart, which they were not supposed to do.

Review of Systems: What could she say? It wasn't like she could ask the patient?

Past Medical History: No health problems; didn't smoke; didn't use drugs or alcohol.

Family History: Diabetes on the mother's side; mother knew nothing of the boy's biological father's medical history.

Social History: One half-brother; four half-sisters; mother widowed, employed, but worried about hospital bills.

How to present all this in a clear, succinct way? This was Laura's focus as she exited the ward, scanning her notes. She hadn't seen the young man barging toward her until he brushed so close that she dropped her notebook. She jerked to avoid him, noticing his muscular build, such a contrast to her unfortunate patient, and his skin was several shades lighter. He was dressed all in black, including a baseball cap that obscured his face.

How rude, Laura thought. Or maybe it was her fault for blocking the entrance. Whatever, she had to concentrate on her report.

She took a couple of steps forward into the hall before coming to an abrupt halt when she heard shouting behind her.

"Mama, what you doin' talkin' to that yellow-hair bitch?" The voice was menacing, rising above the clamor.

With a start she realized that the "yellow-hair bitch" must be her. She'd been the only woman with blonde hair on the ward. So what was his problem? Could he be the half-brother Mrs. Jones reported in the family history?

Curious now, she inched back to the doorway of the ward. Sure enough, the angry kid hovered over Mrs. Jones, shaking a finger in her face. "Told you 'bout the one fucked up Anthony in the 'mergency room!"

What was that all about? She'd never been in an emergency room. That wouldn't be until her third year of med school.

"Johnny, quiet down. Please." She strained to hear the woman's response.

"What was that bitch doin' here?" he shouted as Laura turned to go.

"Stop it, Johnny. You're shouting. They'll throw you out of here."

"Who was she?" he demanded.

"She's just a student doctor, honey. I could tell she was trying to help."

What more could she overhear? Nothing, she decided. She'd be late if she didn't get going.

A few minutes past six Laura Nelson left the surgical conference room with Susan. Neither noticed the stocky young man lurking in the corridor by the stairwell.

"I got an alcoholic with massive esophageal bleeding," Susan explained. "Sure wish I could go to the library to look up cirrhosis of the liver, but Dad's picking me up. I told him to meet me in front of the hospital rather than the basic science building where we usually go out."

Anxious to tell Susan about her patient, Laura walked with her to the hospital exit. "I'd love to research head injuries," she commiserated, "but I need to get home to the kids." She missed her children, even more, after the time spent with the poor Diggs boy's mother. Before school had begun, Laura promised herself that her highest priority, whenever possible, would be to spend the hour before bedtime with her own boys, three-year-old Mikey and three-month-old Kevin. Tonight, she needed that hour with them. Yet she had to present her patient case in the morning too.

Worried about this conflict so inherent in her career choice, she said good night to Susan, waving as she got into a dark blue sedan under the glare of spotlights. Rather than turning back to leave by the basic science building where the school provided escorts to the student parking lot, Laura decided on an alternate route, directly out the main hospital exit, cutting through the doctor's parking lot, and walking the two blocks to her car.

Facing the block of deserted, burned-out tenements, she took a deep breath. Yes, she could still smell the smoldering ash. Or was it her imagination? The fires no longer burned, but there was a curfew. Detroit, still a tinderbox of hostility and tangible fear. With an involuntary shudder, Laura sped up her pace and tried to ignore the shifting shadows that seemed to follow her. She thought of her parents, how shocked they'd be if they knew what this neighborhood was like. Then there was Steve, her husband, who knew full well and who'd insisted that she carry a gun, which she did, but only to placate him. Where Steve grew up in northern Michigan, guns and knives and hunting were second nature.

"Just one more block," she whispered aloud, slowing a bit to avoid the debris littering the sidewalk. Thankful there were no passing cars. Thankful that there was enough light. Anxious to get home to her kids. Anxious to tackle her patient report for tomorrow.

Suddenly she lurched. Her neck snapped backward, jerking her head. A violent, painful jerk. Then she saw the glint of steel in the grayness of threatening rain as a switchblade snapped open just inches from her throat. She tried to scream. Only small, muffled sounds came out as a strong hand clamped over her mouth.

Too stunned to react, Laura felt herself being dragged through a rubble-strewn lot. The powerful hand sealed her mouth and the other arm wrapped around her body, restraining both of her arms. Where was the knife? She didn't know.

A mugging. "Just take my purse," she tried to scream, but the man's grip tightened, choking off her breath. Frantic, she tried to kick, but only stumbled as her assailant pulled her more deeply into the shadows of the burned-out buildings.

She closed her eyes for a second, hoping against hope that this was a nightmare. She opened them when she hit hard on what looked to be the foundation of an abandoned house. She could see crumbling concrete strewn with broken bottles and patches of dirt. Landing on her side, she scrambled to all fours, but the hand on her mouth did not relent. The ground beneath her was jagged and pieces of broken glass cut into her legs. She tried to crawl, but one muscular arm flipped her over and pinned her down on her back. The other clamped even more tightly against her mouth. She tried to bite the big hand, but the pressure intensified and she couldn't breathe. "Take my purse," she screamed silently. "Take my purse and leave me alone!"

Trying to get some leverage, she groped at the uneven ground with her feet, but her assailant had dropped to his knees and dug an elbow into her chest, spreading her legs with his other hand. He shoved up her skirt and ripped off her pantyhose, shredding them.

"I'm being raped!" screamed through Laura's mind the instant she felt a strong hand against her thighs. No, this couldn't be happening to her! This was not a mugging. He was not interested in her purse. He was going to rape her. For the first time Laura realized he was making sounds. Hisses, grunts and some words. "Fuck." "Pay." "Brother." They made no sense. She knew she should pay attention, but he was digging his fingers into her abdomen, groping for her white cotton panties. She flailed and twisted, but he yanked them down past her knees in one effortless move. Then he lowered himself onto her. His face so close to hers that she could feel each guttural breath. His bulk crushed her chest, making it hard to breathe. For the first time, she looked at his eyes, recoiling at what she saw: brown saucers, smoldering with hate.

Pinned to the hard ground, helpless against this man's immense strength, barely able to breathe, she urged herself to think, but how could she as he pushed his body onto hers? He kept spewing obscenities, more focused now. The words "fuck" and "kill" and "cut your throat" interspersed between incomprehensible grunts.

"Kill"? He was going to kill her? She had to get away! Repeatedly, she tried to scream, but the hand crushed her lips and nose. His other hand worked his pants down and he thrust his stiff penis between her thighs.

Her struggle seemed useless, but she wouldn't surrender. She thought of her husband, her children. Was she going to die right here? Her purse strap, wound around her right shoulder, impaired any motion on that side. Pulling her left hand free, she reached up and ripped off her attacker's baseball cap. She tried to tear at his hair, but the head was shaved smooth. She tried to scratch at his eyes, but her nails were filed too short to make an impact. He managed to pin her arm. Something lumpy was digging into her back and she realized that the bump underneath her must be her purse. Desperate now, she felt like an animal, a trapped animal with the powerful instinct of survival taking hold.

He groaned as he shoved his penis inside her back and forth. The cadence of crude obscenities assaulted her. "Fuck you, bitch doctors. Slit your fuckin' throats." Laura realized with horror that her attacker was acting out of hate, not lust. Hate so deep that he wanted to hurt her as much as he could. What was next? Death? Was he going to kill her with that knife? Her heart beat so fast that she thought it would explode in her chest. She had two small children. She wasn't ready to die!

Then the threats stopped, replaced by repulsive grunts. Strangely, the brief lull in the verbal assault allowed Laura time to concentrate despite the thrusting crescendo inside of her. Again she closed her eyes tightly, opening them when he uttered a hideous, incomprehensible howl as if it came from the center of his soul. It was this terrifying, murderous sound that convinced Laura that he was really going to kill her.

She knew that her only hope was to attract attention, but his hand still silenced her. She couldn't free her right arm far enough to pry his hand off her mouth, her purse strap was in the way. How much longer did she have to live?

And then she remembered. Oh God, could she reach it fast enough? He had just exploded inside her. Already, she could feel his erection begin to subside as his body shifted slightly to her left, just enough to allow her to tug the purse from under her. Tensing her body to stop the violent trembling, Laura slipped her right hand into that special compartment of her purse. She found it. Cold and metallic.

Laura felt his body relax and the bulk of his weight collapsed against her, but he kept his hand clamped over her mouth. Hardly able to breathe, she knew she'd have to make her move before she either passed out or he slit her throat. At the instant that she felt her assailant's weight begin to ease off to her right side, Laura lifted the small revolver. Gripping it tightly, she withdrew it from her purse, and in a single motion she put it against the side of his smooth head and pulled the trigger. The noise of the shot was deafening.

There was a jolting motion and a sharp, burning odor. His

heavy frame stiffened. Then it fell against her, pinning her left arm. With all her might, she squirmed out from under him and rolled him completely off of her onto the rubble. There was a momentary quiver and then he lay still, slumped in a fetal position, legs curled. All she could do was lay beside him, panting from her efforts, afraid that her heart would explode, too scared to even look at the dark form next to her.

How long they lay side by side, she didn't know. But at some point she realized that it was getting dark. She felt a drop of rain. She couldn't just lay here next to him. Was he actually dead? Had she killed him? Just the thought that she might have killed him, made her heart stop. But he was going to kill her, cut her throat, isn't that what he said? She could hardly remember. And why hadn't someone come? Someone must have heard the gunshot?

Finally, she realized that she had to look at him. What if he was alive? She should go for help. She'd shot him for God's sake! Slowly rolling to her left, Laura saw it: the jagged hole in her assailant's head. The coppery taste in her own mouth made her gag as she stared at the congealed blood on the ground under the horrible head wound. Laura dragged herself up onto her knees. In the dusk, under storm clouds, it was difficult to tell how much blood pooled on the dark ground. He was dead, wasn't he? Vomit filled her throat, but she swallowed it down, forcing herself to tear her gaze from the body and to look around. Chest heaving, she gasped for breath, eyes hot with tears, ears still ringing from the gunshot.

All she could see were shadows of burned-out buildings. Nothing moving. Another drop of rain reminded her that she had to do something. Her eyes moved back to the crumpled form. A plain black T-shirt covered the upper body; black pants were bunched around his thighs. She looked again at his shaved head; the bullet hole was getting harder to make out and the dust behind her contact lenses made her squeeze her eyes shut. She couldn't bring herself to look at his face.

Had this really happened? The cuts on her legs, and the pulsating pain in her abdomen told her this was reality, not some horrible dream. Using one hand to steady herself, Laura tried to stand up. The ground felt wet and slimy beneath her. Then her stomach turned. Wrenching back her hand, she fell back to her knees. It wasn't raining that hard. She had planted her hand in bits of blood and brain. The horror struck her so profoundly, that she doubled over on her hands and knees and wretched.

Having no idea what she was going to do, Laura wiped her hand on her frayed pantyhose. Then she forced herself to her feet. Still wobbly, she stared at the body. She hadn't touched it, but she knew that it was lifeless, dead. Whimpering, she smoothed her skirt over her naked lower body and waited. Gunshots and firebombs were common in this neighborhood, but she was so close to the hospital someone should come soon. She heard the shrill wail of an approaching ambulance, a sense of relief flooding through her. But then it screeched to a halt nearby, probably at the emergency room entrance. She waited, hugging herself as clouds darkened the sky.

A few more sprinkles. Nobody came. She kept staring at the boy's body. Bizarre, terrifying words coursed through her: rape; murder. This could not have happened. She'd have to report it to the police. Endure the humiliation of a rape examination. Or, she glanced at the dead body, would they arrest her? Would she go to jail? For murder? The gun was unregistered, illegal. No, her mind screamed. I can't go to jail. My children, they're my life! With a shudder she realized that she still held the gun. It felt heinous in her hand and she started to put it down in the dirt, but hesitated. She couldn't just leave it, so she picked up her purse, deposited the weapon inside, and zipped it shut.

Laura gulped the humid air and tried to clear her head. A few more deep breaths and no more whimpering. She wondered if this could look like just one more random killing. She wished that it was, wished that she had just stumbled upon it. If she just got out of here right now, would all of this just go away? Maybe Steve would never have to find out. He was already conflicted about her being in med school in the first place.

She'd met Steve her first day on campus at the University of

Michigan. She a naïve freshmen, he a second year journalism major. They were married one year later. He'd switched majors and now had a Master's Degree in Social Work and a job in inner city Detroit, where they'd moved so she could enroll in the medical school there. Now they had two kids. If Steve found out she'd been raped, she didn't know what he'd do or think. He was idealistic, self-righteous. Would he think that she was tainted? Would he blame her? "Must not find out; must not find out," kept repeating itself in her mind as she stooped to pick up her panties and ruined pantyhose. She stuffed them in her purse. Then she inched away until she felt the concrete of the sidewalk. She felt a few more drops. A storm was coming. There was no one in sight.

CHAPTER TWO

Snake pulled the car over to the curb as Lucy Jones walked out through the heavy gray door of the hospital. He leaned over to the passenger window and called to her. "Mrs. Jones? I'm lookin' to pick up Johnny. He in there?"

"No, Ray," she said, taking out a tissue and dabbing her eyes. "My boy left a while ago. He's supposed to be home with the girls while I go to work."

"Hope Anthony's doin' better, Mrs. Jones," Snake called after her. He hated when the old folks called him "Ray."

"Where the fuck is Johnny?" he asked aloud as soon as Lucy walked away. They had plans tonight, the brothers from the Alexandrine neighborhood. Not real brothers, but closer. Five of them, four now with Anthony down. Lonnie Greenwood, three or four years older than the others, back from Nam with a bullet in the leg, still limping, growing an Afro. Willie Allen, a pudgy seventeen-year-old, who followed the others like a puppy dog. And he and Johnny, the ones gonna bust out of this shit hole. Gonna become famous. Johnny with his music. Him with his painting. Just like Diego Rivera who painted on the wall of the big art museum on Woodward. Snake figured he would be a famous painter too. Make a ton of money doing it. Just like Rivera.

Snake drove Lonnie's beat-up old Mustang in circles around the hospital to avoid the cops that hung around the doors. He'd borrowed the car, originally maroon but now mostly rusted, to take his mother, Leona, to rehab. Her back had gone out on her again, and social services was threatening to take away her benefits if she missed another physical therapy session. How the hell did they think she was gonna get there anyway? Hardly able to walk, no money for a bus, and no car. After dropping her off, Snake headed over to the hospital to pick up Johnny like they planned. Then they'd swing back to the neighborhood and get Lonnie and Willie for the night. He had to give it to Johnny, so good about checkin' in on Anthony every day. Somethin' must be wrong tonight since he was so late comin' out. It'd kill Johnny if that boy died — they'd been so tight. Johnny, nineteen, the same age as Snake, one year older than Anthony. So different, but real brothers lookin' out for each other. As smart as Anthony was, Johnny had always been the big brother — even though they'd had different fathers — fathers they had never seen.

Now Anthony was lying in that hospital and Snake knew that Johnny blamed himself and it was breakin' him up. No way Anthony woulda come out that night if Johnny hadn't dragged him out into the looting and sniping.

"Fuckin' city's on fire!" Johnny'd yelled that second night of the riot as he dumped his bag onto Anthony's bed, two toaster ovens, a transistor radio, a pile of screwdrivers, and a half-dozen flashlights. "All the loot you can carry. Crash in, take the shit, torch, and run. Like nothin' you've ever seen! It's our turn, man! Come on, let's get goin'!"

"People getting shot out there," Anthony told him.

"I tell you, the cops ain't doin' nothin', just standin' back," Johnny argued. "Only shootin' goin' on is us snipin' at the pigs. What's the matter with you?"

"Cops'll shoot back. You guys are fools if you think they won't."

"Hey, there's plenty stores burstin' with school clothes, Mr. College." Johnny knew his brother was desperate to look sharp when he stepped onto campus. Knew he didn't want to step out into the alien, preppy world lookin' like a welfare case. "I can show you where to get 'em. Man, I can get 'em for you."

Anthony shook his head. "You're into too much shit already," he'd said. "Now cool it, the girls are asleep."

Snake saw Johnny grab Anthony by the shoulder, using his strength to persuade him. Anthony, slim, his skin much darker, his hair neatly trimmed like a black poster model. Johnny, stocky, muscular, his head shaved, just like Snake's to make them look mean, rebellious.

"This a day like no other day in the history of the world, man. Don't you get that yet? It's time to shop for free. Let's go, the brothers are waitin' on us." Like Johnny knew he would, Anthony gave in and followed them out into the night. Snake could still feel the weight of the sawed-off shotgun he'd lifted earlier that night and carried wrapped in a rag.

What happened next Snake could see like it was on the big screen. Five of them — him, Johnny, Lonnie, Willie, and Anthony, heading up Alexandrine toward the fiery skies. Swaggering, ignoring the cop cars and fire equipment scattered along the route. Darting in and out of the shadows, cops everywhere, the occasional fire of a sniper's bullet, all blended into an excitement beyond Snake's belief.

The gang turned onto West Grand Boulevard where the streets were jammed with all kinds of people, white and black, men and women, old and young. They were carrying televisions and lamps and boxes and bags full of who knew what. As the group made their way along, entire streets were on fire. Smoke clogged the air and made them cough and wheeze. Cops and guards in uniforms, packing all kind of weapons, from M-2 rifles to short barrel shotguns, swarmed the streets, but they were standing down and just letting the folks loot and burn.

"Remember, just like we seen them other guys do it," Johnny'd yelled, taking charge. Earlier that evening they'd caught the routine used by other gangs. "Smash in the glass. Take what we can. Leave by the back. Willie, you wait in the alley till I say so, then go in and torch the place."

That's when Snake saw Anthony tug on Johnny's shirt, pointing to a building a half a block ahead and on the other side of the street. A burst of gunfire exploded. "Let's get out of here," Anthony shouted.

"Not till we get what we come for," Johnny jerked out of Anthony's grasp. "We go left here, use the alley. Place is on the corner, they got every kinda clothing you can imagine. We hit it, stash the loot, circle back and hit the appliance place couple a blocks down and get ourselves some real entertainment. I told you, the pigs ain't shootin'. See them guys carryin' out the TVs over there. Hell, look how many are whities!"

Snake remembered the old black man with Coke-bottle glasses sitting in a folding chair in front of a men's clothing store on the next corner, a rifle resting in his lap, a piece of cardboard with SOUL BROTHER scrawled in Magic Marker by his side. Even with all the noise and shit going down, he'd dozed off, slumped forward.

"Snake, get the drop on the old man before he goes for that rifle," Johnny'd ordered.

"Man's a brother. We can't loot no brother."

Lonnie moved ahead. "Yeah, well, our brother, Anthony here, he needs shit. In Nam, make no difference what color, you do what you have to do."

"Don't," Anthony coughed from the smoke. "He's got a gun. I don't need the threads, man. Let's just get the hell out of here."

Lonnie was right. Do what you had to do. As the old man dozed, Snake grabbed his rifle.

"You gonna have to shoot me, boy." The old man had surprised Snake by instantly yanking the rifle out of his hand. "This shop's all I got."

Snake had no choice. He swung the butt of his shotgun up and slammed it into the man's head. As he slumped onto the cement sidewalk, Snake grabbed the poor fool's rifle. Shotgun in one hand

and rifle in another, Snake crashed through the gaping hole that Willie had smashed in the store window with a baseball bat.

Behind him, Johnny pushed Anthony inside. Lonnie was already there, pulling clothes off the racks. "Get suits, man," Johnny'd shouted.

"Got another piece!" Snake shoved the old man's Remington into Anthony's hands as he jumped into the racks, grabbing at clothes.

Snake, Lonnie, and Johnny were heading toward the back door just as they heard the booming command, "Police! Drop it!"

They ran like hell out the back of the store into the alley before they realized that Anthony was not behind them. That's when they heard the gunshot. Johnny bolted back toward the shop, and Snake had to hold him back with both arms. It took all his strength to keep Johnny back in the darkness as they waited and watched police surround the building. Almost twenty minutes later a green van with a white cross arrived. Five minutes later two stretchers were carried out of the building — the old man with the SOUL BROTHER sign and Anthony.

The whole world came apart around them as Snake and Johnny threaded their way to City Hospital. Sniper bullets rang out. Fire hoses clogged the streets. Sirens came from every direction. Smoke clogged the air so they could hardly breathe. Buses poured in with hundreds of soldiers, armed with bayonets. Snake was scared shitless and he knew Johnny was too 'cause he puked right there in the parking lot. Then, before Snake even realized it, Johnny grabbed a white coat from an ambulance and disappeared inside the emergency room.

Snake tried to follow, but a cop held out a rifle, barring his way. Then Snake disappeared into the smoke-filled chaos to hook back up with Lonnie and Willie.

Now looking for Johnny to come out of City Hospital, Snake circled the gray concrete building to avoid the pigs. He loitered for as long as he dared by the parking lot where Johnny had puked. Johnny, so tough on the streets, but bleeding inside. So torn up about his brother. Where was Johnny now? To cheer Johnny up, the gang was taking him to Baker's Keyboard to listen to the Doozy Blues. His mother had said he'd left, hadn't she? Snake flipped on the Mustang's wipers; it was starting to rain.

CHAPTER THREE

"Miss Nelson?" Laura jumped at a familiar voice. She felt her knees buckle. Dr. Monroe, the chief of surgery. What was he doing here? Had he seen what had happened?

"Are you all right?" Keys in hand, he was standing next to a dark Cadillac.

Stunned, she said nothing, realizing that she had retraced her steps and was standing in the Doctor's Parking Lot.

"Are you all right?" he repeated, staring straight at her.

"Yes, uh, Dr. Monroe," she heard her voice shake. Out of nowhere came, "I'm studying at the library tonight. I was just going back in."

"That's good. You'd better get out of the rain."

She hadn't even noticed that the drizzle was now a light rain. Her hand went to her hair as if validating the dampness. She'd worn it down, shoulder length. Dampness always made it frizzy and wouldn't it be full of dirt? Is that why he was staring? Or was it the cut on her lip? She still tasted the blood as she bit down on it purposefully. Gripping her handbag tightly, she simply said, "Yes." Then a fresh wave of panic turned her stomach inside out as she felt warm liquid dribble down her left leg.

"Very well. See you at patient presentations tomorrow," he said in that tinge of a southern accent, which had mesmerized her at freshman orientation. And she wasn't alone, the whole class seemed to hang on his every word as he eloquently, and with great pride, expounded on the world-class trauma care they'd see during their training at City Hospital. Charismatic, that's what Susan had called him.

Had Dr. Monroe seen what happened? According to her watch, it was fifteen minutes past seven. About a half hour since she had fired that shot.

Running into Dr. Monroe had interrupted the cycling mantra in her brain. A mindless mantra, "Must not find out." As he climbed into his car and started the engine, Laura realized that she had to do something, go somewhere.

She knew she must look like a wreck. She'd been dragged across the ground and thrown down into the dirt and debris. Her legs were cut, but her skirt was probably long enough to cover most of the damage. Maybe nobody would notice that she didn't have stockings. Miraculously, her clothes were not torn and the red cotton sweater and full skirt would hide any stains.

A wave of nausea hit as she felt that warmish discharge dripping down her leg. She needed soap and hot water, a thorough scrubbing inside and out. Groping in her purse for a dime, she headed for the ladies' room off of the hospital lobby. In the mirror, she checked her face for scratches or bruises around her mouth. He hadn't hit her and Laura didn't see much damage except for the small cut on her lower lip.

With a ripple of repulsion, she forced herself to check her lower body. First she pulled a handful of paper towels from the dispenser, wet them under the faucet, and rushed into one of the stalls. Pulling up her skirt, she dabbed at herself, ignoring the pain as she ran her fingers over her bruised labia, noting the slight bloody discharge. A wave of dizziness caused her to slump against the metal wall of the stall. Her head cleared and she checked out her knees. Abrasions on both, but nothing more serious than a fall on a sidewalk. Two small, jagged pieces of glass protruded from her left thigh. She got them out with the edge of her fingernail.

Rushing from the stall back to the sink, beginning to run on adrenaline, Laura gathered additional paper towels, constantly listening for the sounds of anyone entering the restroom. She was lucky. No one interrupted her makeshift bathing procedure. She tried to urinate, but the attempt was too painful. She bought a Kotex from the machine, but cringed. The clean pad would feel so good, but she'd have to put it against the soiled panties. She pulled them out of her purse and with a shudder, shoved them back inside. She'd risk wearing nothing rather than put them back on. She tossed the sanitary pad and wadding up her torn pantyhose, pushed them to the bottom of a wastebasket. Finally, she washed her face with cool water.

What else? Her hair. She reached into her bag for her brush and moved it, trancelike, through the tangles, dislodging bits of gritty sand.

The wall clock read 7:40 P.M. What should she do? Go to a pay phone and call the police? Call her husband to come pick her up? Slinking against the wall by the hand-drier, she heard the mantra again, "Must never know!" She'd been raped. It wasn't her fault. Yes, but you killed a man, was the response. Who would believe that he threatened to kill you? Would he have killed her? How would she ever know? Maybe he would have just walked away. If only he had just taken my purse.

"I will lose my children," she said abruptly as she leaned her head against the restroom wall.

Suddenly Laura knew what she had to do. Not for her, but for her young sons. They needed her. She could not go to jail. She would tell no one, not even Steve. But was she strong enough to get through this? She prayed she was. Prayed harder than she ever had. Harder than she thought she could. Praying for strength and forgiveness.

Walking into the library, she approached Mrs. Oberly, the librarian in charge of the evening shift, a kindly, rotund woman in her sixties with graying hair. One of the few members of the university support staff with a penchant for assisting the female students, she did everything she could to give the few women in the med school an extra edge. In response to Laura's request, Mrs. Oberly was able to quickly pinpoint the precise reference texts Laura would need to prepare for her presentation tomorrow. Laura's survival plan: to establish that she was in the library preparing for class tomorrow. That was, of course, if she made it to tomorrow.

But first she had to call Steve. The thought of her family made her weak with terror. She should be home with her babies. Maybe she should drop the whole idea of being a doctor? Just stay home. Steve would like that, so would his parents. No, Laura gripped the edge of the table, fighting to resist the collapsing feeling inside as she formulated her story: simply explain to Steve that she was going to be late. Straightening up in her study carrel, she started to sweat as her mind raced. Where to concentrate? Steve's reaction? The murder kept reappearing in her mind. Then she slumped back, nearly breaking into a sob. What to do about the gun? How to get rid of the filthy panties? All of these demands competed for attention as she left the library for the bank of pay phones across the hall.

She dialed home. "Steve, hi, it's me." She knew that she talked too fast when she was excited so she spoke deliberately, not wanting to arouse Steve's suspicions. Steve could always tell when she was lying. Could Steve ever accept that she'd been raped? Or was it her own shame that terrified her? Was this about Steve? Or about her own pride? She didn't know and she was terrified to think it through.

"Hey, where are you?" Laura heard the concern in her husband's voice. "It's past dinnertime. Are you okay?"

"I'm okay."

"You sure? You don't sound it."

"Sorry, honey. Something came up very suddenly, and I absolutely have to stay. No choice. We got a patient assignment, and I have to give a report first thing in the morning. I need to do some research in the library."

"They sprung it on you just like that? Great. Well, the boys are hungry so we'll go ahead and eat. I'll make my special hot dogs. We'll be fine."

"There's enough formula for the baby in the fridge and chips for Mikey in the cabinet. Don't let him eat them all. I'm sorry—" Laura couldn't go on. She'd crossed the line. She could never go back.

"We'll miss you," Steve said, "Tiger's aren't on, so it'll have to be boxing." He hesitated. "Laura, they've lifted the curfew, but you're still in a dangerous neighborhood. Remember that, okay?"

"I'll be careful, honey," she said on the verge of tears. How could she be saying this when she wanted to just fall into Steve's arms and tell him everything? Why couldn't she just do that?

"How long will you stay?"

"Till about ten or so. I'll be home before eleven. Kiss the kids for me. I'll make it up to you, Steve. I promise."

"Sounds good, babe. I'll hold you to that."

Laura hung up, feeling more and more like a criminal, like she'd lost all sense of credibility, of integrity. She was a liar and a killer. She didn't know if she was doing the right thing, but she couldn't risk being separated from her kids.

Suddenly, she had an uncontrollable urge to talk to her mother. Just to hear her voice and feel her strength. She picked up the phone, cradled the receiver in her hand, then set it back. Her mother would know that something was horribly wrong and pull the truth out of her. It's too late, Laura thought with deepening desperation. Too late to take the bullet back; too late to take the safe way back to her car.

It was now 8:35 P.M., an hour and a half after it happened, and Laura returned to her study carrel. Her hands trembled as she fumbled through the pages of the gigantic neurosurgical text in front of her, looking for the sections on skull fractures and brain injury. The bullet in Anthony's brain caused enough swelling and hemorrhage to destroy the brain stem, which controls breathing. Yet he was still alive. The man she shot tonight was not. The brain destruction caused by her bullet was so immediate, so irreversibly lethal. Had anyone found him yet? She almost burst into tears, so she put her face in her hands and sat for a moment as her emotions flip-flopped — one moment logical and the next on the verge of total break-down.

She checked her watch. It was 9:30 P.M. She had one more thing to do: look up exactly what kind of rape precautions to take. Tearing through the *Merck Manual,* a small handbook with all sorts of practical medical information, Laura found nothing, not one sentence. Running out of time, she found what she needed in the *Manual of Current Therapy.* Laura hastily scribbled some notes. There were precautions against venereal disease, prevention of pregnancy, tetanus, first aid for lacerations and abrasions, and a section on psychological stuff that she couldn't worry about now.

Sorting through all this, she focused on venereal disease, shocked and sobered by the high frequency of syphilis and gonorrhea. She resolved to get some penicillin, writing down the exact type and dosage. Then a lump settled in the pit of her stomach. The penicillin had to be intramuscular, she read. How would she ever get a shot? There was the risk of pregnancy, of course, but Laura dared not let herself dwell on that. It simply couldn't happen. The cut on her lip and the abrasions would heal in a few days. Forget about tetanus, too unlikely. So the critical thing, she figured, was to inject herself with a big slug of penicillin.

When she was in that hospital ward today, she noted the medicine cabinets right off the nursing station. Those cabinets were stocked with vials and ampules for injection, and all kinds of pills. She'd seen needles and syringes in the open drawer. Tomorrow she'd make an excuse to go back there and somehow take what she needed.

Right now she had to pack up and leave. No way she'd retrace her earlier path out the hospital door. The terror of that burned-out stretch of buildings made her slump back into her chair. She would walk around to the med school exit and calmly request an escort to her car, an emergency service provided after hours by armed hospital security. Then she remembered the gun in her purse. What should she do with it? She kept a firm hand on her handbag as she left the building.

It was still raining. Laura's tall escort held an oversized umbrella over her as she unlocked the driver's door of the black Falcon wagon. Would he notice how violently her hands trembled? Laura managed a quick wave to him as she jerked the car into gear and lurched out of the parking lot. As she did, a rusted out Mustang veered around the corner, braking hard, swerving to miss her. The angry blast of a horn cut through the rain, and Laura accelerated, never even seeing the three young men in the Mustang.

She struggled to stay calm enough to drive, telling herself that it was an ordinary car, not the police. No flashing lights. She took a deep breath and slowed the wagon to the twenty-five mile per hour speed limit and headed toward the Chrysler Expressway, which took her to the Ford and then to the Lodge, a fifteen minute commute at this time of night.

Rain was battering her windshield, making it difficult to see. The drive home was one of terror mingled with guilt, all mixed up. She came to a stop in front of her home. Was it too late to just go in and tell Steve, confide in him, let him help her out of this? She sat for a long moment, trembling, trying to decide. No, she had made up her mind, "No one must know," pounded in her brain. She had to get through this on her own. Her whole future depended on it.

Loud snores greeted Laura as she crept in the front door and through the living room. She tiptoed directly to the children's room, hoping that Steve wouldn't wake up. Mikey was sleeping, curled up with "Ginky," his beloved tattered blanket. Kevin was asleep in his crib, wrapped snugly in a light blue receiving blanket. She leaned over each child to kiss them softly before creeping off to her bedroom. No, she couldn't risk losing them no matter how many lies she had to tell.

She needed a shower desperately, a very hot and very soapy one. A hot bath would be better, but it would take more time and she needed time to get into bed and wrap herself up, to think about what she'd done, to plan what to do next. But first she had to scrub from head to toe. Then she'd call her mother even if it was late, just to hear her voice. She searched her drawers for a long, heavy night-gown to cover her body, to hide any bruises and the puncture wounds from the shards of glass. She couldn't take the chance that Steve would be interested in sex tonight. Just the thought of it was repugnant. Certainly for now. Maybe forever.

After her shower, Laura slipped quietly into bed. She decided not to rouse Steve from the couch. She'd tell him tomorrow that she had tried to get him to come to bed but he hadn't budged. She wondered how many more lies she would tell. As the events of the night replayed continuously in her mind, she recalculated the chances that no one would ever find out. The "yes" answer chased the "no" around and around her mind. It was past midnight, but she called her mother, who she knew would be reading in bed. Laura didn't tell her what had happened and knew she never would. Instead she asked a couple of open-ended questions and let her mother prattle in that comforting way of hers.

She was still awake at 3:00 A.M. when Steve stumbled into the bedroom, still in jeans and a T-shirt. He headed into the bathroom, then flopped into bed and fell immediately back to sleep. All night long she tossed and turned. What were the repercussions of what she'd done? What would happen if she went to the police? Would they believe her? Or would they make her a poster child? A white woman killing a black man? She hadn't reported the rape to the police. Why not? Was it shame? She didn't really know and that kept her throwing question after question at herself.

When it came to Steve, she felt shame and guilt. She wanted desperately to tell him so he could help her shoulder this horror, but deep-down she knew it would ruin her marriage. He'd resisted her going to med school in the first place, but she had convinced him that she could be a good mom and a good doctor, and she knew she could. Finally, he'd given in. Then she'd pressured him to move to Detroit, arguing that University Medical School offered the real-life clinical training she wanted. That had been before the riots.

Moving to Detroit had been a mistake. Wasn't that clear after the horror of tonight? If only she'd given in to Steve. But no, she'd been bull headed and self centered and risked everything. One thing was certain, if Steve found out she'd been raped, he'd force her to leave school. That would be his justification to deprive her of her dream. When it came to careers, things were different with her and Steve. For him, social work was a job. For her, being a doctor was like a vocation. Something so much a part of her. Something too important to risk losing.

For the rest of the night, these impossible questions flipped back and forth, interrupted only by Steve's sporadic snoring until Kevin's 5:00 A.M. hunger cries.

"I'll get the baby, Steve," Laura whispered, slipping out of bed. Laura and Steve alternated getting up for the early morning bottle. Though it was Steve's turn, he murmured assent.

As Laura sank into the rocking chair in the children's room with her baby in her arms, a miraculous feeling of satisfaction flooded through her. During that brief interlude, everything seemed all right. After Kevin finished half of the bottle, Laura stood and lifted the baby over her shoulder to burp him. As she stood, the serenity dissipated. Pacing, she tried to stave off surges of panic. Mostly about the gun. If they found the gun, what then? She carried the baby into her bedroom. In the dark she reached for her purse, extracted the gun, and returned to the children's room. Juggling Kevin on one shoulder, she found the box of baby clothes stored on the top shelf in the small closet — clothes too small for Mikey and still too big for Kevin. Nobody would think to look for a gun in a box of baby clothes. She'd get rid of the gun later and make up an explanation for Steve. She maneuvered the revolver to the center of the box, walked quietly back to the living room sofa, and fed Kevin the rest of his bottle. Calmer now, as was the rain, gently tapping against the window.

CHAPTER FOUR

Stacy and Sharon Jones had just finished watching *The Millionaire* when they heard pounding at the front door.

"I'll get it," said Stacy. "You better get to bed."

"Okay," Sharon yawned, for once not challenging Stacy's authority. At fourteen, Stacy was in charge of her three younger sisters: Sharon, twelve; Rachel, nine; and Katie, seven.

"Hey girl," Snake said when she opened the door a crack. "Johnny here?"

"No." She thought Snake looked different — older maybe.

"You know where he is?"

"How should I know?" She opened the door wide enough for him to step inside. "He's supposed to be home with us." Mama left strict orders not to let anybody inside, but Stacy thought Snake was cool. And he was Johnny's best friend even though Mama didn't like him hanging around.

"Everyone's down 'bout Anthony, but Johnny takin' it so damn hard, you know? I told your mama I'd watch out for Johnny. And for Johnny's little sister too," he said finally looking her in the eye. "And it'd be my own personal pleasure."

Snake acted sweeter than Stacy ever remembered him being. She knew that he and Johnny messed around with some bad stuff. She was pretty sure they smoked pot. And they got drunk, but that was before Anthony got shot. Ever since, Johnny had changed. He hardly ever came home, and when he did he was mean and ugly. Hateful, rebellious, angry. He even talked back to Mama. Mama said he had a broken heart about Anthony, but Stacy was scared for him. Detroit was still dangerous even though the riots were over, weren't they? Maybe Snake could help.

Alexandrine Avenue was south of the worst of the riots, but looting and fires still popped up around the neighborhood. Red flashing lights and screaming sirens went off, wrecking what otherwise would have been beautiful late summer nights. Stacy was scared for herself and her sisters. The days weren't as bad as they were two weeks ago. Now, they could at least go to the schoolyard to play, finding their way through the rubble; but the nights were scary, especially without Johnny there. Stacy did not tell her mother that Johnny wasn't home at night, trying to keep her from further stress. Her mother worked nights then spent much of the day at the hospital with Anthony. During the day, Stacy had assumed her mother's place, waking up her sisters in the morning and making them eat their cereal. She supervised them as they dressed, and then she walked them to the schoolyard so mama could get some sleep in peace. Stacy would handle dinner and bedtime then tackle her summer reading assignment. Mama expected all As, and Stacy was aiming for a scholarship just like Anthony.

"Snake," she decided to ask the question that nobody would answer. "Anthony's going to be okay, isn't he?"

"You gotta ask Johnny 'bout that. He knows 'bout the doctors that fucked up Anthony when he was layin' in that emergency room. Said he saw it with his own eyes. That it wasn't the bullet. That a lady doctor near killed him. Said she had yellow hair. Something about a tube in his throat. Heard the chief doctor tell her she fucked up. He called her a fucking criminal. You ask Johnny 'bout that."

Stacy blamed the riots for Anthony getting shot. She knew that Johnny blamed the white doctors at the hospital. Really blamed them, and that too scared her.

"What does that mean?" Stacy leaned against the doorjamb, even more confused.

The honk of a horn interrupted.

"Gotta go, girl." Snake looked anxious to leave. "When Johnny gets home tell him we're goin' on down to Baker's to hear some music."

Stacy Jones heard the muffled sounds across the dark bedroom. Katie was crying again. Hoping not to wake the others, she whispered, "What's wrong, little sister?"

"I hear the bang, bang," Katie sobbed.

Stacy struggled to emerge from a restless sleep. Was there shooting going on outside? She held her breath in the sudden pocket of silence soon followed by banging sounds.

"The front door," she mumbled. "Johnny forgot his keys again."

She kissed Katie's forehead on her way out, careful to close the door quietly behind her. Johnny didn't care who he woke up, especially these days.

As she approached the front door, Stacy glanced at the living room wall clock: 4:17 A.M. She shook her head groggily. Since Anthony had been in the hospital, Stacy had slept only fitfully. Johnny was supposed to stay home with her and her sisters, but of course he didn't. Anthony used to be home at night, studying in his room, but then he would be going off to college once he got better.

Stacy wondered if Snake had come back again for Johnny. She'd seen him leave in that Mustang with Willie Allen and that creepy Lonnie guy who supposedly had a real job, like at the car plant. Now the pounding at the door was louder. Stacy didn't have a bathrobe so she pulled the threadbare sheet off her bed and wound it around her. Flicking on the overhead light in the living room, she first peeked into her brothers' bedroom. Both twin beds were empty, so she unlocked the front door and yanked it open, expecting Johnny.

Two Detroit policemen stood outside. "Man almighty," she cried, her drowsiness vanished as she blinked.

"Hello, young lady," said a smooth-faced, young black officer dressed in a navy blue uniform. "I'm Officer Willard and this is my partner, Officer Donovan."

Stacy hesitated. "Why are you here?"

"We'd like to talk to your parents," said the partner, who was white with a stomach that hung out over his belt.

"My mother's not home. She's at work. What do you want?"

The men glanced at each other.

"We need to talk to your mother," Donovan explained. "Is she the head of the household?"

"Yes, she is," Stacy answered. "She works nights at General Motors."

"Uh huh, and when will she be home?" Willard asked impatiently. "It's after four."

The cop's face softened. "I know it's late and all, but we need to talk to your mother. Maybe you can help us get in touch with her."

"How old are you?" Donovan asked, averting his eyes from her thin frame wrapped in the tattered sheet.

"Fourteen," Stacy said without flinching, hoping that her mama wouldn't get in trouble for leaving them alone.

"Is there anybody else here with you?" Donovan asked after Stacy led them into the small, neat, but sparsely furnished living room. Both officers continued to stand.

"My sisters are sleeping," Stacy whispered.

"Okay," Willard replied. "Could you tell us your name?"

"I'm Stacy Jones."

The officers exchanged another look. "Jones?" Donovan asked.

Willard just nodded. "Stacy, who lives here with you?"

"My mother and my brothers and sisters."

"And where are your brothers?" Willard pressed.

"Johnny's not usually out this late," she quickly explained. Johnny would not want Stacy blabbing to these guys. He hated cops, all cops, even black ones. Then she muttered, "And Anthony's in the hospital."

"So you have a brother named 'Johnny'? John Jones?" Donovan asked.

"No," Stacey said cautiously. "Not Jones. He has a different last name than me."

"Diggs, is it?" Willard cut in.

"Uh huh," Stacey nodded.

Willard nodded too. "So just you and your sisters are home?"

"Asleep, like I said. They'd be real scared to see you here. Why don't you come back when my mama is home? She gets home about six, but she needs to get some sleep."

"Whattaya think, Willie?" the older cop exchanged another look with his partner. "How about some coffee and we come back?"

"Why are you here anyway?" Stacy blurted.

"We need to talk to your mother," Officer Willard said flatly. "Does she have a phone number at work?"

"No, she's part of the cleaning crew. They send her to a different place every night."

"Well, it's four-thirty now. We'll just go out for coffee and be back and wait for her to get home. You go on back to sleep," Officer Willard decided. "Be sure to lock this door. You're too young to be here on your own."

Stacy frowned. "Usually my brothers are here."

An old man walking through the abandoned lot had discovered the body as he returned home after a night of poker and beer. His daughter called the police who confirmed the report sometime around midnight. In the back pocket of the dead man's jeans they had found a switchblade and a wallet with the name and address of John Diggs.

One more hysterical mother. One more son lost to the ravages of the troubled city. The police department was obligated to send out a homicide crew, but the chances of an arrest and conviction were slim. The department had an overwhelming backlog due to the riots, and 1300 Beaubien, home to Detroit's 1st Precinct, swarmed with investigators from the President's Advisory Commission on Civil Disorders.

Willard and Donovan would patrol the area for awhile before returning to Alexandrine Avenue. Maybe the mother would shed some light, but they expected a short and uneventful investigation. Even if there had been a witness, no one in Detroit was likely to come forward. After the riots, it seemed the entire population, good guys and the bad, were keeping their heads down and their mouths closed tight.

They'd just pulled up to the Jones house when they saw a woman trudging toward them from the bus stop on Woodward.

"Must be her," Willard said. "Let's get this over with."

Both officers stepped out of the car.

With a start, Lucy realized that there were two police officers in front of her house.

"What's wrong? My girls?" she called, eyes flashing in panic. "Is it Anthony?" She rushed toward the apartment, Willard following.

"What is it?" Lucy fumbled for her keys.

"Calm down now, Mrs. Diggs," Willard began. "We talked to Stacy, just a little while ago. She is a fine girl."

"My name is Lucy Jones. What do you mean, you talked to Stacy?" Lucy stared at the young black cop.

He lifted his hands in a conciliatory gesture. "Here, let me help you with the door so we can sit down and talk." After unlocking the door, all three walked into the empty living room. "Please, sit down," Willard went on. Lucy sank into the lone upholstered chair. Donovan leaned against the edge of a sagging beige sofa.

"Mrs. Jones, we believe your son was killed this evening. That's why we're here," Willard said matter-of-factly.

Lucy gasped. "What do you mean, killed?" She stared up at Willard, who was standing in the middle of the room, legs spread, arms crossed.

"He took a bullet in the brain," Donovan said softly. "He died instantly. He was taken to the morgue at City Hospital. We'll need you to come down and make a positive I.D."

Lucy just shook her head. How could Anthony have been shot last night? That had happened weeks ago. She struggled to make sense of this, but she couldn't. Did they unplug the respirator? She hadn't given permission.

"Anthony," she wailed. "Oh, God, how could you take my boy? He never hurt anybody."

"Mrs. Jones," Willard interrupted. "It isn't—" He turned as Stacy slipped into the room, her eyes huge with fear.

"Please, God," Lucy pleaded. Stacy grabbed her mother's arm.

"Mrs. Jones, I know you're upset and that this is a shock," Willard said firmly. "If you could just give us some information now, you can come down to the station later today when you're ready."

Lucy stared at them in disbelief.

"But we'll need you to come to the morgue to identify the body," Willard added.

"The body?" Stacy whispered. She held onto her mother as tightly as she could.

Donovan approached them. "Please, sit down. We have to ask a few more questions."

Lucy and Stacy sat mutely on the couch.

"Now, Mrs. Jones," he said briskly, "do you know where he was going and who he was with this evening? Let's start from when you last saw him."

A sickening sensation shot through Lucy's chest and spread across her whole being. They weren't talking about Anthony at all.

CHAPTER FIVE

At Grosse Pointe Shores, it was barely eight in the morning.

"David," Cynthia Monroe began, "I'm making our plans for Aruba. How long do you think we can stay?"

David glanced up from the paper. "Sorry, what was that?"

Dressed in a pale green silk dressing gown, Cynthia replied, "I'm thinking three weeks of sun and sand. Some tennis. How does that sound?"

David and Cynthia Monroe were finishing their coffee at the elegant travertine marble table in the spacious dining area just off the kitchen. They could hardly see each other through the over-sized bouquet of gladiolas, thanks to Cynthia's obsession with fresh flowers. Elaborate arrangements were scattered throughout the house with replacements arriving at their estate every other day. This indulgence had always irked David, but he left domestic matters to his wife.

David rose, pulling on his suit jacket. For a moment he considered his wife silently. At thirty-two, she was even more stunning than when he had met her nearly seven years ago. Her shoulder length dark hair hung loose at her shoulders, and her deep blue eyes peered over at him expectantly.

"There's no way I can get away from the hospital this fall." He shook his head slowly. "The surgical schedule is nonstop."

"But certainly—" Cynthia frowned.

David attempted a smile. "We're still getting riot-related emergencies, gunshot wounds, knifings, burns."

"I'm tired of the riot excuse. You've been late every night for so many weeks I've lost count. And when you do show up, you're like some kind of zombie. It's obvious your mind is someplace else."

"I'm sorry," he said, "but it's my job."

"We've missed two dinner parties in the last month," she continued. "You're out being the hero, and I'm stuck here."

"Cynthia, it's not that bad. You play bridge, and you're at the club almost every day. You have many evening engagements."

"It's not safe anymore without an escort."

"Just use the limousine service if you go into the city. But I will make an effort to be home earlier in the evenings."

Cynthia banged the empty silver coffeepot on the surface of the table. "That's a lie, and you know it." Her voice was shrill. "Your work has always been more important than me. I'm telling you, I need a break. Detroit's become so oppressive."

"You know you love this city."

"I love this house because this is where I grew up with Daddy. As for Aruba, I'm booking the flight with the travel agent. If you don't give me some dates, then I'll go ahead and set it up without your input."

"We'll talk more tonight," he said, straightening his tie. "But seriously, Cynthia. I can't get away this year."

"Don't you understand? We need time together," she said, burying her head in her hands. In a small voice she added, "Are you still trying to punish me?"

David knew her moods well, but he did glance back, wondering where this switch from sullen to petulant was heading. "Being chief of surgery comes with responsibility, for God's sake. I'm not 'punishing' anybody." He struggled to mask his annoyance. Simply put, his wife was used to getting her own way. She was a skilled manipulator. "I can't let my faculty and my house staff down. Besides those riots, we just got a new crop of medical students, remember?"

"Oh, how important." She waved her hand at him. "Just go then."

Without another word David walked through the kitchen,

reaching for the car keys hanging on the hook by the door. His face grim, he eased himself into the driver's seat of the shiny Cadillac and pulled the car out of the garage onto the long, winding driveway leading from the French Provincial estate on Lake St. Clair to Lake Shore Drive.

David thought a lot about being a kid, growing up in Charleston, South Carolina, with his younger brother, Nick. Then his father lost his job in a paper mill as the industry became mechanized. The automotive industry, however, needed mechanics, and so the Monroe family moved from charming Charleston to the bustling, increasingly hostile city of Detroit. Ten years later, when David was in college, both his parents were killed driving on Interstate 94 during a winter storm. His dad had never mastered the skill required to drive in Michigan's ice and snow. His parents died instantly when their sedan careened into a jack-knifed tractor trailer. With a small inheritance, David was able to graduate from Duke and enroll in Harvard Medical School where he stayed on for a surgical residency. From there he went to University Medical School in Detroit to be near his brother. Nick had married his high school sweetheart, Denise, and they had four sons who all looked like replicas of Nick and David when they were little. David adored his nephews, but being with them was bittersweet. He'd always wanted children, and Cynthia did not. Her refusal was a raw wound, a profound disappointment.

Cynthia Harriman, the only child of Dr. Bernard D. Harriman and the late Gladys Harriman, came into his life the first year of his assistant professorship. They met at City Hospital's Valentine Benefit Gala when he was thirty-two and she twenty-four. They married eight months later. It was after the lavish wedding when David began to discover the many adjustments that were necessary to endure a vain and willful wife. After Cynthia's father suffered a heart attack and passed away, David came to realize that he had married not only a very rich, but a very spoiled woman. And now she wanted to go to Aruba. Some things would never change.

In time, Dr. David Monroe was appointed chairman of surgery. That had occurred based on his own merit, he wanted to think, but had his influential father-in-law paved the way? Did it matter? Deep down, he knew that it was his own personal vision that had transformed City Hospital in Detroit into the nation's leading Trauma Surgery Center. And of that, he was immensely proud. Except for that incident with the Diggs boy.

How could he forget the night Detroit went up in flames? More than a hundred doctors working around the clock from Sunday evening through Thursday. But no matter the chaos and the pure physical exhaustion of those days, it was inconceivable that a boy with a gaping head wound be left unattended on a stretcher. The Diggs boy arrived via ambulance with a gunshot wound to the head; but in the turmoil he was not logged into the system. Finding his head swathed in a bulky bandage, the emergency room staff assumed he'd been evaluated and judged stable. To compound matters, the female intern who found him in cardiac arrest had a difficult time intubating him, leading to prolonged anoxia.

Each day he halfway expected notification of a lawsuit, or worse yet, a call from an investigative reporter from the *Free Press*, now that that nun was asking questions. Sister Mary Agnes, a friend of the patient's family, had come to see him with what she called an eyewitness report of what had happened. The eyewitness was the patient's brother who'd snuck into the ER and watched the botched resuscitation. David had been honest with the nun, admitting that the hospital had made a mistake that night. On impulse, he'd promised her that the hospital would cover all the patient's medical costs, determined to personally pay if the hospital balked. Mistakes like that should not happen in his emergency room.

Now the Diggs boy had no brain function. Whether from the gunshot wound or the lapse in emergency care, it was impossible to tell. There was no hope of recovery, yet his mother refused to turn off the ventilator. What would he do if this were happening to his son? Well, he'd never have a son and that was that.

*   *   *

As David entered the stop-and-go traffic along Jefferson Avenue, the present came into focus. Today the first year med students would be reporting on their first physical examinations. And he planned to attend although he usually delegated this to the junior staff. Naive students fumbling around with their first diagnostic cases usually made him impatient, but his mind kept returning to a certain student. What was her name? The one assigned to the Diggs boy. That must be why she lingered on his mind. He couldn't shake the Diggs tragedy. And then he'd seen her last night in the parking lot. Looking so strange. Or was it scared? She had such distinctive green eyes. A pretty blonde with that all-American look he found so refreshing. Glancing out the car window at the misty river, David continued to wonder why this woman so intrigued him? Then he remembered her name, Laura Nelson. Amused at the rare feeling he was experiencing, he calmly made his way through the rush hour traffic. The feeling? It was anticipation.

CHAPTER SIX

"There was a call from the dean, Dr. Monroe," David's secretary announced as he walked into his office. Connie Zimmer, a prim woman in her early fifties, had worked for David since his arrival at the school nine years ago. By now, she could just about anticipate David's reaction to everything. "He wants to see you in his office for a short meeting right away."

David sighed with irritation. "What's it about, Connie?"

"He didn't say."

"My schedule's too tight."

"This morning you have the first year students and no other meetings that I know of. I thought you'd appreciate the reprieve."

"Well, you thought wrong." David tossed his leather briefcase on the credenza.

"I'm sorry, Dr. Monroe," she said slowly.

He glanced at the stack of charts on his desk, then turned to Connie with a sheepish grin. "No, I'm sorry. I'll go see what kind of bureaucracy Andrew's dreamed up, but I am planning to make the student review."

"Now what's got into him?" Connie muttered when her boss gave her shoulder an affectionate squeeze on the way out.

Dean Andrew Burke's massive, boxy form overwhelmed even the oversize chair at his desk. The venerable dean of University Medical School needed a course in weight management. Three uphol-stered chairs were arranged in front of him. Ed Collins, the frail chairman of medicine, was settled in one. David valued his counterpart, twenty years his senior, as a trusted colleague, and a mentor in the politics of academic medicine. At the moment, Ed was talking to a man with coppery brown skin, a husky athletic build and intense black eyes. The stranger was middle-aged, with a shiny bald spot, and looked professional in a tailored charcoal gray suit. The third chair was empty and obviously intended for David. He mumbled a hello and sat down, unable to suppress a frown as he noted how pale Ed appeared.

"Good morning, David," the dean began. "Detective Reynolds, this is Dr. Monroe, chairman of surgery. Now, gentlemen, let's get down to business."

As usual, Andrew took charge of the meeting. "Detective Reynolds called early this morning and requested this meeting. I think you ought to hear what he has to say." He gestured with his hand. "Detective, please proceed."

"Sure thing," Reynolds said with a curt nod. "Thanks for seeing me so quickly. I'm afraid I have some disturbing news. Last night there was a shooting, a homicide. It took place only steps away from here. The victim, a young black male about twenty years old, was shot at close range in the head. We have an I.D., but we don't know why this happened, and why here."

Ed Collins shook his head. "Aftermath of these devastating riots, no doubt."

"Could be," Reynolds nodded curtly. "Could be anything. Anyway, I'm here to urge you to do all you can to keep your staff and students safe. I'll be talking to hospital security too, but I wanted to meet with you all first. I know hospitals operate around the clock; but the point is, I'd bet most everybody around here pays little attention to safety precautions. All those long hours add up to exhaustion, don't they? What happened last night is a little too close for comfort. I'd like you all to relay to your staff and students a sense of urgency. You want to tell them to use the help at hand. There's an armed security force, right? And some of our uniforms are still on patrol at the hospital. They're here for a reason. To my mind, Detroit has seen enough killing in the last month to last till the end of time."

Dr. Collins nodded enthusiastically. David glanced at the dean, who was jotting some notes.

"The police will increase their patrol, of course," the detective continued, "but I'd advise re-assessing your security. I admit I have a strong personal interest in this as well, gentleman, because I have a daughter in the first year class here."

"Our security people have already been providing a voluntary after-hours escort service," the Dean replied.

"We can make it mandatory, can't we, Andrew?" Ed Collins asked.

The dean nodded. "Of course, we can step it up. What time did this, er, incident occur, detective?"

"The reports aren't back, of course, but it's estimated somewhere around seven P.M. I'd begin that service at five, Dr. Burke. I realize your doctors and students come and go at all hours. Get them to keep their eyes open. Tell them to report any suspicious activity around the school or hospital."

"Of course," Burke replied. "Thank you."

The detective smiled. "I'm not done. We'll stick around for a while today, looking for potential witnesses, that kind of thing. We'll set up outside and ask your people questions as they come in. You never know if someone saw something unless you ask."

"You can count on our full cooperation," the dean added, always the politician. "Thank you again and we're delighted your daughter is here in our program."

David rose from his chair, offering his hand to the detective. "Her name?"

"Susan Reynolds."

"I'll keep my eye on her."

"I'd appreciate that, doctor."

By the time David arrived at the conference room, freshman students were presenting their material in groups of six to an audience of four surgical residents and one member of the surgical faculty. As per tradition, this session would be grueling, testing the thickness of new medical students' skin. The faculty and the house staff pulled no punches in interrogating the uninitiated as they fumbled to present their first clinical case. David slipped into a chair, quietly observing the end of Susan Reynolds' report. She was tall like her father, with the same coppery skin tone, a beautiful girl. No wonder the detective was so concerned. He found himself nodding an approval of her self-confidence as she aptly responded to critiques of her examination of a patient with complications of cirrhosis of the liver. Miss Reynolds was the only African-American woman in the class and based on today's performance, he judged that she'd do just fine.

"Nelson is next," the chief surgical resident called out as soon as Susan was dismissed.

Laura stood up and hesitantly approached. Her heart beat out of control. Why hadn't she stayed home? Told them she was sick?

She gripped the sides of the podium as the gunshot wound in her patient's head and gunshot wound in the head of the man she'd shot kept mixing and matching in her mind. Should she just turn around now? At the head of the conference table, she froze. Her eyes were so irritated that she'd worn her glasses instead of her contacts, her legs were weak, and her pelvis still throbbed. She wore lipstick to cover her cut lower lip, but licked it subconsciously as she stared at the curious faces of her fellow students and instructors.

"Miss Nelson, are you okay?" Laura's hand flew to cover her mouth. The voice was Dr. Monroe's. The same voice she'd heard in the hospital parking lot last night.

She looked over to him, and he nodded his head in encouragement. The others began to shuffle and squirm. She clenched her teeth, urging herself to focus on what she had to do: report on her patient. After a moment adjusting her glasses, she reached for her notes and began. Her voice shook, but she found herself able to go on.

"Anthony Diggs is an eighteen-year-old black male with a gunshot wound to the head. Since arrival at City Hospital, he has been comatose and on a ventilator. So I took his medical history from his mother."

She could feel all eyes staring, as she prayed that God would help her keep her patient and the man she shot separate. She tried so hard to concentrate on Anthony Diggs and to expunge thoughts on the path of the bullet through the skull of the man whom she herself had shot, that she forgot much of what she'd tried to read in the library last night. She felt herself bungling anatomical terms. She knew her delivery sounded confusing, disjointed. She talked too fast as she rushed to conclude with the report of the neurological examination, concluding that her patient had irreversible brain damage. Then she straightened and braced for the barrage of humiliating questions and criticisms sure to follow.

She didn't have to wait long. An aggressive surgical resident jumped right in.

"What about the Babinsky reflex?"

Laura struggled to recall what she'd read about this strange test, in which it was necessary to take the dull handle of a reflex hammer and stroke the side of the foot from the heel to the ball and then move it upward to the base of each toe. She was pretty sure she had done that to her patient according to the instructions in the manual.

"The Babinsky reflex," she repeated in order to gain some time. "Positive, bilaterally."

"Explain what you actually saw," demanded the same resident.

"Uhh, the big toe flexed and the other toes fanned out," Laura answered from somewhere inside herself.

Another voice piped up. "And what is the significance?"

"It's a sign of deep coma," Laura said. Yes, she did remember that.

"How did you judge the level of consciousness?" Yet another interrogator jumped in.

"The patient did not react to the pinprick test. No reaction, nothing." Laura wished that she'd paid more attention to the section on coma scales. She wanted to leave this interrogation and run home to Steve.

"Okay," the only woman in the group offered. "Your patient was unresponsive. What position was he lying in?"

"Flat in bed. Not moving. I can't remember exactly." Laura stopped, thinking now of how her victim had been curled in the fetal position.

A prolonged silence as Laura left Anthony Diggs entirely.

Finally, the chief resident spoke impatiently. "Okay students, this course is all about observation. Miss Nelson's report is lacking critical details. "Dr. Monroe, any comments?"

"Yes. Miss Nelson, did you note the development of any decubiti when you examined the patient?"

"I'm sorry?" Again that voice from the parking lot focused her. "Decubiti?"

A few subdued snickers could be heard.

"Yes, Miss Nelson, decubiti. Bedsores, to the layman. Were there any bedsores?"

Not really sure what a bedsore looked like, Laura closed her eyes to remember her examination of the patient. "I did see some dark, blotchy areas," she said, opening her eyes and blinking. "Also, there were some oozing sores on his buttocks." She prayed that her answer was at least close to right.

"Fine, Miss Nelson. I want you to prepare a written report on the causes of morbidity and mortality in comatose patients. Hand it in early next week."

David Monroe rose from the conference table and headed for the exit. Now why had he asked for that report? There'd been a certain sophistication as she began discussing the patient's history, but then she'd lapsed into some kind of funk. The additional report might give him some indication. At the door he turned back, remembering the haunted look of this student when he'd run across her last night in the rain. She still seemed shaken, distraught.

Maybe just nervous, but wasn't there something else? Yes, she now wore glasses, adding a scholarly note.

Laura's knees felt week as she left the surgical conference room, and she felt lightheaded. She'd come so close to losing it. Already late for gross anatomy lab, Susan hurried her along.

"Dr. Cunningham — Will — wants to have coffee with me after dissection," Susan was saying. "Do you think that's okay? Being he's an instructor? I don't want to get in any trouble."

"That report," Laura's voice shook. "I was so bad."

"You did okay," Susan said, "but you did seem distracted at one point. Now about Will Cunningham? Should I or shouldn't I?"

"Uh, sorry?" Laura mumbled as they pushed though the swinging doors into a macabre sea of cadavers each laid out on a stainless steel table, covered by sheets of heavy plastic to keep them saturated with formaldehyde.

"Harry," the cadaver they shared with two other students, was centrally located among his peers of forty men and women. Anatomical charts in vivid colors lined the walls of the huge rectangular room. Organs in jars, intact skeletons, and detached skeletal parts filled every nook and cranny.

"Harry's 'perfume' gets stronger every day," Susan stated the obvious as they approached. "At least if I go out with Will, we'll have that 'certain smell' in common. Hey, doesn't your husband complain? I mean, formaldehyde's seeping out of every pore. And my hair stinks."

"It irritates my eyes," Laura remarked, shivering inside her stained white lab coat, not so much because they kept the anatomy lab very cold, but at the pall of death that surrounded her.

"Yeah, and he has to last the whole year."

"About time you two showed up," a friendly voice called out. "We've got to crack the chest wall today."

"So far the morning's been interesting," Susan reported. "Dr. Monroe gave Laura an extra assignment." She gave Laura a friendly punch in the shoulder, but Laura did not respond.

Against big odds, four freshman women had found themselves randomly assigned to a dissection table: out of a hundred and
fifty students. Considering that there were only ten women, and
only one black woman, in the entire first year class, the quartet at-
tracted more than their share of attention. Despite different back-
grounds, personalities, and skills, by the end of the first month the
girls had bonded into a tight clique, founded on mutual respect for
each other's strengths and weaknesses.

Laura Nelson, from Grand Rapids and a graduate of the University of Michigan, was hardworking, pragmatic and family ori-
ented. With her easy smile and even temperament, Laura
engendered their trust. No matter the demands of her home life,
she never let them down.

Susan Reynolds, from Detroit, impressed her colleagues with
her studious nature and professional appearance, complete with
large wire-rimmed glasses. Susan's mother had died when she was
a teen, but she adored her father, a detective with the Detroit Police. Susan was no-nonsense, intensely dedicated to academic success. She never let them slack off.

Vicky Walson, from Grosse Pointe Shores was the most attractive of the ten women in the class. Willow thin with platinum
blonde hair styled as if she'd just walked off a modeling set, she
flaunted expensive clothes and jewelry that should be kept locked
in a safe. She was twenty-five, three years older than her partners
and married to a rich lawyer, who indulged her every whim. Women
tended to resent her flamboyance. Not her partners. Vickie was
their secret weapon, the smartest of the four.

Rosie Santangelo, from Miami, was petite, cute, vivacious,
and funny. Spiked black hair, dancing black eyes, a sexy wardrobe
on the dramatic side, and an outgoing personality all combined to
attract the single guys. She'd already dated so many men from the
class that the girls lost count.

Their subject, Harry — skinny, waxy skin, a garish scar running the entire length of the abdomen, thinning black hair on his
head surrounding a bald spot the size of a nickel, coarse black hair

shrouding his thin chest — looked to be in his fifties. The girls had no idea how he'd ended up on their dissection table, veins pumped full of blue latex-like material, arteries with red.

"Do you get the feeling we're being stared at?" Vicky began to giggle as she made the first incision of the day, carefully dissecting a big sheet of yellow waxy skin, still matted with the wiry black hair that had inspired "Harry's" name.

"I think they're dazzled by those diamonds you have dangling from your ears," Susan said with an exaggerated wink. "And, Susan gestured to Rosie's open lab coat. "A little cleavage never hurts."

"Yeah, yeah." Rosie grinned. With a blunt hemostat she began to scrape away the connective tissue between the ribs. "Hey, two of you are married anyway. And Susan doesn't have time for men. Study, study, study. Except maybe for Dr. Will Cunningham."

Susan glanced up at their young lab instructor, a tall man with toffee colored skin and close cropped hair. Flustered as he caught her eye and flashed a toothy smile, she leaned forward, concentrating on the neurovascular bundle beneath Harry's ribs. "Quit embarrassing me," she said. "Here, give me a hand." It was time to expose the intercostal bundles that lay beneath each rib.

"You know, that scar on Harry's belly mystifies me." Vicky picked up her scalpel, pausing to inspect the gnarly white scar, which traveled all the way down the cadaver's belly to his pubic bone after taking a slight curve to the right around his umbilicus. "Hmmm, must be some gastrointestinal surgery?"

"Maybe an ulcer? Or some kind of malignancy?" Susan suggested. "He's skin and bones."

"Laura, what do you think? Why so quiet?" Vicky inquired. "Kids keep you up at night?"

Laura shrugged.

"Hey, don't these ribs make you ravenous?" Rosie quipped as her instrument made scraping sounds against the underlying bone. "If only we had some barbecue sauce right now." She looked up for a reaction to her ghoulish attempt at levity.

"Oops, sorry, Laura, you don't look too good. I mean, you look like you just got diagnosed with an incurable disease."

Laura flushed. "Just distracted, I guess. That extra assignment."

"You've gotta get more sleep, girl," Susan stopped to scrutinize Laura's face. "Even with those glasses, your eyes look red and puffy."

"I have a three-month-old baby," Laura sighed. "And, yes, I am exhausted."

"That lipstick helps," Rosie said. "You should wear it more often."

"How did you get that information about head trauma? The bullet wound in your patient?" Susan pursued. "You have a medical library at home?"

"Maybe her husband is a secret neurosurgeon," Vicky said.

"Very funny," Laura replied, realizing this to be an opportunity to establish her whereabouts last night. "After your dad picked you up, Susan, I realized that I would be going home to a noisy house, and I panicked about the report." She tried hard to sound convincing. She'd set her course: a life of lies. "So I turned around and headed to the library. Lots of good it did me. I was terrible. I just froze up. I'm so embarrassed."

"Well, my father, for one, was worried about you," Susan said.

A confused expression crossed Laura's face. "Why?"

"Because he's a cop, that's why."

"Your dad, a policeman?" Suddenly she remembered. Orientation, when they'd all introduced themselves. A detective, Susan had said. Laura's heart started to pound. Keeping her head down, she sensed that they were all staring at her.

"That reminds me. Laura, do you think you could give me a ride into school?" Susan asked. "With all the riot problems, Dad's hours are crazy."

"Uh, sure," Laura said. "You live by Mount Carmel Hospital, right?"

"Right. About a mile from you," Susan said, deftly changing blades on her scalpel.

"It'll be good having somebody to ride in with. This city's scary."

Susan nodded. "With all the curfews and ongoing violence, the city's a mess."

Quite the understatement, Laura thought, desperately trying to process the impact of Susan's dad seeing her as she ventured out of the hospital last night.

"Raymond talked to Mayor Cavanaugh last night at a fund raiser. The *Detroit Free Press* is all over the administration, probing into each and every death," Vicky announced. "One of the perks of med school is I don't have to attend all that bullshit stuff. Not that last night was bullshit. It was for the families of cops and firemen killed in the riots."

The girls nodded sympathetically.

"Hey, Susan," Vicky looked up, scalpel in mid air. "Is it politically okay to refer to the police as 'cops'?"

"'Cops' is okay," Rosie jumped in as if an expert in "politically correct." "I've heard worse. Hey, you guys been listening to Stokely Carmichel? Calling for Total Revolution? H. Rapp Brown talking 'Black Power'? Now that's a bit unsettling."

"Yeah. You know, it's not easy being a black detective in this city, especially now. Dad tries to be a good role model for the ones coming up." Susan looked up from her dissection, placed her scalpel on the tray and picked up a forceps. "On the bright side, he does love his job. Thinks he makes a difference. Like your husband, Laura."

Laura said nothing. She'd been going over last night one more time.

"Talking about making a difference," Rosie added. "The mayor's office put out a commendation on City Hospital. Very complimentary, how the hospital pulled together, worked around the clock, that sort of thing. Lots of quotes from Dr. 'Charming' Monroe."

"I heard that 80% of the riot victims were taken to City Hospital," said Vicky. "Here let me retract that rib. And that they ran out of beds in the prison wards."

"True," Susan reported with an authoritative nod. "Dad said that even the doctors were carrying guns."

"I don't believe it," Vicky looked up from her dissection. "Doctors with guns? No way."

"It's true," replied Susan. "The violence hasn't stopped…last week a nurse's aide was stabbed right outside the hospital."

"Susan," Laura interrupted. "Are the police doing anything? About the doctors and guns?"

"Don't know," Susan said. "Strange times. Dad said they put panic buttons at all the nursing stations, but you know my concern right now?"

She didn't wait for an answer. "The Tigers. This three-way race between us and the Red Sox and the Twins is driving me crazy."

"You sound like Steve," Laura said, trying to steady her scalpel. Chat about Steve and the kids, she told herself. That's what they expect. "Any sport will do." She fought the urge to talk too fast like she did when she was scared. "Baseball's his passion. He'll go crazy if the Tigers win the pennant. Did I tell you he was at Tiger Stadium for that double header against the Yankees the Sunday the riots broke out? The mayor called the game."

"I can't stand sports talk," groaned Rosie. "Hey, Vick, I saw you get picked up in a white stretch. Must be tough to have such a rich husband."

Laura didn't hear Vicky's response. For the rest of the session she remained silent. By the time they had finished their work with Harry that morning, she'd run through the details of her alibi three times.

CHAPTER SEVEN

At 6:30 Thursday night, traffic crawled on the Lodge as Laura exited the Ford Expressway. All day long with the exception of her morning presentation, she hadn't stopped trying to consider her current situation in an objective manner. Though it still seemed so unreal, she knew that she couldn't simply wish the horror away. All she could do was move forward, just like the traffic. She had to face the facts and decide.

The facts. Yesterday she had been raped. She had killed the rapist with a gun her husband got from a hunting buddy, a gun with no legal registration. Yes, she had gotten through a whole day undetected. But there were bound to be problems ahead. Laura wanted to sort them out, and for once, she welcomed the tedious traffic as she drove home.

First, Steve. At some point tonight, she would have to undress. Steve might notice the bruises on her ribcage, legs, and arms that had turned a blotchy blue. She had to come up with a believable story to explain them. How about a fall down the back stairs of the med school building? She could tell him that she was in a hurry, missed a step and was lucky not to have broken anything. She'd cut her lip in the fall. At the very least, she decided, she'd undress in the bathroom.

Next — much more horrible — sex with Steve. Tonight he would be expecting it. Even if she could put him off, tomorrow night would be a certainty. Steve couldn't go more than two nights without sex. Laura had found this endearing throughout the entire five years of their marriage, but now it frightened her. The fact was, she might even have some type of venereal disease, and she had not yet had a chance to get the penicillin she'd read about. The mere thought of intercourse made her stomach churn. She felt defiled, like she could never be clean again. What would she do?

One thing was clear. She would do what she had to. Steve and the police must never find out what happened last night. If they did, she'd never be a doctor and much, much worse, she'd risk losing her kids. Just that thought made her so lightheaded that she considered pulling off to the shoulder. Instead she reached into her purse for Mylanta to calm her churning stomach.

Laura eventually turned off the highway and made her way into her own neighborhood.

"Mommy's home!" Mikey shrieked as he saw Laura drive up to the curb and step out of the car. He dropped the toy cars he'd been playing with and rushed from the small front yard to her car, insisting, as usual, on carrying her heavy books.

"Hi, Mikey," she called, leaning down to stack two medical texts in her son's small arms. Each time she looked at Mikey she marveled that she could be the mother of such a wonderful little child. Everywhere she took him people would turn to remark at how cute he was — floppy blonde hair with bright blue eyes, and such a sunny, affectionate personality.

Laura smiled down at him. "Thanks for helping me. You're so strong. I don't know how you can carry so many big books."

"I'm not going to drop them either," he announced proudly as she reached above him to open the door to the unassuming two-story house.

"Thanks, Mikey." Laura glanced inside to the living room. A small couch, a wooden coffee table, and two armchairs in front of the television and stereo console practically filled the room. Where was Steve?

"Did you guys have dinner yet?"

"Nope. We waited for you," Mikey announced, as if that were

a great accomplishment. "Mommy, what happened to your mouth?"

Her lipstick had obviously faded. "Oh, just a little fall. That was so nice of you to wait on dinner for me," she said. Secretly she had hoped that Steve would have fed Mikey and the baby so she could just sit down and play with them, forgetting everything else for a while.

"Where's Daddy?" she called, walking toward the kitchen. No Steve. Heading down the hall to their bedroom she found him napping on the bed, Kevin asleep beside him.

"Hmmm, hey babe," Steve groaned.

Laura lifted Kevin and carried him to his crib, hoping he would continue sleeping for a while. Mikey raced into the kitchen to decide what they wanted for dinner as Laura stopped off in the bathroom to gulp down two tablets of Tylenol. Mikey chose grilled cheese sandwiches, and Laura quickly prepared coleslaw and opened a can of applesauce. She then went into the bathroom and changed into jeans and an old sweatshirt before calling Steve into the kitchen for dinner. As usual, Mikey dominated the conversation as they ate the simple meal, excitedly talking about Uncle Ted's new Mustang convertible. Uncle Ted, Laura's brother, had even sent a picture of the car to Mikey. At age three, Mikey knew every make of car and was very proud of his expertise.

Kevin woke up as Laura cleared away the few dishes. She quickly warmed a plastic bottle of formula.

"Steve, honey, I'm not feeling well. Could you run out and pick up some groceries for the weekend?" Laura improvised. She wanted to keep Steve occupied as long as possible. "We're pretty low on everything."

"You do look a bit peaked. I think you're pushing yourself too hard." He grinned. "I don't feel much like going out tonight. I want to go to bed early. I missed you last night."

"Me too, Mommy!" Mikey chimed in.

Forcing a smile, Laura appealed to Steve's sense of paternal responsibility. "We're short on milk, and we really do need more baby formula, the one with iron. Why don't you pick up a few jars of strained fruit to start Kevin off on solid food. Just look at him attack this stuff. I think he's ready, don't you?"

"Daddy, can I go with you?" Mikey cut in. "Maybe I'll see one of those new Mustangs in the parking lot."

Steve's hands rose into the air. "Okay, okay," he conceded.

Laura tried to smile. "Thanks, hon."

"Mikey, let's roll. I'm outnumbered. See you soon," he said. "Don't forget that my parents are coming this weekend." Steve stopped to grab the car keys off the side table. "That's why tonight is our night." He winked, then hesitated as he opened the door to leave.

"Hey, what happened to your lip, babe?"

"Just a little fall," Mikey answered.

Laura smiled. She explained hastily, embellishing the lie.

Steve was right. She had forgotten all about Steve's parents coming to town for his birthday. Gently squeezing Kevin, who sucked his bottle contentedly in her arms, Laura tried not to cry. She considered her options: Steve could never stay awake past eleven, so she could count on study time after that to do that coma report. She decided to start the research now and hold Steve off for as long as she could. She took a deep breath, holding Kevin close.

Steve arrived back at the house a few minutes before ten as Laura was tucking Kevin into his crib. Mikey had fallen asleep in the car and together they took him straight to bed, Laura wiping away the chocolate smeared all over his hands and face. She had changed to a pale green, full-length nightgown in spite of the humid night, the most unsexy one she had. She had put rollers in her hair, something she almost never did since her hair was naturally wavy and looked best hanging naturally.

Steve came into their bedroom and undressed to his boxer shorts. He headed directly for the double bed. Lying there, he hummed "Happy Birthday" and waited impatiently as Laura busied herself with folding laundry. Finally, she climbed in and turned off the bedside light, lying quietly until Steve tried to remove her nightgown. "No, I'm cold," she whispered. As he began to make love to her, Laura hugged her nightgown tightly around her and endured the weight of Steve's body on top of hers. Their sex was mercifully quick, and while she was relieved that Steve had not noticed her disinterest, she also reflected how so much of the romance had seeped out of their marriage. But then, what did she expect? The stress of Steve's career and the crushing demands of med school were bound to affect them both. With two young children on top of it all. The question forced itself on her: maybe she was attempting too much. And now having to live with being raped and almost being killed.

Later, hunched over her report, tears flowing, the incident played over and over in her mind. She'd been raped by a very angry, very strong man. Somehow it didn't seem random. He wanted to hurt her. Said he would kill her, slit her throat. She rubbed her eyes, wiped off her glasses and tried to tackle her assignment, but she just couldn't do it. Even though she knew that Steve would be annoyed, she'd just have to steal some time out of the weekend to get her work done.

Eventually, Laura crept back into bed. As she lay against Steve's strong, warm body, she began to feel safe. As much as she wanted to, she knew she would never tell him what had happened last night. She had made her decision. There was no going back.

CHAPTER EIGHT

Steve's parents were seated on the worn living room couch when Laura arrived home the next afternoon. Kevin napped as Mikey zoomed his Matchbox cars around the dining room. Jim Nelson stopped fiddling with the TV long enough to meet her with a hug. Helen didn't even get up, but remained seated on the sofa, a mug of coffee in front of her. Sitting down next to her, Laura attempted to chat with her mother-in-law, but she detected tension immediately. There was really something wrong between Steve and his parents, especially his mother. When she excused herself to go change, Steve joined her in the bedroom. "Same old agenda," he said. "Mother thinks you should stay home with the boys. You know, quit med school."

"Your mother's disapproval doesn't phase me. She's a traditional woman who lives mostly in isolation. I wonder if she even knows what's going on in the world." What Laura didn't say was that whatever Steve's mother's parenting skills were, she didn't want them. She swore that her relationship with her sons would be diametrically opposed to that between Helen Nelson and Steve.

"Mother's never worked. She's as old-fashioned as they come."

"At least your dad's normal."

Steve paused before agreeing or disagreeing. "Yeah, I guess. He's slipping though. Not even going deer hunting on the Upper Peninsula this year."

"I hardly know your parents," Laura sighed, slipping into shorts and a T-shirt.

"Neither do I. I didn't choose my parents. But I can choose not to be like them."

"And you're not." Laura went to Steve and hugged him. "You're a terrific dad."

Laura walked back into the living room. She tried to smile and not stare at Steve's plump mother. Her grayish-blonde, shoulder-length hair was slightly disheveled, and she was clasping her hands together tightly. His father had moved to the easy chair in front of the television set, watching the hosts of a local sports show discuss the batting averages of the American League's top players: Carl Yastrzemski, Frank Robinson, and Detroit's own Al Kaline. As she sat down next to her mother-in-law, Laura couldn't help but long for her own mother. She stifled a sigh, anticipating a stressful weekend.

On Monday morning, Susan waved Laura up into her driveway on Lesure, near Six Mile. As Susan climbed into the front seat of the wagon, Laura pushed aside a plastic bag of disposable diapers.

"Sorry for the mess. With a three-year-old you've always got toys and cookie crumbs and God knows what else left behind. I always keep extra diapers for the baby."

"No problem," Susan said. "It's actually a relief to be heading for classes this morning. I've been holed up all weekend, studying. Yours, my friend, is one of the few faces I've seen in days." Susan picked up a cassette case off the floor and inspected it. "Hey, I didn't know you were an Elvis fan."

"Yeah, always have been. Steve too."

"So how was your weekend?" Susan asked.

"Grueling. My in-laws came down from Traverse City for Steve's birthday and I had to work on that assignment from Dr. Monroe."

"Man, Laura, I don't know how you do it. Kids and in-laws.

Distractions totally derail me. Thank God I'm an only child. I can barely eat sometimes."

Laura glanced at her tall, thin friend. "That's obvious, and you'd better watch it. Pretty soon, you'll be as skinny as Harry. But I am beat."

"Too bad you had to be singled out for that extra assignment," Susan said. "Out of all the people in the class, he picks you, mother of two kids."

"I deserved it," Laura admitted with a shrug. "That word, decubiti. I'll never forget it for the rest of my life."

"Sadistic," Susan said. "People may find him attractive, but that Southern charm is lost on me."

"Charm or no charm, I finished the assignment."

"Hey," Susan changed the subject. "I have some rather horrible news from my dad."

A chill went up Laura's spine as she stared out at the looming Henry Ford Hospital. "Bad news?"

"A murder last Wednesday night. Close to the school. My dad's involved. Remember the morning of our presentation?"

"Remember? I'll be scarred forever," Laura said, willing her heart to stop pounding. Not daring to blurt out, "Susan, just tell me."

"Well, I didn't know it then, but Dad had met with Dean Burke, Dr. Collins, and Dr. Monroe earlier to notify them about this murder. He needed their cooperation. You know, interview students and hospital staff for possible witnesses; tell them how dangerous it still is out there."

"What?" Laura stopped breathing.

"Dad said that they were all very accommodating except Dr. 'Charming' Monroe. He called Dad back, warning him not to harass his interns and residents. Said that the surgical team and everyone else were already overburdened trying to deal with the load of riot injuries. Said he didn't want them further stressed by unnecessary police interrogations."

"What did your father do?" Laura struggled to get those few words out. She needed to keep the conversation going; to find out all she could about the police investigation, though that thought terrorized her.

"Well, Dad said he just heard him out. Didn't want to say anything to piss off the big-time doctor, being that his favorite and only daughter's medical career might hang in the balance."

"Was that it?" Laura tried to seem nonchalant.

"Yeah." Susan turned from her view of the dilapidated West Side projects to glance at her pale friend. "Laura, what's the matter? Are you okay?"

"Huh? I'm fine, really. Just tired."

As they turned into the student parking lot, Susan breathed a sigh of relief. "We've made it one more time. Thanks for the ride."

"No problem. Where should we meet tonight? And what time?" Laura asked as they made their way toward the huge gray Basic Science building.

"Oh! I almost forgot. Dad's got people asking questions around here today so don't be surprised. Remember when we were leaving the hospital together on Wednesday, and Dad picked me up in the main lot? You were on your way to the student parking lot, right? He wants to ask you some questions, too."

Laura stiffened. "That won't be necessary. Like I told you last week, I decided to study instead, and I went right back in and used the library."

"But Dad saw you head off in the direction of the other lot. He remembered because he felt guilty that he didn't offer you a ride to your car. Just think, what if you'd actually been there? You could have been hurt. A man was murdered right about the time you left."

"Murdered? Does he know what happened?" Laura failed to control the shakiness in her voice. She slowed her pace, needing to get as much information from Susan as she could before they walked into the building.

"I don't know. I just wish that I'd had the presence of mind to stay and work on my case."

Laura began to feel cold and clammy. "That botched presentation is what got me the extra assignment. I've got to go over to the surgical office now and hand it in."

"Good luck," Susan said, squeezing Laura's shoulder.

"See you in anatomy lab," Laura said, trying for nonchalance.

"Don't forget the 'gross' part."

"How could I?"

CHAPTER NINE

Laura knocked gingerly on Dr. Monroe's door. When he'd given her the assignment on Friday, he hadn't specified its format or length, but she assumed the more comprehensive, the better.

Preparing the report, Laura had been surprised, and then quickly disillusioned at the awful complications facing Anthony Diggs. She tried to divide them into the most serious and the most likely, but found instead that they were all life-threatening. First, there were lung problems because he had no spontaneous respirations. The ventilator settings were decided by intermittent monitoring of his blood gases, but pneumothorax — a ruptured lung, and atelectasis — a collapsed lung were deadly complications. Other lung disasters, such as bacterial pneumonia, pulmonary edema, and pulmonary emboli were common. Laura was aware that Anthony Diggs had problems with his tracheal tube clogging already.

Infection was a constant threat. Not only pneumonia, but a urinary tract infection caused by the Foley catheter draining his bladder or sepsis from the intravenous catheter that remained his lifeline for fluids, electrolytes, and antibiotics. And as she now knew, pressure sores or decubiti ultimately resulted in gangrene unless skin grafts and meticulous nursing care could interrupt the progress of rotting decay.

Her report focused on fatal pulmonary and infectious outcomes, and she also included references to fluid imbalance and possible kidney failure, cardiac arrest, and malnutrition. She found that immersion in this research offered a temporary escape from the guilt and fear that riddled most of her waking hours. Hopefully, this was the type of thing Dr. Monroe wanted.

No one answered her hesitant knock, so she inched open the door and poked her head inside. The small outer office was occupied by a petite, middle-aged woman.

Connie Zimmer smiled as she looked up from her desk. "Can I help you?"

"Yes, please. I would like to drop off a report that Dr. Monroe requested," Laura replied.

"Of course," Connie agreed. "Who do you work for?"

"I'm Laura Nelson, a med student."

"Oh," Connie smiled again. "They're making them younger every year. I thought you were someone's assistant secretary. Please sit down. Is Dr. Monroe expecting you?"

Laura smiled nervously, shaking her head no. She sat stiffly on a wooden chair, desperate to leave. Glancing at her watch, she saw that she had fifteen minutes before her first class. Still shocked that the detective wanted to question her about the shooting, she needed to find a quiet place to pull herself together and to examine her options. Someone must have seen the man grab her and pull her off the sidewalk. Someone must have been hiding in the shadows. Or did the shot attract a witness? Yes, it had been just light enough that someone may have been able to identify her. How foolish she'd been. She should have gone to the police right away and told them everything. After all, she was a victim too. Would they believe it was self-defense? No, it was too late. What were her odds of being caught? She had no idea. But at least she was alive.

"Miss Nelson?" Dr. Monroe interrupted her thoughts as he stepped out from his office. Connie rose and left the waiting area, files in hand, for the inner office.

"I'm sorry, Dr. Monroe. I didn't mean to disturb you. I'm here to hand in the assignment you gave me last week. Maybe you don't remember."

His eyes widened. "Of course. Here's what I'd like you to do." He reached for the folder in her hand. "Leave the report with me.

Then re-examine your patient and be back here at exactly 5:20 to report your findings. I'll have only ten minutes, so you'll need to be prompt and brief. Is that clear?"

Laura nodded mutely and handed him the report.

"Later, then." Without another word, he turned into his office, closing the door behind him.

Laura rushed to the anatomy lab. After her second class, she headed for the women's locker room on the third floor. Overcome by a growing sense of panic, she needed a place to think about Susan's message: the police were coming after her. They knew something. They must. She had made the wrong decision.

CHAPTER TEN

Laura used what was left of her lunch period to rush over to the hospital. She found Anthony in the corner of the congested men's surgical ward. Good, they'd moved him away from the obnoxious shackled patient. This time the human odors and the sickening smell of disinfectant did not turn her stomach, and she ignored the rude catcalls of patients alert enough to notice her entrance. A dull sky seen from the few narrow windows accentuated the grayness of the ward, exaggerating the yellowish-brown stains on the sheets left by leaking body fluids. As before, her patient was totally still, except for the heave of his chest in tandem with the respirator.

The lone chair next to Anthony's bed was empty; and though she felt badly that Anthony was alone, Laura was relieved that she would not have to try to comfort his mother. She had to examine his emaciated body, specifically looking for decubiti. She located the blotchy area she'd seen on the thin dark skin over the sacral bone. Shrinking back, she saw that it was much larger and that the open sore in the center was deeper, and she now knew that those ulcers could eventually become gangrenous.

She approached the nursing station to inquire which nurse had been assigned to Anthony Diggs that day. The ward clerk indicated the opposite side of the long, narrow bank of desks. Laura's gaze settled on a stately woman in a starched white uniform.

Laura walked toward the woman, slightly taller and about ten years older than herself, her dark skin shining vibrantly against her white uniform. GLORIA JACKSON, R.N. was inscribed on her name badge. The nurse stood beside the counter by a wall cabinet whose open door exposed shelves of plastic tubing and various bottles. Laura paused, remembering her need for penicillin in case her rapist had a venereal disease. She had forgotten all about the penicillin. What about Steve? They'd had sex already. She shook her head, not wanting to think about that, and focused on the woman in front of her.

"Miss Jackson, may I interrupt you for a minute?"

The nurse looked up. "How can I help you?"

"I'm Laura Nelson, a first year med student assigned to Anthony Diggs for my physical examination course. And I, well, I just wondered if I could ask you a few questions."

"I saw you the other day. We'll have to talk while I prepare these dressings." The nurse stifled a yawn. "What I wouldn't do for a cup of coffee right about now. I've worked right through lunch and now it's, what, almost 3:30. But these are my problems, Miss Nelson. What are yours?"

"I know it's been really tough since the riots," Laura replied sincerely. "Here, let me help you with that." She reached for the bandage scissors and cut the adhesive strips that the nurse was struggling to arrange.

"I'm late on my injections, so I appreciate the help. Now, what is it you want to know?"

"Well, when I examined Mr. Diggs today, I was struck by how much his decubitus, I mean decubiti, have progressed since last Thursday," Laura stumbled.

"Yes, Anthony's bedsores are worse," Miss Jackson replied sadly. "We just don't have the resources to keep turning him in bed like we should. I don't have the proper air mattress. It's all I can do to keep his airway free so that the ventilator can function."

"And what about Anthony's future?" Laura went on, recalling his devoted mother. "Do you feel he has any chance for recovery?"

Gloria Jackson's gaze held Laura's. "I don't think so. Maybe a clogged airway would be for the best, I don't know." She hesitated, speaking slowly. "Anthony is a special patient to me. I know his family from the old neighborhood."

"I met his mother," Laura said quickly. "She told me a little about him. It's tragic."

The nurse sighed. "Anthony was a role model for the younger boys in the neighborhood. Headed straight for college on a full scholarship. A miracle in that neighborhood. Guess some dreams are too good to be true."

Laura nodded. "His mother said a policeman shot him. Is that what happened?"

"I just don't know. Those days were crazy. Everything out of control. The report says he was involved in some looting, but he'd never been in any sort of trouble. His brother, however, is another story. I just pray this violence stops before the whole city is lost."

"Sounds like you know the family well?" Laura commented as she placed folded dressings onto a developing stack.

"My sister and Lucy, his mother, go to the same church. Lucy is a good woman, but the poor thing has had more than her share of troubles. My heart goes out to her."

"I thought I'd find her here."

"She's at his brother's funeral."

"What?" gasped Laura. "His brother?"

"Johnny was shot last week. Lucy had to come up with the money for the funeral before they could bury him. Lucky for her, she could rely on the church. Sister Mary Agnes, God bless her, found help. Have you met her? She's a saint."

Laura shook her head.

"Well, you hang around, and you'll get to know Sister. She comes every day to see Anthony."

"What happened to his brother? To Johnny?"

"Shot in the head. Killed outright. They don't know who did it. The kid was a real hothead though. I had to call security on him that very night to get him out of here. He was causing a big commotion right here on the ward. He barged in, cussing and yelling about

white people as usual." She lowered her voice. "He was just plain
bad, that one. Lucy tried to calm him down, but he was out of control."

"Oh, the poor woman," Laura could picture the woman's
kind, tired eyes. Now this?

"Everybody on the street knew that he was involved with a
bad crowd. Neighborhood punks. Smoking dope, that type of
thing. Now he's dead."

The completed wound dressings were arranged on the tray,
and the nurse now turned her attention to the array of small vials in
an open cabinet drawer. Some were labeled penicillin. Laura
watched the nurse's every move as she checked a chart, chose one
of the vials, peeled off its metallic rim, then wiped the top with alcohol soaked cotton. With a smooth practiced motion, she punc-
tured the red rubber center of a vial with a hypodermic needle and
drew the contents into the syringe to the proper calibration mark-
ing. When the nurse turned her back to reach for the next batch of
charts piled up on the counter, Laura grabbed an empty syringe, a
packaged needle, and a vial marked penicillin VK, and slid them
into her pocket. That was the first step. The second was to get up
the nerve to inject herself. She'd look up the right dose, and hopefully, she would not hit a nerve or a major blood vessel, or worse yet,
have some kind of horrible allergic reaction. Wouldn't that serve her
right for stealing drugs?

"Thanks for the information, Miss Jackson," Laura said. "I
don't want to hold you up any longer."

"And thank you for the help." The nurse smiled as she finished preparing the injections. She arranged them on her tray, carefully checking each label on the plastic sleeves, before wheeling
her cart toward the patient beds.

As Laura followed her out of the cramped prep station, a
young black girl stepped into the ward, accompanied by a short,
chubby nun in a black habit. The nun clasped her hands together
behind her back as they proceeded toward Anthony's bed.

Gloria paused. "Over there," she said to Laura. "That's the

oldest of the four Jones girls. And that is Sister Mary Agnes. She's a real hero around these parts. Came from a very wealthy family, an only child. Turned her back on that whole life and joined the order. She came down to this godforsaken neighborhood, oh my, must've been seven years ago. Now she's the principal over at St. Joseph's. I tell you, you've never seen someone do so much for so many people, kids and parents alike."

Both women turned to follow the pair's progress across the room.

"She's too young to be in here, but she's with the Sister, so it's okay by me." A shadow of concern crossed the nurse's face when she noted a third visitor, a young black man with a shaved head, carrying a spray of flowers with a sash that read, "Rest in Peace."

"St. Joseph's?" Laura asked, wanting to show an interest. "Is that near here?"

"It's over by Warren Avenue, just north of here. It used to be a big black hole in the city. Now it's a thriving parochial school." Gloria nodded as the two women visitors pulled chairs close to Anthony's bed and the young man stood. "The guy with them is Ray Rogers. Calls himself 'Snake.' Trouble, just like Johnny."

"Johnny? Anthony's brother?" Laura clarified.

"That poor girl," Gloria said. "One brother shot by the police and another murdered just a block away from the hospital. Those flowers must have come from Johnny's funeral."

Laura jerked. She nearly crushed the vial of penicillin she was fingering in the pocket of her lab coat. Her knees started to buckle, and she lurched forward. Gloria almost lost control of the cart as she reached out to grab her. Laura tried to recover her balance by leaning against the refrigerator unit.

"What's wrong?" the nurse blurted. "Are you okay?"

"Yes. I'm fine," Laura stammered. "I've got to get going."

"Not until you settle down, girl." Gloria steered Laura to a nearby bench. "I knew you looked tired. You been up all night studying? You sit here while I give these injections. I'm already a half-hour off schedule."

Laura sank onto the hard bench against the wall, momentarily complying with the nurse's order until her attention was diverted to the young girl and the man with her. They were both staring and he was pointing at her.

Then the girl called out, "Sister, she's the one in the emergency room Johnny told us about! The yellow-haired doctor. She's the one—"

Laura stared back. What was she talking about? Laura had never been inside an emergency room. Then her heart thundered as the words "yellow-haired" doctor reverberated. She'd heard those words before.

"Stacy, not here," the nun said, glancing at Laura. "Johnny said a lot of stuff. I told your mama I'd check out what he said. Hush, child."

Laura's eyes clouded with confusion as she watched the young man reach over and put a hand awkwardly on the young girl's shoulder. She grappled with the impact of what she'd just heard. Horrified, she now knew whom she had killed and left in the rubble. Johnny Diggs. Anthony's brother. Lucy Jones's other son? It had been self-defense, hadn't it? But could she ever know for sure?

Laura did not wait to hear any more. She bolted off of the bench and ran off the surgical ward.

CHAPTER ELEVEN

Laura headed for the auditorium in a daze. She had one more class, histology, before she had to report back to Dr. Monroe. The lecturer used 35 mm slides, and the lights were dimmed as he worked his way through endless carousels. Laura sometimes dozed off during these lectures, but today she needed to get into that darkened room to sit and think.

She heard nothing of the lecture on the integument: the dermis, the epidermis, and the sweat glands. The layers of the skin seemed irrelevant as she began to reconstruct in detail everything that happened last Wednesday night, from the time she left the men's surgical ward to the time she was attacked. On the very edge of her memory was the shadow of a young man with light brown skin. Not tall, but stocky. Did he have a shaved head? She couldn't recall. He had barged into the ward, practically knocking her down, and yelled something that didn't make sense about a yellow-hair doctor. Then she had gone off to her conference.

The lights suddenly came on in the auditorium. Laura blinked rapidly and dabbed the gathering tears from her eyes. The professor was now illustrating the tissues of the skin on the green chalkboard. He used different colored chalk to point out the five layers of the scalp. Suddenly Laura jerked forward and caught her breath as she realized that her assailant had worn a baseball cap. Underneath his head was shaved just like the scalp the professor was drawing.

She jerked again as someone poked her in the arm. The student sitting next to her had a note in his hand that he was trying to pass to her.

"What? Oh, thanks," Laura muttered as she reached for the note, her name written on the outside. The message read:

I remembered your "special" meeting with Dr. Monroe later (I can't wait to hear how it goes) so I told my dad to pick me up because I need to get home early. That's all for now . . . Oops, not yet. I shouldn't be telling you this, but my dad is going to stop by your house tonight to ask you about that murder last week. Dr. "Charming" doesn't want him approaching any of us at school, as I told you this morning. That's why he's coming to your house. Dad's a great guy, so no problem, but please don't let him know that I told you. Act surprised, etc., and tear up this note. See you, tomorrow.

Love, Susan.

Once again, nausea coursed through Laura. She felt faint and shaky, but managed a glance and a slight wave in Susan's direction, mouthing an "Okay." She then got up abruptly and made her way to the exit. She just had to talk to Steve before Detective Reynolds got to him. She hurried through the halls until she found a pay phone. But when she called his office, Steve was not there.

What was she going to do? The gun that killed Johnny Diggs was still in her house. She had to make sure Steve didn't tell the police anything about it.

"Well, Miss Nelson. You're punctual," David Monroe remarked as Connie showed Laura into his office.

"Yes, Dr. Monroe," she mumbled after an awkward pause. With a sweeping arm motion, he invited her to sit in the lone chair opposite his ample oak desk.

"I've read your report." Dr. Monroe said. "The prognosis, as you've pointed out, is dismal. Did you find anything in your examination today that points to the contrary?"

"Nothing," Laura said quietly.

"The Diggs boy will surely die from complications caused by massive brain injuries. You've done a good job of listing them.

There's no hope of recovery of any cerebral function. We've requested permission from his mother to disconnect the respirator. It'll be best for her and for the patient. But she continues to hold out hope."

He paused. Laura remained silent.

Then Dr. Monroe simply informed her that her report was acceptable, wished her success and dismissed her.

Laura rose from her chair, mumbled a "thank you," and hurried out of his office. She headed toward the nearest pay phone to try Steve again. What she did not notice was that Dr. Monroe had followed her into the hall, watching her run down the corridor. As he turned back to his office, a slight smile crossed his face.

"Steve, I'm glad I caught you in the office," Laura said too rapidly. "You doing okay?"

"Not bad. What's up with you?"

"I'm fine. Listen, I was thinking that it would be nice if we had dinner out tonight." She tried not to sound desperate. "How about Abacus? We love the food, and the service is pretty quick. It's been a while since we've been out."

"What? Is this my wife I'm talking to? Go out for dinner on a weeknight?"

"I had an easy day," she lied. "Besides, I'd like a chance to talk to you. I'm sure Carol can watch the boys. She's always anxious to make a little extra money."

Carol Slade, her husband and toddler son lived upstairs in the house on Washburn that Steve and Laura rented in the northwest section of Detroit. To Laura's enormous relief, Carol had been delighted when Laura approached her about babysitting. For Laura, it meant that her children would never even have to leave the house when she went off to school.

"Tell you the truth, I'm pretty tired. The weekend, all that parental strain." Steve gave an exaggerated groan. "Maybe tomorrow, babe."

"Please, Steve, will you do it for me?" Laura tried to sound excited rather than anxious. "We need it after that weekend. Meet me there at 7:00?"

"Feels like you're twisting my arm, but okay, come home first, and we'll go from there."

"There's a book at the Providence Hospital library in South-field that I need," she bluffed. "Sometimes I go there when the books I need are already out down here, so I'll be out that way already." Laura felt a sick guilt. Was she getting too good at making up lies? "Leave the boys with Carol and just meet me there. Okay?"

"Oh, one more thing, honey. Will you stop at the supermarket on the way and get some jars of baby food for Kevin? Fruit, like applesauce and pears? We also need peanut butter, jelly and paper towels. And, oh, I really hate to do this to you, but I'm in desperate need for pantyhose. Remember, size A. Get suntan or taupe, not beige. Beige makes my legs look sickly."

Laura knew that Steve would balk at the pantyhose request, but the unseemly task might get him out of the house earlier. Hopefully, Susan's dad would not show up before then. She waited in silence.

"Hey babe, that's asking too much. I'll be dammed if I'm going to stand around trying to pick out pantyhose like some kind of weirdo."

"Steve, please. Get me about six pair. Please, honey?"

Steve grunted. "Yeah, I'll do it just this once."

Laura hung up the phone with a sigh. She had one more thing to do before leaving. Stopping in an empty restroom near the building exit, she settled herself down on an uncovered toilet seat in one of the stalls. Cringing, she clumsily assembled the apparatus that she'd secreted in the pocket of her white smock earlier, then plunged the needle through the pink rubber cap of the vial and drew up what she thought was the right amount of milky white fluid. Without the benefit of swabbing the site with alcohol, she stood, bent forward and stabbed the needle into the upper, outer part of her gluteal muscle, pushing the plunger until the chamber of the plastic syringe was empty. Wincing, she prayed that her ignorance would not cause her to strike a critical nerve or a major blood vessel. She expected a sore behind, but at least she wouldn't end up with syphilis or gonorrhea.

CHAPTER TWELVE

Laura and Steve were ushered into a small comfortable booth at Abacus. They both enjoyed this restaurant, nestled in one of the new shopping malls in the Detroit suburbs. The atmosphere was small town, and it reminded both of them of the cozy, comfortable restaurants back in Grand Rapids.

After placing an order for chicken chow mien, fried dumplings, and a couple of beers, Steve began to talk politics. They'd evacuated Hanoi, had Laura heard? The fact was, she hadn't, but she really didn't care at the moment. She just shrugged.

Steve then launched into a breakdown of the recent riot statistics in Detroit. Forty-three deaths. Steve said that there were commissions set up to investigate what went wrong. A lot of finger pointing, but on the positive side, more funds might be allocated for programs his clients desperately needed.

"I'm glad," Laura interrupted him. "Listen, honey, there's something that I need to talk to you about."

"You didn't get your book, huh."

"What?"

"The book you needed? You didn't get it?" He smiled.

Laura faked a laugh. "No, it's not that."

His smile faded.

"Hey," she said quickly. "It's just that something happened around school. Not at the school itself, but in the neighborhood. A guy was shot and killed about a block away from the hospital. Between the main exit and the student lot where I park."

"Did you know him? Somebody from the school?"

"Nobody I knew," she said, taking a deep breath to make sure she spoke slowly.

Steve was already shaking his head. "God, Laura, I keep telling you. You're in such a dangerous section. Look at you, you're scared." He reached across the table for her hand.

"It happened the night I worked late in the library. Remember I called you? You know, for that report I had to do."

Steve listened silently, holding off on asking questions. He frowned, his blue eyes flashing. "That school is too damned dangerous. You could have been killed. You know, all this racial tension and insane violence were not part of the equation when we decided to move to Detroit, but here we are. I tell you, it scares the hell out of me that you have to stay out so damned late." He lowered his voice. "Just because the mayor's lifted the curfew doesn't mean the danger is over. At least you have protection."

Laura felt her face drain. "I'm fine, Steve, really. But I wanted to tell you this so you'd know what was happening. If I hadn't decided to turn back and head for the library at the last minute, who knows what would have happened. God, was I scared when I heard that."

"Damn good thing I gave you that gun. That's exactly why I insisted that you take it, even if you keep giving me misery over it."

"Shush Keep your voice down."

"That neighborhood is unstable and dangerous. Anything can happen any time," he insisted. "You're lucky you didn't get caught in the crossfire."

"You're right. I am lucky," Laura said. "The police are all over the school. The dean's added more security. That's good. But what's not good is that they want to talk to me about this killing."

"Why you?" Steve's eyebrows shot up. He set down his beer and scrutinized his wife.

Laura forced herself to speak slowly. "After our conference, I left the hospital with Susan. Her dad was picking her up there. Susan's dad, who happens to be a detective with the Detroit Police, saw me walk toward the student parking lot before I changed my mind and headed for the library. It was a snap decision, and thank God I made it. I was so torn about being home with you and the boys and pulling together a decent report, you remember, right?"

"Yes, I remember that night. I fell asleep on the couch waiting for you and even had a crimp in my neck in the morning to prove it." He smiled broadly at his wife, the tiny laugh lines around his eyes softening his gaze. It had been a long time since the two of them had been out like this. No kids. Just having dinner.

She smiled back. "The bottom line," Laura continued, "is that Detective Reynolds wants to talk to me. Tonight. At home. Susan clued me in, but I'm not supposed to know, so whatever you do, don't give it away that we're expecting him. Anyway, in case he talks to you, I just wanted to make absolutely sure that you wouldn't mention anything to him about the gun." Laura had lowered her voice. The next booth was empty, but she couldn't afford to be careless.

"Why would I do that? I'm not about to mention an unregistered gun."

"Well, it's just that you are very honest and so am I. If we get asked whether we own a gun, what will you say?"

"We'll both say 'no.' There's no reason to spill our guts about something that is none of their business. I don't want to be harassed just because I want to protect my family. Not by these Detroit cops. From what I've seen some of them are worse than the riffraff. And I'm not too thrilled with them coming to my home to question my wife about something she knows nothing about, either."

This was the reaction Laura had prayed for. Steve being supportive. For a moment, she toyed with telling him the whole story, but the moment quickly passed. She would guard her horrible secret.

Laura nodded. "Okay, but for the time being I'm going to stop bringing it in to school."

"Come on, Laura. You've got to protect yourself. Isn't that what this conversation is all about?"

"Just until this blows over," Laura promised. "I don't want any cops catching me with an illegal weapon."

He grumbled a reluctant assent and went on to tell her about their new neighbors, Sally and Lionel Watkins, a middle-aged black couple and their two young grandsons, who had just moved in next door. Mikey was excited about having new playmates: Keith was four, and Charlie, two.

Laura was only half-listening. Had he said that he liked the Watkins family already? That was good. But she had lied to Steve yet again, which filled her with insidious guilt.

A dark blue Chevy Impala was waiting in front of the Nelson house as Steve pulled his '58 Pontiac sedan into the narrow driveway. Laura parked the Falcon on the curb. They walked hand-in-hand to the door, and it wasn't until Steve turned the key in the lock that two men appeared behind them. One was tall and husky with a shiny bald spot, probably in his fifties, looking professional in a gray striped suit. Must be Susan's dad, Laura figured. The other was slim and younger, pale with watery blue eyes and a long narrow nose, slipshod in baggy dungarees and a wrinkled sports jacket.

Laura tensed as Steve squeezed her hand and turned toward the men. "Can we help you?"

"Mr. and Mrs. Nelson?" the older man inquired.

"Yes," Steve answered.

"I'm Detective Reynolds and this is Detective Kaminsky." He flashed a badge with picture I.D. "Could we come in and ask you a few questions?"

"What's this all about?" Steve said.

"Excuse me, Detective Reynolds, but, you are Susan Reynolds's father?" interrupted Laura, smiling innocently. "Steve, Susan Reynolds is a classmate of mine."

"Yes, I am, Mrs. Nelson."

"Are you here for something specific?" Steve asked. "We're running a bit late, and the babysitter will be anxious for us to pick up our children."

Detective Reynolds nodded tersely. "I know. The lady upstairs answered your bell when we rang. Said you were out to dinner, so we waited outside. Please, take your time to get settled."

Steve began to say something, but Laura stopped him. "Steve, go on up and get the kids. Come on in, detectives."

As Steve headed upstairs, Laura escorted the men into the living room and offered them a pop or beer. Anything to keep her busy in the kitchen, away from their probing stares.   '

"A pop would be great," Reynolds answered. Kaminsky nodded.

"So what brings you here?" Steve asked after Mikey had been put to bed. He joined Laura on the sofa where she sat with Kevin nestled in the crook of her arm. "Has something happened in the neighborhood? Crime's rampant all over Detroit, but so far this neighborhood seems okay."

"No, no, nothing like that," the younger detective said. He had a habit of bobbing his leg as he spoke. "It's not this neighborhood."

"We're investigating a shooting that occurred down by the medical school last week," Detective Reynolds stated flatly. "There was a homicide. Mrs. Nelson, we thought you may have seen or heard something the night of the murder."

"No," Laura responded with an exaggerated shrug. "When did this occur?"

"Wednesday night." John Reynolds studied Laura for a moment before sipping his Vernor's ginger ale. "Mrs. Nelson, I personally saw you in the vicinity of the murder site that night. When I picked up Susan, I saw you walk directly toward the scene of the crime, the direction of the student parking lot. That's why I'm here. Are you sure you didn't see or hear something?"

Laura shook her head.

"That school should have a mandatory escort service for you young ladies. And I don't mean after hours, I mean all the time. I've told that to the dean. If I'd had any sense, I'd have driven you to the lot that night, and we wouldn't be having this conversation."

Laura nodded. "You needn't have worried about me. I turned right around and headed for the med school library."

"What made you do that?" the younger detective asked.

"I had a presentation to prepare."

Reynolds nodded. "When did you turn around? How far had you gone?"

"What? Oh, not even a block."

Kaminsky swallowed the last of his pop and jumped in. "Did you see anything unusual? Did you hear anything?"

Laura paused. "No, it's always pretty scary around the school and the hospital, but nothing unusual. When I eventually went home that evening, I got an escort and left by the exit on the other side of the building, my usual route to the student parking lot."

Steve put a hand on Laura's arm. "Laura, I never want you leaving alone. No matter what time. Promise me."

The detectives alternated asking the same questions from multiple approaches. Did she hear a gunshot? See anyone running? Did she see anybody lurking around?

Laura sat quietly on the sofa while repeatedly denying that she saw or heard anything unusual. She strained to appear casual, secretly relieved that the cut on her lip had already healed. She reminded herself to be consistent as the men peppered her with questions. The last few questions became more direct, more intrusive. "Did anyone see you walk back in?"

"Well, I saw the chief of surgery, Dr. Monroe, in the doctor's lot by the main door. Naturally, there were all kinds of people inside. Relatives visiting patients, that kind of thing. I saw people I knew in the library."

"Exactly how far did you go toward the student lot? And how long do you think you were out there before coming back into the hospital?" Kaminsky pressed, his leg still bobbing.

"I don't know exactly. I went straight to the library and worked there until I left to go home. Why are you asking me all of these questions?" Laura tried to keep both the irritation and the panic out of her voice as she tugged gently on Kevin's plastic bottle,

removing it from his mouth with calm deliberation and lifting the
infant over her shoulder. A diversion to give herself a moment to
get composed.

"We're just trying to find out if you saw anything connected
with this murder, ma'am," Reynolds said more softly. "Now, is
there anything you can recall about last Wednesday night that
might help us?"

"I just don't see why this is so important," Steve began.

"Someone died. That's important, Mr. Nelson," Reynolds answered, "and we're following up on leads. The shooting took place
in the general time frame your wife left the hospital. If the shooter
saw her, he might figure that she also saw him. I hope you understand this line of questioning is for her protection."

"We appreciate that," Steve said. "But my wife has already
told you she saw nothing."

Detective Reynolds scratched his head, got up and faced
Laura directly. "I hope you're not hiding anything out of fear, Mrs.
Nelson, because if you saw someone, you'd be much better off let-
ting us know now. Remember, I'm here to help you, not hurt you. I
don't want anything like this happening near the med school again.
Not to you, not to Susan, not to anybody."

"I saw nothing," Laura repeated, her eyes averted.

Reynolds glanced at Kaminsky, then back at Laura. "My
guess is somebody did. There were signs of a struggle. Like someone had been dragged. Might have been a sexual assault." He
stared at Laura's blonde hair falling in waves to her shoulder.

"Oh," was all she could think of to say. She made a mental
note to toss out the shoes she'd been wearing that night. Her pantyhose and panties were long gone.

"To tell you the truth, we lost a lot of evidence because of the
heavy rain. Body'd been out there a few hours, but there was still
blood. Of course, we bagged the hands anyway."

"What does that mean?" Laura asked picking up the empty
plastic bottle and squeezing it with both hands.

"For testing. First we swab the hands for gunpowder residue, see if the guy maybe shot someone else. At the same time, we also check for anything lodged under fingernails." Reynolds looked intently at Laura, holding the stare for an uncomfortably long time.

Laura forced herself to respond levelly. "So what did you find?"

"Investigation's still ongoing," Kaminsky dismissed her question, but Reynolds said, "Blood, not the victim's, and fibers, not from his clothing."

"Well, that's all very interesting, detectives, but it's got nothing to do with us," said Steve, standing up abruptly.

Reynolds crossed his arms over his chest. "We also found the bullet at the site. You don't own a thirty-eight caliber gun, do you, Mrs. Nelson?"

"A gun? No, I don't," Laura said quickly, getting up to stand by Steve. That was true; it was Steve's gun, wasn't it? By then she was thinking of the red sweater. She'd have to get rid of it and the skirt.

Reynolds' intense black eyes did not waver. "Okay, folks. Give us a call if anything comes to mind about that Wednesday night, even if you think it might be trivial."

"Thanks for the pop," he called as he and Kaminsky headed out the door.

In the Chevy, Reynolds frowned.

"So whattaya think?" Kaminsky asked as they drove away. "Anything strike you as off?"

"Not exactly."

"That blonde hair though. First glance, looks like it could be a match to the strands we found."

"Sure. And a match to the thousands of other blondes in the city."

"So whatta we got?"

"What we've got is a beat-up thirty-eight that went through the victim's skull."

"Okay, the victim. Who saw him last? Hospital security. We

talked to them separately, right? Stories gibe perfectly. The Diggs kid mouths off. They escort him out, thinking he's just a punk. Kid disappears, winds up dead an hour later. Pants down to his thighs. End of story."

"End of his life, you mean," Reynolds added. "So the kid runs off and grabs a woman? Maybe a girlfriend pops him off? A prostitute? Like maybe the kid doesn't pay up and the pimp offs him?"

"Or a stranger? Like you'd expect with a rape, right?" Kaminsky said. "Only our boy ends up the victim."

"Gotta be sexual assault. They found juice on his skivvies, like he lost it not too long before he bought it, too."

"Right. So maybe it's a rape. There's his juice and somebody's vaginal fluid. He's got a blade, but it's tucked away in his pocket 'cause he doesn't think he'll need it. Looks like maybe the woman was carryin', surprises him with the thirty-eight when he's not payin' attention, and he ends up dead."

"Which means we've got a murder victim and a rape victim," Reynolds said.

"Maybe a third party to make it complicated. Say the girl gets raped. Boyfriend shows up. Pops the perp."

"We already checked out the hospitals. Plenty of rapes. Nothing fits. So what do we really have?"

"We've got B-negative blood embedded under a nail on the left hand," Kaminsky summarized. "Victim's O-neg. And red cotton fibers and a long blonde hair."

"All of which puts us nowhere." Reynolds shook his head. "1300 Beaubien won't be happy. Crazy the politics now. Congress and the President breathing down our necks for what went wrong. Governor Romney looking for the Republican nomination next year."

"Mayor's on the hot seat." Kaminsky smirked.

"You voted for Cavanaugh, did you not?"

"Sure did. Thought he was gonna make real progress, then look what happened. Fuckin' city'll never get over it."

Reynolds stared out the car window. "Maybe so, 'Minsky, but

politics or no politics, we've got our jobs to do. Let's head over to the kid's neighborhood again and see what we find. Buddies, girl-friends, whatever. The kid had a family, right? His brother's layin' in a hospital bed right now. We've got plenty of other people to talk to."

"What about the Nelson woman?"

"Good question. Check out the library story. Before that, she was in class with my daughter. That I know."

CHAPTER THIRTEEN

Later that night, the cold steel blade of a knife cut through her throat. All five layers of the skin slit, muscles severed, the jugular sliced. It was so quick compared to the hours of meticulous dissection they'd afforded Harry's neck. Laura tried to scream, but the big, muscular hand firmly cupped her mouth so no sound could emerge. The faint glow of the moon exposed the glint of the blade dripping blood. Anticipating excruciating pain, she was incredulous as death came quickly, and she floated upward.

Her spirit drifted over the room and lingered as her body was displayed in a simple ivory-colored casket. She was wearing her violet knit dress with the high neckline that covered the horrible slash across her throat. Her hair looked okay, except the part was on the wrong side. She doubted that anyone would notice the difference, but it would feel odd if she were still alive.

Steve stood stoically as he greeted the procession of relatives, friends, and classmates. His eyes were red and puffy. He was dressed in his dark blue suit and the new tie she'd given him for his birthday. Everybody talked in hushed voices. Everything seemed sad, but rather serene. Then what was so terribly wrong? She answered her own question. She couldn't see Mikey or Kevin anywhere. She needed to find them, but she couldn't penetrate the thick cloud down there. The harder she tried the farther away she drifted.

Laura awoke — soaked in sweat, tears covering her cheeks. She struggled to fight off the memory of death. Steve had awak-

ened and propped himself up to hold her as she sobbed. The nightmare lingered stubbornly as she lay against him, finally quieting
down. Slowly, reality seeped through the fog and her resolve reap-
peared. Had she said anything out loud?

When Steve went back to sleep, Laura crept into the kids'
closet and retrieved the gun. It felt cold and heavy as she held it
with two hands, turning it over. She should have paid more attention when Steve tried to teach her about guns. She'd so objected to
carrying one, she'd tuned his instructions out. She didn't know
about bullets and shells and how bullets were traced to guns. She
didn't know whether she should try to take out the remaining bullets. Even if she dared to try, how would she explain the missing
bullets to Steve? Even worse, the single missing bullet? No, she'd
have to keep the gun hidden. Replacing the thirty-eight in the kids'
closet, Laura padded to her own closet, reached into the far corner,
and pulled out the red sweater and filthy skirt. She stuffed them in
a plastic bag and for a minute thought about putting the gun in
there too. But how could she explain a missing gun to Steve? So she
took the heinous bag and shoved it into the middle of the accumulated week's trash. Pickup was early tomorrow. She'd put the can
out before she left for school and hope to God that it disappeared
forever in some dump.

When Laura returned to bed, Steve stirred. "Feeling better
now, babe?" he groaned, flopping over, resuming an irregular snore.

CHAPTER FOURTEEN

DECEMBER 1967

The winter had begun as it always did, crisp autumn nights followed by a stretch of Indian summer before a white Thanksgiving. As Christmas approached, the great expanse of Michigan was blanketed in snow. In Detroit, the bitterly cold nights sent much of the city's population indoors, allowing a false sense of security amid the hushed downtown streets for the first time since the riots.

David Monroe arrived home in Grosse Point Shores earlier than usual. He'd settled into his favorite leather easy chair in the study, wondering if he had the energy to start a fire. After four months the surgical service at City Hospital had drifted back to normal. Still incredibly busy, but the last of the riot victims had finally been discharged, except for Anthony Diggs who had died that morning.

Surprised at the depth of his grief over the poor Diggs kid, David felt inadequate, almost despondent. If the kid had been logged into the ER and treated promptly, could he have been saved? No, he answered his own question. The bullet had destroyed too much brain tissue. Still, David felt personally responsible for the breech of protocol during that chaotic night. And now, after dedicating his life to making City Hospital's trauma care the best in the world, the hospital's reputation might be tainted. He blamed himself; he should have been more discreet. Instead, he'd openly chastised that intern, a pudgy woman with brassy blonde hair, who'd bungled Digg's intubation. Instead of slipping the plastic tube in the trachea, she'd shoved it into the esophagus, depriving the boy's lungs of oxygen. David learned later that Digg's brother had been watching. The brother had heard him tell the intern, "Inconceivable that this could happen in this ER. Criminal. If this boy lives, he'll be brain dead."

Well at least the mother would not have to deal with his medical expenses, and so far that nun hadn't filed a lawsuit or gone to the media.

"David, you're home early," Cynthia's voice interrupted. "Is everything okay?"

No, David wanted to say. Everything's not okay. I'm depressed. I'm not happy. I don't know why I came home early tonight. But he said nothing.

"Kate Davis just dropped me off. I didn't expect you, but I am glad you're here," she said while removing her cashmere coat and holding it out for the maid. "We have to talk, but I need to change. Dinner's at seven."

They sat on opposite sides of the lavish sofa in the drawing room of their mansion after an evening meal. Cynthia again brought up plans for an Aruba getaway.

"Cynthia, it's just not possible."

"Darling, I just don't understand. The med school is closed, is it not?"

"That doesn't mean I'm free."

"You told me yourself, the students have all gone home. Everybody has gone home. It's a week before Christmas. Normal people rest and relax with their families. Don't tell me you can't get coverage for the surgical schedule. That's absurd."

"Families," David echoed. "Except you have no use for mine."

"Let's not get into that." Cynthia pushed back her shining hair. "I've already booked our flights. We leave for Aruba on the 27th. That way we can still go the Yacht Club on Christmas Eve and, if you insist, to Nick and Denise's on Christmas. We'll be in the islands in plenty of time for a New Year's Eve party the Wilson's are throwing. I bought a sensational new gown!"

"I told you before, I just can't spare the time."

"Explain to me exactly why?" Cynthia's voice now at a shrill pitch. "We didn't take one trip the entire fall."

"Sorry, not this year."

"Well, we need to get away. All you think about is that hospital."

"I have responsibilities, you know that."

"I'm thinking about us. Maybe it's time to try," her voice became softer. She leaned forward and said, "I'm telling you, David, this is really important for us." She let the "us" linger.

Ten years earlier, when they first dated, he had found her manipulative side amusing. Cynthia, the prima donna of Grosse Pointe Shores, and he, the idealistic young doctor. As he lifted his brandy snifter, his glance fell on the shadows in the corner; David wondered if he had ever really loved her. At that moment he was aware that he felt both pity for and guilt about Cynthia.

"What could be so important to us?" He gazed absently at the Manet on the wall in back of her.

Cynthia glared at him. "You just don't understand."

"Don't understand what?"

"What's at stake."

The lights were dim, and the candles on the coffee table flickered.

"What are you talking about?"

David felt a pang of sadness while he studied Cynthia's profile. What's at stake is that you can't make me trade my responsibilities for a beach vacation. Had they grown so far apart that they'd lost all semblance of communication?

"Oh, what does it matter? My friends are right." Cynthia was almost screaming. "You don't give a damn about me. You're too busy feeding your perverted obsession with those naïve little nurses who treat you like a God."

David's clenched his fists, but he kept his tone placating, patronizing. "Cynthia, it's late. Let's not quarrel." He rose and started up the spiral staircase. When they so chose, which was often now, they slept in separate suites.

"You ruined my life," she said softly. "Now that Daddy's gone, what is there to live for?"

"Cynthia, stop talking like that."

David grabbed the back of an armchair. After her father died, Cynthia had threatened suicide a few times when she did not get her way. Although he considered her earlier threats a mere ploy for attention, he had taken precautions to keep all sedative medication in the house to a minimum. Because they kept no guns, he felt relatively secure. Right now she was just blowing off steam because she wasn't getting her way. He'd come to realize that he should never have married her.

If only they had had a child. And now, years had passed, David's dream of children had faded, replaced by bitterness. Standing in the living room of his opulent home, David felt suddenly desolate. His life, so carefully planned, so full of the promise, was empty.

He dimmed the lights and watched in silence as Cynthia stood up and brushed past him at the foot of the stairs. "You'll be sorry," she seethed. "I was really going to do it this time. For you."

David opened his mouth but no words came. As he stood in the dark foyer watching Cynthia climb the staircase, he was too drained to repress the memory of the darkest moment in his life.

Six years ago was the happiest period of their marriage, or so he thought. His career was blossoming. She was wrapped up in the social scene. Elated by an enthusiastic response to the research he'd presented at a surgical meeting in San Francisco, David had taken the red-eye back to Detroit to share his excitement with Cynthia. He'd taken a cab to Gross Point Shores, longing to surprise Cynthia and just slip into bed beside her.

Letting himself into the house, he'd crept up the circular

staircase, already unbuttoning his wilting shirt. He'd heard the moan coming through the open bedroom door. Could Cynthia be having a bad dream? She used to have nightmares frequently about her mother's death. He'd rushed to her side to comfort her.

"David, thank God," Cynthia's normally strong voice trembled. "How did you know?"

"Darling? Know what? What's happened?" At Cynthia's side, he could see she was writhing in pain, her dark hair splayed across the pink silk pillowcase. But it was her pallor that had scared him the most. He dropped to his knees, fumbling for her hand. "What's wrong?" he pleaded. "Tell me, Cynthia."

"I wanted to go through with it, but I got scared." The words came out in chokes, interspersed amongst moans. It wasn't until he turned back the sweat soaked sheet and saw the pool of dark red blood that had leaked out around saturated sanitary napkins, that horror replaced panic.

Grabbing Cynthia by the shoulders, failing to control the anger in his voice, he'd demanded, "What have you done? You must tell me."

"Yesterday," she said. "But I didn't think it would hurt like this. David, did they do something wrong? I'm so scared." Tears filled her deep blue eyes, saturating the pillows. "Please don't let me die!"

"You had an abortion! You killed the baby? Our child?"

"Why did you do this?" he'd sobbed.

"I thought I could do it. I knew you wanted a baby. You were away. I got scared. Found a doctor. Please don't let me die." Her words came out thready, halting. She continued to writhe, and he knew he had to help her.

"You're going to need blood transfusions, antibiotics. I'll have Ed Barrone admit you to the hospital. Call it a miscarriage."

"David, please understand. My mother. I was a little girl when she died. She died giving birth. She bled to death. Daddy always told me not to get pregnant. I tried — for you. I got too scared."

How could he ever forgive her for intentionally killing his

child? Cynthia was a healthy young woman. Using her mother's tragedy was not an acceptable excuse. At least to him, but was he being fair? It was Cynthia's body. Was she really that terrified or was she simply selfish? Or was he the selfish one? He honestly didn't know.

Since then Cynthia had taken the pill and, over the years, they'd had sex less and less frequently. He had simply busied himself in his work. Contrary to Cynthia's taunts, he'd had no other women. But six years later, David could still feel the rage.

CHAPTER FIFTEEN

"Daddy, Mommy is taking me and Kevin to her school today," Mikey announced on the Tuesday morning before Christmas as Steve sauntered into the small kitchen whose borders were decorated with paper cut-out snowflakes.

"There are pancakes in the oven for you, hon," Laura offered. She had made them as a kind of peace offering now that the semester was over and she had some time off. Things with Steve had been increasingly tense over the past few months. She just couldn't shake the panic that was always there, accentuated every time they made love. So she struggled to come up with ways to put Steve off. She sensed the downward spiral this put on the intimacy of their marriage, but she was helpless to reverse it.

"It's great being home and having a real breakfast for a change," Laura said tentatively.

Steve sat at the table. "Feels like forever," he said with a smile. "Don't think I've had pancakes since—"

"Since the Tigers lost the pennant." Laura, smiling herself, finished his sentence. "I made them the morning after that split doubleheader."

"Ouch. Sending Boston to the series just to lose to the Cards. Mark my word, the Tigers are going all the way next year. Right, Mr. Mike?"

"Right, Dad. I like Al Kaline."

Steve patted Mikey's blonde head. "Sure you want to go in today?" he asked.

"Susan called yesterday and said that the first semester grades will be posted at nine this morning. They're also mailing them. But we're going up north and the suspense is killing me. I figured I'd just drive in to get them."

"Sure you can handle the boys?"

"Yes. There'll be plenty of parking spots right outside school."

"As long as you're careful," he said, swallowing a mouthful of pancakes. "Mmm, these are great. You're not having any?"

Laura hesitated. "Guess I'm just not hungry. I'll grab something later."

For a month or so, Laura had suffered constant nausea. Sometimes it was hard to keep food down, a situation she had initially attributed to the memory of that awful night and then the stress of final exams. And now she had missed three periods. She was due this week, and if she didn't get it she'd have to see a doctor. Surely she'd feel better once she knew she had made it through the first semester.

"Come on, Mommy, let's go. I want to see your school." Mikey began to smack his fork impatiently against his plate. "Let's go now!"

Laura marveled at the child's enthusiasm. How could anyone — even a kid — consider the tedious drive downtown exciting? With a sharp pang, she remembered how she herself had felt on her first day of class when life was simply brimming with possibility. Now she was just relieved not to have been implicated in the murder of Johnny Diggs. As each day passed the fear inside her subsided a bit, but it never dissolved, and she knew it never would.

Laura carried Kevin and led Mikey along the walkway that connected the hospital to the med school where they entered the elevator that would take them to the third floor.

"What's that funny smell?" Mikey inquired as soon as they stepped off.

"I don't smell anything," Laura answered before realizing that it was the all-permeating odor of formaldehyde escaping from the anatomy lab. She no longer even noticed the smell. Poor Harry, she thought, he's still in there half-dissected. She wondered if his soul had gone to heaven or hell.

"It stinks," insisted Mikey. He pushed against the elevator wall. "I love elevators."

"Me too, Mikey. Here, you can push the button."

The administration posted the semester grades outside the cafeteria on the wall. All grades were listed by social security number in order to preserve confidentiality.

"Come on, Mikey," she urged, reaching for his hand. Her son had stopped to look at posters outside the physiology department office. Laura didn't think she could stand the anxiety any longer.

"Mommy, what are these pictures? They look like bodies with no skin."

"Right, Mikey. That's what you look like inside, underneath your skin."

"Are you sure? Yuck," he declared, picking up his pace.

Hurrying along the nearly empty corridors, they soon arrived at the cafeteria. Laura spotted the posted list and shifted Kevin over to her other shoulder. Mikey was beside her, still holding her hand. She stared at the long list of numbers. University Medical School had a pass-fail system for each class, with an option for the occasional honors.

Laura stood still for a few moments, silently reciting a Hail Mary. She then raised her eyes to each listing, starting with biochemistry. Thank God, a pass. Moving to anatomy, she gasped and let go of Mikey's hand. Honors. Better than she'd ever dared dream.

"What's wrong, Mommy?" Mikey squeaked.

Taking Mikey by the hand again, she stood and went back to the charts. Histology, a pass. physiology, another honors.

"I don't believe this," she let out. One more list, physical diagnosis.

The shock of another honors registered.

"Laura," a familiar voice called out. It was Rosie. "I knew you'd show up. Oh, these must be your kids. Hello, Mr. Kid," Rosie stooped down to say hello to Mikey. "So, what's the good word?"

Laura was still stunned. "Well, okay. I mean, really okay. How about you?"

"All passes, thank God. I was really worked up about biochem. I can finally breathe again."

"Me too," said Laura.

"Want to go inside? Maybe Mikey wants an ice cream." Rosie spelled out "ice cream." "I'm finishing some experiments in the lab, and right now they're on automatic pilot. It's a special project because I'm thinking of going for that combined M.D./Ph.D. in biochem. Figured I'd get a head start since I can't seem to keep a boyfriend."

Laura laughed. "Sure, let's go for it. Mikey, you go with Rosie for some ice cream, and I'll take Kevin and find a table."

Thrilled, Mikey ran ahead.

"They have chocolate," Mikey came running back. "That's what kind I want."

Inside the cafeteria, the foursome settled down. Laura took off the boys' snowsuits, waking up Kevin in the process. Then they went to work on Dixie cups of chocolate ice cream.

"So give me the facts," Rosie said. "What did you get? I know you were concerned about physical diagnosis. What did 'Dr. Charming' give you?"

"You mean Dr. Monroe?" Laura grinned. "Well, this you'll never believe. Honors. Even though I bungled that report."

"That's wonderful!" cried Rosie, jumping up to give Laura a hug. "If anybody deserves it, you do. Now I've got to run. Congratulations again, and I'm so glad I finally met your kids."

As Laura settled back to spoon out ice cream for Kevin, she noticed an entourage of white coats heading toward one of the larger tables in the corner, a group of surgical residents. In the center was Dr. Monroe himself.

What should she do? Naturally, he would see her. Children

were not supposed to be in here, and Mikey's squeaky voice had already caused a few people to glance her way. She wanted to thank Dr. Monroe for her grade, but not in the presence of his disciples, and certainly not with her children in tow. Besides, she looked a mess. Almost as bad as she did the last time she'd run into Dr. Monroe unexpectedly, in the parking lot. Remembering it now, her heart slammed against her chest, just as it had that awful night.

CHAPTER SIXTEEN

The surgical group had just completed morning rounds and had a few spare minutes before the next case. It was rare that Dr. Monroe joined the residents for a cup of coffee in the cafeteria, but today was one of those days because the med students were off and the schedule was less hectic. It also gave David a chance to talk with Ed Collins, whose pallor and frailness over the past semester had increasingly concerned him.

The group settled around a circular table and began chatting about the world's first heart transplant that had taken place in Capetown, South Africa, of all places. Someone asked David if he knew Christian Barnard. But he did not answer. He had turned to stare at the young woman with a baby and a small child sitting across the room.

David Monroe recognized Laura immediately. If it were not for his snooping, he would have been surprised by the sight of the children. He had requested her admission file from the med school administration office and learned that she was twenty-three years old, married, and the mother of two children. Graduating from the University of Michigan with a 3.8 grade point average, she'd been given a full scholarship and access to the maximum amount of loans available to first year med students.

What surprised him was that she was married and had children. She'd intrigued him from the start. More and more, she reminded him of himself at that age, intensely committed and passionate about learning.

Originally he had linked his special interest to her report on the unfortunate Diggs case. Then the murder of a young black man near the medical school campus had brought forth questions from that detective, Reynolds. Coincidence that the victim turned out to be the brother of Anthony Diggs?

After informing David that his investigation had unearthed the fact that the victim had been forcibly removed by hospital security less than two hours before his murder, the stubborn detective questioned him very pointedly about Laura Nelson. What did he know of her whereabouts that night? Had he seen her outside the hospital? David told Reynolds that he had. The detective pushed him about timing. Exactly what time had he seen her? David simply could not remember more; he chose not to describe her somewhat disheveled appearance, her wild eyes. Whatever the case, there was no way she could have shown up the next morning had she witnessed a murder. The detective was barking up the wrong tree.

David's attention remained focused across the room where Laura had started to put the baby into a light blue snowsuit.

David rose. "Excuse me a moment," he said, walking toward Laura's table as she struggled with Kevin's zipper.

"Need help with that contraption?" he inquired softly.

Laura blinked. "Dr. Monroe," she blurted, "I'm just getting ready to leave."

"No, Mommy," Mikey said as he stared at the tall man in the white lab coat, "there's still some ice cream left!"

"That's okay, Mikey. We don't have to finish it."

David Monroe smiled broadly.

"Dr. Monroe, I want to thank you for the physical diagnosis grade. I didn't expect it."

"You shouldn't be surprised, considering you handed in a fine report."

Laura blushed.

"I don't give compliments lightly," he said in that charming drawl. "You probably know my reputation."

"Thank you," she said, blushing more deeply.

"Mind if I sit down?"

"Sure." She gaped at the messy table. "Mikey, would you help clean the table and put all our Dixie cups into the trash?"

As soon as David sat down, Mikey leaned closer to him, and the chief of surgery reached out and patted the small blonde head.

Mikey nodded proudly, lifting the tray upon which Laura had collected their leftovers. After he walked off, David spoke slowly, "I thought you might be interested in an update on the Diggs boy. He died just before rounds night before last. It's a blessing, really."

"Oh, no, his poor mother. Such a hard-working woman. And so much tragedy in her life." Laura sighed deeply, looking away for a moment. Forcing down the panic triggered by that name. Then Mikey returned from his errand. She reached up to brush a strand of hair off her face.

"Aren't you going to introduce me to your young companions?" David abruptly changed his demeanor. The distinguished professor vanished and a gentle man emerged.

"Yes, of course," Laura said, taken by the boyish smile David directed at her kids. "This is Mikey and the baby is Kevin. Mikey, this is Dr. Monroe, one of my professors."

"Hi, Mikey." He reached down to shake the little boy's hand, then softly touched Kevin's silky blonde hair just as the baby broke into a smile. "You're a happy fellow, aren't you? But here's the guy I want to talk to." He turned to Mikey. "What's your favorite color?" he quickly asked.

"Green!" Mikey shot back.

"Mine too," he said. "If Mommy says yes, we can go right over there and I bet we can find something green." He pointed to the vending area in the corner of the room.

Laura smiled and nodded as David held out his hand and led the boy away. Mikey, thrilled, found something green among the machines. Walking hand-in-hand back to Laura, he thanked his new friend in an excited, squeaky voice, and gave Laura a pair of lollipops.

"Well, Mikey, it was sure nice meeting you," David beamed down at the little boy, then faced Laura with a smile. "Laura, have a nice holiday vacation."

Laura blushed at his use of her first name. "You too. Thanks again, Dr. Monroe."

As the Nelson trio made their way toward the exit, David sat still for a moment.

"What the heck's going on over there, David?" Ed Collins called. "Who's the pretty lady with the kids?"

Startled, David turned his head. To avoid Ed's questioning eyes, he stood and glanced up at the cafeteria clock.

"Listen, Ed, why don't we meet for a chat after Grand Rounds this afternoon?"

"Sounds good. Now get back to your group of young protégés over there." Ed nodded toward the knot of surgical residents hovering by the doorway.

"Let's get back to it, people," David called as he approached the group. He quickly led his entourage toward the surgical suites to prepare for the next case. All the while, images of Laura and her sons played through his mind. They were soon replaced by more images of Ed. He really did look thinner, even more gaunt than when David had seen him a week ago.

CHAPTER SEVENTEEN

CHRISTMAS EVE 1967

When Laura awoke on the day before Christmas, snow had carpeted the earth overnight. More than ten inches had fallen since their arrival at Steve's parents' house in Traverse City. After learning that Steve's elusive Aunt Hazel would be joining the Nelsons for the holiday, Laura wanted to drive over to the shopping center to pick up a few last minute gifts. Traveling in the Far East, Aunt Hazel had been unable to attend their wedding, but she had sent a substantial check. From what Laura had heard, Hazel was the opposite of her reclusive sister, Helen.

Despite the idyllic winter scene, Laura's mood darkened. She desperately missed her parents, especially her mom. Janet and Ted, her younger siblings, would have left their respective colleges by now, and her family would all be in Florida. Today, they'd have the traditional game of touch football on the beach. Tonight they'd all go to Midnight Mass where her mom sang in the choir. She sipped her second cup of tea, since coffee made her sick now. Laura put in a call to Florida, promising herself that next year she and Steve would take the kids south for the holidays.

She was dialing when Steve burst into the room. "It's safe to go now. The roads are plowed." He plopped down beside her on the double bed, nuzzling her neck with an unshaven jaw.

Awkwardly, Laura caressed his hair. "I'm not feeling too well, hon. Could we wait a bit? I need to get something to settle my stomach."

Steve bolted up. "I knew it! My God, you're pregnant! You've been sick to your stomach for a couple of months now. Explains your moods too. Babe, why didn't you say something?"

"Steve, I don't know," she managed. "I'm just tired and stressed. I can't possibly be pregnant."

He looked into her eyes. "Why not? We've had enough sex, haven't we? Even with all your excuses. No wonder you've been so tired."

Laura attempted a smile. "Yes, but you know I've been careful with the timing and all."

He sat down, slung an arm around her. "Never mind that. I just know it'll be our first girl. Let's go tell Mother and Dad."

"No, your mother will just get on my case about staying home," Laura said, settling in the crook of his arm. "Let's be sure first. You know I don't really want to have another baby right now. I thought we agreed."

"Maybe you'll spend more time at home."

"In the middle of a school semester?" Laura's voice trembled. The nausea and vomiting, worse in the morning, now plagued her every day. After two pregnancies Laura certainly knew the symptoms, but she had ignored this unwelcome reality as long as she could.

"Everything will work out, babe."

Laura stared at him. What did he mean? Was he actually happy about this pregnancy?

Steve drew her close. "Now lie down, I'll bring you some more tea and toast."

After Steve left, Laura shut the door and collapsed on the bed, her tears quickly soaking the pillow. What did Steve mean, spend more time at home? Was he going to make this an excuse for her to quit school? Maybe he was right. This was an impossible time in her life to be pregnant. Would the school kick her out? No, thought Laura with stubborn resolve. She'd worked too hard to get this far.

She was aware that these were selfish concerns, dwarfed by a reality so frightening that she had forced it into the deepest recesses of her mind. Yet she'd have to face up to it. To go back and carefully calculate the onset of her last menstrual period and compare that to the onset of her morning sickness. Then she would have to ask the dreadful question: Who was the father?

Staring out the window at the calm white expanse, Laura ruefully wished she had started on the pills her gynecologist had suggested she take after Kevin was born. She'd procrastinated, blaming her indecision on the Church, whose anti-birth control stance had stopped her from taking anything.

A sharp knock on the bedroom door interrupted her thoughts. Steve walked in carrying a pot of tea on a tray with toast and jelly. Helen Nelson trailed sheepishly behind.

"Laura," she offered, "I didn't know you weren't feeling well. I did say to Steve's father last night that you were looking so peaked," she persisted. "Steve tells me that they're working you way too hard. Hopefully you'll be able to slow down now."

Slow down? She meant leave school. Obviously, that's what they all wanted. Laura blew her nose and dabbed at her puffy eyes. "Thanks. I'll be okay."

After shopping and napping, Laura finally reached her mother on the phone. The sound of her voice made Laura want to cry, though she tried to sound as positive as she could. Still, her mother immediately knew that something was wrong. "Honey, I don't want to pry, but you've been sounding just so awful for too long. Your father and I have been wondering if the whole med school thing is the best idea just now. The boys are so young, and you and Steve have so many responsibilities." Laura squeezed her eyes shut. Everything seemed to conspire against her. Now even her own mother, "I just miss you and Dad," she cut in. "I wish we were in Florida for Christmas."

"So do I, honey," Peg Whelan said.

"Can I talk to Jan and Ted? Are they there?"

"No. They're still at the beach."

Laura sighed, longing to tell her mother about this pregnancy, but not trusting herself to hold back the truth. Instead, she said a quick good-bye and hung up the phone.

That night, Aunt Hazel, enveloped in a full-length fur coat, charged into the Nelson household without ringing the bell. The drama of her entrance, combined with her flamboyance, stunned Laura. Hazel Harmon was the absolute opposite of her plain, plump sister, although they both had wavy blonde hair, almond-shaped eyes, and near identical facial features.

Aunt Hazel headed for Laura with open arms. "I finally get to see my niece! My God, you're beautiful. Much more beautiful than the pictures Helen sent me."

After kissing Laura on both cheeks, Hazel greeted Mikey who had ventured to her side, fascinated by her dangling jade earrings. The startled look on his face as she swooped him up, quickly turned to one of joy.

"Mikey, why, thank God I arrived before you grew up completely. I'm your Aunt Hazel, and I intend to be your favorite aunt. And Steve, darling, you look absolutely fantastic. You really are the definition of handsome. Hard to believe it's been five years since I've seen you. Much too long. You were a gangly young man with cute freckles then. Now this, a father two times over. I simply can't believe it!"

Both Steve and Mikey beamed as she handed the boy to his father. Hazel then turned to her sister and brother-in-law. "Jim and Helen, I'm so glad you invited me for the holidays. It's been so long."

"Happy Holidays, Hazel." Jim Nelson rose slowly from his chair to stiffly return Hazel's hearty embrace.

"It's good to see you, Helen," Aunt Hazel said quietly. Because Helen held the baby, Laura assumed, the sisters did not embrace. "It's been too long."

Laura witnessed this scene with curiosity. A faraway look had crossed her mother-in-law's face as she greeted her own sister. Was it admiration or irritation? Suddenly, the Nelson household was infused with energy. Intrigued, Laura planned to spend time with Aunt Hazel. Maybe she held the key that would unlock some of the secrets that lurked beneath the restrained facade of the Nelson family.

CHAPTER EIGHTEEN

In Detroit, the bitter cold and blanket of snow made for a quiet Christmas Eve at the Jones home.

"I hope Mama comes home soon," Katie repeated for the third time. Her two older sisters tried to be patient. It was only 8:00. The youngest of the Jones sisters, Katie hadn't quite grasped the impact of the tragedy that had struck the family. She still believed the holiday would bring magic.

"Remember last year? We had the biggest tree. There was a present for everyone."

"She'll be here soon. Don't be a baby," Rachel said glumly. She knew that everything was different this year. Her brothers, Anthony and Johnny, were in heaven. Now there was no Christmas tree and no presents. Her mama wasn't home yet and neither was her oldest sister.

"Mama's gonna be real mad about Stacy," Rachel added. "She's not supposed to leave us home alone."

"Stacy said she'd read me a Christmas story before bedtime," complained Katie.

"She will, honey," responded Sharon. The second oldest, she assumed the responsible role. Pulling out the fish sticks that she'd warmed in the oven, she offered a plate to her little sister. "Here, Katie, if you eat these, I'll let you have some ice cream."

"Okay, but I want Mama to come home. Christmas is almost here!"

"We can play Parcheesi while we wait for her," Sharon said. "I'll go get it. Rachel, play with us."

There was no sign of holiday festivity in the Jones house. The small black and white television in the sitting room had been broken for a week. That would have been a good distraction for little Katie. They could have watched some Christmas specials. Maybe it didn't matter. The Jones family would be excluded from the rest of the world's holiday celebration this year anyway. It wasn't fair, but Sharon knew she had to try to keep up their spirits the best she could.

"Okay, roll the dice to see who goes first." She laid out the well-worn Parcheesi board as Rachel joined them at the kitchen table.

More snow began to fall in northern Michigan on Christmas Eve as the Nelson family sat down to a traditional Christmas Eve dinner. Helen had roasted a turkey and fixed all the trimmings. She refused to allow either her sister or her daughter-in-law to help her in the kitchen so Hazel and Laura had time to chat. When the family did sit down to eat, Laura could not help but notice that Steve's mother had not even said one word to her sister. What could have happened between these two sisters to cause such tension? She was anxious to get Steve aside so she could ask. So when Mikey fell asleep during dinner, she followed Steve as he carried him upstairs to the bedroom that used to be his own. He lay the child down on one of the twin beds, and tiptoed over to check on Kevin in the crib. Then he went to the window and for a long while he stared at the snow-covered oak tree that dominated the back yard.

"Honey, are you okay?" Laura whispered.

"Yes, I'm fine." At the sound of her voice, Steve jerked and turned toward the door. "Let's get back down to the others."

Startled, Laura decided to hold her questions. Something was bothering Steve. Was it about her pregnancy? Did he sense something suspicious?

Helen served the dark chocolate mousse cake when they returned and Steve gulped his piece in two huge mouthfuls. He then reached over to Laura, grabbed her arm, and announced, "Well, folks, Laura and I are going to bed. Thanks for dinner, Mother. We'll see you all in the morning."

"I've got to help your mother with the dishes," Laura insisted, pulling her arm away. "She did everything herself, and I want her to relax." Laura had watched her mother-in-law grow increasingly tense through the course of the meal.

"You look tired, and it's getting late." Steve stood abruptly, waiting for Laura to do the same. "Kevin will have us up soon enough."

"See you in the morning," Laura mumbled as Steve reached for her arm again, practically forcing her up.

"What was that all about?" she demanded, tugging her arm away from his as soon as they had closed the door to their bedroom.

"You need your rest. Besides, Mother and Aunt Hazel need time to talk and get caught up."

"Helen hasn't said a word to her all night, or haven't you noticed? I was just getting to know your aunt. I really like her. She's so different from your mother even though they look so much alike. Underneath the make-up and the styled hair. Are they twins?"

"They are," he said, going to the closet. "You stay here while I get the presents down to the tree."

As he left the room with an armload of gifts, Laura lay down with a mind full of questions, but sleep came along and took them away.

When she awoke, a thin film of perspiration covered her neck and arms. A dark form had pressed her down and slashed her throat. She was paralyzed, unable to reach the gun in her purse. When she managed to turn her head and open her eyes, Steve was snoring beside her. She didn't want to wake him, yet she was afraid to go back to sleep. She slipped out of bed and tiptoed out of the bedroom. The grandfather clock in the hallway was visible in the dim light. It was 2:30 A.M. To her surprise, there was a light on downstairs.

Laura headed toward the living room. She could make out someone sitting in the large comfortable chair traditionally reserved for Steve's dad. It was Aunt Hazel, dressed in a black satin peignoir. Her hair hung down to her shoulders, and she looked quite beautiful. In her hand was a brandy snifter. With a wan smile and a nod, she gestured for Laura to sit down in the chair next to her.

"Aunt Hazel, what are you doing up so late?"

"Lost in memories I suppose. I grew up in Traverse City. Left in '52 for good, and I haven't even been back to visit in over five years. I had hoped things would change, but except for you and your darling children, they haven't. Helen hates me. She still blames me for everything."

"Blames you for what?"

Hazel studied her. "You don't know, do you?" she said softly. "I'm the evil sister. Totally to blame for Phillip's accident. And for what happened between me and Jim."

Hazel stiffened before leaning down to lift the brandy bottle from the floor. She refilled her glass. "You're in this family, and it's time you knew some things."

The rest of the house was completely quiet as Laura sat on the couch and listened to Aunt Hazel. An hour later she walked Aunt Hazel to her room before returning to Steve's side as he slept in the double bed. She took care not to rouse him and lay awake for another hour, watching the moonlight fill the room. She thought about Aunt Hazel's story, amazed and hurt that Steve had never told her what had happened. Long ago, Steve had been through a terrible trauma. But so had she, and hadn't she promised herself never to tell him? Could she blame him for keeping something like this to himself?

CHAPTER NINETEEN

By 11:00 P.M. on Christmas Eve, Lucy Jones was exhausted. She had worked two additional shifts at General Motor's headquarters this week, which meant that she had not had a day off in more than three weeks: except for Anthony's funeral. After pushing the heavy, industrial vacuum cleaner through endless offices and hallways, she was physically and mentally numb. She hadn't counted on the extra mess and debris strewn about during the office Christmas parties. Besides the plastic glasses, empty bottles, and wrapping paper, ashtrays overflowed. The restrooms, always a mess at the end of the day, were littered with paper towels, spilled cosmetics, and even some forgotten gifts. These she wrapped carefully in paper towels to take home for the girls.

Working this extra time was the only possible way Lucy could afford a Christmas tree, which had to be small enough so she could carry it home. Last year she had two healthy boys to accompany her. Anthony and Johnny had hoisted the tree over their strong young shoulders, laughing and joking.

On the way home, Lucy got off the bus on Woodward near a roadside stand and selected the best of the scrawny trees still available. Then she began her journey's last leg, half carrying and half dragging the small but unwieldy tree the last four blocks to home. Wet snow soaked Lucy's feet. As she began to shiver, despair began to seep inside. With each step, she sunk deeper and deeper into darkness. She pushed herself to go on; the few colored lights burning along her path only deepening her depression.

Lucy soon came to the corner funeral parlor where Johnny, and then Anthony, had been laid out. She shuddered, frozen with grief. Years ago, she had buried her husband here. Poor Daniel. Just about to get his associate's degree from Detroit Junior College. Just about to decide what to do with the rest of his life. He had instilled a love of learning in her. It was Daniel that let her really dream for the first time in her life. There was a way out of poverty, and it was by learning. Lucy sobbed. After the deaths of her sons, she kept on going each day for the sake of her daughters. Her pace slowed to a halt, and she found herself suddenly slumped against the concrete wall of the building as the snow fell. She half lay and half sat in a semi-conscious heap, the meager Christmas tree and the last-minute gifts in a bag at her side.

A dark blue Buick careened around the corner. A tall nun in the black and white habit of the Sisters of Mercy was at the wheel — a shorter passenger, also attired in a full habit, beside her. The two nuns had been friends since their novice days, though they now lived in different worlds. Still, they'd made a pact to return to the motherhouse in Bloomfield Hills each year to spend Christmas Eve together. Tonight, after attending early services at the chapel, they'd walked over to Sister Portia's nearby convent to relax and reminisce. Portia always played hostess, for her quarters at St. Mary-of-the-Woods Academy, where she taught art and music appreciation, were plush and comfortable. As usual, she drove Sister Mary Agnes home to her convent near St. Joseph's, driving tensely through the ghetto streets of inner city Detroit.

"Portia, what's wrong with you?" Mary Agnes inquired. "Your driving is atrocious tonight."

As Portia slowed the car, her companion focused on a crumpled body slumped by a building.

"Oh, my good Lord. You almost ran over that person. At least I think it's a person. My Lord, Sister, how many glasses of wine did you have?"

"I only had two, I swear." Portia pulled the car to a stop a few yards beyond the street corner.

"You swear? I think it's a woman. What could she be doing here?"

"What should we do?" Portia's voice trembled.

"Let's get out and see if we can help," Mary Agnes said matter-of-factly.

"Do you think we should? This is such a terrible neighborhood, and it's so dark."

"Whoever that is over there needs help. This is my neighborhood, Portia, remember? I've been here fifteen years, and I'm telling you everything will be fine. Back up now, please."

These foreboding streets were home to Mary Agnes. Though the neighborhood terrified many others, she knew that she would leave the order before ever returning to a middle-class assignment. Principal at St. Joseph's School for the past five years, she lived with three other nuns in a nearby dilapidated building that served as a convent.

Sister Mary Agnes was already stepping out of the car and hiking up her long skirt. Her reluctant companion followed tentatively.

"Oh, good Lord Almighty, it's Lucy," she called. "Portia, get over here quick. I need help. Here, here, Lucy. It's Sister Mary Agnes. What happened?"

"Oh my, oh Sister," Lucy responded slowly.

"What happened?" Portia blurted. "Have you been mugged?" She glanced around furtively.

"Lucy, are you okay?"

Lucy Jones struggled to stand with the nun's help. "I'm so embarrassed. Really, nothing is wrong, I been working too many hours, that's all. I guess I just ran out of steam carrying this tree."

"Why don't you get into the car, and we'll take you home," Sister Mary Agnes suggested softly.

"No, no, that's too much trouble," Lucy said. "I can make it."

"You're being silly. Here, get in the car." Sister Mary Agnes held open the back door on the passenger side.

Mary Agnes helped Lucy into the back of the Buick, ignoring

her feeble protests. She then reached for the tree and the bag of gifts and put them in the trunk.

"Thank you so much," Lucy said. "That's our Christmas this year."

The nuns exchanged a glance before climbing into the car.

"Thank you for coming to Anthony's funeral mass," Lucy said to Mary Agnes as Portia started up the engine.

"I can't tell you how grief stricken we all are. Anthony was the best student to ever come out of St. Joseph's."

"Excuse me, Sister." Portia's voice was shaky. "I need directions. Also, will you lock the doors?" The car began to creep along the road.

"Keep going straight, Portia," Mary Agnes directed. "It's only a block and a half away."

"I'm terribly sorry to put you to such trouble, Sisters."

"No trouble at all," Mary Agnes said. "This is Sister Portia. She's from St. Mary-of-the-Woods Academy out in Bloomfield Hills. Now, tell me how you ended up huddled on that street corner?"

"I'm not sure what happened," Lucy's voice dwindled as she spoke. "I've been working some extra shifts so I could afford to buy the tree for my girls. I was walking home, and I just started thinking about last Christmas with my boys and I remembered when Daniel was alive, and I guess I just sort of gave up."

"Here we are, Sister," Mary Agnes said. "Lucy, that's your place on the right, if I'm not mistaken?"

"Yes, this is it. Thank you again."

Sister Mary Agnes noticed a dim light in the small flat. "Is Stacy home with the younger girls? Or do you have someone else stay with them when you're working?"

"Stacy's home, Sister. I have no one else."

Sister Mary Agnes hesitated. "Lucy, did you know that Stacy has not been in school for the past few days. We tried to reach you, but there's been no answer. Is Stacy ill?"

Lucy jerked. For a long moment she said nothing.

The blue sedan had come to a stop. "Here we are, safe and sound!" exclaimed Portia with relief.

Lucy responded in a slow, faltering voice, "Sister, Stacy is not ill. She's at home now. I'll have to ask her about school. There must be some mistake," she continued. "You know what a good student Stacy is."

"Yes, I do. She's been an excellent student in the past. But she's had some problems lately."

"She'll be okay," Lucy said defensively. "She's a good girl. All my girls are going to be just fine."

Lucy dragged herself from the car and turned toward the front door. "I do have to go on in now and get the tree ready. I don't want the younger ones to be disappointed in the morning."

Mary Agnes nodded. "Okay. Then let's get this tree in the house right now. Portia, could we bother you to open the trunk again?"

After the tree and the bag of gifts were taken out and the trunk slammed shut, Portia sidled up to her companion. "Sister," she said, "we really have to get going."

Mary Agnes replied sharply. "We're not going to leave Mrs. Jones out here to struggle with this tree. You can see she's exhausted."

Mary Agnes grabbed the tree with both hands before either woman could object. She held it firmly by the trunk and headed for the front door. Portia grabbed the gifts. Lucy Jones followed hurriedly, fumbling in her purse for her keys.

Inside, Lucy was surprised to find Sharon asleep on the sofa as she turned on the small table lamp.

"Where would you like the tree?" Sister Mary Agnes whispered.

"You can put it anywhere," replied Lucy almost absently as she turned away and headed toward the two small bedrooms off the main living area.

Portia placed the bag on the one upholstered chair, and Mary

Agnes stood holding the tree. Lucy returned almost immediately, panic etched on her tired face.

"What's wrong, Lucy?" the short nun asked.

"I can't find Stacy, Sister. I—"

"Oh dear. Portia, go out right now and make sure the car is locked, I don't want your car stolen. Then come back inside, and we'll decide what to do."

She turned to Lucy after gently setting the tree against one wall. "How long have you been gone today?" the nun asked.

"Since 6:00 this morning. The girls were still asleep. I left a note for Stacy like I always do. Lord, something terrible must have happened. She knows better than to leave the younger ones alone." She wrung her hands together. "Oh, God, please don't take another one of my children."

Sharon stirred on the sofa, and the nun went over to her. "Sharon," she said gently. As the child's sleepy eyes opened, the nun continued. "Surprised to see me here?" She flashed a smile. "I just gave your mother a ride home. Sharon, honey, do you know where Stacy is?"

The child sat up slowly, rubbing her eyes. She glanced fearfully at her mother.

"She's not here, Sharon. We really need to find her. Your mother's very worried."

Sharon looked directly into the nun's kind eyes. "She went out, after lunchtime. She told me to fix dinner for Rachel and Katie but that she'd be back for bedtime. I read a story to Rachel and Katie and made them go to bed even though they wanted to stay up. Katie still believes in Santa Claus, even though she says she doesn't."

A strangled sound rose from Lucy's throat.

"Do you know whom she went out with, honey," pressed Sister Mary Agnes. "Any idea at all?"

Lucy did not move as the nun gently questioned her daughter.

"That Snake guy and Willie. You know, Mama, Johnny's friends."

Lucy groaned. Snake and Willie had grown up a few doors down from the Jones household. Lucy sank into the chair in the corner beside the forgotten Christmas tree. "Those boys are too old for Stacy. This is all wrong."

"Mrs. Jones," Sister Portia said, after quietly stepping inside and closing the front door behind her, "why don't you put Sharon to bed, and we'll talk about what to do?"

Sister Mary Agnes assumed charge when Lucy returned a few moments later. "Do you have any idea where Stacy might be?"

"No, I don't," she said. "She has never done this before, she's a responsible girl. I just don't know what to do."

"We could call the police," Mary Agnes murmured, "but they're not likely to do much. After all, we have no reason to believe that anything's happened to her."

"How do we know?" Lucy whispered.

"Let me see what I can do," Mary Agnes said, pacing the room. Then she snapped her fingers. "Portia, I'll need your car."

"But it doesn't really belong to me," she protested.

"This is more important," Mary Agnes snapped her fingers again. "And you're not going with me. By the time I get back, I expect you two will have decorated that tree over there. Lucy, you have ornaments and lights?"

"Uh huh. But where you going? I should go with you."

"You stay here with your daughters. Sister, hand me the car keys," she said to her reluctant companion.

CHAPTER TWENTY

Over the years, Sister Mary Agnes had gone to great pains to earn the trust of the teens in the neighborhood. Her casual, everything's cool approach disarmed even the most streetwise kid. Her role as an educator and religious figure brought her into the street on an almost daily basis and she knew about the sordid places where the kids hung out.

It didn't take long to find Stacy. Sister Mary Agnes drove barely more than a mile beyond the west side ghetto to a burned-out building near Warren Avenue on Theodore Street, not far from the Art Institute. It was an old, decrepit place, now abandoned. The kids had swooped in and turned it into a drug den. After stepping past a maze of half-conscious bodies in the dark hallway, the nun entered a graffiti-covered, smoky room. Noxious odors intermingled in the air as loud music assaulted her ears.

The only child of aloof, affluent parents, Sister Mary Agnes had never forgotten their indifference to the one person in her life who had shown her true devotion and introduced her to a selflessness born of dignity: Agatha, her parents' maid. Agatha's hapless plight formed the foundation of the nun's dedication to bring education to the underprivileged. So be it if she had smoked some reefer to engender trust among her teen network. She just hoped her younger students never found out. In return, many of the older kids unloaded on her, and she never violated their trust. So when she came striding in that Christmas Eve, conversations stopped mid-sentence. Dressed in her long black habit, stiffly starched white collar and black veil, she strode into the pack of teens and young adults lounging on battered old beanbags and cardboard boxes. She paused briefly as her vision adjusted to the darkness. The pungent smell of marijuana mixed with other unidentifiable odors wafted over her. There were a few murmurs of "Hello, Sister" as she walked past, finding her way into the center of the dark space.

Silently nodding in recognition, the nun's eyes darted back and forth. She had a single focus, and she refused to be distracted by the woozy scene before her. Finally, she spotted Stacy slumped against a far wall. The nun walked quickly over to her.

"Let's go, Stacy," she quietly urged, attempting to get the young girl to stand up. Stacy resisted.

"Here, Lonnie, help me get her into the car," the nun ordered one of the older boys hovering in a corner nonchalantly, sharing a bhong with Snake and Willie. He had a part-time job at the Ford factory that he'd landed with the nun's help after his stint in Vietnam. Seeing him here caused her heart to plummet.

"Ah, shit, I don't wanna do nothin'," Lonnie grumbled. "My babe's right over here, can't you see?" He pointed to a girl with huge gold hoop earrings.

"Snake, Willie, can I talk to you for a minute?" Sister Mary Agnes gestured. They swaggered over to her.

"Look, guys," she said, "I hope you're not too stoned to get this message. I don't want you messing with Stacy Jones. You hear?"

"Shit, Sister," Snake shot back. "The girl's already messed up, and that ain't my doin'."

"Well, I'm asking you to leave her alone. She's too young to be involved in all this. Her family's been through too much already, and you know it."

Snake puffed out his chest. "I been tryin' to help her. She so messed up cause her brothers got snuffed, ain't nothin' to do with us. It's the white man that's fuckin' us all up. S'cuse my language."

"Hey Sister," Willie cut in. "Who hit Johnny out there on the street, do ya know? We all knew 'bout the muthafuckin' pigs that got Anthony. But the brothers don't know who got Johnny. Pigs use'ta come around askin' questions, but not no more."

"No, I don't know," the sister answered honestly as Lonnie helped lift Stacy up.

"Asshole pigs don't give a damn," Snake cut in. "But Johnny was a brother. You hear things, I know that."

"I haven't heard anything," the nun repeated. "Anthony was caught looting, which I still find hard to believe. Maybe you know more about that than I do," she ventured.

"Unh unh, don't know nothin'," Willie slurred, slowly shaking his head.

"Somebody gotta take out the stupid pigs and the fuck-up doctors," Snake angrily shot back. He nodded at Stacy. "She knows what I'm talkin' 'bout."

The nun willed herself to remain dispassionate. Lucy had repeated to her Johnny's eyewitness report about the hospital being at fault in their treatment of Anthony, but she did not know how much to believe — there was such havoc all over the city during the riots. On Lucy's behalf she'd poked around the hospital, even made an appointment with Dr. Monroe, the chief of surgery. Johnny'd claimed that he'd worked on Anthony that night. And the doctor admitted it right off. Like he had nothing to hide. Then he told her that for a while Anthony had been left in the hallway that night. That he'd had a cardiac arrest. They'd resuscitated him, but he'd already had too much brain damage from the bullet.

"Dr. Monroe," she'd then confronted him. "Anthony's brother was there. He said that a female doctor made mistakes. That you, yourself, called her a criminal."

"Sister," he'd said respectfully, "let me assure you that there was nothing criminal. The doctor in question had a hard time intubating Anthony. This is not uncommon. I had to do a tracheotomy. I'm not sure what the patient's brother saw or didn't see."

In the end, Sister Mary Agnes advised Lucy to just try and forget Johnny's story. Without Johnny's actual testimony, it was unlikely that a case could be made against the hospital. The boy had been so lost and hot-headed anyway. And now, finding Stacy in this hellhole, would mean one more tragedy for Lucy.

"Okay, guys," the nun said, hands on her hips. "I'm taking Stacy home. I'm going to say this one more time. I don't want her hanging with your gang. She's too young and you know it." She looked Snake sharply in the eye. "Leave her alone. For her mother's sake, please."

"Sister, don't give me that." He shook his head. "Stacy here makes up her own mind. She's no little girl. Besides, looks like we got an interest in common. You seen that mural on the wall outside the building? That's mine. It's called *The Cakewalk*, get it? We're all walkin' to freedom. You see I'm usin' all the same colors Diego used on his. All them blacks and reds and yellows and whites. Equals the races that make up North America, 'specially here in Detroit. We've all got somewhere to go. Get the picture? Stacy been helpin' me paint now and then. I started that paintin' to remember my man Johnny, you know? Stacy 'preciate that, her bro goin' down in the Detroit streets."

The nun remained silent as Willie and Lonnie helped get Stacy into the car. She glanced over at Snake's mural, a seemingly imprecise rendering of several human figures on a road, reaching their hands towards the sky. She was not close enough to see their expressions or the other forms that filled the painting, but she could make out that it covered the entire first story of the building. Once the engine turned over, Sister Mary Agnes thanked God that the battery was intact and that the car was still in one piece.

Lucy's haggard face flooded with relief as the nun helped Stacy into the living room at home. Just as quickly, she frowned at her daughter's skimpy outfit, a short black skirt and tight sweater.

"Where did you get these things?" she demanded.

"Best to just get her to bed, Lucy," said Sister Mary Agnes.

While she waited, Sister Mary Agnes noticed the small Christmas tree now standing in the corner, nicely decorated with several colorful ornaments and a lot of silver tinsel. Sister Portia sat next to the tree on the shabby sofa, arranging a tiny pile of small wrapped gifts, a satisfied smile on her face.

"It looks terrific, Portia." Quietly she asked, "How did it go with you and Mrs. Jones?"

"Lucy is quite a woman. She told me all about her family. To think, two young sons dying, and she's all alone to take care of four daughters. And her job is so hard. But what's the matter with Stacy?" Portia lowered her voice to a whisper. "Good Lord, I was worried about you out there by yourself."

"She's high." The weary nun sat down next to Portia. "Another promising life going to waste."

Portia shook her head. "Not yet, Sister. Maybe there's something I can do."

Mary Agnes looked up. "From that opulent school of yours?"

"Seriously, Sister. Mrs. Jones told me how intelligent Stacy is. An all A student until recently."

Mary Agnes nodded. "That's true."

Excitement lit up Portia's eyes. "What if I could get her a scholarship at St. Mary-of-the-Woods? She could live in the dorm with the other girls and get out of this horrible, dangerous neighborhood."

Mary Agnes slapped the couch. "What a wonderful idea. Do you think you could really do it?"

"Well, I can try. I'll pull every string I can."

Tears welled in the nun's eyes. Only an hour ago, Portia wanted to race away from this neighborhood as fast as she could. Sister Mary Agnes never failed to marvel at the strange and mysterious ways of God.

CHAPTER TWENTY-ONE

A few miles away, the elite social circle of Grosse Pointe celebrated the holiday at their exclusive Yacht Club. For most of the country, Christmas Eve was a family occasion, but attendance at this lavish gala was a status statement. Judging by the crowd, David observed that very few chose to be home with their children on this magic night of reindeers on rooftops. In fact, it seemed that even the scourge of the Detroit riots had not dampened the social customs of this insulated community. At his wife's insistence, the Monroes were among the revelers.

Standing at the doorway, David's mood was far from celebratory. He was physically exhausted, wishing only to get some sleep tonight. He wanted to sneak away early this evening, hoping that the intensive care unit at the hospital didn't call about its own chairman of medicine. Just in case, he'd kept his beeper on. David had performed emergency surgery last night on Ed Collins. It was a high-risk procedure, an attempted repair of a ruptured aortic aneurysm.

Yesterday, Ed had barely made it back to his office after finishing afternoon rounds before collapsing onto a chair. Connie urgently paged David, who came running from the recovery room as Ed labored to describe the searing pain which migrated from his chest to his back, accelerating with each beat of his heart before he lost consciousness. The loss of all pulses and absence of blood pressure gave David little choice but to rush him to the OR. The aneurysm was massive, and Ed's prognosis was extremely poor. So far they hadn't been able to wean him off the respirator, and his kidneys had shut down. If the ICU called tonight David would respond and Cynthia, no doubt, would explode in one of her tantrums. That he didn't need, especially so soon after their last blow up about the Aruba trip.

Cynthia stood at his side, looking simply marvelous. Her red velvet sheath showed off her figure, and her hair was arranged in a cascade of loose curls held in place by a giant diamond pin. A ruby pendant dangled on her neck, calling attention to her cleavage. Cynthia certainly knew how to garner attention.

"Darling," Cynthia took David's hand in hers as two women approached. "You remember Ruth Davis and Ann Wilson?"

"Good evening, ladies."

Ann Wilson, a striking strawberry blonde socialite flashed David a practiced smile. Beside her, Ruth Davis was standoffish. Her coal black eyes failed to return his smile. He guessed she was older than Ann, in her late thirties or early forties. Her short dark hair and lanky build made her attractive in an aloof sort of way.

"Would you be a doll and get us drinks?" Cynthia flashed David a bright smile. "A martini for me. Ruth? Ann?"

David dutifully sauntered off to fill their drink order. Three martinis: one for him, Cynthia, and Ann. A gin and tonic for Ruth.

"My, he is the handsome one," remarked Ann. "You'd better keep a close eye on him, Cynthia darling. I can't help but think of all those gorgeous single nurses milling around him all the time."

"Ann, stop," Ruth chided. "Cynthia's the gorgeous one. You look just divine tonight." She moved closer to Cynthia and slipped an arm around her waist. "You shouldn't have to put up with that nonsense. David doesn't deserve you."

Cynthia smiled full force at Ruth. "My goodness, that's wonderful to hear. David's a very attractive man, I know that," she said. "My main complaint is that he's married to that hospital. But he is the chief of surgery. That's what I wanted for him."

"Look over there," Ruth cut in. "Raymond Walson and his wife. She's a medical student, isn't she, Cynthia?"

"And who is Raymond Walson?" asked Ann, searching the crowded room.

"Raymond and I are law partners," Ruth replied, pulling her arm away from Cynthia as David approached, leading a tuxedoed waiter carrying a silver tray with four drinks. After glasses were clinked, David picked up the conversation he'd barely overheard.

"Does that make you an attorney?" he inquired, intrigued with Cynthia's friend. There weren't many female law partners in this city. With her lanky figure and sharp features, she might look imposing in a business suit confronting a legal opponent. Tonight she wore a simple deep blue gown without any accessories but black pearl earrings.

"Yes, it does." Ruth responded coolly. "Patterson, Stewart, and Mays. Do you know the firm?"

"I can't say that I do. But in my line of work, that's probably a good thing." He smiled.

Ruth did not smile back. "You don't have to worry. We specialize in labor negotiations and union contracts."

"Good," he said, shifting his gaze in the direction where his wife stared. Surprised, he recognized one of his students, the lovely woman carefully removing her full-length black sable coat to reveal a sequin studded red silk sheath. Vicky Walson, one of the smartest, if not the smartest in the class, looked stunning. Her long platinum hair hung shoulder length and was brushed back over her ears to highlight huge Burmese ruby earrings.

Taking her arm, Vicky's escort headed toward them.

"Hello, Ruth. I didn't think either of us would make it." Turning to the rest of the group, he explained. "We had an arbitration that had to be settled before we could leave the table. If it weren't Christmas Eve, we'd still be in there now, I'm afraid."

"Let me make the introductions," Ruth offered. "Ann, Cynthia, David, this is Raymond Walson, and his wife."

"Mrs. Walson, we've met," David said, smiling brightly.

"A pleasure to see you here, Dr. Monroe."

"So you two know each other?" Raymond Walson prodded.

"Yes, indeed," David responded. "Mrs. Walson, I believe that you are one of the top students in the freshman class."

Raymond beamed at his wife as she blushed at the compliment. "She works really hard, I assure you. But I must say that it's great to have my wife over the holidays. I know once classes start up, I'll be back on bread and water with an occasional frozen dinner."

"You? A medical student?" Cynthia Monroe suddenly asked, eyeing Vicky with one of those head-to-heel looks that only women can affect.

"Yes," Vicky responded just as coolly.

"How can you do that?" Cynthia demanded.

"Do what?" Vicky said simply, reaching for Raymond's hand.

"Well, I think it's a disgrace," Cynthia huffed. "Taking up valuable places meant for men who will make real contributions to medicine."

Vicky's cheeks flushed with anger. She opened her mouth to reply, but Raymond broke into the conversation instead.

"Great meeting you, Dr. Monroe. Take good care of my wife, she's a hell of a hard worker. She's also a fabulous dancer, and I want to get her out on the floor before the orchestra quits. Come on, darling."

David's jaw clenched. Cynthia tried to snuggle up to him, but David held her stiffly at arm's length, willing himself not to renounce her then and there. Instead, with an exaggerated effort, he glanced at his watch and announced that he had to check in with the hospital. Cynthia trailed behind him. Reaching for his sleeve, she suggested that he return quickly.

"I'll not be back," he seethed between his teeth as he pulled out of her reach.

Cynthia followed David out of the elegant ballroom to the bank of phones discreetly located in a small alcove. As he picked up a receiver, she grabbed his arm.

"Listen, Cynthia, I'm serious." David hissed. "Your rudeness to my student was inexcusable."

"But darling," she attempted.

David cut her off and wrenched his arm from her hold. "I'm too angry to discuss it right now. Go back inside. I have an important phone call to make."

"I'll just bet you do," she retorted hotly, grabbing him again by the sleeve.

David yanked his arm from her grip. "It's Ed Collins. I'll be spending the night at the hospital, so find a ride home. Tell your friends I had an emergency. In fact, make up whatever story you want, I don't care."

"How could you?" Cynthia's right hand flew up and struck him across his face.

David calmly and firmly pushed his wife aside. He quickly retrieved his black cashmere overcoat. Instead of calling the hospital, he'd head right over.

Cynthia, suddenly alone in the alcove, struggled to pull herself together. Angry tears welled in her eyes, threatening to destroy the carefully applied make-up. She headed for the powder room, a forced smile on her face. Image was everything, after all. The Monroes were the perfect couple. David, the perfect gentleman. Always impeccably dressed. Always exuding charm. Cynthia couldn't erase the image of Vicky and her handsome young husband. It made her feel old and ugly. One hand moved slowly down her torso as she turned sideways to view her profile in the mirror. Her four-inch spike heels started to wobble, and she leaned on a satin covered chair to steady herself.

"Cynthia, are you all right? Ruth was waiting outside the powder room when Cynthia emerged several minutes later, a forearm crossing her abdomen protectively. "You look like you've just seen a ghost. Let's sit down." Ruth nodded toward a table in an adjacent empty ballroom. "Something's terribly wrong, isn't it?"

"It's David. He had to leave for the hospital. Of all nights, Christmas Eve," Cynthia stammered as she sat down.

"Some kind of an emergency?" Ruth pulled up an identical chair. She sat down and placed her hand over Cynthia's.

"No, not really. I mean, I don't know. Yes, that's what he said," Cynthia contradicted herself.

"Maybe it's for the best," Ruth said soothingly. "I felt the tension between you, and I couldn't help but notice the way he treats you. You deserve much better than that," Ruth inched her chair closer and placed an arm around Cynthia's shoulder.

"Everybody is always saying how wonderful he is. But I can tell you, he's no saint."

"Of course he isn't. Doesn't he realize how beautiful you are?" Ruth stroked Cynthia's smooth bare arm.

They ordered drinks from a roaming waiter and after their glasses had been drained, their conversation strayed to vacation and travel talk. When Ruth offered to drive her home, Cynthia gratefully accepted. The two women left the ball together following their requisite farewells. Upon arrival at the Monroe estate, they had another drink in the candlelit living room, Vivaldi playing softly in the background.

Ruth's consoling embraces soon progressed to a sensual exploration of Cynthia's soft, silken body. After a few tentative moments, Ruth held Cynthia close and they kissed. Arm and arm, they climbed the stairs to Cynthia's suite. Slowly and deliberately they undressed each other and lay down on the bed. Through a fog of alcohol, Cynthia glimpsed backward through the years to her days at Smith. She recalled intimacies shared with her roommate, Elsie Vane. Elsie had short hair, like Ruth's. But they were much, much younger then. Cynthia reached for Ruth.

The next day at noon David returned home physically and emotionally drained. Up most of the night, he had lost his friend and colleague, Ed Collins. With a heavy heart, he showered, shaved, and dressed. Reluctantly, and with trepidation, he headed for Cynthia's room, tapping lightly on her door, expecting an ugly scene.

In the past, the Monroes had visited David's brother, Nick, his wife, Denise, and their four children on Christmas Day, an annual outing that had grown to be nothing more than a source of contention. Cynthia considered Nick and Denise beneath her social class and had no interest in their children. David fiercely loved his brother and admired his sister-in-law, but mostly he adored his nephews — Jonathan, Paul, Scott, and little Bobby. After that scene last night, David assumed that Cynthia would refuse to go. They'd have an argument. He'd go alone.

"I'll be down shortly, darling," Cynthia responded. "We're heading out to your brother's, right?"

David was baffled by his wife's pleasant response but too exhausted to dwell on it.

CHAPTER TWENTY-TWO

On Christmas morning Laura waited until after they'd returned from Mass and all the presents were opened before approaching Steve about Aunt Hazel's surprising story the night before. Experiencing an uncommon reprieve in her morning sickness, she suggested to Steve that they take a walk. The boys were mesmerized by their gifts, and this was the first opportunity to have any real privacy with Steve since their arrival.

"Your Aunt Hazel is quite a character," Laura began.

Steve wrapped an arm around his wife as they walked down the driveway. "You can say that again."

"She told me some things about the family after everyone was asleep last night." Laura felt Steve suddenly stiffen. "She told me about Phillip."

Steve froze in his tracks, looking down at his feet.

"Why hadn't you ever told me?" she asked softly.

Steve's voice cracked when he finally spoke, "Because I'm still ashamed. Even though I was only a kid, ten years old. No one ever talked about it after it happened, so I never told you. I never told anyone."

"I'm your wife, why don't you tell me now?" Something must really be wrong with their marriage. She'd been in the dark about how Steve's twin had died. He'd never know how she'd been raped. Or how she had killed.

Slowly, tentative, with eyes cast down, Steve spoke in a monotone.

He and Phillip were identical twins. Phillip had been the aggressive one, outgoing and charming; Steve was quiet and timid. Phillip had always made the decisions: what games to play; what they wanted for dinner. Steve was like the perpetual shadow. Not that Phillip was cruel, he just expected that Steve would follow.

One day the twins were playing cowboys up in the tree house their dad had built for them. They loved to play there with their new puppy, Lucky, a yellow Lab that the twins took everywhere. Steve adored Lucky with a special passion. Perhaps he related to the puppy's subordinate status. And perhaps, in retrospect, the twins should have been given two puppies rather than one to share. There was a scuffle over which twin Lucky loved best, and uncharacteristically, Steve shoved Phillip. It was an angry, forceful shove, strong enough to propel Phillip backward and through the opening in the railing at the ladder. The fall was only ten feet; but Phillip's neck snapped on impact, and he died instantly.

Steve's mother had not been home. Aunt Hazel was visiting and was watching the boys while Helen had her hair styled for a Knights of Columbus dinner. His mother returned home to the flashing red lights of emergency vehicles. Phillip lay lifeless under the old oak tree. His father was on his knees, his face blurred by tears, leaning over his dead son. Steve was huddled in Aunt Hazel's arms in the rocking chair on the large back porch, moaning, "I didn't mean to hurt him." And he hadn't. He had just wanted to show Phillip that he would not be bullied when it came to Lucky.

Steve wasn't really sure what happened next, but his mother was hospitalized. They called it a nervous breakdown. For two months, Aunt Hazel stayed with Jim and Steve.

"She told me, Steve. How at first she was restless, not used to confinement in a small town and anxious to get back to her job as a fashion coordinator for Macy's in New York City. About how she fell in love with your father. About how they had an affair."

Steve admitted that he became very attached to his aunt during that time. She gave him love and attention in a way he'd never received. Just him, no competition with Phillip. As for his father and Aunt Hazel, he'd only been ten, but had suspected an intimate relationship, and when his mother returned home, Hazel left Traverse City. Steve sounded so terribly sad when he explained how his parents never again mentioned Phillip. For some time, Helen wanted nothing to do with Steve. She made him feel like a ghost, as if he were invisible. His dad made the meals and took him fishing, but he was always sad. He dismantled the tree house and, worst of all, got rid of Lucky. Had his parents known the tussle was over Lucky? Steve didn't know.

His mother slowly improved, Steve said. The depressive episodes became shorter and less frequent, and he and his father learned to tiptoe around her moods. Steve told Laura that he coped by trying to be the perfect son. Compliant with rules, afraid that if he upset his mother, his dad would take her away and leave him alone. An irrational fear, Steve now realized, but it was real back then. Steve said that a childhood like that made him want to be a strong father to his own sons.

"You are a wonderful father," Laura wrapped her arms around Steve, kissing him on the forehead, and with a mittened hand she wiped tears from his eyes. "Honey, why didn't you tell me this yourself? I mean before? It would have helped me understand your parents."

Steve pulled back to face her. "Don't you understand? This is about me. I killed my twin brother. I live with that shame every day. I don't want anyone else to know. Especially the kids. You have to promise me."

"Oh Steve, I'm so sorry," Laura said.

"I don't want your pity," Steve said, reaching to take her back into his arms, holding her tightly in the still, white wilderness. "I just want your promise."

"You have my word," she whispered, letting loose a steaming, frigid breath.

Following their walk together on Christmas morning, Steve became distant and introspective. He brooded for the next few days, and Laura went out of her way to appear cheerful and affectionate. But once they left Traverse City, Steve snapped back into his normal self, horsing around with the boys, grumbling about the striking Detroit newspapers.

Steve's story had served to distract Laura from her most grievous concern, but only temporarily. What if the baby was not Steve's? She simply couldn't cope with that possibility. Since there was absolutely nothing she could do but wait, she forced herself to bury her terror in a dark compartment deep inside.

"Okay, little guys, vacation's over," Laura announced on Tuesday morning, the second day of 1968. She tried to sound cheery and upbeat. "Mommy has to go back to school today, and you guys get to go upstairs. Carol's waiting for you." She forced a smile at a sleepy-eyed Carol, who stood at the top of the stairs holding her son, Teddy, still in his pajamas. Laura kissed both her children goodbye, trying not to impart to them the fear roiling inside her.

Steve had already left for a caseworker conference in Lansing where he'd been asked to recruit administrative assistants to take some of the load off the social workers. The only junior social worker asked to attend, it was a welcome boost to his ego.

As she pulled out of her icy driveway, Laura headed directly to the Lodge Expressway. Susan had called last night to say that she was staying with a friend downtown and would find her own way to school in the morning. Laura couldn't help but wonder if that "friend" was Dr. Will Cunningham. With Susan on her own, Laura would have the very rare chance to be alone, if even for an hour. She desperately needed that time after that phone call this morning. Compartmentalize, she told herself. This was her defense mechanism: one thing at a time.

But the moment she'd started the Falcon, a cavalcade of thoughts competed for her attention. She'd seen her doctor. Yes, she was indeed four months pregnant.

She gripped the wheel of the car tightly as she drove south on the freeway. Since Christmas Day, she had begun to feel somewhat better, experiencing less nausea and vomiting, but she knew she'd start to show soon. Would she be able to continue school? If she told no one, she could finish the semester, but what about the next one? She'd be just about at term, waddling around with a bulging belly. Could she get by wearing those ugly loose muumuus?

"Face the real issue," she said aloud. "Quit putting it off." There was a fifty-fifty chance that her baby would be biracial. Laura had no idea how she would handle this. At the moment, she could only beg God that it wouldn't happen. No matter what, she would love the baby and protect it. Of that she was certain. But how would Steve react?

First, she would have to admit the rape. Would she have to tell the police? If so, would they tie it to Johnny Diggs' murder? Then what? She could go to jail. She could lose Mikey and Kevin. And who would take care of the new baby? She couldn't expect Steve to do it. Certainly his parents wouldn't. What about her own parents?

She moved through the familiar, frustrating traffic, crying openly now. Hot tears blurred her vision as she pulled into the school parking lot. She sat for a moment, dabbing at her eyes, careful not to dislodge her contacts. As she set the parking brake, her stomach lurched as if the car were still in motion. Before she went into school, she had to focus on the morning's alarming call. She turned off the engine and closed her eyes.

She picked up the phone just as she was about to leave the house.

"Hello?" she'd answered, thinking the caller to be Susan, saying that she'd changed her plans and needed a ride. "What happened?"

"Mrs. Laura Nelson?" A male voice. "Detective Reynolds here."

"Uhh. . . . good morning."

"Happy New Year to you and your family."

"The same to you, detective," Laura said quickly. "Does Susan want me to pick her up?"

"No, I'm not calling about Susan," he said. "I have a few more questions about that night back in September we spoke about. Nothing really."

"Shoot." Laura froze. Had she really said, "shoot"?

"Well, I wanted to go over that afternoon. About how you were in the hospital to examine a patient late in the day. I know it's a while ago, but does that ring a bell?"

Laura's mind raced as her heart pounded. Where was he going with this? "Yes. Physical diagnosis." She'd tried to keep her voice steady. "We saw our first patient that day."

"Mrs. Nelson, do you remember your first patient? "

Laura swallowed. "A young man with a gunshot wound to the head."

"Named?"

Should she tell him? Of course, he's a detective.

"Anthony Diggs."

"That's right. And the boy killed was Johnny Diggs. Brothers. You knew that?"

"How awful," Laura said, after holding her breath so long she felt faint. "Yes, I did know."

"Strange coincidence?" Susan's father asked.

Without waiting for a response, he asked, "Now, the question that keeps coming to my mind is: why were you in that parking lot, not once, but twice that night?"

"What?" Laura held her breath, struggling to formulate a response, a response consistent with everything she'd told him months ago. "Detective, as you know, I went out into the hospital parking lot with Susan where you picked her up. Then I went back inside to the library. Later, I left by the student parking lot. I was escorted by security. But I've already told you that."

"Sure, sure. But bear with me, Mrs. Nelson, something's not adding up. You said you'd seen Dr. Monroe, out there. Right?"

"Yes." Laura felt lightheaded. She tried to remember. She told Detective Reynolds that she'd seen Dr. Monroe in the hospital lot. Right?

"Then why didn't I see him? That's what leads me to believe that you were out in the hospital parking lot at least twice that night. Once when I saw you. Once when he saw you. You follow?"

"I don't know what to tell you, detective." Laura could feel the tremble in her voice as she spoke more rapidly than she could think. "I follow what you're saying, but I think you're making a mountain out of a molehill. Apparently, Dr. Monroe was leaving the hospital just after you pulled away. That explains it, don't you think?" she said quickly. "Detective, I was just on my way out for school."

The call had rattled Laura terribly. What had precipitated it? Why now, when she was beginning to feel a little more secure that no one knew about that night?

At school, Laura became gratefully distracted. First on today's schedule was gross anatomy. As she swung open the double doors of the lab, the pungent odor of Harry and his colleagues nearly suffocated her after the holiday break. The stench was even more appalling than she'd remembered. The partially dissected cadavers, soaked in formaldehyde and covered with heavy plastic sheets, had definitely ripened. The odor and the unpleasant task triggered a surge of nausea. To make matters worse, Laura began to wonder if there could be some kind of toxic effect on her poor baby.

"Vacation is officially over," Rosie groaned. A look of disgust crossed her perky face as she held one hand over her nose and slid the plastic off Harry with the other. "Finally, we attack Harry's skinny abdomen. Find out what kind of surgery lies under that mysterious scar."

Ever practical, Susan reached for her scalpel and said, "Let's get started. Hope you all had a nice holiday, 'cause this semester's not going to be easy, and I do mean the horrors of neuroanatomy."

Vicky let out the breath she had been holding, thanks to Harry. "I've heard that the emergency room field class is like an education in itself too."

"Yeah, I wonder what that's going to be like," Laura said. "I didn't think we were going to see the inside of the ER until our third year." Scalpel in hand, she made the first midline incision from the bottom of the sternum, right over the wide band of scar tissue to the pubis. She continued along the base of the penis and through the midline of the scrotum then paused so they could all inspect the layers of the abdominal wall. "Thank you, Harry, for being so skinny." They were well ahead of their colleagues who had to carve through layers of greasy, lumpy fat.

"So with this new program," Rosie responded, "we hang around the interns and see what real life is going to be like?"

"Uh huh," Vicky nodded. "Like a real-world experience except the real world here at City Hospital is worse than the real world everywhere else."

"It starts on a Friday night and goes through the end of classes on Monday," Susan added. "And don't expect to get much sleep."

"How do you know so much? A little extra help from Dr. Will?" Laura teased, making an effort to take part in the conversation.

Susan glanced about the sea of cadavers. "Will and I are seeing each other," she admitted. "But we can't let on since he's our instructor. He could get in trouble. You know?"

Rosie glanced up. "Aha, I did detect a certain glow. Our lips are sealed, as long as you give up the details at lunch. Right girls? By the way, guess who I went out with over the holidays?"

"Only one somebody?" Vicky snickered.

"Well, no, but somebody in med school . . . Okay, I'll tell you. Tim Robinson. We went to another war protest."

"The senior, red hair, always hanging around the cafeteria like he's on the make?" Vicky laughed. "Good luck with that one."

"Sounds like the male version of you," Susan said. "Oops, pull that tissue out of the way will you. Better yet, cut it away."

"Okay," Vicky leaned in with a tiny scissors to cut the fibers of fascia that Susan held in her forceps. "Listen, girls, I've been dying to tell you about my Christmas Eve." She paused for effect. "Raymond and I went to a big party at our club. Black tie and all."

"Ooh la la," Rosie murmured.

"And," Vicky paused. "Guess who we ran into?"

"Not a clue," Susan responded, looking up from Harry's shrunken, knobby liver.

"Anybody else want to take a guess?" Vicky pressed.

"Somebody important, obviously," Laura answered, glancing at the others. "Somebody we know?"

"Not likely that we'll know anybody in Vick's elite circle," Susan said, maneuvering her hemostat to expose the common bile duct.

"Here, Laura," Susan said, "grab the hepatic portal vein and push it aside so that I can get through all these adhesions."

Laura pushed aside the big blue vein with a deft move. Incredibly, dissection had already become so routine it was almost mechanical.

"This particular society person you all know," Vicky again paused and they all looked up at her. "Dr. David Monroe and his wife. By the way, he looks divine in formal wear." Vicky turned toward Laura. "And Laura, if the grapevine is not mistaken, I heard Dr. Monroe threw an 'honors' your way."

Vicky smiled at Laura as Rosie added, "Yeah, but only after he scared the daylights out of her."

After a dramatic pause, Vicky continued, "His wife practically attacked me."

"What?" Rosie demanded. "You're exaggerating, yes?"

"Not at all. When Raymond and I were being introduced, it came up that I was a student here. Well, Cynthia, that's his wife, completely freaked. She said something like, 'how come you're taking up valuable space men could use'. I've never been so insulted. I almost gave it right back to her," Vicky went on. "Fortunately, Raymond got me out of there but fast. Imagine two women in evening gowns going at it in the middle of the ballroom floor."

"I heard he was married to a real snoot," Rosie said. "Very rich and high society."

"Yes," said Vicky. "'Snoot' is an understatement for that woman."

"What did Dr. Monroe do?" Laura asked quietly.

"Well, I'm not sure," Vicky replied, relishing her words. "No one saw him for the rest of the evening."

"How embarrassing," Laura murmured.

"I was pissed," said Vicky. "I think that Dr. Monroe was mortified."

"What does his wife look like?" Laura ventured.

"God, Laura, she looks sensational. Older than us, of course. Like somebody who spends close to a hundred percent of her time making herself look gorgeous. Probably shops in Paris. But frankly, she's a bitch if I ever saw one."

Rosie snorted with pleasure.

"Yeah, I've seen her picture a few times in the *Detroit Free Press* society page," Susan confirmed. "She always looks great. That is, great, as in rich."

Everyone nodded.

"Interesting, but let's get back to work. Okay?" Laura said.

Vicky smiled with obvious pleasure at her report. "You're right, Laura. We have to kick butt this semester now that we've got a reputation to maintain." She reached for the six-inch tissue forceps. "So," Vicky continued, "let's hear about the Nelson's Christmas, hmm? Did Santa Claus make it? Susan, hand me the scalpel. I'll dissect the hepatic artery while you retract the rib cage."

"Yes," Laura answered Vicky, "We were at Steve's parents in Traverse City so we had lots of snow. Oh, oh, here come the predators."

Over vacation, word had spread that the ladies had taken more than their fair share of class honors. Now a group of men walked over to their dissection table. Although the banter was light, the women grinned at each other. The men in the class were going to treat them with a different mix of resentment and respect. As they approached, they began to fan out, revealing none other than a redheaded student named Tim Robinson in their center, who added another obvious element to this mix, romance. He tucked a cluster of bright flowers into Rosie's lab coat.

At that moment, poor Harry was forgotten by everyone.

CHAPTER TWENTY-THREE

After her first week at St. Mary-of-the-Woods Academy, it was plainly evident that Stacy Jones was unhappy. Now, watching Stacy's belligerent face, Sr. Portia wondered whether it had been a mistake to take her away from home. But hadn't the events of Christmas Eve made it clear that something had to be done? She couldn't just stand by and let this bright young girl be lured into a life of self-destruction. On the other hand, Portia cringed at the emotional struggle of this fourteen-year-old, whisked away from her home in the middle of the school year. One of only five black students among four hundred girls. Sr. Portia could only hope that she was doing more good than harm.

The nun had summoned Stacy into the small parlor off the spacious reception area where the girls received visitors on week-ends and holidays. The room was cozy and comfortable with a blazing fire in the stone fireplace. Stacy sat across from Sister Portia on a large overstuffed sofa, glaring at the fire as she fidgeted with the strap of her book bag.

"How are things going?" Sister Portia began, knowing this would be difficult. Stacy had little in common with the wealthy, rather spoiled young ladies at the academy. For the nun, meeting the Jones family on Christmas Eve had renewed a passion for her vocation. If she could make a difference with this one girl, she kept thinking.

"I hate it here. I don't belong here."

"Yes, you do, Stacy. You know that your mother wants you

here and you know why," the nun said softly. "Everything will work out just fine. You've got to give it more time is all."

"I miss Mama so much. She needs me." Stacy's brown eyes filled with tears. "I promise if you let me go home, I'll be perfect. No more trouble. Please, just let me go back." The tears began to trickle down her cheeks, and Sister Portia handed her a large white handkerchief from the pocket of her habit.

"I've just got to get out of here," Stacy went on. "Everybody's white. All the girls hate me."

"They don't hate you," reasoned Sister Portia. "They just don't know you that well yet. There are some other black girls, and I'll make a point of introducing you."

"Don't. They're just as snobby as everyone else," Stacy insisted as she blew her nose and dabbed at the tears.

"Stacy, you've been sullen and unfriendly since you arrived. You haven't even talked to anyone."

"That's not true."

"Well then, why did you refuse to play on the basketball team? I know you played at St. Joseph's. Sister Mary Agnes told me so. Just give the other girls a chance, Stacy. Trust me on this."

Stacy sniffled.

"Listen," the nun said in a conspiratorial tone. "I'll try to bend the rules and take you home this weekend. You can see your mom and your sisters." She detected a flicker of hope in Stacy's eyes. "I spoke to Sister Mary Agnes just today. She tells me everyone really misses you too. Says your classmates are eager to hear how you're doing, to congratulate you on your scholarship. You've become a celebrity!"

"Well, I don't want to be a celebrity," Stacy responded, her eyes flashing defiantly. "Everybody here is white, except for a couple girls. It doesn't matter — I hate them, and they hate me. I'll stay here until next weekend, then I'm going home and I'm not coming back." She shook her head, anger creeping back into her voice.

"My goodness, Stacy, Sister Mary Agnes is white and so am I. And I know you don't hate us. Honey, you've just got to trust us.

You'll be fine. It will just take a little time." She glanced at her watch. "But right now, why don't you go down to the gym? The basketball team is just beginning practice. Show them what you can do."

Usually, Portia detested sports because they distracted her students from the study and appreciation of art and music. She knew, however, that basketball in the academy's league was competitive. If Stacy turned out to be half as good as Sister Mary Agnes had predicted, it could be her ticket to instant acceptance.

Stacy reluctantly agreed to go down to the gym. As she changed into a scratchy gym outfit, she swore to herself one thing: there was no way she was coming back after the weekend.

"Steve Nelson. I gotta talk to Steve Nelson," Snake barged through the smudged glass door leading to the Department of Social Services in downtown Detroit. Shaved head swinging from side to side, he seemed to yell at anyone and no one.

It was just before quitting time in the middle of a hectic workweek made worse by the recent holidays. The secretary did not look up from her typing and simply pointed over her shoulder, past the counter that doubled as a privacy barrier in the cramped office.

Steve looked at his watch and frowned, but he walked forward and lifted a hinged portion of the countertop and motioned to Snake.

"I'm Steve Nelson." He shifted an armload of files he was returning to the battered green cabinet in the corner of the room he shared with three other social workers. "What can I do for you?"

Steve was in a hurry. He had driven Laura's Falcon, and he needed to get his Pontiac out of the repair shop before it closed. He'd skipped lunch and arranged his day so that he could walk out the door exactly at five. If he got there in time, the mechanic had promised to help him out by driving one of the cars home for him. Save him lots of aggravation as Laura would be too busy for such mundane matters.

"It's my mama. Somethin' wrong with her disability situation.

You gotta help straighten it out 'cause they cut her off for no good reason." The words tumbled out of Snake's mouth. "Somethin' 'bout forms. They say she can't get her money now 'cause she didn't get the forms in when they wanted, like she don't got nothin' else to worry about. Mama got my little bros and groceries to worry 'bout. Who says they can take away money just like that?"

"Hold on," Steve held up his hand. "Let's go a little slower. Take a seat." He gestured to a orange molded plastic chair in front of his scratched desk. After Snake threw himself into it and crossed his arms defiantly across his chest, Steve sat down, put on an "I'm listening" expression and hoped that this would not take too long.

"Who exactly is your mother, and why has her disability been terminated?"

"Leona Rogers. And like I said, she missed sendin' in papers, and now they won't help her out."

Steve finally placed the young man. This was Leona's oldest son. Roy or Ray? She had two more at home but much younger. This one didn't go by his given name though. Leona had told him once that she hated the nickname.

"I gave him a fine name," she complained. "Why he wants everyone calling him 'Snake', I'll never know." Leona had described how this son, a sweet, creative boy who loved to draw, had grown up into a man who spent too much time on the streets and too much time smoking pot.

Steve almost smiled when he remembered the nickname, hoping that it might break the tension and then ease him out the door on time. "Snake, isn't it?"

Snake nodded and seemed to relax a bit. Steve opened a desk drawer, pulled out a file, and began flipping through the pages. As Steve scanned one form after another, Snake picked up a framed photograph of Steve with Laura and the kids from Steve's desk.

"This your old lady?" Snake said, looking at Laura's face intently.

Steve barely looked at Snake as he retrieved the photo and set it back on his desk and answered off-handedly, "Yeah, my family. The social worker, the doctor, and their two boys."

Snake's eyes opened wide.

Steve finally looked up from the paperwork. "You know, your mother missed her last two appointments with me, and I got a call from the disability office saying she had failed to show up there, too. There's no phone number in the file so I couldn't call to check."

"There ain't no phone, so there ain't no number. But what dif do that make? There ain't no hot water either. Look man, she'll fill out the papers when she can."

Steve dropped the file back into the drawer with a sigh. Then he stood up and said, "She has to file them on time, just like everyone else. She has to follow the rules. Tell your mother that if she wants, I can help her file a reinstatement application."

Steve grabbed his coat off a hook on the wall and pulled it on. He leaned across his desk to offer his hand to Snake, but Snake refused to take it.

Steve shrugged. "I really have to go now." He was out the door, buttoning his coat against the already dark and brutally cold January evening, when Snake burst out after him.

"What do you know about following rules? My mama busted herself up following rules, taking care of those old folks. You even know 'bout that she's a nurse aide? She works hard, on double shifts 'cause nobody want to take care of them old people downtown. She works so hard she ruined her back. Then the rules say, you can't lift, you can't work. She keeps working, 'course, had to work, pain or no pain. Then she starts taking meds, man, for the pain, cause she has to pick up the old folks and do her job."

Snake stayed right beside Steve as he walked toward his car, and Steve stiffened as Snake leaned in close, almost shouting. Then Steve suddenly felt queasy, mentally measuring whether he would be able to defend himself. He picked up his pace.

"Hey, you ain't listening. How's she gonna do any forms when she's laid up in the hospital?" Snake shouted. He grabbed Steve's arm just as Steve reached the Falcon and started to unlock the driver's side door.

A jolt of fear that ran up Steve's arm as Snake latched onto it disappeared as quickly as it had come. It had never entered Steve's mind that Leona might have a good reason for not meeting the deadline. A surge of embarrassment rushed through him followed by something else: compassion for his client. Something he felt less and less frequently since living in Detroit.

"Okay. What happened?" Steve asked.

Snake's breathing slowed, and he let go of Steve's arm. As he did Steve noticed the blue crescents outlining the young man's hands and wondered if he had some kind of disease. Maybe he'd ask Laura if blue fingernails were a sign of something horrible. Distracted by the blue, he'd almost missed Snake's response. "Car accident. She'll be okay. They say she'll be out soon."

Steve opened the car door and said, "I'm glad. I really have to get over to the garage to pick up my car and get this one back to my wife, but I'll call around tomorrow, explain the extenuating circumstances."

"Now, man. She needs help now," Snake shouted in Steve's face. "You and your cars can just wait."

Steve stood his ground. "You're right," he said. "Your mother does need help. She needs my help and I will make those calls tomorrow, when the disability office is open. Right now it's closed. But she needs your help, too. If you got a job, she wouldn't have to rely on the measly amount of money the city can give."

Snake took a step back and Steve took that opportunity to slip into the station wagon. Before he closed the door, he added, "You did a good thing today, coming to see me for your mother's sake, but you're no helpless kid. You care so much about your mother, get yourself a job." Steve yanked the car door shut, turned on the engine, and pulled out.

Snake watched the car pull away, the billowing clouds forming around the exhaust pipe. It was cold outside, that was for sure, but inside he was all heated up. This whitie blew him and his mama off as usual, Mr. Important Whitie and his yellow-haired doctor wife in that picture.

The doc from the hospital the day he visited Anthony. Stacy thought she was the one that Johnny saw in the emergency room, the one who messed up Anthony so bad. Johnny was the only one who'd know for sure. But Snake did know two new things: he knew who owned the black Falcon wagon that near hit him comin' out of a parking lot the night Johnny was lyin' dead just a block away; and he knew the name of the yellow-hair doctor he'd seen with Anthony.

Stomach growling, fingers drumming the steering wheel as he waited for a break in traffic, Steve suddenly remembered. During one of their sessions Leona Rogers mentioned that her son wanted to be an artist. He was working on some sort of outdoor art project instead of looking for a real job. Painting on a wall near the Art Museum. Steve realized that the blue color on Snake's hands must be paint. Too bad the hotheaded kid had no sense of work ethic. For Steve, Leona had become a prototype in this society of matriarchs: undereducated; back breaking work for a pittance; an obstinate social welfare system; now more medical bills. No wonder he was becoming more and more disillusioned. How could he help these people?

Traffic started moving and Steve considered the more optimistic view. Maybe the Snake kid would make it out. Maybe he'd become a great artist. Right. More likely, Mr. Snake Rogers would end up in jail. Leona said he already used drugs.

As Steve approached the garage, he wondered what drove people to do what they did? Snake, painting? Laura, medicine? Obsessions that he could not comprehend. Once Laura had tried to explain to him that medicine was like a vocation. Like being a priest or a nun. Bullshit. She was a mother for God's sake. Why wasn't that enough? Why hadn't he been honest with her about her ambitions from the beginning instead of telling her to go ahead when he'd really resented her decision.

Or was there something lacking in him? All he wanted was to be a good husband and father. A good provider and a stronger father than his own. That's all that mattered to him. Sure, he wanted to do his job well, but if something better came along, he'd have no problem giving it up. Unlike Laura, there was no passion about what he did every day. He'd started college as a communications major. Why had he changed to social work? Because he wanted the security of knowing he'd always have a job. Well, it's a good thing he had a job, because he had to pay all the bills, including a full-time babysitter so Laura could go to school.

As Steve parked Laura's Falcon outside the shop, he breathed deeply. A smile played on his lips as Laura's scent erased his irritability, and he envisioned his wife's beautiful smile. Yes, despite it all, they were a great couple. Laura with her emerald green eyes, her golden hair. Together they'd made two beautiful kids: Mikey with Laura's green eyes and Kevin's blue, like his.

CHAPTER TWENTY-FOUR

Heavy snow had been falling steadily. By 6:00 P.M. , five inches had accumulated. Snowplows were out on the main roads. The freeways should be clear, but the back streets would be a mess.

Laura and Susan both grimaced as they reached the heavy gray doors of the basic science building and looked out at the clogged, unplowed street. In the entranceway, Dr. Monroe stood talking to a man in an expensive cashmere coat.

"Hey, I know that guy," Susan whispered.

"He looks familiar. Who is it?"

"Can't put a name to him. Cripes, Laura," Susan said, "it's going to be tough driving in this."

Laura nodded as she watched the pair of men shake hands and walk their separate ways. "Yeah. I wish we hadn't stayed so long."

"My fault for taking so long in micro lab."

Laura glanced down at Susan's thin black flats. "You wait here. I'll go get the car. Okay if I leave my microscope here with you? It's so darned heavy. I sure wish I'd finished my histology project so I didn't have to lug this home tonight." She shifted the pile of books she held in her arms.

"Of course. Go ahead," Susan said glancing down at Laura's feet. "Girl, you were smart to wear boots. Didn't realize snow was in the forecast."

"You had Dr. Will in your forecast. I want details on the ride home," Laura called as she headed out the door.

Trudging as fast as she could through the heavy snow, Laura found her car nearly obliterated by a blanket of white. She used her glove to wipe the snow off the lock to find the keyhole then managed to unlock the driver's door and open it, sending white powder in all directions. Dumping her books onto the front seat, she reached for the snow scraper. Something seemed amiss. It was an eerie, unexplainable sensation.

Resolutely, Laura grabbed the scraper and trudged to the back of the wagon. She cleared the rear window as best she could while more snow fell. She saw a few other students in the nearly empty lot doing the same thing as she made her way to the front windshield, passenger side first. Finally reaching the driver's side window, the scraper encountered something — a piece of cardboard lodged under the windshield wiper.

Laura reached for the cardboard. On one side, there was a faded Dole pineapple label. She turned it over and noticed some writing there but it was too dark to make out the words. Probably one of her classmates with a smart remark about last semester's grades, she thought.

After pushing the bulky white snow from the doorframe, she got in and started the engine, setting the heater and defroster to high. She wondered what kind of message was scrawled on the cardboard scrap. A note for Susan from Will perhaps? She flipped on the overhead light, pulled off her gloves, and examined the soggy piece of cardboard. The ink was wet and runny, the words in red marker, disconcertingly reminding her of blood. Through the blur, the letters were crude but unmistakable. A wave of terror pulsed through her as she read, YOU CAN'T HIDE — KILLER BITCH.

She froze. Just when she thought she was safe. Somebody must know. Laura sat immobilized as the car heater began to blow warm air, creating an arc of clear window in front of her. She now saw that there were no other cars close to hers. "Stay calm. Put the car in reverse, back out of this spot and pick up Susan," she said aloud.

The falling snow had already obscured her rear view, but she was too scared to get out to brush the snow off the back window. She shifted the automatic transmission into reverse. Nothing happened. The station wagon did not move. She had expected some sliding on the icy surface underneath the accumulated snow. She'd grown up in Western Michigan where a few inches of snow was nothing, so why wasn't anything happening? She almost floored the gas pedal. The car lurched.

Something was wrong. She checked the gauges. There was no blinking oil light, and the engine had started just fine. The gearshift mechanism seemed okay, and there was plenty of gas. She again put it in reverse but made no progress. Was it a flat? Remembering the threatening note, Laura started to get out of the car to check the tires. Just as quickly, she jerked the door closed.

She couldn't just sit in the deserted parking lot. She slid her frozen hands back into her gloves. Cautiously, she again pushed open the driver's side door. She'd already turned on the headlights, figuring she'd need some light to find out what was wrong. She stepped out, petrified that at any instant a retaliatory bullet would rip through her. She approached the rear wheel on the driver's side and with her gloved hand brushed aside enough snow in order to look closely at the tire.

She'd been right. It was flat. She'd expected that the car would be listing to the left, but it wasn't. Why not? Pushing away more snow, she checked the other rear tire. She leaned down and heard her own heart pound like a drum. The second tire was flat, too.

Rising abruptly, Laura made her way back to the driver's door. Hastily brushing her gloves together to free them of snow, she reached inside, grabbed her purse and yanked the keys out of the ignition. She saw the pile of medical texts and her priceless class notes on the front seat but chose to leave them, not wanting to waste any time. She closed the door, locked it and rushed back toward the school. A few yards away, she allowed herself a furtive glance back toward her car. With a wave of dismay she realized that she'd left the headlights on. Two new tires would cost plenty. She did not want to risk having to purchase a new battery too. Turning back, she trudged as fast as she could to the parked car. Keys ready, she approached the door, opened it, and reached in to turn off the headlights. The cardboard note was lying on the floor of the front seat. She grabbed it and stuffed it into her coat pocket.

Susan was waiting just inside the heavy doors, trying to keep warm. Her expression turned to one of surprise as she saw Laura push through the big door.

"Geez, I am so sorry. I didn't even see the car pull up," she apologized. "Guess I was too preoccupied about stuff. I've got physiology lab tomorrow. We're going to do cardiac stimulation experiments on a dog, and I've been chosen for the actual surgery."

"You didn't miss anything. We've got a problem," Laura said.

"What kind of problem?"

"I've got two flat tires. The car won't move. God, Steve'll flip. His car was just in for repairs yesterday. Now this."

"Oh, no, that's awful. I'll call my dad. He should still be at the precinct. Maybe he can swing by and pick us up."

Laura panicked. A ride home with Detective Reynolds after their recent conversation? She managed what she hoped was a civil reply. "Nah, don't bother him. I'll get in touch with Steve. He can pack up the kids and drive down to get us. Then tomorrow, once the lot is plowed, he can come down and change the tires."

"Laura, that's silly. In this weather? It'll take forever. Here, you watch our stuff. I'm calling my dad. The station is all of five minutes away." Not waiting for an answer, she headed for the pay phones in the hallway.

Laura waited anxiously, her hand wrapped around the damp piece of cardboard in her pocket.

When she returned, Susan smiled. "Dad is on his way. Caught him as he was leaving," she explained. "He'll be here in a few minutes, just enough time for me to run for a candy bar at the vending machines. Can I get you one?"

Laura started to tremble. "No thanks. I'll wait here."

*   *   *

Ten minutes later, the detective pulled up in a dark blue Pontiac. To Laura, it looked like the perfect unmarked police car, and her palms began to perspire inside her gloves. He certainly wouldn't question her again about that night in front of his own daughter, would he?

Laura loaded her wooden microscope box into the back seat and climbed in beside it as Susan hopped up front with her dad.

"Hello, detective," Laura began, "it's nice to see you again."

"Same, Mrs. Nelson," he responded politely, turning around to meet her gaze. "Sorry about your car. Flat tire?"

Laura nodded briefly and looked away.

"Not one but two flats, Dad." Susan added. "Can you believe it?"

"I wanted to get in touch with Steve, but Susan insisted on calling you first. Anyway, thanks for picking us up."

"Anything for my most favorite daughter and her friend," he replied. "I'm glad you two caught me in time. The roads are really getting treacherous."

"Dad, I'm your only daughter," Susan said. She gave her father a generous smile and turned to face Laura. "And, Dad, how about 'Laura'? 'Mrs. Nelson' sounds way too formal."

Laura nodded and tried to smile as Detective Reynolds glanced back before heading toward the student parking lot rather than the entrance ramp to the Chrysler Expressway.

"Okay, then, Laura. I just want to take a look at your car." Reynolds had pulled into the parking lot, his heavy-duty snow tires rolling easily over the snow. "Where is it?"

"Oh, don't go to any trouble," Laura responded hastily. "I must've run over some broken glass. It's all over the place."

"Just take a minute. I want to make sure nothing else is going on here. I assured Dean Burke some months back that my uniformed men would continue to patrol the area around the med school carefully, and I intend to keep my word." He had slowed to a crawl, the snow crunching beneath the tires.

"It's the small station wagon over there," Laura managed. She pointed to one of the four snow-covered vehicles still left in the lot.

Laura shivered. She had read enough detective novels to imagine him deciphering the clues that must be all around, and said a silent prayer that he would not notice anything amiss.

John Reynolds slipped on a knit cap and got out of the car. Shining his flashlight around the ground, he then moved the beam methodically over the hood and to the left front tire and then along the driver's side to the rear tire. Carefully, he walked around the entire car. Laura began to panic as she watched him pay particular attention to the two front tires, pushing aside the heavy wet snow with his gloves and boots. Then, he shone the penetrating light directly into the car, checking the driver's side lock. Circling once more, he directed the beam onto the ground around the car. Would there be footprints other than hers? Laura had not even looked, but then, the falling snow would have obliterated them. Right? She squeezed her eyes shut, not daring to look. Then she felt a spray of snow as Detective Reynolds opened the driver's door of the sedan. He stuck his head in, turning to Laura in the back seat.

"Laura, you left a lot of books in the car. Don't you need them?"

"I'll get them in the morning," she blurted.

"Why don't you give me your keys? I'll get them for you now."

"Sure, let Dad get the books. Laura, you're bound to need them tonight, especially the class notes."

Reaching into her purse, Laura reluctantly retrieved her keys and handed them to Susan's father.

"Here they are," Reynolds announced as he climbed back into the driver's seat of the Pontiac. He flipped on the interior car light, then turned fully around to face Laura and hand her the books and her keys. Their faces were no more than a foot apart.

"Laura, you have four flat tires," he announced. "I'm not sure how this happened. It's not likely that you simply ran over broken glass. I suspect foul play, and I don't like it. I'm going to send a couple of uniforms over to investigate tomorrow. I don't want you to move your car until we've finished investigating."

Laura tried not to show the fear that curdled inside her. The accusatory note. The four flat tires. What was happening? And now, the police were involved. She tried to think. Was someone out to harm her? For a split second she thought about telling Susan's dad about the note. Would the police protect her? No, they'd arrest her, she decided. She was too far into lies and deception. She'd have to face this new threat alone.

"It's your safety, Laura, that's important," the detective was saying as he glanced at Susan beside him. "Strange situation."

"I need my car," Laura said, trying to divert attention away from why someone might have done this. "Steve will have to replace the tires tomorrow."

"Your husband needs clearance before he touches the car. We need to consider it as evidence, are you following me?"

"Evidence for what? Don't you think this is just a prank?" Laura's voice was starting to tremble as much as she was.

"I don't know, but I plan to check it out."

By the time Detective Reynolds pulled to a stop in front of the Nelson house, nearly a foot of snow had accumulated. Steve's car was almost buried in the driveway.

"Thanks for the ride, detective," Laura said. "Susan, I'll get Steve to drive us in tomorrow. He can change my tires then and we'll be back to normal."

"Laura, remember what I said about the car. We need to check it out for evidence," the detective said somewhat brusquely. "In fact, I'd like to come in and talk with your husband about it now."

"That's not necessary," Laura said as sweetly as she could manage. Steve was already upset enough about the violence in the city. Walking in with Detective Reynolds would only make things worse.

"Come on, Dad," Susan intervened, "it's late. I've got a lot of homework. Laura can give Steve the message. She'll explain everything, right Laura?"

"Sure. You two go on home," Laura urged. "I'll talk with Steve. He'll call you if he has any questions, detective."

Reynolds frowned. "Okay, girls. Guess I'm outnumbered."

Inside, Steve fed the baby his formula while Mikey raced around playing cars.

"Four flat tires!" he exploded.

"That's not all," Laura grimaced. "We're not even supposed to change them until the police authorize it. Here, let me take over." She lifted Kevin from his arms.

Steve slumped down in his easy chair. "I'm telling you again, Laura. That goddamn school is not safe. I want you to drop out. At least until after the baby is born."

"Let's not overreact, okay? Pranks like this can happen anywhere. We can put the tires on our Bank Americard. I'll cut back on other things." She tried to sound optimistic. "Besides, we'll save money if you could come down tomorrow to change them yourself."

"Does sound like typical adolescent vandalism," Steve stated matter-of-factly. "That parking lot needs better security. I thought they had stepped it up."

"Me too. So will you drive me and Susan in tomorrow?"

He scowled. "Yeah, but I've really had it with you going in there everyday. You're pregnant for God's sake."

Laura breathed a sigh of relief and ignored his last comment as she walked into the kitchen to start dinner. Mikey followed, zooming around like a human race car. Instead of being amused, she was irritated. It had been a very long day.

The next morning, Steve called the police station after taking time before work to pick up two new tires to replace the front ones. He was hoping to get the two rear flats repaired since the tires were practically brand new.

"Mr. Nelson, about your car," an officer stated. "There's a problem."

"What's going on?" Steve asked. He was standing at an open pay phone on the street. Though it had finally stopped snowing, the wind was brutal.

"Well, Mr. Nelson," the male voice responded. "Those tires are not just flat. All four were blown away with a twenty-two caliber automatic."

"What the hell?" Steve was incredulous. "Is this somebody's idea of a joke?"

"Hold on, please. Detective Reynolds wants to talk to you," the unidentified voice announced as Steve was clicked onto hold.

"Mr. Nelson, John Reynolds here. Remember me? I spoke with you and your wife last fall about that shooting down near the med school."

"Yeah, I remember," Steve responded. "Thanks for giving Laura a ride home last night. Helluva storm."

"My pleasure. Mr. Nelson, do you have any idea why someone would deliberately shoot out your wife's tires?"

"No, of course not. But with violence rampant in the city, nothing surprises me."

"Just a hunch, Mr. Nelson. I'm wondering if there's some connection to that situation last fall. That's what I'm investigating."

"Detective Reynolds, I need four new tires. My wife needs to drive that car home tonight. I'll be there on my lunch hour to replace those tires."

"I'll make sure my men clear your car by then, but if you or your wife come up with anything else, anything at all, I want you to call me right away, agreed?"

"Absolutely," Steve said, "but I can't imagine how this could be related to that kid that was killed last fall."

After he hung up the phone, Reynolds gingerly fingered the strand of blonde hair he'd found on the headrest in the back seat of his city

Pontiac when he'd reached back to grab his overcoat the previous evening. After pondering for some time, he sauntered up the stairs to the evidence room and checked out the Diggs box. Selecting a blonde hair from an envelope, he removed it with tweezers and placed it in another envelope he'd marked 'A'. Into another envelope, he'd marked 'B', he placed the lone strand from his car. It was a little longer than the first, but to the naked eye looked otherwise identical in color and in texture. He then took both envelopes over to microscopy and with no explanation other than the request itself, asked an old and trusted colleague whether the two specimens could be from the same individual.

After a short glance under the microscope, the criminologist nodded. "Not only could be, but highly probable, my friend."

Later, Reynolds returned the specimen to its original envelope but retained envelope 'B', otherwise unmarked, and placed it in a folder piled high with nearly illegible notes in his private drawer. He closed his eyes, any doubts he'd had drifting away. So it was Laura Nelson's hair found on the victim. But hair was not admissible as evidence. Legally, what you could say was: This is similar to her hair. But not: This is her hair.

Reynolds then reflected that it was possible that the victim had carried a strand on his clothing from the bedside of his brother out of the hospital after Laura had examined the comatose young man that night in September. Possible, yes, but probable? And how did any of this connect to the blown-out tires in the parking lot last night? Sit tight, he told himself. Wait for what ballistics finds on those bullets from the .22.

Reynolds opened his eyes then. Was Laura Nelson in danger? And what about Susan, riding in with her everyday?

All morning Laura looked for an opportunity to destroy the cardboard note. Finally, between anatomy and biochem, she ducked into a toilet stall in the women's restroom and shredded the note. Part she flushed, part she distributed in the various waste containers. Finally, she was satisfied that there was no trace of it left behind, and her heart quit beating so wildly. If only she could deal with the gun so effectively. Steve was back on the kick that she carry it with her again. She still kept it hidden on the top shelf of the closet in the kids' room. Only now she kept it in a locked box.

CHAPTER TWENTY-FIVE

After a weekend at home, Stacy Jones returned reluctantly to St. Mary-of-the-Woods Academy. As soon as Sister Portia made the offer to bring her home for the weekend, Stacy had planned to beg her mother to allow her to return for good. She'd promise anything. Straight As. Home right after school. Never to go out, not even on weekends. Anything to get her out of the white girls' prison. But she hadn't succeeded.

Lucy, of course, was overjoyed to see Stacy, and her little sisters were beside themselves, each one vying for her attention. What the nun had said was true. Stacy was like a celebrity. All the neighbors stopped by to say hello on Saturday. Both flattered and frightened by so much fanfare, Stacy tried to answer all their questions. What was it like going to such a snooty school? What were the other girls like? Were there other black girls? The older girls were especially interested in how she could survive in a school with no boys, but everybody became silent with awe when Stacy told them that she had a friend who knew Diana Ross.

At bedtime, she sat down with Lucy to state her case. She tried to explain why she hated the academy. How lonely she was. How she had no friends except for Monica Williams. How she missed her old friends and family.

"Why baby, that's just normal." Lucy put her arms around her daughter and gave her a loving hug. "Stacy, honey, my heart is just busting with pride. You're going to make something of yourself.

You're so smart." She paused. "Just think of how proud Anthony and Johnny would be of you."

"But Mama, you need me here, you know you do," Stacy implored. "How can you manage alone with the girls? I know I messed up once, but I'll never do it again. I learned my lesson. I promise, Mama, please!"

"Not for you to worry about anymore, honey," Lucy said as a smile played on her lips. "Your mama's got herself a new job starting next Monday."

"What kind of a job?"

"Stacy, it's a real good job. God has answered our prayers. I'm going to be an administrative assistant."

"A what?" Stacy's eyes narrowed.

"I haven't started yet, but, no more cleaning, scrubbing, and mopping. No. This job requires skill and ability."

"What skill do you have, Mama? You never even graduated from high school," Stacy challenged.

Lucy nodded. "That's what I told them straight off, but they asked me to take a test, and so I did. They said I did real good, and I got the job. And the great part," Lucy continued, "is that it's day work, baby. Do you know what that means? I can be home every night with the girls, and no more weekend work."

"Where'd you get this job?" Stacy demanded.

"I'm so excited to tell you, could hardly stand it with all these people around today." She tried to embrace her daughter again, but Stacy recoiled.

"Mama, please."

"Here's how it happened. You remember those nice Sisters that came over on Christmas Eve? The night Sister Mary Agnes brought you home?"

"Of course I remember," Stacy said.

"Well, Sister Portia came back with little presents for the girls on Christmas Day when you were still sleeping and talked to me a lot about you and what was happening. I told her how smart you were and how worried I was with all this crime and the killings that's going on. Of course, Sister Mary Agnes came too and she already knew how smart you are. That's when we decided to try for that fine school you're attending. To help you get in, they had to contact the Social Services Department to make arrangements. So I went down, and this social worker interviewed me so the scholarship would go through. One thing led to another, and I told him about my job and my worries, about you, about your little sisters, everything we been through with Anthony and Johnny." Her face clouded over. "Well, that social worker started to talk to me about my schooling, what I felt about the welfare system, all the crime in the neighborhood, all the drug problems. Before long he says, 'Mrs. Jones, you just had your job interview.' Just like that. Then he told me there was a job opening in his department. I told you he was a social worker, didn't I?"

"Uh huh." Stacy was incredulous. "So what is this job?"

"It's being an administrative assistant, like I said. I had to go in three separate times and talk to lots of people in the office. I didn't know nothin' about being an administrative assistant before, but now I have some idea."

"Well, I don't. What is it?"

"What I'm supposed to do is to take care of things for four of the social workers. I had to meet them all. Mr. Nelson was so nice. He introduced me to everybody and made me sound real good even though he knew I don't have any decent experience. But here's the amazing part, honey," Lucy confided. "I'm the one who will answer all the calls when the social workers are out in the neighborhoods. I also have to fix up their schedules and make sure that the most important problems, like when people get their benefits cut off or they have no money to eat, get the most attention. I start work on Monday."

"Why, Mama, that sounds like a fine job!" Stacy threw her arms around Lucy and hugged her.

"I know it. But let's not talk about it anymore tonight. I'm not supposed to tell you this because everybody wants it to be a surprise, but there's a party for you at St. Joseph's tomorrow afternoon. All of your friends will be there."

Stacy frowned. Things were already different with her friends. She'd been away barely more than a week, but everybody was already treating her strangely. Maybe it was the new hairstyle. Monica, her friend, had helped her straighten it so her dark curls hung loose and full, long enough to pull back into a trendy ponytail. Wait until they found out that Monica knew Diana Ross.

Stacy felt weird at the party in her honor. Maybe she didn't fit in anymore. Maybe she didn't fit in anywhere any more. But one thing was for sure, her girlfriends were begging her to get them into a Diana Ross concert. Smugly, she promised them that she'd try.

When she arrived home after the party, Snake and Willie were waiting for her on the front porch steps. They were wearing armbands in protest against the war. Knowing her mother would not want them in the house, she sat with them on the porch. They talked about her brothers, and Snake and Willie swore they'd find out who'd killed Johnny.

"Stacy, get in the house now," Lucy Jones eventually called out the front window. "Ray and Willie, go along home and stay out of trouble."

"Mrs. Jones, we're just sayin' hello," Snake called back. "No problem here, we got to go anyway."

"One more thing," Snake whispered to Stacy. "I saw that yellow-hair doctor lady again. 'Member the one from the hospital screwin' with Anthony? Gave the bitch a fuckin' surprise."

Willie snickered as he stepped down into the street. "You show them whities, bro."

"What did you do?" Stacy asked, shrinking back as Snake leaned in close.

"Shot the motherfuckin' tires outta her car is what I did. Turns out her old man tried to screw with my mama. Teach them to fuck with me," he nodded. "Tell you that right now."

Stacy's eyes widened. "You shot the tires out? You mean you got a gun?"

Snake stood and spun around on the step. "Keep it down, girl. That's what I mean."

"You askin' for trouble?" Stacy shook a finger at him. "Your mama needs you around to help with your brothers. You're just asking for it walking around with a gun on you."

"Hey, whose side you on, girl? You said yourself you wanted that lady doctor to quit comin' around and screwin' with your bro."

Stacy shook her head. "I just wanted her to leave us alone is all. Haven't we had enough trouble around here to last forever? I've got to go now." She stood up.

Snake grunted and brushed his hand across Stacy's breasts as he passed her on his way off the steps. "Now you get in and tell your mama to get you out of that white girl school. You hear?"

When Sister Portia drove down to the Jones home on Sunday night to take her back to the Academy, Stacy went, unable to disappoint her mother. All the way back, Sister kept talking about some old Flemish paintings at the Detroit Art Museum. Stacy was barely listening. The truth of it was, she'd already started to look forward to playing in the basketball game Wednesday night. The St. Mary's girls had a new motto: "Sisterhood is Power," a phrase they heard on TV while watching an antiwar demonstration in Washington, D.C. They'd taken to greeting each other with these words. They just had to beat those cocky girls at Mount Mercy.

CHAPTER TWENTY-SIX

By the middle of February, Snake's mural had grown and changed, along with its name. He'd originally called it *The Cakewalk* because during slavery, that dance, with its basic strut, shoulders thrown back and head held high, had been a way blacks made fun of the high and mighty attitude of the whites. But Snake now took the painting much more seriously, and he had added more figures. At this point they not only reached for the sky, some also walked along a road that resembled railroad tracks. The painting was called *The Railroad*. While slavery had never existed in the state of Michigan, Detroit's proximity to Canada had helped establish several escape routes that ultimately led thousands of slaves to freedom.

Willie stood nearby with a small fire burning in an old trashcan to keep warm as Snake made more changes to the painting. It was a windless, frozen day.

"Look here, Willie," Snake said, "first I'm gonna paint in Diana Ross. That'd be something Stacy'll like, right bro? Then, I'm gonna get the brother in there, Dr. Martin Luther King Jr., man."

"Hot shit," Willie answered. "Can't believe he showed here, bro. Can't believe he just up and showed at Cobo Hall last week with nobody even knowin' he was comin'."

Snake smiled, cupping his hands over his mouth to warm them. "Can't blame him. Up to see the Queen of Soul, Miss Aretha Franklin. What about that, man, what about the mayor calling it Aretha Franklin Day. 'Bout time we get the respect. Someday, my name gonna be added to that list. I keep paintin' this thing and eventually they'll take notice, and I'll be gettin' outta this fuckin' hole."

Willie, as usual, listened to his friend's dreams with a look of awe on his face. He'd seen Snake's determination to create this big painting deepen as the months passed. Regardless of the weather, he painted every day. He was looking for a real job now, too. If anyone could find a way out of the neighborhood, it was Snake.

As 1968 progressed, David spent more and more time at the hospital. By choice now, rather than necessity. Although the streets of Detroit still provided the usual gunshot wounds and stabbings, especially on weekend nights, casualties related to the riots had finally ceased. But as the post-riot governmental probes and the volatile political rhetoric escalated, City Hospital continued to absorb the victims of poverty and violence as spring approached. It was here in the crowded examining rooms, that University Medical School students were exposed to every conceivable medical scourge, every traumatic horror inflicted by guns, stabbings, auto collisions, burns, and diseases the civilized world considered eradicated — the result of indigence and neglect and nowhere else to go.

And this was David's domain. He took tremendous personal pride in the trauma treatment center he had pioneered where victims, whose chances of survival were almost nil elsewhere, survived regardless of their ethnicity. The enormity of the challenge provided by the Detroit riots had carried the accomplishments of City Hospital into national focus. As a result, the hospital had been contacted by a network producer, Ted Compton, about doing a documentary. Something realistic, something that would highlight the need for improved management of serious violent injuries. Compton had been watching the local news coverage and was determined that Dr. Monroe be the real-life central character.

At first David had balked, shying away from more publicity. Hadn't the riots been enough? Why prolong the city's agony. Detroit was still plagued by civil unrest and instability. Fires were still sporadically reported, followed by occasional curfews. Racial hostility was still palpable. Compton argued an opposite point of view — that his program would showcase the expertise of the medical school, helping to rehabilitate Detroit's damaged image. Finally, as a tribute to his colleague Ed Collins, David had agreed to allow Ted Compton to produce the show. He hoped it had been a wise decision.

With a cup of coffee in hand, David sat for a moment in his office to reflect on his decision. Alone, in the dark, his mind gradually floated toward a recurring image. Since that impromptu meeting with Laura Nelson and her two kids in the hospital cafeteria, the same picture kept invading his consciousness. It was Laura. Try as he might to submerge the image of her, it returned. A vague sense of guilt ultimately followed his reveries, and to combat them, he had pushed himself harder, working longer hours. Laura was young, she was married, she was out of his reach, she was out of his life.

It was also strange, he reflected, how accepting his wife had recently become of his grueling, sometimes eighty-hour workweek. Since that dreadful scene at the club on Christmas Eve, Cynthia seemed so much more accommodating, even understanding. They had never discussed the ugliness of that night, but after she'd taken that trip to Aruba with her attorney friend, Ruth, in mid-January, Cynthia had become much more pleasant. She and David still slept in separate rooms but that suited him just fine.

As David sipped his coffee, images of Laura drifted into his mind.

David had actually seen very little of her during the second semester. There had been no reason for them to interact. He smiled to himself, aware that he had made it his business to know her class schedule anyway. A simple drop-by visit to the administration office had provided him an easy opportunity to scan class rosters. From then on her schedule was imprinted on his mind. He always knew where she would be, and he occasionally created opportunities to see her. At these supposedly "chance" encounters, Laura had always been pleasant but in a remote, cool sort of way.

Lately, David had noticed that Laura looked healthier than last semester. She obviously had adjusted well to the incredible stresses a first-year student faced. She radiated a fresh glow and had even gained some weight. He recalled how painfully thin she'd looked during the first semester final examinations, her clothing nearly hanging off her body.

David glanced at the clock. How long had he been sitting there, foolishly wasting time? It was 8:00 P.M. He was hungry, and he had to catch the ER head nurse to warn her about the invasion of the television crew tomorrow.

CHAPTER TWENTY-SEVEN

"Ready for the weekend from hell?" Susan quipped as she climbed into Laura's Falcon for their daily journey into the epicenter of Detroit. "Will told me this program is the newest brainchild of Dr. 'Charming.' You get to stay up all night and pretend you're a real doctor working the ER. Does he think it's going to scare us into quitting? Like separate the men from the boys?"

"My stuff's in the back seat," Laura replied. "Not sure if that makes me ready though."

"I can't wait for my chance," Susan said. "You're lucky to be going first. I'm not on for another two months."

"Maybe I'm nuts, but I guess I'm glad to get it over with. Steve's making the time to spend the weekend with the boys, planning an all-male agenda. I suggested that he take them over to the Henry Ford Museum tomorrow. You know how much Mikey loves cars."

"Uh huh, he and every other guy I know."

"Would that include Will Cunningham?"

Susan blushed. "It would. It's scary how much I like him. Just one problem."

"He's an instructor, right? Can he get in trouble for dating a student?"

"Once I finish anatomy, I can date him out in the open. It's not like he's tenured faculty, he's just a post doc. But that's not the problem. We have a major life-style incompatibility."

"What? You guys seem so well-suited for each other."

"Sports," Susan smiled. "He's clueless. Doesn't know the Pistons from the Lions. With their mediocre standings, who cares? But the Tigers, almost winning the Pennant? And the Red Wings? Four Stanley Cups. Imagine."

"You're the only one who's more crazy about sports than Steve," Laura said.

Susan smiled mischievously. "So what about Will? What if we had kids? How could he teach them to throw a football?"

"Uh, Susan, speaking of kids," Laura interrupted. "I have something to tell you." She turned sideways to look her friend straight in the eye. "Promise not to tell anyone?"

"Yeah . . ." Susan hesitated. "What's up?"

"I'm going to have another baby."

"You can't be serious?"

Laura blinked. "Maybe I'm crazy, but it's true."

"But . . . why?"

"Because I want more kids," Laura said quickly, avoiding Susan's blatant stare. "What's so awful about that?"

"You already have two. You're only twenty-three." Susan sounded very logical. "Still lots of time on your biological clock, so I mean, why now?"

Laura gripped the wheel. "I'll be twenty-four. Why so negative? Why not now?"

"Because you'll have to drop out of med school, that's why not now. You're already stretched beyond reason. Med school's an eighty-hour-a-week proposition." Susan's foot began to drum against the floor. "Girl, after how hard you worked. I mean, why?"

"I know what you're thinking," she said, fighting tears to reason with her friend. "But I'm already an experienced mother and I got through the first semester okay, right?"

"So when is the baby due?" Susan asked.

"Late May. I'll be able to finish the second term, have some time off for semester break, and be back in September for the next term. Great planning, huh?"

Laura suddenly realized that she was rehearsing these words

for the school administration office. She feared that as soon as they learned she was pregnant, they'd ask her to leave and reapply in the future. If only this were her sole concern, she thought. The real issue was whose baby she was carrying. Her whole world hinged on the answer to this question. Right now, there was no answer; there was nothing she could do but bury the question as deeply as she could.

"I suppose," Susan said flatly. "When are you planning to tell the school?"

"I'm going to wait as long as I can. Maybe another month. Then it'll be too late to kick me out. I'll guarantee them that I'll be back in September." She glanced at Susan. "Please don't tell anyone, including Rosie and Vicky."

"You have my word. Your little secret is safe with me."

"Thanks. You're a true friend. My only concern now is whether it will be a boy or girl." Laura flashed a smile she hoped looked sincere.

"Wow!" Susan pointed ahead. "Take a look at the hospital parking lot, would you? It's jammed. You can hardly even see the entrance with all those vans lined up. What's going on?"

"Who knows, but I've gotta get out of this miserable traffic," Laura said. She skillfully weaved her way off the Chrysler Expressway.

"Lots of activity," Susan reported. "Not more riots, I hope?"

"Whatever it is, I hope it doesn't interfere with my ER call weekend. I guess you can understand why I'm anxious to get this weekend behind me. Now remember — nobody knows but Steve, my parents, and the in-laws. I've been dying to tell someone, you have no idea."

"Well, I'm glad you told me." Susan stared pointedly at Laura's abdomen. "You definitely do have a bulge. No wonder you've been wearing those oversized muumuu things. Don't think Vicky hasn't commented."

"Let's just hope I can find an extra large scrub gown for tonight."

*   *   *

The emergency room bustled with frenetic activity on Friday, March fifteenth, as cameramen stationed themselves strategically to best capture a series of dramatic vignettes. The more sensational the story the better, from the time an ambulance screamed its arrival at the hospital to the closing of the operating room doors. Bright floodlights illuminated the ER entrance area, casting an eerie daylight image throughout the usually dim interior. To make matters more intense, the heat generated by the powerful lights overwhelmed the ancient thermostats, and a sheen of sweat covered every face as the hospital staff and film crew moved about.

The triage area, where the most urgent cases were separated from more minor ones, was the documentary's focus. Cameramen, lighting technicians, and reporters all waited to descend on the next unlucky trauma victim. A large movie camera on a swivel focused its telescopic lens on the panorama of treatment cubicles. A separate huge, wide-angle lens camera covered the production command center that had overtaken the main nursing station.

The network was not disappointed. By midnight, it was evident that inner city Detroit had produced its typical Friday night violence resulting in a parade of ambulances, sirens screaming and lights flashing. Already four gunshot cases, in addition to six stabbings, had been admitted. These were on top of the usual car crashes, heart attacks, concussions, and fractures.

Despite the commotion caused by the production crew, the ER trauma team functioned at its best. Professional and practiced. Each crisis was more urgent than the former, and life and death traded places so often that no one could keep count. The shoot was going so well that Ted Compton planned to wrap it up for the night after filming one last case. By midnight, a growing pallor had overtaken his usual ruddy complexion, the result of too much blood and gore.

In the meantime, David walked past a crowded waiting room to a cramped, curtained cubicle in the main ER. He had to squeeze around the patient's family and a uniformed policeman to do so. When he parted the curtain, he saw Dr. Doug Kaplan, a staff urologist, bent over a young patient with a big Afro, who lay with his pants down by his knees, gripping the edges of the examining table so hard his knuckles were truly white, his face a sweaty study in agony. David watched as the urologist attempted to insert a plastic catheter into the stump of what had been a normal-sized, functioning penis. Until tonight. The patient's name, David had noted on the log-in record, was Lonnie Greenwood, age twenty-three.

Because of the din created by bickering members of Lonnie's family and his girlfriend's family, Dr. Kaplan had to shout to be heard by the four medical students at his side. "The shaft of the penis is totally destroyed!"

Meantime, a young police officer was trying to take a statement from the victim's girlfriend, Maya Johnson, a moon-faced girl with large gold hoop earrings.

"A clean break we might be able to repair, but not this," Dr. Kaplan continued in a matter-of-fact, clinical tone. He paused for a moment to respond to one of the student's questions.

From what David gathered, Lonnie's girlfriend had been the cause of the awful wound.

"There's not enough tissue to piece together. These fragments are already necrotic; we'll have to excise them," the urologist went on. "This man would be dead if he hadn't been hit so precisely. Would have severed the femoral artery. We'll take him to the OR and secure a patent urethra so that there'll be bladder drainage.

David could not help but overhear the involved families squabbling over whose fault the incident was: Lonnie's, for messing around with another woman, or his girlfriend's, for taking revenge. David learned that the policeman on duty had driven the victim and his girlfriend to the hospital in his squad car rather than wait for an ambulance. He had just been joined by a dark-skinned detective named Morris Willard. Willard, who wore an ill-fitting brown suit, a pair of shiny shoes, and a scowl, attempted to ascertain some details about the gun that Maya Johnson had allegedly used against her boyfriend.

"It's not alleged, it's true, I did it, and I'd do it again! That sorry ass butterhead thinks it's just fine for him to bang Glenda."

"Who's Glenda?" the detective asked.

"She was my best girlfriend! But no more."

"Excuse me, Miss," Willard interrupted. "Your name please?"

"What? My name is Maya Johnson. No relation to the President of the United States in case you was wondering."

"Miss Johnson," the detective continued, "you have just admitted that you attempted to murder." He waited for the officer to supply the name. "Lonnie Greenwood."

"Like hell I did," she spat, "I was attemptin' to shoot his dick off!"

The detective, a mask of sweat already covering his face, turned to the young cop. "Have you read Miss Johnson her rights?"

"Not yet sir."

"Miss Johnson, are you still in possession of the weapon that you used?"

"Course not. That weapon, like you say, disappeared real quick. Got no idea. Go ahead and arrest me, I don't care, nothin' else left for me now."

"Maybe not," Willard said roughly, turning to the uniformed officer. "Cuff her. Find that weapon."

David had intended to observe Doug's case and to assess it for the camera crew, but once he saw the nature of the wound, he knew that television was out of the question. However, his attention was soon diverted. First there was the scene with Lonnie's girlfriend and the police. Then there was Laura Nelson, right here in the ER, witnessing the awful spectacle. On weekend rotation, he realized, as it dawned on him that he had neglected to keep the students out of the way of the cameras and reporters on this unusual night.

The students wore the traditional green surgical scrubs worn by staff. Crumpled and baggy, the outfits were hardly flattering, but to David the scrubs made Laura look younger. Her blonde hair hung loosely to her shoulders, looking fresh and soft, her cheeks bright. Her eyes, however, shone with what he imagined was utter horror at the sight before her.

"Doug," David called to make his presence known.

Surprise registered on the students' faces as they recognized the chief of surgery.

"Thought I'd check on your case for the film crew."

Doug frowned. "I don't think so, Dr. Monroe."

"I agree. This one's not fit for TV viewing," David said, grimacing at the gory stump and agonized face before him.

Lonnie groaned.

"He's on his way to the OR," Doug said, turning to the students still standing at Lonnie's side as the sedative took effect on the patient. Two students helped the traumatized young man lay back, finally closing his eyes. "You students go on up and scrub for the surgery."

David cut in. "Doug, may I borrow one of your students? I've got an interesting case."

"Of course."

"Mrs. Nelson, would you come with me?" David said, pausing at the door and motioning to the detective inside. "This place is overly crowded tonight. I'm getting concerned about security. Is it possible for you to get more officers here?"

"Soon as I'm done dealing with this circus, Doctor." He sounded more annoyed than cooperative.

At that moment, a familiar figure walked with authority through the ER doors and after a moment's hesitation, approached them. It was Detective Reynolds. Laura felt her knees buckle. What was he doing here? Did it have to do with her?

"What's all the hoopla about?" Reynolds directed his question to the cameras. "You should have told me, I would've sent some uniforms over."

A thin smile crossed David's face. "Hello, Detective

Reynolds. In fact, I was just discussing that very possibility with that officer over there." He nodded inside the room. "Sorry I didn't catch his name.

"Willard," Reynolds grunted. "I'll handle it."

David turned to Laura. "We have to be going," he announced, leading her out into the hallway.

Only then did Laura release her breath. Susan's dad had not said a word to her.

Scratching his head, Reynolds watched as the enigmatic Laura followed Dr. Monroe. "Now what is that all about?" he mumbled.

"John, what are you doin' here?" Willard frowned as he joined Reynolds at the cubicle door.

Reynolds reached out to shake Willard's hand. "It's your first night on, Detective. 1300 Beubien assigned me as lead, must have thought you needed a role model. How about that?" Reynolds paused to more closely inspect his new charge. "Now for your first lesson: wait for me before you leave the precinct. That way we don't waste time."

The younger detective reached for Reynolds' outstretched hand and rolled his eyes. "No reason I can't go off on my own. It's not like I'm a rookie. Specially since the perp's from my old neighborhood."

"No matter. I'm senior detective in homicide and you'll do your teething with me. And in case you're thinking different, just because we're both Americans of African descent, I'm not cutting you any slack. You're gonna do things my way. Understand?"

"Got it. Truth is, there's no homicide here. Bastard got his prick shot off by the dumb bitch over there. She spilled it."

Reynolds took in the scene with a glance. A handcuffed and tearful young black woman surrounded by her shrieking family. "What makes her dumb, detective?"

Willard stared at Reynolds. "She shot her man's dick off. Then she admits it to me in so many words. How dumb is that?"

"Second lesson, watch your mouth. You move up in the ranks,

you have to watch what you say. Keep the gutter out of your language. You have to be both a detective and a gentleman, Detective Willard. And one more thing, since you're gonna be my project, I assume you're wearing a vest under that suit."

Confusion passed over Willard's face.

"The kind that stops bullets." Reynolds lifted both hands in mock surrender and spoke softly. "I wear one all the time. The riots may be over, but the danger out there isn't."

CHAPTER TWENTY-EIGHT

"Cup of coffee?" David asked, joining Laura as she waited outside the urology cubicle.

"Uh, sure, okay." Anything to get as far away from those detectives as possible.

"Let's try to sneak through this maze of reporters," David said. "They wanted to film one more case before leaving."

"I saw them outside earlier. A documentary, someone said. It must have been a tough day for you," Laura ventured. What the heck was she supposed to say to Dr. Monroe? And why had he pulled her out of her group?

David nodded. "Yes, it was in a way. But in another way, it was exhilarating. We've created a model trauma center here. It's good to see it recognized on a national level."

They fell silent for a few moments as they proceeded along the hallway. Laura blinked rapidly beneath the fluorescent lights, her contacts suddenly dry and scratchy.

"What case do you want me to see, Dr. Monroe?"

"None in particular," David responded. "I needed an excuse to get away from this crowd and sit for a few minutes. I thought that a companion would help ward off the reporters and keep that producer away. Sort of like a decoy. I hope you don't mind," he admitted in a conspiratorial tone as they worked their way through the throng of white coats that intermingled with cameramen lugging their heavy equipment.

"Of course I don't mind," Laura said quickly.

"Good." David smiled broadly. "And don't worry, we'll be back in the thick of things in a few moments. You'll see your share of trauma medicine. It's barely half-past twelve. In the ER, the night is young."

"It is amazing. So what's going to become of all this filming?" Laura asked, struggling to keep the conversation going, feeling strangely awkward.

Pointing to a table for two, David responded, "I'll get the coffee, then I'll tell you all about it. How do you like yours?"

"I'd prefer a hot chocolate," Laura said as she sat down. "And maybe a muffin or something?" She couldn't believe her brazenness, but there'd been no time for dinner and she needed something in her stomach.

"Here we go," David announced as he returned with their drinks and two muffins wrapped in cellophane. "I survive on coffee this hour of the night."

"I'm usually a coffee drinker too," Laura said pouring the powder into her mug, "but somehow hot chocolate seemed right."

"I bet you miss your children when you're away all night like this," David said. "Cute kids. How old is the baby now?"

Laura blushed, remembering their last cafeteria encounter. She'd thought about it often, more often than she cared to admit. "Uh, yes, I certainly do miss them. Kevin's ten months."

"Must be difficult. Kids — the stress of med school? To tell you the truth, I was worried about you a few months ago. You were very thin, but things must be agreeing with you now. You look like the picture of health."

"It is difficult," Laura responded. "Impossible, no. Worth it, yes. Definitely. You know, everybody must think I'm a lousy mother, but I'm not, really." She gave a shy smile. Self-conscious, yet comfortable.

"What you think and feel is important, not what everyone else thinks. I don't know how you handle it all. What type of work does your husband do?" David asked. Then he held up his hands. "Stop me if I'm prying."

She smiled. "It's fine. He's a social worker with Wayne County Social Services. He finished his Master's last year, and I'm hoping he'll go on to get a doctorate. Once I've finished med school, of course."

"That's great. Well," David glanced around, noting and ignoring a few inquisitive stares from the ER staff. A discarded magazine lay on the table, open to a picture of Bobby and Ethel Kennedy and a passel of toothy kids. "So do you think Robert Kennedy will be our next president?"

Laura shrugged. "Sure would make for an active White House."

"That family has had more than it's share of tragedies."

"I've always admired Rose Kennedy," Laura said finishing her hot chocolate and trying to find the courage to ask him why Detective Reynolds was here.

"Me too," said David, pushing back his chair. "That was just what I needed. It was a pleasure to chat with you, Laura."

He'd called her 'Laura'. Just like the last time in the cafeteria.

On the way back to the ER, Laura saw a balding man in a plaid shirt and baggy pants issuing orders to a cluster of cameramen. He looked familiar, and she squinted to get a better look. Yes, he was dressed differently, but this was the same man she and Susan had seen with Dr. Monroe the night her tires were slashed. That had been more than two months ago, and she was no closer to knowing who'd left that terrifying note.

Suddenly David took her arm and led her toward the man.

"That's Ted Compton," he said, "the producer. Let's see how the filming is going."

"Dr. Monroe, we've been looking for you," Compton shouted over the noisy din. "I just talked to my guys. We have ample material. We're going to pack it in."

"That's fine," David said, joining him near the triage station. "I'd like to introduce you to Laura Nelson. Mrs. Nelson is a first year medical student. We have a unique program here at the medical center that you may find interesting. Laura, this is Ted Compton."

Before Compton could respond, the heavy double doors of the ER crashed open. Amid spewing obscenities and a general commotion, a huge, bald man in handcuffs barged inside. Two police officers, one on each side, struggled to contain the hulk as he thrust violently from side to side, crashing into walls, upsetting equipment carts in his wake. A crazed expression twisted the giant man's pasty face as all conversation stopped.

David grimaced. Was there any police back-up? What had become of Detective Reynolds and that other detective? David turned away from an ashen-faced Ted Compton to see Carrie Wilson push the hidden security button beneath the nursing station desk. Soon, hospital security would swarm the area.

The man broke loose with a tremendous jerk of his shoulders, sending the officers careening in opposite directions. Still flailing, the huge man lurched forward, one foot striking a cart full of oxygen canisters, which clattered to the floor. Struggling to stay upright, he lunged in the opposite direction, heading straight toward Laura. Before anyone could react, his powerful head and shoulders slammed into her, propelling her to the ground. Her head hit the concrete floor with a loud thud. As she lay crumpled on the ground, the giant scrambled to escape, bringing a thick work boot down solidly on Laura's abdomen.

David dove toward Laura as the policemen rebounded and grabbed the crazed man. Meantime, reinforcements raced through the door. Four men pinned him in a prone position and forced him into a straitjacket.

"That's 'Schizoid George,'" a lanky young psychiatric resident called from the nursing station. "Get me a syringe with Valium. He's a schizophrenic."

The pair of officers secured one of George's powerful legs as the resident injected yellow fluid into his thigh.

"This is what happens when he goes off his Haldol and tries

LSD instead," the resident explained to gawking onlookers.

David was on his knees by Laura's side. At that horrible moment, his medical instincts totally abandoned him. Why Laura? Why not him? They had been standing next to each other. Why didn't he step in front to protect her? It had all happened so fast. He tried to be logical and clinical, to fight off panic as ER personnel surrounded Laura.

Laura was unconscious. David quickly examined the blow to the head. No bleeding. A concussion. He had no idea how severe. As a nurse held out a blanket, Dr. Monroe said, "Not yet. Let me do a quick evaluation." Her abdomen concerned him the most. It had taken the brunt of the blunt trauma.

Carrie Wilson had already inflated a blood pressure cuff around Laura's left upper arm and reported a normal reading. Oblivious to the increasing circle of observers, David wiped sweat from his face with his sleeve before checking Laura's pulse. "Normal," he mumbled softly. Someone handed him a stethoscope. "Heart and lungs okay."

His practiced hands moved to Laura's abdomen. David prayed that he wouldn't find evidence of a ruptured spleen or worse yet, a ruptured liver. He pulled up her surgical scrub gown, deftly palpating for signs of injury. When he noted the abdominal distension, his heart sunk and he felt a rush of panic. Something was really wrong. There had to be a huge amount of internal bleeding for this much swelling to happen so quickly. "Repeat the blood pressure," he demanded. His hands palpated the four quadrants of Laura's abdomen.

"One-ten over seventy, Dr. Monroe," Carrie Wilson reported in a clear, clinical voice. "Pulse steady at one-twenty."

Then David saw the blood on the floor, an expanding pool of bright red blood. Where was it coming from? That's when he knew. The distended abdomen. Must be vaginal bleeding. She was pregnant.

"Put her on a stretcher and admit her immediately to Dr. Barrone's service." Edward Barrone was chairman of obstetrics and gynecology at University Medical School. "Page whoever is on call for obstetrics. STAT," he ordered. "STAT," David raised his voice as he looked up at the bank of incredulous stares directed down at him. Those eyes included Detective Reynolds' and the wide-eyed other detective, David absently noted. The police had pushed George into a wheelchair and rolled him out through the big doors he'd passed through moments earlier.

"That's Laura Nelson," Detective Reynolds said aloud.

"Type and cross-match her blood and have six units on standby. Do a complete blood count and metabolic panel. All STAT!" David continued to shoot off orders. "Find Dr. Baronne, wherever he is."

"Of course," the head nurse responded. "Dr. Monroe, we do need information on the patient."

"Laura Nelson. First year med student. This was her ER orientation."

Two orderlies had come forward and carefully lifted Laura to a stretcher covered with clean white sheets.

"Dr. Monroe, could you repeat that? I couldn't catch it all with the background noise," Compton requested.

"Get the cameras out of here," David shouted. "Get Mrs. Nelson to Labor and Delivery. STAT."

CHAPTER TWENTY-NINE

Less than five minutes had passed since the deranged man barged through the ER doors and barreled into Laura. Clear intravenous fluid was dripping into her veins by the time Dr. Danny Morgan, chief obstetrical resident, responded to the STAT page from the ER.

"Dr. Monroe, sir, could you tell me what happened?" the cherubic-faced resident inquired as he approached Laura and immediately started to palpate her rounded abdomen.

David quickly recounted the nature of the injury and the outcome of his screening examination.

"She's pregnant all right," Morgan confirmed. "I'd say six, maybe seven, months. We'll get her up to labor and delivery right away. So far the fetal heart tones are okay. I guess I don't have to tell you," he added, "this is a high-risk situation. A lot will depend on whether we can control the hemorrhaging. We'll start transfusing her now."

Laura stirred on the stretcher, her eyes suddenly flickering open.

David moved to her side.

"Laura, lie very still." Reflexively, he grasped her hand.

"Dr. Monroe, excuse me," a new voice interrupted. It was a transfusion nurse. "We need to get another IV line in to start the blood. We have two units on the way."

As David nodded and stepped back, Carrie Wilson appeared.

"Dr. Monroe, Dr. Barrone is on the line. You can take it in the nurse's station if you like."

"I'll be right there," David said. "Make sure he holds. Tell him it's important."

He stepped closer to Laura once more. "You're here in the emergency room," David tried to explain as gently as possible. "You've had some blunt trauma to the abdomen."

Laura's eyes were now fully open and still struggling to focus. Both of her hands slid to her belly. The skirt of her green surgical scrub dress had been pulled up and was bunched around her waist. Her lower body was covered by a heavy white sheet, and intravenous lines were connected to each arm.

"What happened?" she gasped.

"You were struck by one of the ER patients," David said softly. "You hit your head on the wall and were unconscious for several minutes."

"Huh? I've got to get home." Laura struggled to sit up.

"Please, Mrs. Nelson, you must try to lie very still." Dr. Morgan protectively pressed his arm over her chest.

"Laura, this is Dr. Morgan, the chief ob-gyn resident." David hesitated briefly. "We realize that you're pregnant. We're going to do everything we can to make sure that you and the baby are okay."

Mrs. Wilson appeared once more. "Dr. Monroe, Dr. Barrone is quite impatient."

"Do not let him hang up. Tell him I'm coming right now." David patted Laura's hand gently. "You're going to be admitted to the obstetrical service once we get a blood transfusion started."

As David hurried out to take the phone call, Detective Reynolds approached Laura's gurney on the heels of a transfusion nurse, carrying a plastic pack full of blood. As the nurse hung the dark red blood on a pole, the detective was close enough to read the label.

"B-negative," he mouthed with a deep frown.

Laura was now conscious enough to realize that something

was horribly wrong. Her head hurt terribly, and the pain in her abdomen was severe enough to make her pant. She could also feel something bulky lodged between her legs. Her mind was still fuzzy, but she made the disastrous connection. Bleeding? Vaginal bleeding? Waves of alarm flooded her. If only she could return to that blackness again.

An orderly appeared and began to push Laura's stretcher toward the bank of elevators beyond the ER doors. Mrs. Wilson and Dr. Morgan stayed by Laura's side during the ride to the fourth floor and through the double doors marked labor and delivery.

The silent orderly maneuvered the stretcher into a small room made up of plain white walls with a grayish hue, dull green floor tiles, a single bed, and two chairs. It was clean but absent of any attempt at décor, so different from the shiny obstetrical suites at the private hospital where Mikey and Kevin had been born. Dr. Morgan and the orderly helped Laura transition from the stretcher to the narrow bed. A cheery labor nurse arrived and bustled about, unaware of the circumstances.

"I can't have the baby now," Laura declared, looking up at the strange faces.

"When is your due date, Mrs. Nelson?" Morgan asked softly.

"Not for another two months. It's way too early."

"Right now we'll get you stabilized and do whatever we can to delay premature labor," he said, patting her arm. "Let me introduce you to Mrs. Myers. She's the chief obstetrics nurse, and she'll take care of everything. Joyce, this is Laura Nelson."

The wiry, fortyish nurse with auburn hair and freckles plumped Laura's pillow, keeping up reassuring bantor as she checked vital signs. "Everything's going to be okay, honey. You're in good hands. Dr. Morgan is the best chief resident we've ever had around here. I hear they've even got the big chief, Dr. Barrone, on the way."

"Hello, Ed? Thanks for holding."

"David, what's going on? I'm in the goddamn kitchen of the

Limelight Restaurant waiting for you to pick up. How the hell did you track me down anyway? Come to think of it, old man, you should be here too. Cynthia said you'd be stopping by after you finished whatever you were doing there at the hospital. Sorry to hear Cynthia's decision. I tried to reassure her that it would be okay."

Had Cynthia told him about something going on at the Limelight? Sorry about what decision? Must be about one of her fundraisers. No matter, she could fend for herself.

"National television, no less," Ed continued. "You're becoming goddamned famous."

"Look," David interrupted, "something happened in the ER, and I need your help. One of our students has been seriously injured. Another patient caused it. We're responsible, so I'd really like you down here."

"I see. One of the women, eh?" he asked in a more serious tone.

"Laura Nelson, one of the freshman observers on call tonight. Massive blunt force to the abdomen. A huge bull of a psychiatric patient crashed into her headlong. Turns out she's pregnant. Heavy bleeding. I'd like for you to come down as soon as possible."

"Hold on there, David. Danny Morgan is top-notch. It's his night on call. Get him to evaluate the woman and give me a call later at home. I'll see her first thing in the morning."

"Ed, I need you here now. You, and not a substitute. This girl's in real trouble. And I don't want to take any chances. Look, will you please get down here right away?"

"Okay, David. I'll be there. It'll take me an hour or so. I'll have to drop my wife at home. And I'll offer Cynthia a lift, but perhaps her lawyer friend can take her. Damn it, David, you're working too hard."

Cynthia was with that lawyer again, David thought absently. "It's been a tough night in the ER what with the TV cameras crawling all over the place."

"Cynthia will be disappointed," Ed added. "I think she's expecting you to show up."

"She'll be fine. She knew I wouldn't get there," David responded irritably. To the best of his knowledge, Cynthia hadn't even mentioned going to the Limelight.

CHAPTER THIRTY

Laura started having regular mild contractions during Dr. Morgan's exam. He was worried about severe hemorrhage. The blow to her abdomen might have ripped the placenta from the uterine wall, abruptio placenta. In that case they'd have to do an emergency Caesarian section. But if the rip were less extensive, or if the bleeding was not from an abrupted placenta, the best decision would be to temporize and delay as long as possible. He was carefully monitoring her vital signs and her clotting factors and so far they were normal. Laura half-heard this clinical report on her condition. Her focus was elsewhere. She now knew this pregnancy was not going to be normal. And she still had not dealt with the possibility of a biracial child.

"Mrs. Nelson, I'm going to strap on this device to monitor your contractions." The resident went about the procedure in a confident manner. Since she was a med student, he tried to distract her with chatter about new diagnostic medical technology. "I'd love to have that new equipment to get a better fix on just where that placenta is sitting. You can see a moving image of the baby in real time. It's called ultrasound . . . the commercial version's due out soon . . . Dr. Barrone gets one right away seeing as he did the clinical trials."

"Am I in labor?" Laura interrupted.

"Too early to tell," he answered. "Let's hope not. Now, just relax. We're going to give you another blood transfusion."

A sharp knock on the door interrupted them. Mrs. Myers opened it.

"Come in, Dr. Monroe. Dr. Morgan is just completing his work-up."

David nodded to the nurse and walked directly to Laura's side as Danny Morgan stepped back.

"How's it going?" David asked.

"I don't know. The last thing I remember was standing in the ER with you. Then I woke up on a stretcher."

David was pale. "We were speaking to that documentary producer when a psychiatric patient was brought in. He bolted from the police escorts and crashed directly into you. You went down and hit your head on the wall. I am terribly sorry—"

"But," Laura began, looking up at both doctors, tears moistening her eyes.

"Mrs. Nelson, your condition is serious," Morgan explained. "Your baby is at extremely high risk. We'll do everything we can to delay labor, I promise you, but right now you need to remain calm. I'll be back to check on you soon," he said as he motioned for Mrs. Myers to follow him out with the chart.

"Has anyone contacted my husband?"

"Dr. Barrone will surely call him when he gets here. Which will be any time now. Unless you'd like me to call now?"

"No, not yet. He knows I won't be home until Sunday," Laura explained tearfully. "He'll wonder why I didn't call. You know, to check on the boys. But I don't want to upset him. Maybe everything will settle down, and I'll be out of here tonight."

David glanced at the wall clock. It was already 1:30 A.M.

Mrs. Myers knocked before pushing open the door. "I'll be just a minute, Dr. Monroe," she said. "I've got to check vitals every fifteen minutes."

They were quiet as she took Laura's blood pressure and pulse. She then swung the flimsy curtain around, checked for vaginal bleeding, and replaced the obstetrical sized sanitary pad.

"Hasn't stopped," the response to inquiring eyes as she

moved busily around the bed, straightening the sheets and plumping the pillows before leaving.

"Dr. Monroe, I'm scared," Laura began. "There's something really wrong, isn't there?"

David nodded and started to say something, but Laura interrupted.

"Can I talk to you about something? Something personal?" she asked almost choking on the words.

"Of course," he replied. "Only, please call me David. Okay?"

She nodded, hesitating only slightly. "You're the only one here that I can discuss this with. The only one who can help me. I don't know how to say this. You'll be so shocked."

"Laura, I'll help you in any way I can."

Eyes brimming with tears, Laura's voice shook as she spoke. "Seven months ago," she began, "I was raped. By a black man." Her eyes stared at the bare white wall beyond the foot of the bed as she spoke. "I never told my husband. At the time, I thought it would damage our marriage. When I realized that I was pregnant, it was too late to tell him."

Laura finally looked at David. "I can't be sure about the father of this baby. It could be the man who raped me."

"Dear God." David instinctively reached across the bed, laying his hand on hers. "How terrible for you." He paused. "Who else knows about this?"

"Nobody."

"Nobody? All this time? What about the police?"

"I didn't report it," Laura simply stated

After a long silence, David leaned in closer to Laura and spoke in a low tone, "Did this happen that night I saw you in the parking lot?"

Laura nodded, tears flowing freely, soaking the pillow.

"Lord have mercy," David groaned, gripping the metal bar surrounding her cot. "How can I help?"

"After the baby is born, is there a way that you can keep my husband away from the nursery until I'm awake enough to deal with the situation? Dr. Monroe, if the baby isn't Steve's, I want to be the first to tell him. He mustn't know until I have talked to him."

Laura's eyes held David's. She took a sharp breath as another contraction gripped her. "I don't know what I'll say or how he'll react. I know I should have told him back then when it happened, but I just couldn't."

David nodded. "Good God, yes, I'll try. They won't let him in the delivery room, but when they take the baby to the nursery. . . . Yes, I'll find a way."

"When Mikey and Kevin were born I was awake and pretty alert. I figured I would be awake enough to see the baby and know and go from there."

"That's your plan?" There was a long silence. "I'll do anything I can," David vowed. "I'll stay in close touch with Dr. Barrone."

"Thank you," she murmured, turning away. "No matter what, I want to give this baby the best life I can."

"Are the other children going to be okay while you're in the hospital? Is there's anything I can do to help?"

"How good a baby-sitter are you, Dr. Monroe?"

"I guess I'd be okay," he stumbled.

Laura managed the slightest of smiles as David pulled out his handkerchief to dab at the tears running down her cheeks.

CHAPTER THIRTY-ONE

"David," the booming voice filled the cubby-hole room. "You're still here."

Dr. Ed Barrone, a big, robust man with thinning red hair, barged into the cramped hospital room. He looked out of place in a maroon sports jacket over a broadly striped shirt. A rosy glow tinged his cheeks, a lingering sign of a pleasant evening of food and drink.

"Well, this must be my new VIP patient, Laura Nelson."

Laura looked up. "Yes."

"A med student, no less," Dr. Barrone commented, picking up the chart. "So far, young lady, you've been in good hands. Dr. Monroe and my chief resident, Dr. Morgan, quite the dynamic duo."

The bulky obstetrician approached Laura and bent over the bed. With a practiced hand he pulled down the sheets to expose her distended abdomen.

"What a rare opportunity indeed," he looked up at David with a grin. "To work with Dr. Monroe, the famous media personality. David, are you staying?"

David looked at Laura, who nodded.

Ed Barrone then methodically palpated and probed Laura's abdomen. Without sacrificing concentration on his patient, Ed chided David on his latest notoriety. After completing his examination, Ed Barrone motioned for David to follow him out of the room.

Mrs. Myers returned, chatting amiably while she adjusted the IV board taped to Laura's wrist and helped her don a fresh hospital gown. She had brought in a pack of the usual hospital amenities — soap and skin lotion, mouthwash, and toothpaste, and she'd located Laura's personal belongings in her locker. She helped her remove her contact lenses, replacing them with her glasses. When Laura checked her appearance in the mirror under her tray, some pink had returned to her cheeks. The blood transfusion was almost complete, and she did feel better, yet the rhythmic contractions were definitely more frequent.

When Ed Barrone and David Monroe returned, Danny Morgan and three other residents followed and were introduced to Laura. Two were ob-gyn residents and one was a pediatric resident rotating through neonatology. Laura noted with some comfort that one of the young residents was a woman.

Dr. Barrone spoke. "Here's what we're going to do. You know you're having uterine contractions?"

Laura nodded.

"Okay. Since they've increased and the bleeding hasn't stopped, we're going to treat you with intravenous alcohol." The obstetrician pulled up a chair beside Laura's bed and sat down. "We're hoping to delay labor. Every day that we can give the baby counts. Meantime we'll keep up the blood transfusions."

Laura was barely understanding the implications.

"Now, while on the alcohol drip, you'll feel like you're drunk. The alcohol will have no deleterious effects on the baby at this stage of development."

Laura interrupted him. "How long?"

"We don't know. We're all on call to deliver you either via a regular delivery or a C-section should the alcohol not work. We think that the blunt trauma to your abdomen caused an abrupted placenta, but we can't rule out a placenta previa; that's when the placenta blocks the cervix, until the last minute. Now I'd like to call your husband. I expect he'll want to be with you."

She glanced quickly at David once more. "Okay."

The team left. As the door closed behind the entourage, David returned to her side.

"I'm worried about the IV alcohol," she hurried to say. "Could you stop by to make sure I'm not blabbering? I mean, I don't know how I'll react to feeling drunk. I hardly ever drink anything alcoholic." David nodded as she spoke. "If I'm talking, you know, saying anything about what happened to me, will you please try to keep Steve out? I can't afford to say anything about rape or murder."

"Did you say murder?"

"What?" Laura froze. "Oh no, just that I was afraid that I might be murdered. You know, when I was raped."

David hesitated. "Is there anything else, Laura?"

"No. I would never ask you to do this, but I'm desperate. I just don't know. Maybe when this is over, I should drop out of med school. Maybe I should stay home and take care of my kids."

"You don't have to worry about that now," David said. "I'll be here for you. Everything else can wait."

The door opened again after a single knock. A young technician walked in carrying a basket full of needles and tubes. She quickly went to work hooking up the intravenous alcohol drip and inserting the needle straight into the pink rubber connector of the I.V. tubing already in place.

Once the alcohol drip infused at a measured rate, Laura drifted into a heavy twilight sleep. She remained oblivious to the constant stream of hospital personnel in and out of her small room. Periodically, she would float toward consciousness long enough to realize that people were talking about her. Steve and David would appear and then float in and out. It was all so peaceful. So disconnected. Whatever was happening didn't matter anymore, not while she was cradled in this warm, wonderful cocoon.

CHAPTER THIRTY-TWO

"Do you hear me, Laura?" It was Dr. Barrone. "The alcohol's not working anymore. We want you awake when we deliver the baby."

Dr. Monroe's voice penetrated her chemical oblivion. "Laura, it's been four days and we haven't been able to stop the contractions. You're going to the delivery room now."

A forceful contraction made Laura grit her teeth and try to hold her breath so she would not scream out. This was worse than any labor pain she'd ever experienced.

"Laura, we can't risk giving you anything for pain right now, the baby is too premature." Dr. Barrone spoke with authority.

"What? How long will it be?" she gasped.

"Not long," he replied. "We'll send your husband in for a few minutes while we make the last-minute preparations."

Another intense contraction followed Dr. Barrone's exit. Seconds later, a blurry but clearly distraught Steve appeared in the doorway, eyes red from lack of sleep, shirt crumpled. His disheveled appearance shocked Laura. Steve always looked so neat and well-groomed.

"Steve," she gasped, "I'm so scared."

Two nurses in baggy blue scrub gowns hurried in, almost pushing Steve aside. They worked rapidly and efficiently to strap Laura onto the stretcher and wheel her toward the delivery room.

On the other side of the delivery room door David waited. He stepped forward to join the obstetrical team as they completed preparations. He managed to hold Laura's hand as the anesthesiologist adjusted the panel of dials that controlled the flow of anesthetic gases in various canisters in the event it was deemed necessary to perform a C-section. Dr. Bill Kelly, senior staff neonatologist, had joined the team.

Once she was situated, David left the room for a moment to give Steve a last minute update on Laura. He had established a trusting rapport with her husband over the past few days, and now as he rushed back into the crowded delivery room David's eyes met Laura's, and he moved to her side. The attendants were putting her feet up in the stirrups in the standard lithotomy position.

"Laura," he whispered close to her ear just as the anesthesiologist strapped an oxygen mask over her face. "I remember everything you told me."

Barrone proceeded cautiously yet speedily. All conversation ceased. Everyone was ready to go into action as he gingerly proceeded with a pelvic examination.

"No praevia; no C-section," he announced as the group held their collective breath. "We'll have this baby out with the next contraction."

"Laura, that's good news for you," the doctor said as the others exhaled in relief.

"Okay, people," Dr. Kelly alerted his residents, "we're going to be in an intubation situation with the newborn."

"Ready, Bill?" Ed asked.

"Ready."

For his part, David had never felt such intense involvement, such passion, such closeness to another as he agonized over Laura during the last four days. He alone knew her terrible secret. What if she was right and the baby wasn't Steve's? He couldn't even conceive of Steve's response to a biracial baby. Just the thought terrified him. How could he help Laura? He didn't know, but he'd move heaven and earth if he had to.

David had abandoned his OR schedule along with all research to be with Laura around the clock. He had explained to his secretary and to the surgical staff that because the incident happened in the ER during the filming of the documentary, he not only felt responsible, but that the hospital was liable. No matter that actuality, David just had to be there.

As David coached Laura through the next contraction, his heart lurched as he saw a small, fuzzy head emerge.

"Now for the shoulders," Dr. Barrone recited to his obstetrical students.

"I'm right beside you, Ed," reassured Bill as the baby's abdomen and feet delivered almost precipitously. "Team's ready."

"Here, Danny, cut the cord while I suction," Dr. Barrone instructed his resident before turning to hand the small inert bundle, slippery and blood-streaked, to the neonatal expert. "Take the baby, Bill."

Ed Barrone turned his attention back to Laura to deliver the placenta. Following that, he would apprise her of the baby's condition. Less than three pounds, the infant was terribly premature and hadn't breathed on its own. Suddenly, the seasoned obstetrician frowned. Laura's next contraction was much too forceful. Dr. Barrone instinctively reached forward to palpate Laura's abdomen through the blue surgical drapes. Unexpectedly, she bore down.

David saw a shadow of concern darken Ed's face.

"Dr. Kelly, we've got another one," Joyce Myers announced as Dr. Baronne delivered the second baby amidst chaos and confusion as the neonatal team rushed to find an incubator and to set up another set of tiny resuscitation instruments.

The second small bundle appeared as lifeless as the first.

Once the placenta had been expelled, Joyce released Laura's wrists and lowered her legs. Ed Barrone stepped over to check on the babies. Not a sound had been heard from either.

"Hey, Ed," Bill Kelly murmured, "why no heads-up on this? Lord knows we weren't prepared for two."

"None of us were. We couldn't do a proper exam for fear of catastrophic hemorrhage. If I can avoid it I don't expose a fetus to

radiation, especially given her history of two full-term uncompli-
cated deliveries."

Bill Kelly looked down at the flaccid neonates. "At least you
were able to hold off delivery a few days," he said softly. "That'll
give them an edge."

"But enough?" Ed gestured toward the neonatal team as they
pumped measured aliquots of oxygen through the small airways inserted into the motionless forms.

David intersected Ed as he walked back to Laura's side.
"Whether or not these babies will ever take a breath is doubtful,
isn't it?"

"We've got them intubated and on ventilators, but . . . David,
I'm just remembering the unusual family history. The father, an
identical twin. The paternal grandmother, an identical twin. I can't
tell for sure right now, but these babies seem identical. I should
have suspected it."

"Come on, Ed. Identical twins are a chance occurrence. It's
fraternal twins that have a hereditary tendency."

"Still, if only I had access to that new ultrasound technology."

"We'll be one of the first centers, Ed," David called as he
moved closer to the bevy of activity surrounding the babies.

"Well, you certainly surprised us, my dear. None of us expected twins." Ed Barrone smiled weakly at Laura. "But they're
very premature," he cautioned. "They'll be going to neonatal intensive care." That's all he said before walking back over toward
the babies.

Laura tried to pull herself into a sitting position but could not.
She managed to turn her head toward the urgent activity in the corner.

"Now, now," Mrs. Myers warned, suddenly at her side.
"There's plenty of time for that. This is the time for you to rest."

David hurried back to Laura's side. He bent over and gently
stroked back the strands of hair that had fallen over her pale, per-
spiring face.

"Laura," he whispered. "You have twin girls. They're very small, but they look just like you and Steve. Do you understand?"

She gasped. "Oh, thank God. Can I see them?"

"Not now. Your husband is waiting for you right outside," David said, squeezing her hand, not knowing what else to say.

CHAPTER THIRTY-THREE

After the birth of Laura's twins, David felt dejected and empty. At first he hadn't even gone home, claiming a series of surgical emergencies, throwing himself into a frenzy of activity, anything to keep his mind occupied. Yes, he was relieved that there hadn't been a need to buffer the situation with Steve and that Laura's secret was safe and would remain so with him. Yes, he was enormously thankful that Laura would be okay and that her tiny babies were now breathing on their own. But the painful truth — the Nelsons were a family. There was no place for him in Laura's life.

When Compton's *Motor City Trauma* aired accolades poured in, as did donations to the foundation that David had established in honor of Ed Collins. But rather than savoring success, David began to sink deeper and deeper into melancholy. He was unable to sleep, had no appetite, and no sense of pleasure whatsoever. Just an overwhelming feeling of hopelessness, even worthlessness.

"Tough it out," he mumbled, oblivious to nature's optimism in the perfumed air of an unseasonably warm April day as he approached his estate.

"Well, well, look who's decided to come home," Cynthia lashed out as she met David at the door. She wore a black silk sheath with a bold oriental sash of red and gold. Her raven hair was brushed back into a dramatic swirl. For a moment he panicked. Had he promised to escort her to some function or another?

"Hello, Cynthia," David said, taking off his jacket. "Going out?"

"Yes. Ponroy's. Dinner with Ruth since you are no longer gracious enough to let me know when to expect you." Cynthia paused to scrutinize him. "If you do want to join us, I think you'd better shower and change. You look, well, like hell."

Breathing a sigh of relief, David kicked off his shoes and leaned back against the sofa. It was true. He did look unkempt. Hair too long. Nails unfiled. Clothes wrinkled. "I am beyond bushed," he said. "Too beat to go out. I'll just fix myself something and go to bed." Turning to head upstairs, he remembered something he'd been meaning to ask Cynthia, "Oh, one thing. Ed Barrone mentioned something."

The sound of the doorbell interrupted.

Without waiting for it to be opened, someone came sailing in. "Cynthia, I'm here," Ruth's clear buoyant voice rang out. Her hair was longer and combed straight down in a trendy cut. "Oh, I'm sorry, David. I didn't realize you were home. Glad to see you." Ruth walked over and gave him a perfunctory peck on the cheek as he stood to greet her. "Am I interrupting anything?" she asked.

"Nothing important. I was just going upstairs. Don't let me interfere with your dinner plans, ladies."

Ruth arched an eyebrow at Cynthia. "Everything okay?"

"Fine," Cynthia said quickly. "Let's go."

By April, Snake's mural was half done. With Willie's help he had constructed a scaffold out of trash cans and old flooring from the hangout on Theodore Street that enabled him to paint even higher up the wall. Once Lonnie got out of the hospital he helped Snake transport and mix the paints. People passing would stop and look at the colorful pastiche that sprawled across the abandoned building, and Snake reveled in the attention. A local black paper, the *Inner City Voice, The Voice of Revolution,* had just come by and taken pictures and printed them on the front page. Snake was ready to burst with pride when that happened. The ICV was more than just a paper, it was backed by serious political activists dedicated to making life better in Detroit. The more attention there was, the sooner Snake would be free, really free.

Whenever he had some extra money, which was not often, Snake would dress smartly and make his way out to Baker's Keyboard Lounge on Eight Mile and Livernois. It was one of the oldest clubs in the city, offering the smoky blues and hot jazz that Johnny had loved. As he swayed along to the beat, Snake missed Johnny even more. Anthony had his books; Johnny had his music; Snake had his painting. Invariably Stacy would float into his reverie. With the brothers both gone, he'd tried to protect the Jones girls, but then Lucy had Stacy dragged off to that nun school. At first she hated it; but now, to Snake's growing despair, she was more and more excited about going back. All she talked about was her best friend Monica Williams. Monica was black, but very rich and even knew Diana Ross. Both those girls should have more black pride now that Dr. Martin Luther King got gunned down. The next time he saw Stacy he'd tell her that.

In honor of Stacy, Snake had painted a blind pig into the painting. Back during Prohibition days the illegal bars charged admission to anyone willing to pay to see a blind pig perform. Only a few bars actually had a pig in a cage on the bar, and they were soon replaced with dancing girls. Snake painted a black pig and put it behind bars. He painted it beside his image of Diana Ross, somebody he knew Stacy loved. The feelings he had for Stacy made him feel trapped, like he was in a cage. He couldn't wait to tell her he landed a job on the assembly line at one of the Ford plants. It was a miserable job and only part-time, but she would be proud. But not as proud as she'd be when she saw his mural. That's when he'd tell her how he felt about her.

In early May, a young, radiant group of eight sat around a lavishly appointed table at the Grosse Pointe Yacht Club. A fresh bouquet of peach colored roses dominated the table, surrounded by candles nestled in gleaming silver, casting a warm, inviting glow.

"I'd like to propose a toast to our four guests of honor, the most beautiful and the most successful women ever to grace the halls of University Medical School," the male host of the party announced.

"Here, here," the other three men joined him.

"Thank you," beamed Rosie. She looked lovely in a red satin dress, her short dark hair feathered to frame her pixie face. "Girls, let's drink to that. We deserve it after the hell we've been though," she said, flashing her perky smile at Raymond Walson, their host.

Rosie had invited Tim Robinson, her on-again, off-again, boyfriend who had just finished his third year at the med school. An unpredictable couple, deserving of one another: she flirted outrageously; he ogled every female in sight. Over the last six months they'd broken up and made up so many times that the girls had lost count.

For Susan, this was her first public appearance with Will Cunningham. Glancing around furtively at first, Will eventually settled down and kept one arm slung casually around Susan's chair throughout the meal.

"Oh, this champagne is wonderful." Laura smiled and looked relaxed as she held up the fluted crystal for inspection. The decor, the ambiance, and the champagne made her feel like a celebrity.

"I guess you deserve this little celebration more than anyone else does, Laura," Vicky said, striking as usual in an elegant emerald green suit of raw silk. Her hair arranged in a French twist, she could have walked right off the cover of *Vogue*. "Perfectly adorable twins ready to come home from the hospital, and great grades. What could be better?"

"We'll let you know once we get the babies home," said Steve, his tone far more serious than the others. "So far, we've had to buy a house and hire a live-in baby-sitter. Good thing the hospital's covering the medical bills."

"We did buy a new house. Five bedrooms. Enough room for our live-in. Up in Highland Park, on Puritan."

"I have no idea how you manage," Vicky said, leaning forward to confide. "Someday Raymond and I would like to have children. Right, darling?"

"Someday," Raymond said with a wink.

"Wow, owning your own house already," Rosie sighed. "I can't even imagine. Lucky you can afford it."

"Well, we got it for an outrageous price. It's in one of those so-called changing neighborhoods. Still we couldn't have done it without Steve's promotion and all my loans. It's really a pity," Laura reflected, "what the real estate business is doing to Detroit with those racial scare tactics. I'm afraid it will get worse now that Martin Luther King was killed."

"What do you mean?" asked Vicky quickly glancing at Susan. The three white girls had often remarked on Susan's reticence when it came to the topic of race.

"Pure and simple exploitation. Rumors are planted about blacks moving into the neighborhood, followed by orchestrated vandalism. Bigoted whites start selling. The first wave of blacks pay full price. More vandalism. Landslide selling. Property values plummet. Everybody loses. Except the greedy real estate industry. And the process marches on, block by block."

Susan nodded. "Hey, at least it worked for you," she said with a tone of finality as she reached for Will's hand.

A waiter came by to refill champagne flutes, and Will stood ceremoniously to raise his. "Let's toast to the guy who brought us all together, dear old Harry."

"Hopefully, properly buried by now," Vicky raised her glass.

"Too bad the school doesn't have some kind of service," Susan said, "like a memorial, that we could all attend."

"Just remind me never to donate my body," Vicky said before glancing at Raymond's strangely contorted face.

"Okay, ladies, give Steve and Raymond a break," Tim nodded toward a very pale Steve. "Enough cadaver talk. Oh, oh, look who's over there."

Vicky tilted her head in the direction of the corner. "With his super bitch wife," she added. "I'm not sure whether to stare her down or ignore her."

"Ignore her, honey," said Raymond. "Remember, three more years to go before graduation."

David and Cynthia were being seated at a romantic table for two, the only table in the lavish dining room featuring two dozen long stemmed red roses. Cynthia looked stunning in a long silver gown, her hair swept dramatically to one side and secured with a jeweled clasp.

Will withdrew his arm from Susan's shoulder and sat upright in his chair. "Well, Susie, looks like this'll be our coming out party."

"Geez, I've never seen Mrs. Monroe in person before," Susan whispered. "She really is beautiful."

"That may be so, but Vicky's right," Raymond said. "She's a witch. We had one hell of a run in with her on Christmas Eve."

"We heard," said Susan with a smirk. Then she leaned in toward Will, "I wonder if Dr. Monroe will stop by and say hello."

"I hope not." Will replaced his arm around Susan.

"I'm with Will," Rosie chimed in. "Dr. Monroe makes me nervous enough at the hospital."

"I must say he looks a little down," said Vicky, turning slightly to keep the Monroes in view. "Sort of out-of-it. Probably just exhausted. I heard an ER nurse say that he's often at the hospital round the clock."

"Before we leave, I'm going to say hello to him," Steve said with determination. "I can tell you he was by Laura's side night and day when she was in City Hospital."

All three of Laura's classmates exchanged knowing glances. They'd all discussed their experiences when attempting to visit Laura in the hospital, where Dr. Monroe had practically stood guard at her door. They'd all agreed that he must have felt personally responsible for what happened to Laura in the ER, but they also wondered if there was something more lurking there.

Laura, for her part, gave no secrets away as she sat silently, a deep flush crossing her neck and face. She gripped her napkin, suddenly absorbed with the menu selections.

Assorted appetizers preceded Caesar salads for all, followed by sensational entrees and elaborate desserts. The atmosphere became festive, the banter light, and the mood relaxed. Only Laura felt on edge. The company was wonderful, and it was the first time since moving to Detroit that she and Steve had been out socially with friends. Next week Natalie and Nicole would be discharged, and she'd be home with them and Mikey and Kevin for summer break. So why did she suddenly feel so apprehensive?

After dessert and coffee, Steve abruptly said, "Thank you, Raymond, for a wonderful evening. We should really be getting home." To Laura, he said, "Let's go over and say good night to Dr. Monroe."

Laura flushed again. "Maybe we shouldn't bother him."

"It would be rude to ignore him. After all he did for us, we owe him that," Steve responded, standing.

Laura rose slowly and followed Steve across the room to the intimate table.

"Dr. Monroe," Steve said, "Steve Nelson. I just wanted to thank you for everything you did at the hospital. The babies are doing just fine."

Laura tried to smile at Cynthia. Neither she nor David said a word, or even looked at each other. David rose politely and reflexively extended his hand to Steve. David had last seen him unshaven and distraught, so different from the blonde young man in the tapered navy suit. And Laura looking superb in a white pleated dress studded at the waist by a band of crocheted pink baby roses that cast an air of innocent charm.

"They're each four and a half pounds now," Steve continued. "Almost ready to come home. Good thing. Laura spends so much time with them in the hospital, the boys and I hardly ever see her."

"I'm delighted," David finally said. "Allow me to introduce you to my wife. Cynthia, this is Steve and Laura Nelson." He deliberately avoided mentioning that Laura was a med student.

"Good evening," Cynthia responded in a curt tone.

Much to Laura's relief, Steve said, "Nice to meet you, Mrs. Monroe. We just wanted to express our gratitude to your husband."

"Thank you, I appreciate it," David said. He shook both of their hands and sat back down.

Briefly, David and Laura's eyes met, a fleeting yet intense gaze, an exchange captured by Cynthia.

After a few angry words, the Monroe's left the club minutes later. Once more, David had been unable to clarify Dr. Barrone's comments about Cynthia's decision the obstetrician had spoken of the night of Laura's horrendous accident. In the end, he figured that whatever it was Cynthia had decided she wanted, she would find a way to get it.

PART TWO

CHAPTER THIRTY-FOUR

AUGUST, 1969, FIFTEEN MONTHS LATER

Early Monday morning, August 18, David arrived at his office earlier than usual, but not earlier than Connie, who'd been there since the crack of dawn.

Traipsing to his desk, an uncharacteristic buoyancy in his step, "Top of the morning to you," he called to her.

Connie looked up. Usually it was, "Connie, where's my coffee?" She hadn't even gotten around to brewing it yet.

"And to you, Dr. Monroe," she called, a wide grin crinkling her face. I do think he's going to be okay, she said to herself. "Your mail's ready."

Connie was adept at reading her boss's moods, and she was confident now that he was out from behind that dark cloud of depression he'd suffered through last year. She'd never probed, but she was positive that he'd never seek psychiatric care, so she'd just helped him ride it out. Supporting him the best she could, covering for the meetings he'd missed, the lapses that she knew were part of his affliction.

Connie watched as he flipped though the stack of mail, smiling broadly as he extracted the third year medical class roster.

"So they're starting back tomorrow," Connie remarked. "The beat goes on."

After a six-week vacation, the third year medical students would return to launch their clinical training. They'd be spending their days and nights on hospital rotations, away from the lecture hall and tedious labs. Nothing they had experienced so far could match the intensity that now lay ahead. Except for learning how to do a physical examination and their on-call weekend in the ER, all their training had been basic science classes.

Ignoring Connie's chitchat, David hurriedly scanned the roster. The class was divided into four groups in order to rotate through four major medical areas: internal medicine, surgery, pediatrics, and obstetrics/gynecology. David took a breath when he saw Laura's name on the second section list. That meant she would do surgery first. He felt his heart race as he realized that she would be in the operating suites every day. He no longer agonized about controlling his irrational feelings about her. He was helpless to do so.

"Earth to Dr. Monroe," Connie intruded. "Are you okay? No, of course not. Haven't had your coffee. I'm on my way."

While waiting for Connie to return, David re-checked the roster. He still cringed at the memory of that remark, the one she'd made about dropping out of school. Thank God she had not. Even though she now had not two, but four young children and would be facing a grueling year with night call every third night. Last year he'd watched her from afar, and she seemed to be doing perfectly well without him. Honors in physiology, microbiology, and pathology, passes in everything else. How she did it, he'd never know. As usual, when David fantasized about Laura, he replayed that horrendous weekend back in March of '68. Her twins would be a year and a half now. Walking, he assumed. Starting to talk. And the two little blonde boys, Mikey, so bright and chipper and Kevin, a cuddly baby the one time he'd seen him in the cafeteria.

"Coffee," Connie announced. "And a special treat. I made a stop at Dunkin' Donuts." Connie knew that Cynthia didn't approve of junk food, but that never stopped Dr. Monroe from enjoying empty calories.

"Thanks, Connie," he said, biting into a raspberry filled donut. "I don't have any surgery scheduled today, so I think I'll go over to the labs and check on the head trauma research."

"That?" Connie grimaced. "You still throwing cadavers down elevator shafts? I think that's the most ghoulish experiment I've ever heard of."

"How am I going to convince you?" David smiled. "It's about saving lives. The results have already improved automobile safety."

"Remind me not to donate my body to science," she said. "I've seen your tabulations of broken bones and ruptured organs."

In collaboration with the anatomy and pathology departments, Dr. Monroe was the lead investigator in a government-sponsored study on the effects of high impact, high velocity injuries. To simulate the impact of high-velocity accidents, the research team utilized materials that were easily accessible to them: cadavers and elevator shafts. The research took place in the med school basic science building on weekends when few students were around. Because of the study's bizarre, rather ghoulish techniques, it was considered something of a secret project. The research itself, however, was well-designed and meticulously implemented.

"Okay, Connie, but when seat belts are mandated in all cars, you'll appreciate me more."

"Hey, you run along. I'll keep things in shape here." Connie paused, hesitating before going on. "And Dr. Monroe?"

"What's that?" he asked already stuffing papers in his brief case.

"I'm glad to see you back."

He turned, an eyebrow raised.

"I mean, you seem yourself again."

"Thanks, Connie, and thanks for hanging in there with me."

David gave Connie's arm a squeeze as he walked by her desk. "After I'm finished over there, I'm going home to work on the New England Journal paper. The editor's starting to badger me."

"Sounds good, Dr. Monroe."

It was almost noon when David finished going over the cadaver data with his research associate. Feeling a sense of accomplishment, he decided to head home, ask the housekeeper to fix him a sandwich, go directly to his study, put on some Mozart, and focus on that manuscript. He took a chance that Cynthia would be off doing the charity work that had swallowed up most of her time this past year. David was so grateful that she had found a vital, worthwhile interest. Together, Cynthia and Ruth had begun an entirely new charity devoted to the welfare of unwanted or abandoned children. Though he'd been surprised by Cynthia's choice, it pleased David. Perhaps he'd been too hard on Cynthia.

As he left the building and drove east on Jefferson Avenue, David felt a mellowness. Like a dark cloud had lifted. That maybe he'd be okay. Maybe not happy, but okay.

Ruth's white Cadillac sedan was parked beside the front door in the middle of the circle at the end of the long drive leading to the Monroe estate. David recognized the car immediately, somewhat annoyed. He'd hoped to avoid Cynthia, now he'd have to face them both.

Inside, he wandered around the quiet, seemingly empty house for a bit. Cynthia and Ruth must have used the limo service. He looked around for the housekeeper. Maybe she was out shopping. He'd have to make his own lunch. No big deal. The Monroe refrigerator was never empty. Actually he enjoyed making his own lunch.

But first he loped up the stairs, planning to change into some comfortable clothes. Thinking he heard noises from Cynthia's suite, he realized that he'd been wrong, and she must be home. Opening her door, he cringed. The scene of six years ago flashed before him, the scene of Cynthia in bed, writhing in pain from a botched abortion. What he saw in front of him now was Cynthia in bed, but she was not alone. He saw two women, their naked bodies entwined. In the center of the bed, Ruth's strong, lanky form partially covered his wife's slim body, Cynthia's hair cascading over the edge of the bed. He saw Ruth cradling Cynthia, stroking her breast, fondling her.

David stared blindly at the tableau. Cynthia's eyes were

closed and neither woman heard David approach until he groaned. Cynthia opened her eyes slowly, languidly. With a sudden jerk, she saw David. Panic flashed across her face as she struggled with the sheets and the weight of Ruth's body, trying to pull herself up to a sitting position.

Ruth glanced up at Cynthia's face, her hands still caressing until she looked in the direction of Cynthia's awful stare. There was David, his face ashen and contorted. Cynthia had grabbed the sheet and was now sitting there pulling it around herself, staring at David.

Naked, Ruth slipped off the bed and strolled insolently toward the chaise, where she reached calmly for her clothes. Folding them over one arm she strode toward the bathroom, closing the door behind her. Cynthia and David stared at each other. For a long time David stood planted like stone, utterly speechless.

"Cynthia, I'm leaving now," Ruth said matter-of-factly as she emerged from the bathroom, fully dressed. "Call me when you have a chance." Walking to the side of the bed, she reached toward Cynthia.

"Get out of my house this instant," David seethed. "This is all wrong."

"Your house? Wrong?" Ruth turned and faced David, her eyes wide with rage. "Oh, no. Cynthia's house. And not wrong."

Ruth gestured toward Cynthia. "And to think that just last year she was hell-bent on having your baby, but you couldn't be bothered. I'm the one who went to Aruba with her. She wanted to have your child, you asshole. She thought that's what you wanted. But refusing her did prove one indisputable thing: I love her; you don't."

CHAPTER THIRTY-FIVE

The Plaka Café on Monroe Street in Greektown, with its white façade, aqua trim, and inexpensive, tasty food, had long been a favorite lunch spot for med students. During the past two years, the foursome had always chosen it for occasional small celebrations. Today, the first Tuesday in October, the burly Greek owner seated them at a large table in the center of the room with a view of the street.

"Well, here we are! We finally did it," Rosie exclaimed. "Basic science is history. And we're all still hanging in there."

"Hard to believe," Susan said, "it's already been six weeks since we started back. Doesn't take long to get swallowed up in pediatrics. My little patients keep me up day and night." She paused to sip her coffee. "At least the Tigers won't be keeping me up. Remember last year? World Series: four to three over the St. Louis Cards. Denny McClain with the Cy Young Award. Now why couldn't we do that again?"

Vicky yawned. "Such an impractical hour, girls. I just about rebelled when Laura left the message with my housekeeper," she tried to sound indignant. "Breakfast indeed. Don't you guys know I'm pregnant?"

"It's the first time I could find that we're all free at once since the semester began," Laura explained. "This night call is a killer. Besides, Vick, you said you weren't having any morning sickness. You're so lucky. I was always miserable."

"I'm not," Vicky said, "but I'm as hungry as a horse. I'm going to gain a hundred pounds if I keep eating everything in sight. You won't believe what I put away last night."

"Oh, can it, Vicky. We don't need the details," Rosie chided. "Cripes, Laura had twins and we didn't even know she was pregnant, much less what she was eating."

"I just can't believe you ordered eggs and corned beef hash. I could barely eat chicken broth when I was four months pregnant," said Laura with an exaggerated grimace.

"I remember. You did look awful," Vicky replied. "We just didn't know what was wrong with you. We were diagnosing you all the way from stress to leukemia. Pregnancy never even entered our minds. But then, you suddenly looked great, and we forgot all about it."

Their food arrived.

"So Vicky," Susan turned to Vicky between mouthfuls, "how's internal medicine?"

"Love it. Morning rounds. Drawing bloods. Putting in catheters. I never get home before nine, but that's okay. Sometimes I'm even home before Raymond, sometimes not. He's been ultrabusy at work since that partner of his took a combo of Valium and Seconal. Almost died. Supposedly, she checked herself into some psychiatric place and is being treated for depression. Raymond's covering her practice on top of his own. The only good thing is that he doesn't complain about my coming home so late."

"Valium and Seconal? Obviously trying to kill herself?" Rosie asked.

"Who knows? Lawyers are inscrutable if you ask me. No matter what they say you know they're really thinking something else. That's the rule I go by," Vicky said. "So Laura, what's up with surgery?"

Laura swallowed a bite of toast. "Well, I like it a lot. All I can say is, thank God I had such great anatomy partners." She smiled broadly. "It's all coming back to me, you know, the nerves and veins and muscles. Stuff we thought was so useless to learn. Actually, they're letting me do a lot, more than I'd ever dreamed—"

"For example?" Rosie asked.

"For example, a resident talked me through an entire appendectomy yesterday. From the initial incision to the last suture placement. It was so neat."

"What's it like being back in the trauma area where you were attacked?" Susan asked.

"Doesn't phase me a bit," Laura said. "What happened to me there was just a bizarre thing. I guess if things had not turned out so well I would feel differently, but that whole episode is behind me now."

"And how's your Prince Charming?" Rosie asked with feigned innocence.

"Pardon me?" Laura paused, coffee mug in hand.

"You know, Dr. Monroe," Vicky prompted with a wink at Rosie. "You must see a lot of him now that you're on the surgical service."

"No, not really," Laura said. "I've scrubbed in on a couple of his procedures, but that's about it."

"Incidentally," Vicky said, "on a different, but related, subject. You know that partner of Raymond's I just mentioned? Ruth Davis? She's a good friend of Dr. Monroe's bitchy wife. We've seen them together a few times, Mrs. Monroe and Ruth, I mean. They're involved in some sort of charity."

Laura held her breath. The mention of David's wife gave her a queasy feeling. She didn't know why. To herself, she did have to admit that she thought about David a lot. How could she ever forget after what he'd done for her? Suddenly she realized that all three girls were staring at her. She jerked back into the moment. "Susan, tell us about pediatrics. Then we have to split."

"Yeah, and you haven't said a word about Will the entire time we've been here," Rosie teased. "Don't tell me you're single again?"

Susan hesitated, stirring her coffee. "Not exactly. I really like him. He even wants to get married. After graduation, of course, but

I don't know. It's times like this that I miss my mother. She'd understand."

"Yeah," said Laura, thinking of how much she missed her own mother and how terrible that loss must be for Susan. She was an only child, and her mother had died of a blood clot when Susan was sixteen. "What does your dad think?"

"He really likes Will. What's not to like? Other than he doesn't know beans about sports. Enough about me. Rosie let's hear the latest. And I mean Tim Robinson."

"That jerk?" Rosie grinned. "Roller coaster as usual. He's pissed at the moment. I blew him off for an anesthesia resident last Saturday night."

"You'll never change," sighed Laura. "Tim's crazy about you."

"Yeah, and every other girl that catches his eye. Besides, I don't want to get tied down," Rosie grinned. "Simple as that."

"Take it from me," Laura said with a sudden frown. "Don't rush into anything."

"Vickie's eyebrow shot up, "Meaning?"

"Meaning that I got married my freshman year of college. That's all."

Each year, the Department of Surgery selects the most promising third year student and three residents to attend the annual surgical meeting. This year the meeting was to be in Montreal in early January. The selection committee had proposed students in the order of their accomplishments. Laura Nelson was at the top of the list. In early December there was a brief discussion of logistics. Since the attack in the ER more than a year and a half ago, followed by the birth of the twins, Laura's family responsibilities were public knowledge, and the committee hesitated to advance her name for that reason. This concern was brought to David's attention. He told them to proceed with her selection and to leave it up to her whether to accept or not. It was a prestigious honor that she well deserved, and David was quite sure that she would not decline.

As department chairman of one of the country's largest medical schools, he knew his schedule at the meeting would be demanding. If Laura were there, however, he would plan to decline optional invitations and refuse unnecessary commitments, leaving himself as flexible as possible. He had already scheduled one luncheon meeting with great reluctance; the president of Stanford University was flying in to interview David for the position of dean at the medical school there. While appropriately flattered, David refused to let himself think about it seriously. Did he want to be a dean of a medical school? Yes, some day, and Stanford was certainly a prestigious school. Did he want to move away from Detroit? Of course he did, who wouldn't? But the thought of leaving disturbed him terribly.

What Cynthia thought was not an issue, not after he had discovered the nature of his wife's relationship with Ruth Davis. She could go with him to carry on the sham of their marriage or stay in Detroit, he simply did not care. Admittedly, he was used to her management of the household affairs and arrangement of their social life. Perhaps she'd want that to continue. On the other hand, if she chose to stay behind he would simply be free of her.

Ruth's tirade about Cynthia's decision to have a child finally clarified that remark Ed Barrone had made on the night Laura was attacked. Something like "sorry about Cynthia's decision, old man." Proof of the hopelessness of their communication. So after all these years — and the abortion of her first child — all that she'd needed from him had been a little support to start another. Maybe, maybe not. He couldn't tell. He no longer cared, really.

When Laura told Steve about the meeting in Montreal, he grudgingly agreed that she should attend even though he was scheduled at a conference in Chicago the second Saturday and Sunday in January, and he needed to check in Friday evening. Laura's travel plans, leaving Wednesday morning and returning Friday, would place her back in Detroit by 3:00 P.M. If Steve picked her up at the airport and then left immediately afterward, he could manage the four-hour drive to Chicago. If there were any problems, they could rely on their new, live-in babysitter, Mrs. Starke. She was an older widow with fifteen years experience taking care of kids, a fact that made Laura grateful and Steve resentful — he did not like the idea of a stranger living in their home.

Since the birth of the little girls, Laura watched Steve distance himself from them. So unlike the doting father that he'd been to Mike and Kevin when they were babies and toddlers. While this disappointed Laura, she was too busy to pay it much attention. Despite a vague, free-floating anxiety about her marriage, Laura was pleased that they'd gotten through another difficult year. Only a year and a half to go, and she'd be a doctor. Every single day that passed without a phone call from Detective Reynolds or Detective Willard made her feel more and more secure. Each day she thought less about the scribbled warning on that cardboard box. But still, not a day went by that she didn't think about Johnny Diggs and Anthony Diggs. And every day she said a prayer for their mother.

Laura suspected that Steve might be secretly pleased that she'd be away for a couple of nights. Recently he seemed more and more apathetic. Maybe it was the demands of four active children. Maybe he'd become disillusioned at work. Maybe if he got that supervisory promotion that was opening up. At least it would get him out of the field every day. He was burned out, he said, by the hopeless problems of his Detroit clients, not enough staffing, and cutbacks in funding.

There was nothing she could do about Detroit's problems, but once she finished her grueling surgical rotation, things would be better between them. Maybe being away a couple of days would be a good thing.

CHAPTER THIRTY-SIX

A soft powdery snow began to fall shortly after Laura's plane touched down at Montreal's International Airport on Wednesday afternoon, January 7, 1970. The three surgical residents, one of whom was Rosie's beau, Tim Robinson, were on her flight, and the foursome fell into a comfortable banter as they shared a cab to the Bonaventure Hotel. Laura was captivated by the elegant décor and muted colors of the hotel lobby, and she indulged herself a few moments to take it all in until her companions insisted that they move on to the reception desk. A bellman said something in French as he assisted her with her bags. Laura smiled and uttered a hushed "thank you." Overhearing that exchange, the check-in clerk spoke in English with a hint of snobbery, as he handed her two written messages.

One was a form letter advising that registration for the meeting was located on the mezzanine floor. She had already carefully selected the sessions she most wanted to attend. One was a symposium on Emergency Treatment of Gunshot Wounds chaired by Dr. Monroe. The other message was tucked into a sealed envelope with her name scrawled across the top. As the bellman moved off with her luggage, Laura broke the seal of the second envelope and pulled out a single piece of paper. It was handwritten and read,

Laura,

Welcome to Montreal. I look forward to spending time

with you to talk about your career. Also, I hope you brought pictures of the twins. I have a chairman's dinner tonight (Wednesday). Are you free for dinner tomorrow after the President's Reception? Please confirm by leaving me a message. I'm in Room 1501.

Best, David Monroe.

Laura stood riveted to the floor, oblivious to the stares of her three traveling companions.

"Mademoiselle," the bellman called from the elevator area. "S'il vous plaît."

She looked around, suddenly realizing that she was holding up the whole group. Tim Robinson put a patronizing arm around her shoulder and guided her toward the bank of elevators across the opulent lobby.

"You okay?" he asked.

"Uh huh, Tim, I'm fine," Laura quickly folded the unexpected message and stuffed it into her purse. She scanned the lobby, looking for David. Was he nearby?

"Well then, why don't you go unpack and meet me for a drink in the cocktail lounge?"

Until then, Laura had barely been listening. She glanced over at him. "What?"

"I'll grab a table for two, and we can go over the program."

"Sorry, Tim, I have to go register for the sessions. Then I want to check out the exhibits."

"I'll go with you, beautiful. We can do the exhibits together, then go for that drink."

"Aren't you forgetting something, Tim? I'm still a student. I had to get special permission from my cardiology professor to attend this meeting. I've got case reports to work on. No cocktail time for me." She quickened her pace in the direction of the elevators.

"No, my sweet Laura, you don't understand. These meetings are for partying. Everybody knows that." Tim also quickened his pace.

Laura let out a sigh in the elevator. "What about Rosie?" she asked. My friend, Rosie? Remember her?"

"What about her?" He smiled and looked around. "We're the only ones here in this winter paradise."

Laura's mouth fell open, but she remained silent.

Tim rode the elevator with her to the eighth floor.

"Thanks for the escort," she said flippantly as she stepped into the hallway. "Are you following me?"

"Looks like we're neighbors." Tim stopped at the door next to Laura's and inserted a key into the door with a smirk on his face. "Let me know if you change your mind. Even serious students need to have some fun, beautiful."

Once Laura entered her room, she checked to make sure the door to the adjoining room was locked. What would Rosie make of Tim's outrageous advance? Maybe nothing since she was such a flirt herself. Would Steve ever pull something like this at one of his conferences? No, she answered readily. He'd never flirt with another woman. She just knew it.

She sat down on the edge of the bed and slowly removed David's note from her purse. After reading it once more, she picked up the phone on the bedside table and dialed the operator.

"Please leave a message for Dr. David Monroe," she said. "The message is, 'I accept your invitation'. Please sign it, 'Laura.'"

The next day's meeting schedule offered several options among concurrent sessions. The attendees could choose among symposia on every aspect of surgery from 'New Trochar Technique for Emergency Craniotomy' to 'Gastric Resection in Intractable Peptic Ulcer Disease.' Laura had chosen carefully, wanting to get the most out of this meeting. Rushing excitedly from session to session all day helped keep her mind off her dinner date with David. Every time the fleeting thought rose into her consciousness, she distracted herself. When the sessions ended at six, she went back up to her room to call Steve and check on the children. Because she had been inside all day, Laura hadn't noticed the deepening blanket of snow threatening to bury Montreal. She barely had time to glance out the window before Steve picked up the phone.

"Hello there, honey. How are you doing?"

"Hey, Babe." His response was flat.

Laura tried to remain bright. "I've had an absolutely fascinating day," she offered. "You wouldn't believe that so much exciting research could be going on in surgery. It's incredible. So how's it going on the home front?"

"Things are fine here too," Steve said, "but there's something I need to talk to you about. I have to be in Chicago earlier than I'd planned. They want me on a panel on 'Post-Riot Homelessness'. Mrs. Starke can only stay until five because she's got to leave to take care of a family emergency. Something about her sister having a hysterectomy," he said with irritation. "She said she discussed it with you."

"My plane gets in at three. I'll take a cab home or maybe I can catch a ride home with one of the guys attending the meeting. That'll work."

"Yeah, just so you're here on time."

"I'll do my best," Laura said and quickly added, "And hey, congratulations. I know how important the Chicago meeting is to you, okay? Everything will work out just fine."

"Okay," Steve agreed reluctantly. "So who's there?"

"Three guys from the hospital and a hotel full of surgeons."

"Married?"

"What? How would I know about their personal life? I've scrubbed with one of the residents on a case or two, but that's it." She paused. "Except for Tim Robinson, you know, Rosie's friend?"

"Oh, yeah? Well he's a single guy, eh? I've heard about what goes on at conventions at those luxury hotels."

"Hey, this is no picnic. I'm going to have to make up three days of lectures and case studies." Was she being too defensive?

"Maybe you shouldn't have gone."

"Steve, we talked about this. Remember?"

"Yeah, but with all that's going on—"

"I'll be home Friday afternoon. Now can I talk to Mikey?"

Trying to erase the annoyance from her voice, Laura said goodnight to Mikey and couldn't help but smile as he recited the details of his day — Keith and Tyrone had come over from the old neighborhood and had brought a whole box of Matchbox cars that they lined up for a parade. After Tyrone crashed them, Mrs. Starke gave them all Oreo cookies and then the boys went home. Laura felt a stab of loneliness as she hung up, followed by a pang of guilt. She hadn't told her husband about her plans for the evening.

The telephone rang right after she set it back in the cradle on the nightstand. Laura picked it up, expecting it to be Steve, calling back to apologize for sounding so grumpy.

"Laura, it's David." His voice was buoyant as she said hello. "Just called to welcome you to the surgery meeting."

"I had a wonderful day, Dr. Monroe. There's so much going on, particularly in experimental surgery."

"That's why we sent you here," he said slowly, "to get you hooked on surgery."

"Well, I do appreciate that."

"Listen, I'm sorry to bother you, but I'm calling concerning dinner tonight," David continued.

"Oh, that's alright. I know you're busy. I've seen your name throughout the program." She tried to keep the disappointment out of her voice.

"It's been a hectic day," David agreed. "The reception tonight will also be chaotic, that's why I'm calling. Instead of trying to locate each other in the middle of all the confusion, let's meet in the front lobby at eight o'clock sharp, and bring your coat. Okay?"

"Oh, okay," Laura replied, a smile creeping onto her face. "If you're sure you're not too busy."

"Absolutely not, Laura. I'm really looking forward to talking with you."

"Eight o'clock, front lobby." Had he heard the anticipation in her voice?

CHAPTER THIRTY-SEVEN

Laura wore a black chiffon cocktail dress to the reception. It was short with the full skirt swirling just over her knees. The scooped neckline almost revealed a glimpse of cleavage. She had only worn it once before, to her college graduation dinner dance just after Kevin was born. She smiled as she patted her much flatter stomach and observed her svelte profile in the mirror as she left the elevator. Her hair was brushed back away from her face, and she couldn't help but notice that many eyes followed her as she wended her way through the cluster of surgeons. There were a few women in the crowd, but Laura was clearly the youngest and, perhaps, the most attractive. Hoping to spot one of the other guys from Detroit, she circled the room, stopping occasionally to accept one of the hors d'oeuvres offered by the circulating waiters.

Tim Robinson approached Laura as she reached across the open bar for a Coca-Cola with a twist of lemon.

"You deserve something stronger than that, beautiful," he said, wrapping his arm around her waist.

Wriggling out of his overly intimate hold, Laura swung around to face him. "I'm actually glad to see you," she said. "I don't know a soul here."

"Hell, 99% of the guys in this room wouldn't mind changing that. You look gorgeous." He squeezed her arm, and she caught a whiff of his breath. Tim Robinson was already three sheets to the wind.

She extricated herself again. "Stop it, Tim. Where are the others? I haven't seen them all day."

"They're around. I told them to get lost because I wanted you all to myself."

"Come on, Tim. Give me a break."

Tim ordered a replacement for his whiskey sour. "Let's face reality, eh? We're next door neighbors with adjoining rooms. All we have to do is flip the little switch and voila, we have a two-bedroom suite."

"Get real, Tim, and go slow on the booze."

"Come on, Laura," Tim grabbed for her again, but Laura sidestepped him, then had to reach out to steady him as he nearly lost his balance.

"You know very well I'm married, and everybody at City Hospital knows I have children. And you have been dating one of my best friends. So cool it, will you?"

"Nobody will ever know. Not your husband. Not our mutual girlfriend. Can't you accept fate?"

Laura stared at him stonily.

"Okay, okay," he capitulated. "At least have dinner with us. I told the guys that if I struck out with you, which they predicted I would, we'd meet at the Cafe on the second floor. It's really casual. They serve burgers and salad and stuff."

"Thanks, but no thanks," Laura tried to sound resolute. "I've had my fill of hors d'oeuvres right here so I'm skipping dinner. But I do want to talk to you about tomorrow. Our flight's at 12:30. Can we share a cab back to the airport?"

"No problem, but let's not think about going home yet." He still hadn't stopped gaping at her. "The night is young." Laura shrugged, not sure if the guy was a genuine jerk or just a harmless, lecherous drunk.

"Tell the others I'll make arrangements for a cab at eleven in the morning. I'll be able to get two lectures in by then. We can meet in the lobby and go from there. I can't miss that plane. So you'd better not be hung over."

"Home to hubby," Tim grumbled.

"Yes. And home to your girlfriend for you. Now behave your-self, Tim. God, why do I suddenly feel like your mother?" Glancing at her watch, she saw that it was 7:45 She needed to get to her room, check her messages, and grab her coat.

David had seen Laura walk into the crowded ballroom. He held her in sight the whole time while attending to obligatory chats with his colleagues, working his way around the room, sipping a glass of white wine. He couldn't hold back the silly smile that lit up his face in the middle of a serious debate when he spotted Laura walking in the direction of the elevator bank.

Laura arrived at the lobby entrance at exactly eight. David was waiting, his gray cashmere topcoat slung casually over one arm.

"You look wonderful," he said slowly.

Laura had arranged her hair into a sweeping swirl with a pearl studded clip. She rarely wore makeup, but tonight a hint of smoky eye shadow framed her eyes and her lashes were enhanced with just a touch of mascara. Black three-inch heels were a stark differ-ence to the white rubber-soled nurse's shoes she wore at the hospi-tal. David stared at her legs.

"You look fine, yourself," Laura returned the compliment with a wide smile, not knowing what else to say. He did look more relaxed than she'd ever seen him, and as usual, extremely hand-some.

He held the door for Laura as he signaled for the doorman to summon a cab.

"Merci," he discreetly passed the uniformed man a five-dollar bill.

"Of course, monsieur. Mademoiselle, allow me to help you. It is slippery out here."

David took Laura by the left arm, and the doorman held her right elbow until she was situated comfortably in the cab.

The wide circular drive leading from the grandiose hotel

lobby to the street had been plowed, but new snow was accumulating rapidly. The effect was stunning. Thirty inches of soft, new snow covered Montreal. Traffic was only inching along — the occasional snowplow labored relentlessly only to have its path obliterated by the new falling white fluff.

"We've gotten over two feet since noon," the burly cab driver declared. It's a beaut."

"My God, I had no idea," exclaimed Laura. "It's so beautiful."

"Oui, Mademoiselle. Beautiful it is, but driving is not so good. I put on my chains about an hour ago. Without them I'd be just like those guys." He pointed to the growing collection of cars that were either stuck or abandoned in the drifting snow.

"Lucky you two aren't going far. It's just a block up the street here."

"Thanks very much." David added a generous tip and asked the driver if he would return for them at ten and wait. He would pay him well for his time, he quickly reassured.

"Sure, buddy. Now, you two lovers have a good dinner." He winked at David. "Don't worry. I'll be back for you."

David took Laura's arm as they walked into the lobby of the restaurant. It took a few moments for them to adjust to the candlelit dimness of the room, but their mood was immediately buoyant. Those who had braved the snow had settled in for a special, cozy evening, nodding pleasantly to fellow diners.

David and Laura were escorted to a secluded table for two in the corner of an elegant dining room. The glow of long tapered candles, embellished by the elaborate fresh flower arrangements at each table, created an aura of romance.

The luxury of their surroundings evoked conflicting emotions of awe and sadness in Laura. She had never experienced such ambiance. And she was not with Steve. Not that her husband would have appreciated all of this; he'd probably be annoyed by so much formality. He'd sit through it, but would be anxious to get back home and plop himself down in front of the television. Still, she missed her husband. She missed the Steve that she had married more than six years ago, the one who had sincerely cared about what she wanted, what they wanted together. But that was another Steve altogether than the present Steve, if she admitted the truth. At any rate, no Steve was here tonight, and Laura told herself to just enjoy these exquisite surroundings. "This is wonderful," she said as she gazed around the sumptuous room.

David looked up as he perused the extensive wine list and smiled at her. "I'm glad you like it. Do you mind if I order a bottle of wine or would you rather have a cocktail?"

"Wine would be fine, thank you," Laura responded.

"Good. That's settled," David said with another smile. "Now, I'm anxious to find out what you think about the meeting so far."

The wine steward appeared to assist with the selection. After a brief discussion of the French and California options, David chose a California chardonnay.

"Hope you'll like it. It's a sixty-six. Should be nice," David predicted. "Now, where were we?"

"You had asked me what I thought of the meeting."

"Right." He smiled once more. "So do you think you'll end up in surgery?" he pressed, just as the bottle of chilled white wine was presented for his approval.

After David had tasted the wine, Laura responded. "You know, Dr. Monroe, I really think the answer is 'yes'. But surgery was my first rotation. I'm not sure how I'll feel when I finish the other three."

"May I ask you something else?"

"Sure."

"Remember when you promised to call me David?"

"Well," Laura hesitated. "I guess—"

"Laura," he said softly, "could we be friends?"

"Well, yes, of course," Laura stammered.

"You know that we got to know one another pretty well during those four days."

"Yes, and I can never thank you enough," she responded after a momentary pause. "You did so much for me."

"I'll always feel responsible for your injury, Laura. I'm only grateful that you and the babies are okay."

"What happened to me wasn't in any way your fault," she interrupted. "I just happened to be in the wrong place at the same time that crazy guy decided to go berserk. Now you're making me feel guilty because you're feeling guilty."

"Okay." David was grinning broadly. "Let's call a truce. No guilt on either side. Now, how about taking a good look at this menu?"

The waiter unobtrusively topped off their wine glasses. Laura raised hers, flashing David a big smile. "Sounds good," she agreed.

CHAPTER THIRTY-EIGHT

The wine, the candlelight, the fabulous menu and the charm of her dinner companion conspired to create a festive mood. Laura ordered a shrimp cocktail appetizer and filet mignon as a main course. David started with smoked salmon with caviar followed by the rack of lamb, medium rare. The pair settled back after selecting the Grand Marnier soufflé for dessert.

"Tell me about the children," David asked as soon as all culinary decisions were made. "The twins must be pushing toward the 'terrible twos' by now."

She nodded. "They are. Natalie, older by a few minutes, and Nicole." Laura pulled out the pictures she kept in her wallet. "Here they are with Mikey and Kevin." All four, blonde. Mikey with a capricious smile, Kevin with an angelic expression that obscured his mischievous nature, and Natalie and Nicole, identical toddlers with curls circling their dimpled faces.

"Adorable. How can you tell them apart?" David asked the inevitable question.

"Most people can't, but I have no problem. Their personalities are very different. You can almost tell by their pictures. See the different smiles? Nicole, the aggressive one, wants everything her way. Natalie's as sweet as can be."

"How are the boys handling little sisters?"

"Great. Mikey's ultra-protective and Kevin, who's only a year older than the twins, loves to tease them and play little tricks."

Laura paused pensively and continued, "It's only Steve that's having a problem adjusting."

"Your husband?"

"Afraid so." Without the liberating effect of the wine, Laura would never have ventured this far. "I think it's because they're twins."

"Oh? What's that about?"

"Something happened when Steve was ten years old," Laura hesitated, recalling her promise to Steve, her promise to tell no one about the tragedy that shattered the Nelson family.

"What does that have to do with your daughters?"

After a few conflicted moments, Laura opened up. She relayed the story of Steve's twin brother, Phillip, suggesting that Steve's repressed guilt over his brother's death accounted for his apathetic, even distant relationship with his own twin daughters.

"He doesn't mistreat them or anything. He just doesn't want much to do with them. A relationship so distant compared to Mikey and Kevin. I'm afraid that it will affect their development."

"Do you think it could have anything to do with the other problem you told me about?" David gently explored. "What happened that night?"

Laura paused reflectively. Their appetizers arrived, the waiters hovering until everything was satisfactory. David ordered another bottle of wine — this time a Merlot to accompany their main course.

"David." Laura still didn't feel right calling him by his first name. "I don't think so. You know it's a funny thing. During my pregnancy, I was so haunted by the unknown. The father of my babies could just as well have been the man who raped me. But as soon as the babies were born and you told me everything was okay, I've tried to erase that incident from my memory. Having twins was just too overwhelming. What a complete shock, I mean, nobody expected two."

"Yes. And the babies were so fragile."

"They're healthy little toddlers now, thank God," Laura murmured. She stared at David boldly. "Do you realize that you are the only person on the face of the earth who knows about that night?"

David stared back. "I wasn't sure whether you'd ever told anyone else or not," he responded slowly. "It's been so long since we've had a chance to really talk."

Laura nodded, her face flushed. "I've never told anyone but you. I know that I never thanked you enough. After the babies were born, I mentally tried to obliterate the whole experience. I was totally absorbed in dealing with the babies, the boys at home, and finishing that semester. The truth is, I hardly looked back, but it could have been so different." Her voice trailed off.

The waiter cleared away their dishes and replaced their glasses as he poured from the second bottle of wine.

"I'll never forget what you did for me," Laura continued.

David's eyes shone. "In a way, those four days were the most important days of my life. I learned a lot about myself. I cherished those days."

Laura's head whirled. Was Dr. Monroe telling her he really cared? About her? Is this what her friends had been trying to tell her? All those innuendoes about a special relationship, but she had laughed them off. Laura reached for the crystal wine glass but stopped midway, knowing she should pace herself.

"Anyway, Laura, something's been bothering me ever since you told me about that, uh, situation." He hesitated. "I'm sorry, I don't want to open old wounds, but I'm not sure when we'll get a chance to really talk again."

"That's okay, Doc . . . David."

He spoke softly, "If you don't want to talk about it, that's okay, but remember when you said that there was more that you'd tell me at another time."

Laura hesitated. Should she tell David the whole story? She knew instinctively that she could trust him. It was so tempting to be able to share her worst nightmare with someone.

Laura experienced a few more moments of hesitation before their entrees arrived with a flourish of silver domes. They were silent as the waiters completed their work with a slight bow and retreated.

As they ate, Laura finally said, "David, I'm going to tell you something that will shock you. You must promise first never to repeat a word of it to anyone."

"Of course."

"Promise?"

"I promise."

And then Laura related everything that happened that night nearly two and a half years ago. David listened intently, interrupting only to clarify a point or to emphasize his support. As Laura concluded, her eyes brimmed with tears. David had moved from his chair across the table to sit beside her. He placed his arm protectively around her.

"You were incredibly brave," he reassured her. "Who knows what would have happened if you went to the police? What with the racial volatility and the political witch hunts. But to face this alone without even telling your husband? I just don't understand."

"I didn't tell Steve because I was scared that he'd make me quit school. And I was ashamed. I'd been raped. I killed a man. I was so mixed up."

David reached for Laura's hand and leaned in closer. "Honey, you made the decision. A tough decision. Right or wrong, a decision you'll have to live with. Are you absolutely sure that no one knows?"

"Detective Reynolds, Susan Reynolds's father, is still suspicious, I think." Laura stopped speaking. David was holding her hand in his and he'd just called her "honey." Holding her breath, she didn't know what to do. She couldn't believe she'd told him that she'd killed a man, and she couldn't believe she was sitting so close to him.

"Right, the detective. I'm aware that he's tried to put the pieces together, but exactly what pieces, I really don't know. He did question me about seeing you that night. I simply told him I did. Nothing else."

"Not about how horrible I must have looked?"

"No, but, you did look so flustered. I did notice. I don't know why, but I told them not to harass you at the school. I didn't want you intimidated."

"I'm so grateful for that." Laura inhaled sharply, realizing how close David had come to exposing her, however innocently.

"He also questioned me again about your schedule at some point."

"He did?"

"Yes, he and that other black detective." David frowned. "Can't remember his name. They came back after you were attacked in the emergency room. 'Loose ends,' they said. Nothing else."

Laura's heart pounded. "Why would they do that?"

"The detective, actually both of the detectives, now that I think of it — were there in the ER that night. Well, that's all in the past, isn't it? I'm sure Detective Reynolds has more pressing matters to deal with."

Laura took a deep breath, her heart still pounding. She chose not to tell David about the bullets in her tires in the school parking lot and the threatening note, though she certainly recalled the terror she felt then, and knew deep inside that the incident was connected to Johnny Diggs. What other explanation could there be?

"Je regret, monsieur," the headwaiter interrupted. "I am sorry to interrupt your dinner, but your taxi driver is outside. Would you like him to wait? The weather's gotten worse, and cabs may be difficult to find later."

"Please ask him to wait. Better yet, could he wait inside at the bar? I'll buy him coffee and the dessert of his choice." David discreetly pressed a twenty-dollar bill into the hand of the headwaiter.

"Certainly, monsieur."

David rose slowly. "I'll be right back," he said softly.

"Thanks, buddy," David met the cab driver in the foyer and slipped him a hundred dollar bill. "I really appreciate your returning for us. How about something to eat?" David pointed toward the trolley in the corner laden with tempting desserts.

"Merci," replied the cabby, gazing at the large bill. "No problem. You and your lady take all the time you want. Never thought I'd see the inside of a place like this."

David returned to the secluded corner table, where Laura sat with a worried expression.

"I'm sorry to bother you with my problems," she apologized.

"I'll always be there for you, Laura," he said reassuringly. "I got to know you pretty well when you were in the hospital. There wasn't much I could do for you but pray. I'm a lapsed Catholic, but I think God must've heard me."

"Steve and I are Catholic too. Otherwise I'd have taken birth control pills."

"Once in a while I drop into Old St. Mary's over by the hospital. The Holy Ghost Fathers there make me feel welcome. Someday. . . . Ah, look, here comes the soufflé."

They watched as the waiters presented the flaming extravaganza, and the mood at the table immediately lightened. David seized the opportunity to move the discussion toward Laura's plans and away from any more talk of Detective Reynolds. She responded readily, chatting about the electives that she'd like to take during her senior year and plans beyond med school.

David couldn't take his eyes off Laura as he listened to her long-range plans. She was asking his opinion of residency programs in Florida. She might do her postgraduate training there to be closer to her mom and dad.

Twirling his wineglass between both hands, David wondered at that moment if she would also consider a residency program in California. And then for another moment, he allowed himself to wonder if there were any similarities at all between what Laura wanted and what he wanted.

CHAPTER THIRTY-NINE

As they approached Laura's hotel room, David reached for her key as she retrieved it from her purse. He opened the door, stepping away as he handed the key back to her. Laura turned slowly toward him, and he reached to place his hands on her shoulders. He held her like that for a very long moment. Then he leaned forward, gave her a brief hug, kissed her tenderly on the cheek.

"Thank you for a wonderful evening," he murmured. Then he turned and headed toward the bank of elevators.

Laura walked into her room with reeling emotions. Dinner with David had electrified her in so many ways. She had even confided her darkest secrets to him. Hope and hopelessness clashed within her as she closed the door. Talking about the detective again had brought up that old terror. Would she ever be free from what happened that night?

It wasn't until she had hung up her coat and slipped off her shoes that she noticed the envelope that had been slipped under the door. She carried it over to the side of the bed and sat down to open it. Then she noticed the blinking red message light on the telephone on the bedside stand.

Was it Steve? The detective? Pangs of guilt shot through her.

She ripped open the envelope and read the note: 'Laura, where are you? We've tried to find you everywhere in the hotel. We're leaving at 9:00 P.M. to catch the last plane out of Montreal before they close the airport tonight. The hospital left word that the residents needed to be back for weekend coverage. Hope you'll be there too. Tim and the guys.'

Laura gasped. "Close the airport!" She rose quickly to flip on the television to an English station. It was 11:30 P.M., and the storm was the big news. Another six inches were expected overnight, more tomorrow. The airport was closed indefinitely; certainly through tomorrow.

Picking up the telephone to retrieve her messages, Laura tried to remain calm. She just had to get home.

"Three messages, Madame."

"Could you read them for me, please?" Laura asked the operator.

"Certainly, Madame." the charming French accent agreed.

Two were from Tim, the third from Steve. It had come in at 11:05.

Laura immediately dialed home.

"Where the heck have you been?" he demanded.

"I was at dinner," Laura responded softly.

"At eleven at night?"

"The weather's bad here, honey," Laura reasoned. "It was hard getting taxis. Listen, we have a problem. I just found out that the airport here is closed. I don't think I'll be able to get out of here tomorrow. There's almost three feet of snow."

"Oh, man, that's not good," Steve snapped. "I've gotta be at that damned conference tomorrow. I just found out I'm chairing that session I told you about, for God's sake. That's why I called. Good news for a change. I got it."

"Got what?"

"I got promoted to supervisor."

"Oh honey, congratulations! I'm so sorry I'm not there to celebrate with you. Steve, you know I'll do what I can here, but what if it's physically impossible? How's the weather in Detroit?"

"Fine," he grumbled. "Just try to get home. What'll it look like if I screw up my first big responsibility?"

"Of course I will," she answered. "I'll check the flights first thing in the morning. I'll camp out at the airport if I have to."

"You never should have gone to Montreal," he sputtered. "The connection was too tight."

"I'll call you in the morning," she said firmly. "We'll just have to find a back-up baby-sitter."

She hung up the phone and sat unmoving on the bed. She'd check out of the hotel in the morning and try to get to the airport and wait for a flight to Detroit. At least she'd be right there to grab the first opportunity she could. She'd have to miss tomorrow morning's sessions, but what else could she do?

Things were no better in the morning. The snow was relentless, and the airport remained closed. Laura called Steve before leaving her room to check out. He was angry and resentful because he could not find a baby-sitter. He had even tried Carol from the old neighborhood, but she was out of town. If he did not find someone soon, he would have to miss most, if not all, of the conference. Laura suggested that he call their neighbors, maybe someone at work, or even Susan, if need be.

"Mademoiselle, are you sure you want to check out?" The clerk at the checkout desk politely inquired. "The hotel's full, and I have people waiting to check in. If you change your mind, you'll never be able to get your room back. The other hotels are full too."

"That's okay. I have to try to get home."

"But we're in the middle of a blizzard," the young clerk advised.

Laura eventually made it to the airport after creeping along in one of the few cabs that had ventured out to combat the deep drifting snow. She'd agreed to pay more than twice the usual fare even though she barely had enough cash to cover it.

The airport was jammed. People standing, sitting, lying down everywhere surrounded by piles of luggage. When she finally made it to the ticket counter, the haggard clerk confirmed that all flights were suspended for at least twenty-four hours. That meant the earliest she could leave would be Saturday morning, too late for Steve to make his meeting. This was awful news. Chairing a session at this important meeting would be good for Steve's new position and his self-esteem.

Hauling her luggage, Laura found her way to a drafty corner beside the Hertz rental office. She sat down on her suitcase and did what everybody else was doing. She waited.

Three hours ticked by slowly. Laura kept busy by studying her notes on cardiovascular disease.

Taking a rest from memorizing the classes of drugs used to treat cardiac arrhythmias with all their complicated indications, contraindications, and warnings, Laura decided to call Steve at work. Maybe he'd found a baby-sitting solution. If only her mother and sister were nearby, she thought sadly.

CHAPTER FORTY

Steve Nelson looked up into the eyes of Lucy Jones.

"Mr. Nelson, this is terrible. I know how important that conference is to you. The whole office has been talking about it, with you chairing the Post Riots session and all." Lucy Jones commiserated with Steve over a cup of steaming coffee Friday morning. "Maybe I can help," she offered tentatively.

"Thanks, Lucy," Steve flashed a smile of appreciation, "but you've got more than your share of family responsibilities. The last thing you should have to worry about is my wife's travel schedule."

"But you can't miss that conference." She shook her head. "It just won't look good for you not to be there."

"There's a blizzard in Montreal. Our baby-sitter has to leave this afternoon, and that's that. Thanks for caring anyway, Lucy. It's nice to know someone does."

Lucy smiled in spite of his last remark, wondering what brewed beneath its surface. Clearly protective of Steve Nelson, Lucy Jones felt she owed her job to him. And to Sister Mary Agnes. Just the memory of her cleaning job at General Motors made her cringe. Well, best not to promise yet, but at her next break, she could at least make a phone call. Maybe there was a way to help pay Steve Nelson back for all he'd done for her.

At her mid-morning break Lucy phoned St. Mary-of-the-Woods, insisting that Stacy be called to the phone immediately.

"Mom, what is it?" Her daughter sounded breathless. "I had to run up three flights of stairs. I was at the board, doing this trigonometry problem. Something happen to you? The girls?"

"Everything's fine," Lucy quickly reassured. "I'm at work so I don't have much time either, but I need to ask a big favor of you, baby."

"What is it?"

"Well, you know I wouldn't ask this of you unless it were very important to me."

"Shoot, Mom."

"I need you to baby-sit for my boss's kids tonight and part of tomorrow. His wife is stranded in a blizzard, and he has to go to an important conference. It's Mr. Nelson, baby. You know how much I owe him."

Stacy sucked in her breath. She had her own plans for tonight — at Baker's Keyboard Lounge with Monica.

Lucy ignored her daughter's silence. "He could pick you up at St. Mary's around two, drop you at his house and then drive on to Chicago as he had planned. Then, when his wife gets home, which could be on the very first flight to Detroit tomorrow, she can take you back to school."

Stacy hesitated. "Okay, Mom. What's this guy's full name so I can tell the nuns when he shows up to get me? Better yet, you'd better tell them yourself. They're strict about security around here."

"Whatever it takes. I'll let Mr. Nelson know," Lucy breathed a sigh of relief. "I knew you wouldn't let me down, baby."

Stacy slowly hung up the phone and sank into a nearby chair, gazing aimlessly around the school office. Now what was she going to do? Monica Williams had awakened on her sixteenth birthday to a brand new cherry red Mustang. She and Stacy were so excited about taking it out, that Stacy'd arranged to meet Snake. He'd called to tell her he'd gotten a real job, and she could hear the pride in his voice. Wanting to let him know that she was proud of him, she'd impetuously suggested that they go to Baker's Lounge, Johnny's favorite hangout. Now, walking slowly down the hall back to class, she wished she'd kept her mouth shut.

After trig, Stacy found Monica, and they walked toward their lockers. "Oh man," she fretted, "I've got to get in touch with Snake, but they don't have a phone."

Monica's eyes widened. "Really?"

"Really. He's going to show up at Baker's and I'm not going to be there? Man almighty, he'll be so pissed. Listen, I'll describe him to you, and you can tell him something urgent came up, okay?"

"What? I'm not going without you. I'm not going to Baker's alone, Stacy."

They agreed that Monica would try to find another friend to go with her; with any luck, she would figure out who Snake was. Oh, why had she ever agreed to meet him anyway? He still smoked dope, but she didn't. Drugs were definitely not on her agenda. Did she think she could save him? Get real, she told herself. Maybe it was all for the best that she couldn't go. If Mama found out she was seeing Snake, she would never trust her again. Trouble was that being practically locked up in a girl's school there was no way she could meet nice black boys. Her classmates were mostly white with only white boys in their lives. And that left her out.

In Montreal, David grabbed the only available taxi and directed the driver to the airport, searching for Laura. He had called her after his session earlier this morning to let her know that all outgoing flights from Montreal were cancelled for at least 24 hours. His face clouded over when the hotel clerk told him that Laura Nelson had checked out of the hotel and left for the airport.

"Sorry, sir, but the young lady said she simply had to get home," the clerk said. "I told her that we'd have to give her room away, but she didn't care."

Eventually, David found Laura among the throngs at the airport. She was still seated in the corner, her eyes half-shut as she made her way through the gigantic medical text she had lugged to Canada. She looked small and alone in the milling, disgruntled crowd.

*   *   *

"Laura, what are you doing here?" The alarmed voice startled her and a flash of adrenaline jolted her awake.

"Oh, you scared me." Laura struggled to get up. "My flight's been cancelled so I'm waiting for the next one out. I'm so sorry that I missed your session. But what are you doing here? You weren't scheduled to leave until Saturday, I thought."

He nodded. "Let's go get some lunch, and we'll talk."

Eventually, Laura succumbed to his argument that no planes were leaving that day and that she could stay in the second bedroom of his hotel suite. He promised to get her to the airport first thing the next morning. They could have dinner at the hotel, and she would have a comfortable night's sleep. Laura wasn't sure whether it was the memory of the last evening or the horrible gnawing hunger in her stomach that eventually convinced her to leave with David.

"I have to make one call before I leave," she told him as he carried her suitcase toward the waiting cab.

"Why don't you wait until we get back to the hotel? This place is a zoo," he glanced toward the line of people waiting for access to the bank of pay phones located near the exit.

"I'm sorry, but I have to do this here," she insisted. "It's important."

David stayed with Laura as she waited her turn for the next available pay phone and then walked away as she dialed Steve's phone number at work. One of the office clerks answered, which was not unusual. Steve was often in the field working with clients.

"Oh, Mrs. Nelson," the friendly voice replied. "I almost forgot. I'm supposed to transfer any calls from you to Mrs. Jones."

"Where's Mr. Nelson?" Laura questioned.

"He left a few minutes ago for the Chicago conference."

"What?"

"Here's Mrs. Jones right now," the cheery voice announced.

Lucy explained to Laura in her most reassuring voice that

everything was fine. By now, her considerable talent in dealing with distressed clients was serving her well.

"You're sure that your daughter can handle four young children by herself?" Laura repeated the third variation of this question.

"Yes, Mrs. Nelson. My daughter is very responsible, and she's had lots of experience. She took care of her three younger sisters almost by herself when I worked a different job. So don't you worry none. Your husband's gone to pick her up at St. Mary-of-the-Woods, where she goes to school."

St. Mary-of-the-Woods Academy had a reputation as the best girl's high school in the Detroit area. That made Laura feel a little more secure.

"But why don't you call her tonight to make sure everything's okay? I'll call her too just in case she needs any advice. Now, don't you worry. Everything's going to be fine," Lucy reassured.

Her voice tentative, Laura finally thanked Mrs. Jones. Steve, she knew, had a lot of confidence in his assistant so hopefully she could trust his judgment in deciding to leave their children with a stranger, a young girl they'd never met. Funny though, while she was talking with the woman, she felt somehow like she knew her. Unlikely, considering she'd never even been to Steve's office. Mrs. Jones? But Jones was such a common name.

David unlocked the door to his lavish suite on the eleventh floor of the Bonaventure. He held it open as Laura walked in.

"This is beautiful," she marveled, "and so big." Her eyes rapidly scanned the spacious, elegantly appointed parlor. Two large oriental vases flanked the ornately carved mahogany door that opened into the huge room. The far wall was dominated by a blue veined opalescent marble fireplace with a collection of more oriental vases on the mantle. Plush sofas in expensive brocade created an intimate, gracious effect. A huge arrangement of fresh flowers in muted yellows and pinks adorned the large rectangular dining room table, also a rich mahogany. Heavy draperies framed the bay windows, allowing just enough sunlight to make the Waterford crystal sparkle in the large display cabinet. Laura had never even imagined that hotels had magnificent suites like this.

"Leave your luggage here and let's go down and get some lunch. You must be starving," David suggested. "Here, let me hang your coat in the closet."

"Do I need to change?" Laura glanced down at her jeans and bulky turtleneck sweater.

"You're fine," he said. "I'm putting your things in the bedroom. There's a private bathroom in there. Do you need a couple of minutes to get settled?"

"Sure. Thanks." Laura waited silently in the bedroom as David deposited her suitcase on the luggage rack, then closed the door behind him.

The room had been recently made up. A billowy down comforter lay atop the huge king-size bed. Rich draperies of white brocade framed the large window. The attached bathroom featured a large porcelain tub set off by brightly polished brass. Fluffy white towels embellished with stylized gold monograms were piled high in glass and brass racks. Right or wrong, here she was. She looked into the mirror and dabbed on some lipstick.

"Is there another bedroom?" Laura asked as she stepped back into the parlor.

"You're standing in it," David replied. "The sofa makes a nice bed and with the bathroom over in that corner, I'll be all set."

"Oh no, I can't take your bed," Laura objected. "I thought you said there were two bedrooms."

"I didn't mean to deceive you, Laura," he said with a smile. "I stretched it a little and counted this as one. It'll be just fine. Believe me, I sleep in a lot less comfortable situations at the hospital."

Lunch was casual and pleasant. Laura ordered a Roquefort cheeseburger with French fries and a Coca-Cola.

"Thanks, David. I really needed that," she said as she swallowed the first few bites. "Now I can start to think straight. First, how and when am I going to get home?"

David Monroe frowned. "Is everything okay?"

"Actually good news. Steve got a big promotion at work. And, he got a baby-sitter for tonight."

Laura recounted her conversation with Steve's assistant. She tried to convince both herself and David that everything would be fine but had trouble hiding her anxiety. They'd stopped in the hotel lobby where Laura retrieved Steve's last telephone message explaining that his assistant had stepped in and saved the day.

"Well, here's your key. I've moved my things out of the closet so it's all yours. Please feel free to use the phone. You'll want to check with the airlines frequently. Also, call home as often as you feel like it. My guess is that'll make you feel better. I have a meeting all afternoon so the suite is yours entirely."

"Oh, that's really nice of you," Laura said. "I am sorry I missed your session."

"Same thing I teach at the med school," he responded. "Everything's over at five. I'll meet you around then, and we'll decide what to do next, okay?"

"I'll be fine," Laura said, "just go about your business. I do appreciate the use of the phone. You have to keep feeding the pay phones Canadian coins. I'll pay you for the calls if you let me know how much."

"Your not worrying is payment enough," David said.

CHAPTER FORTY-ONE

David found Laura was curled up on the bed with the phone when he returned to the suite. He paused at the door until she said her good-byes.

"Here's the latest from home," she told him. "Mikey says the baby-sitter is okay with him. She sounds bright and confident."

"Talk to Kevin too?"

"Sure did." Laura smiled. "He's my real information source. Said Stacy's going to make them hot dogs for dinner. Seems he beat her at Fish, and he's feeling very smug."

"How about the twins?"

"So far, so good. I told Stacy what to feed them and left her with detailed instructions. As long as Mikey and Kevin are with them, they're happy."

"Good deal." David hesitated before stepping into the room. "Now that you're up to date, what do you say we get something to eat?"

"Oh, and did you see the huge bouquet of flowers that arrived?"

David said he had. "Just protocol for these suites. My secretary got in the habit of reserving VIP accommodations when I used to travel with my wife, but I don't need all this special treatment."

The mention of David's wife stopped Laura. "David," she began. "I had to make a decision today that I want you to know about. I decided not to tell anyone back in Detroit that I was still here at the hotel. I've led everybody to believe that I'm still at the airport since I'd already told them I'd checked out. That means nobody can contact me."

David grimaced. "Is that wise?"

"Well, let's be perfectly honest," Laura shifted on the bed, "if Steve ever found out that I'd shared a hotel room with another man, he would go berserk. As innocent as my staying here is, he would never understand. I'd always be under a cloud of suspicion."

"I understand. I suggest you call home often then," David advised somewhat uneasily.

Laura nodded. "A little while ago the phone rang, and I didn't answer it. My God, I thought, it could be your wife. Or maybe your secretary and she would recognize my voice. The message light's not on, so I can't say who it was, and I'm sorry."

David waved his hand. "No problem, Laura. If it were important, whoever it was would have left a message."

An ominous feeling washed over David as he recalled a scene two years earlier when Cynthia had unexpectedly walked into his hotel room in Las Vegas. Suspicious as always, she had expected to find him with another woman, a cute ER nurse who had accompanied him to the annual seminar on chest trauma. Cynthia had stormed into his room at two in the morning. The anxious cloud that envcloped him quickly dissipated as he realized that Montreal was inaccessible. Laura couldn't get out. Cynthia couldn't get in. Not that she would even try, not anymore.

The only option for dinner was one of the hotel dining rooms, so David made a reservation at the French gourmet restaurant on the top floor. Before leaving for dinner, Laura checked home one more time. All was well at eight o'clock.

They entered the restaurant chatting comfortably. To a stranger's eye, they looked like a happy, successful couple. Cocktails were followed by a four-course dinner, exquisitely prepared and elegantly served. David ordered a bottle of Cabernet to accompany the Beef Wellington they had each ordered. Coffee and dessert followed. Once again, it was a delectable meal, enhanced by the candlelight.

Their conversation became intimate. David expressed a growing desire to learn more about Laura — about her background, her dreams, her hopes, everything she liked, didn't like. Likewise he opened up to her, telling her about his childhood and early professional career. His pain was obvious as he recited as objectively as he could the status of his relationship with Cynthia. He couldn't avoid the focus on his overwhelming desire for children. Cynthia had been unwilling. He explained how Cynthia had always been terrified of pregnancy. How her mother had died in childbirth. Tears clouded his eyes as he described the pregnancy that she'd terminated. How he thought that she might have reconsidered having a child, but how he hadn't even listened closely enough to what she was trying to tell him. Finally he told her about Ruth Davis, openly confessing his shame and disappointment. It felt strangely comforting to be able to share those feelings with Laura.

Laura listened, shock and sadness intermingling. A dynamic and passionate man like David should have a perfect wife, a woman to cherish and understand him. She asked a few sensitive questions, including whether Cynthia's lover was Raymond Walson's law partner, the one who had attempted suicide.

"Yes," David readily admitted. "How did you know?"

"Oh, just a guess. Based on something Vicky Walson once said."

"I don't think Cynthia will risk any future liaisons with Ruth," David predicted. "It has to do with social status. Divorce is hardly acceptable in our circle, and homosexuality would be unthinkable. So, I'm just trying to live each day as it comes."

Laura took a sip of wine before blurting, "Are you sleeping with her?" She shocked herself with such an intrusive question.

"No, Laura," David responded slowly, sadly. "No, not since then. Actually several months before that. We have no desire to be with each other that way at all."

"That's very sad. I hope to God that my relationship with Steve never gets that bad" She looked away.

They left the restaurant at 11:00 P.M. arm-in-arm. Neither really cared if anyone saw them. Absorbed in each other, having divulged so many private details about their lives over these past two days, it had become clear to them that they knew more about each other than any person on earth.

"I think it's too late to call home again tonight," Laura concluded as she settled herself on one of the large overstuffed sofas in the expansive suite.

"Agreed, but I'm going to check with the airlines," David announced as he opened the brocade draperies covering the large picture window. As they parted to expose the city below, Laura inhaled sharply. The night sky was a clear midnight blue. Gone were the low, heavy snow clouds, having dumped their contents on their way northward. The moon was full and golden light flooded the hotel room as David made his call.

"Good news," he reported. "I've booked you on the first flight out of here to Detroit tomorrow morning. Ten o'clock. They only had one seat on this flight, and you have it. The roads will be cleared by morning, and I promise I'll get you to the airport."

"Oh, thank you, David. Knowing that, I feel so much better." She'd see the children by early tomorrow afternoon and drive the babysitter back to St. Mary's. Steve should be home Sunday afternoon, and then everything, as if that were possible, would be back to normal.

CHAPTER FORTY-TWO

It was already dark in downtown Detroit, but Snake had time to kill before meeting Stacy at Baker's. He worked full-time now, and tonight he had extra money in his pocket. He bought himself a pint and walked over to Theodore Street to look at his mural. The painting had taken him much longer than he'd anticipated. Having a job got in the way of your life, but it was finally finished. Tonight he would convince Stacy to take a ride over so she could see it for herself. He had a new name for it, *The Happening*, and he would explain it all to Stacy, tell her all about the Supremes song of that name that inspired him, tell her how the song came out just before the '67 riots but that it was almost like the song was a warning to the city when he heard it, about all the trouble it was in. He would show her how *The Happening* revealed the heart of Detroit, the struggle, and the deep yearning for freedom — his own struggle.

In Highland Park, Stacy flipped on the color television set in the Nelson's living room and plopped down on Steve's recliner, a bag of potato chips in hand. Being alone in front of a TV was a rare treat. So different from her dormitory where all the girls had to congregate in the activities room and jockey for a decent view. There was always a fight over which channel to watch, and the nuns monitored the programs anyway. The rules: no profanity, no sex, no violence.

Some day, Stacy dreamed, she'd have her own house. Somewhere with no fear, no crime, no prejudice. Yes, she would have her own kids, too, and bring them up with plenty of food, nice clothes, and a safe place to live. No longer did this seem like an impossible dream. She was definitely as smart as the white girls at the academy as she had proved to both her teachers and herself. If she could only get a scholarship to college, maybe she could get a really good job. It was possible, right?

Her mama had told her that Steve Nelson's wife was a doctor. Maybe that's what she wanted to be, too. Like Anthony was going to be. Monica told her that a career like that took eight or ten years of school before it even started. Almost a lifetime. But then Mrs. Nelson had four kids and a husband, and she was doing it. Stacy thought she might ask for some advice from Mrs. Nelson when she met her tomorrow. So far, the nuns at the academy were her only adult link to the successful, white world. Although they tried to be helpful, only Sister Mary Agnes, back home at St. Joseph's, seemed to know what it was like in the streets. How else could she have found Stacy that horrible Christmas Eve night two years ago?

She cringed. Well, she was doing okay now, and she had learned about the polarization of cultures, knowledge that had already changed her life. Her dedication to her mother and sisters stuck in Detroit's ghetto had only grown. She knew her mother was working hard to get them out, and Stacy continually tried to reconcile this struggle with her own dreams.

Shuddering slightly, she realized how close she had come to a dangerous liaison tonight. She should never have agreed to go out with Snake. But Johnny used to tell her about Baker's, and she'd always wanted to go there. Snake had been a friend to both her brothers; somehow when she was with him, she felt closer to them. Crazy, she knew, but Snake was the only person who could bring back those bittersweet memories. How she still grieved for them both, especially Anthony. With his scholarship, he would have paved the way for the whole family to move to a safe and comfortable life. Now it was all on her. When she was a doctor, she'd specialize in gunshot wound cases, Stacy fantasized.

A sudden pounding at the back door startled her, and she jumped up. The pounding continued, louder now. Tentatively,

Stacy approached the door. The clock on the wall read five minutes past ten. She heard a loud male voice but couldn't make out what he was saying. Checking to make sure that the chain lock was securely engaged and noting the bolt mechanism across the door, Stacy finally called out, "Who's there?"

"Stacy, open the motherfuckin' door."

Stacy gasped. "Snake?"

"Damn right. The motherfuckin' fool you blew off tonight. You don't open this door right now, I'll kick it in."

Hands shaking, Stacy slid off the chain, unlocked the bolt, and quickly opened the door. Snake barged into the kitchen. As usual, he wore black and his head was shaved, just like Johnny's had been. She could tell he'd been drinking. She could smell it on his breath.

"Man almighty, Snake. You'll wake the children." She tried to keep her voice calm as he moved forward, shoving the twins' high chairs across the room.

"Now, wouldn't that just be too fuckin' bad." Snake pushed past Stacy, as he stalked into the dining room. He picked up a photograph framed in crystal, then threw it onto the hardwood floor scattering fragments in every direction.

"Snake, please," Stacy pleaded, tugging at his arm. "Come on, sit down."

Snake shrugged her off and walked over to the wall lined with framed pictures of the Nelsons. "This who you think you is, or what?" he demanded.

"Stop, Snake," she pulled at his arm again. Tears welled in her eyes. The phone rang then, but Snake grabbed her.

"Forget it. I want you to look at this, look at all them white faces. See the difference? See how there's no color in their faces at all? That the world you want to live in? Honky world?"

Snake stopped speaking abruptly as he stared at a portrait of the Nelson family. On one end of a couch, Steve sat next to the kids, Laura on the other end. "You see who that is, girl? Look close."

Stacy had no choice but to look. Snake had pulled her next to him. The phone finally stopped ringing.

"Oh my goodness, it's that doctor," Stacy said.

"Yeah. It's her all right. That yellow-hair doctor lady from the hospital. And here you is, baby-sittin' for the bitch who near killed your brother?"

Stacy's eyes were wide with confusion and fear. "How did you know where I was?"

"Yeah, I waited for you tonight," Snake began, "waitin' and waitin'. Finally some fine woman comes up and says, 'Snake? Could your name be Snake?' I says, 'Yeah'." And she says, 'Stacy said to tell you she couldn't make it tonight. She's baby-sittin' for her mother's boss, Mr. Steve Nelson.' All I had to do is dial information and get the motherfuckin' address."

"That was Monica. I asked her to let you know. So you wouldn't be upset."

"Upset? I'm fuckin' pissed you blew me off for the honky lives here. "

"Mama asked me as a favor."

"I got more information for you. Same Mr. Steve Nelson from the Social Services Department last year, lecturin' me bout my Mama and welfare, tellin' me to get a job like I wasn't already lookin' for one. Took me forever part-time to get to full-time and look where I find you when I do? In the honky's own house."

"Please, Snake," Stacy whispered. Snake had tightened his grip on her arm. "That hurts."

"I'm not good enough for you, huh? It's that fucking white school. Guess you think you're one of them now. Too good to go to Baker's with Snake."

He dragged Stacy into the living room. The phone started ringing again. Snake pushed Stacy onto the sofa then headed back toward the kitchen, where he yanked the phone off the hook.

Stacy was sitting on the sofa when Snake returned. "Look . . . I'm really sorry about tonight," she stammered. "This job came up. It was an emergency. This Mr. Nelson is my mama's boss. I didn't know anything about his wife, the doctor. I wanted to call you, I mean, but I know you have no phone so I couldn't. I sent Monica."

Snake sat down next to her and reached under his shirt. From under his belt, he drew out a gun, inspected it, and casually shifted it from hand to hand.

Stacy recoiled. "What are you doing with that?"

"This's my ticket to respect. Nobody gonna dis Snake they know I'm packin'."

"But it not legal? Is it?"

"Girl, where you from? Of course it's not 'legal'." Snake kept fondling the weapon. "This say, I'm bad. Don't mess with me."

"Could you please put it down," Stacy said. "I don't want to be anywhere around guns. They scare me."

"I promised your mama that I would find the motherfucker who gunned down Johnny. I swear I will. I promised your mama I would look out for you too." Snake's voice softened and he reached over and placed his weapon on the side table near the steps. "Now you're old enough," he said, pulling Stacy toward him. "Old enough to be Snake's woman."

"I can't go out with you, Snake," Stacy said edging away.

"Sure you can," he said. "You're sixteen now."

"No, I can't," she blurted. "Mama won't let me."

Snake stared at her. "You know what you're sayin'? You babysittin' for the white bitch who messed up Anthony, the motherfucker who fucked up my mama's welfare. Girl, you dissin' your brothers."

He drew her closer against his body. She could feel his breath, the rapid beat of his heart. Feel his hand caressing her breast. "Anybody ever touched you like this?" he whispered.

"No," she whispered back, scared to move, scared to resist, scared of the gun.

Snake drew her closer to him, slipping his hand inside her bra. "Feel good?" he prompted.

"Snake, don't," Stacy finally managed. "I don't want you to do that."

"Baby, you're gonna love it. You're a big girl now."

He nudged her onto her back, straddling her, kissing her lips.

Stacy struggled to sit up. "No." she said, louder, firmer. "I said, stop."

"Baby, I'm not gonna hurt you. You just lie still," Snake tried to kiss her again, but she jerked her head sideways.

"No." she screamed. "Don't. I don't want you to do that to me."

"I promise, baby, you'll love it. Snake will never hurt you. You just keep quiet. Okay? Don't want to wake the whitie children." His body now lay on top of hers, both fully clothed. "I'm not going to force myself, Stacy. I want you to want me. Real respect, baby."

Neither Snake nor Stacy saw Mikey, clad in blue flannel pajamas and grasping his beloved Ginky, sneak down the stairs. Without a word, he lifted the gun off the table and carried it back upstairs.

CHAPTER FORTY-THREE

It seemed so natural, so right, as David sat beside Laura on the sofa in the spacious living room of the dimly lit suite Friday night. His arm softly encircling her shoulders as if to protect her from an imaginary chill. The fireplace created a romantic glow in the room, and aside from its sparking embers, the rest of the world seemed to be standing still.

Neither spoke. David's arm around Laura's shoulders tightened ever so slightly. Soon, Laura's head rested on his shoulder. She snuggled a little closer and lifted her head slowly. The expression on David's face, outlined by the fire, was one of pure pleasure mixed with real pain.

"It's getting very late," he said. "Do you think you should get some sleep?"

"I feel so totally wonderful that I never want to move," she said simply.

"I don't either, but I promised you your own room, and I don't want you to think I deceived you." He took her hand and brushed it lightly over his cheek. "The truth is, I don't think I can protect your honor if we stay like this much longer."

"Thank you," she murmured, then kissed him lightly on the lips. She stood up slowly and walked into the bedroom, closing the door behind her. Then she lay face down on the king-size bed and began weeping softly into the pillow.

After a while she undressed, brushed out her hair, and pulled on the only nightgown she'd packed, a sheer knee-length. Quietly opening the bedroom door, she moved silently into the darkness that was interrupted only by the flicker of fading embers. David was still sitting on the sofa, holding a glass of wine in both hands, staring blankly ahead.

When Laura reached down to touch his face, she felt hot tears. Wordlessly, she reached for his hand. After removing the glass and placing it on the coffee table, in a low, husky voice she invited him to come with her into the bedroom.

Laura motioned him toward the bed. Neither said a word as she adjusted the small lamp in the corner of the room to a muted glow and slipped out of her nightgown. David slowly removed his clothes and joined her. Floating on a mattress of dreamy desire, their bodies came together. Unhurried, yet aflame in a passion that Laura could not have fathomed. They made love, their bodies joined, savoring every exquisite sensation.

Knowing that this may be their only night together, they lay in each other's arms until the sky lightened. David rose first. He left the bedroom and headed for the telephone in the adjoining room. When he returned, he leaned over and kissed Laura very tenderly. The kiss lingered.

"I've called the airlines," he finally said. "Your flight's still set for ten. It's going to Chicago first. That's the best they can do. The first direct flight to Detroit doesn't leave until three this afternoon, if it takes off at all today with everything being so backed up. I think you should go via Chicago." David's voice was resigned and forlorn.

Laura reached for him and nodded silently. What if she didn't go back? What if she stayed just one more night?

"Laura, you know I don't want you to go," David said, echoing her longing. "Could you stay one more day?"

Tears flooded Laura's eyes. "I don't want to leave you." She threw her arms around David then, clinging to him. Her whole world had changed.

CHAPTER FORTY-FOUR

Snake Rogers was used to having his way with women. He was starting to live the American dream. Carried a piece. A real artist. A real job. Prospects to deal drugs on the side. But he was prepared to wait on Johnny and Anthony's little sister. Stacy was something special. He wanted to make her proud.

When he'd barged in tonight he'd planned to let her know he was a man, show her the piece, teach her a lesson about dissin' Snake. But he could never hurt her. Scare her, sure. But when it came to takin' her, he wasn't gonna force it. Don't matter if she don't give it up the first time. Keep pursuin' her. She'd be his woman, just wait and see.

Trying not to crush her with his weight, he lay on her, angled close enough to feel every breath, every heartbeat, and he never wanted it to stop. As he kept murmuring that he would never hurt her, she stopped resisting and Snake was sure that she was enjoying herself.

"I'm gonna take care of you forever, baby."

When a pair of detectives arrived in the residential neighborhood of Highland Park around eleven on Friday night, the streets were calm and quiet. One, a tall, lanky man with watery blue eyes named Kaminsky, and his partner, a tense black detective named Willard, proceeded to the scene without haste. Scowling, Willard was annoyed at being summoned on a call usually assigned to patrolmen. It had something to do with his partner Reynolds who was out sick.

Exactly what, he didn't know. Probably just a prank call from a kid.

"What exactly did dispatch say anyway?" Willard asked.

"A kid, as in little kid. Said somebody was hurting his babysitter. Said the guy had a gun."

"Hurting her how, like what is this guy supposed to be doing? And who lives here anyway?"

Kaminsky shrugged.

"Leave the heater running while we run a check on the name and address," suggested Willard.

Kaminsky bobbed one of his legs as he gulped down the last dregs of cold coffee from a Tigers mug. He picked up the radio and called in.

"No shit? Reynolds has a special alert on this address?" Kaminsky stiffened as he hung up the radio.

"What is it, 'Minsky?"

"John Reynolds wants a heads-up anything happens here. Homeowners name is Nelson: Stephen and Laura."

"Nelson?" Willard repeated. "Rings a bell." He frowned as he glanced out at the house. "Laura Nelson? Oh yeah. Goes to med school with Reynold's daughter. Reynolds thinks she knows something about a homicide case. Cold case. '67 riots."

Kaminsky's eyes widened. "I questioned a Nelson a couple years ago when I was on with Reynolds. A young couple, that's all I remember. How many Nelsons you figure live in Detroit?"

"Plenty. But how many on Reynold's hit list?"

"The med student did it?" Kaminsky laughed.

Willard frowned. "Don't laugh. Reynolds thought so."

"No shit. Another thing. Central got another call on this address after we dispatched. Baby-sitter's mother. Said there was no answer here when she called almost an hour ago. She's been trying ever since."

Willard checked his watch. "Let's go!"

"What the fuck?" Snake's head jerked up, interrupted by the buzz of the doorbell. "Who the fuck is that?"

Loud knocks at the front door followed a repeat buzz.

"A neighbor?" Stacy guessed.

"You better not be fuckin' with me, baby," he said, sliding off Stacy.

"I'm not," Stacy shook her head. "Just get out of here. Go out the back door. The way you came in. Go, go." Stacy was up now, tugging at Snake. "Oh no, there's broken glass all over the dining room floor. I was going to sweep it up."

Behind her, Snake grabbed for the gun he'd left on the end table. "My piece? Where the fuck is my piece?"

"What?" Stacey responded. "Your gun? Get it and get out." A look of desperation shot across her face as she followed the source of Snake's menacing gaze. It led to the top of the stairs.

Again the buzz of a doorbell and a second round of pounding, now louder and more insistent.

"Get rid of whoever it is," Snake yelled as he lunged up the stairs. "Where the fuck? One of those honky brats musta lifted my piece."

Snake bolted up the stairs.

"No, Snake, stay away from the children." She rushed up behind him.

"You hear that Minsk? Sounded like something hit hard in there. Let's go in. On three!"

Willard had weighed the options. There'd be hell to pay if they forced their way into this place without due cause: destruction of private property; no direct order to proceed; no search warrant. But what if something nasty was really going on in there? They'd look like fools just standing out there like idiots. And why was John Reynolds involved?

Crashing through the front door with blunt force, the pair practically fell over Stacy's unconscious body sprawled at the foot of the stairs. Blood streamed from an ugly gash on her head.

"Shit. Check this floor," Willard ordered. He was already bending over the slim, still body. "Toss me that blanket."

Kaminsky grabbed a blanket from the sofa and tossed it to Willard before hurriedly assessing the surroundings. "Broken glass in dining room. Phone off the hook in the kitchen."

"What the fuck is happening here?" Willard did a hasty examination of Stacy before covering her with the blanket. "This one's out cold. Hit her head pretty bad. Call for back up, an ambulance."

"I'll check upstairs. A kid called this in, right?"

Snake took the stairs two at a time, not looking back until he felt a tug on his shirt. Spinning around, he faced Stacy.

"Snake, please," she pleaded. "Come down, go out the back door."

"Get out of my way, girl."

She didn't let go of his shirt. He pushed her away. He hadn't wanted to hurt her, and his eyes widened in horror as he watched her tumble backward down the stairs. She hit hard at the bottom and for a fraction of a second, he just wanted to go to her, to cradle her in his arms, to tell her he was sorry. Of course, he couldn't. He had to get the gun and get the fuck out. Fiery anger blasted through his veins. Right now he should be at Baker's with Stacy, groovin' to the music, not tearin' through this honky's house, trying to find his piece.

Upstairs Snake faced a hall with three doors on each side and a bathroom with the door open at the end. The first door on the right was closed but not locked. Snake barged inside. Two cribs, each with a sleeping kid. He yanked the kid out of one crib and tossed it onto the floor like a rag doll. The thud reminded him of Stacy and his heart lurched, but a crash at the front door jarred him back to reality. He had to find his piece and get the fuck out. He rushed into the next room. Only a neatly made, empty double bed. He heard male voices downstairs. As he jerked open a third door, his heart slammed in his chest. The unmistakable static of a police radio.

"Stop, mister!" A kid stood facing him from across the room. "This is my room. I'll shoot you." In the kid's hand was the twenty-two, aimed point-blank at his chest. Could a kid that small shoot a gun? Yes. Some relative of Lonnie's had wasted his own grandmother. He needed to get that piece. He hadn't admitted to Stacy that it was Lonnie's, and the poor fuck loved that gun.

"Gimme the gun, little boy."

"I'm five years old, and my Daddy taught me how to shoot." The kid's voice was squeaky, but he did not back off.

Snake took a zigzag step forward before he heard the heavy footsteps on the stairs. He pivoted when he heard, "Heading upstairs, Minsky."

Trapped. He had to get out. Now. Only way, the window. and leaning against the windowsill he saw a baseball bat. With one eye fixated on the kid, Snake lunged for that bat.

Willard heard the crash as he reached the top of the stairs. Gun drawn, he edged into the hallway and slid along the corridor. In the dimness of the hall night-light, he could make out three doors on each side. All but two were ajar.

"Halt! Police!" he yelled. Immediately, he became distracted by the screams. Sounded like a baby and his heart sunk. He'd seen too much child abuse, hated domestic violence. Gun ready, he jerked his body across the corridor and peered into a child's bedroom. He could see two cribs amid shades of shadowy pink. One was empty, and the other held a bellowing red-faced toddler.

Willard flipped the light switch by the door and scanned the room.

"Holy shit," he breathed as he saw an identical-looking child, silent and motionless on the hardwood floor. Dropping to his knees, he quickly determined that the limp body was breathing, that there was no obvious blood. "Lord have mercy," he whispered.

Hadn't a kid called this in? Where was this kid? Willard crossed the corridor again and eased himself into the room directly across from the one with the babies. The one he judged the source of the crash, which had sounded like breaking glass. Backing against the wall, he crouched low, gun drawn and ready. Suddenly he froze as a little boy looked up at him in wonder. The kid's hands shook, and in his hands was a revolver.

"Easy," Willard whispered, wondering what to say that wouldn't scare the kid. "I'm a policeman. Okay, son?"

"I was gonna shoot the bad man," the kid announced, clutching a gun as if it were a stuffed animal. "He went out my window."

Willard's gaze drifted to the broken window as Kaminsky came barreling up the stairs. "Careful, Minsk, go slow," Willard warned. "Check out the room across the hall. There's a baby in there. Call another ambulance, and secure the rest of the upstairs."

Lowering his voice, Willard approached Mikey. "Okay kid, you did great, but it's time to give me that gun."

"How come you don't have a uniform?" the kid asked, clutching the weapon precariously. Willard could feel the damp sweat spread under his arms.

"I'm a detective," Willard said, breathing easier now that the kid let the gun's barrel slump toward the floor. "I don't have to wear a police uniform. Okay?"

"Okay then." The kid shrugged and handed Willard the weapon.

"Minsk!" Willard called, wrapping the gun in his handkerchief and stashing it in his jacket pocket. He grabbed Mikey by the hand and rushed out into the hallway. "Take this kid. I'm in pursuit!"

Kaminsky appeared and reached for Mikey, taking him into the bedroom where one toddler screamed up a storm and the other lay silent and motionless on the floor.

Outside, the streetlights provided just enough glow to see a beat-up Mustang, tires squealing, race off. He was too far away to get the license number, but something clicked. He'd seen that car before.

CHAPTER FORTY-FIVE

By the time room service arrived on Saturday morning, Laura had showered and dressed in a pair of navy blue wool slacks and a crew neck sweater. David too had dressed, but in a conservative suit. They waited silently at the bronze and glass table in the parlor of the suite as the room service waiter arranged the fruit, served the Eggs Benedict, and poured coffee from the ornate silver service.

"Will that be all, sir?" the waiter inquired.

"Yes, this is fine." David signed the check, added a gratuity, and pulled out a five-dollar bill for the waiter as he followed him to the door.

Seated again, David said, "Laura, you leave for the airport in forty-five minutes. I've arranged a driver, and if you don't mind, I'll go with you and make sure you get on the plane."

"Yes, thank you," Laura murmured.

David's hazel eyes never left her. "I know this is not the right time to ask, but could we have a future together, Laura? I mean, a real future."

"No," she said firmly, yet her tone was tender. "I'm married and so are you." She reached for David's hand, the one without the gold wedding band. "But David, I want you to know I'll never regret last night."

"But it doesn't have to end. I know that I love you. I'm so very sure." David struggled for the right words. "I think I've loved you ever since I first saw you. I was certain of it as I got to know you, especially during your time in the hospital. But now, after last night, I am so, so sure."

Laura moved close to him, barely touching.

"Laura, please marry me? I know that sounds crazy. I know it can't be now, but someday? You know how deeply I feel, not only about you, but also for your children. We can work this all out. There has to be a way to work this out."

Laura's face was inscrutable. "That's not possible. I can't leave Steve. He loves me, and our children, and I care about him." She paused. "Not the way I know that I love you, but I'm married to him, and I can't even think of leaving him. Please understand, David." Did she mean this? Could she just let David walk away?

He stood and pulled her to him. Ignoring their untouched breakfast, they held each other on the sofa.

"Will you at least continue to see me then?" David asked in a low, hoarse voice, tightening his grip on her.

"No, David. I can't. Not ever, and I'm not even sure I can return to school," she said. "Maybe I should drop out. It'll be too hard to see you all the time around the hospital and know I'll never be with you again, not like last night." She paused, lowering her head. "I just don't know what to do."

"No!" After a moment, he met her eyes once more. "Laura, I'm going to be leaving Detroit. I'm taking the position of dean at Stanford University. I'll be moving to California as soon as it can be arranged." He hesitated, "Unless you tell me not to."

"What are you talking about?"

"Yesterday I met with the President of Stanford. He came to Montreal to offer me the position."

"You're leaving Detroit?"

"I didn't accept at the time, how could I? But it seems the timing is right if this is what you want."

Laura hugged him tighter. "You know it's not."

"Please, won't you reconsider? We don't have to decide this now."

"Promise me something," Laura spoke in a whisper. "Please, we have to act as if last night, our whole relationship, never happened. You must understand, it's the only way I can go on. There are so many innocent people involved."

"I don't know if I can do that, Laura. It's asking too much. I don't think I can."

"You must."

Holding her hands in his, he felt his eyes fill with tears. "We'll both make a promise then. If you need anything, anytime, anywhere, for any reason, or if you change your mind, you'll let me know." His voice was low. "I'll make sure that you always know where to find me, wherever I am."

She reached up with both hands and held his face tenderly. "I promise."

Neither spoke much in the car on the way to the airport, but their hands held tight. The roads seemed miraculously clear of snow.

The airport was mobbed. After waiting for nearly ten minutes in line, Laura was finally able to call home once more, where the telephone at the Nelson home was not answered by Stacy Jones, but by Susan Reynolds. Laura's first thought was that she'd dialed the wrong number.

"It's no mistake," Susan said quickly, "I'm at your house. Some things happened here last night. But listen to me very carefully, Laura," Susan continued firmly. "Everything is okay."

"What are you talking about? What things?" she stammered. "What are you doing at my house?"

"It's going to be okay," Susan reassured her.

Laura gasped as she saw a horde of people pushing through the gate area to board the Chicago flight. "There's no time. The plane's leaving."

"Just give me your flight details, Laura," Susan urged. "I'll be here when you get home and explain everything."

"The children?"

"Fine. I swear."

Hurriedly, Laura gave Susan her flight information. "I'll take a cab home," she said quickly, barely daring to ask one more question. "Steve?"

"Steve's fine," Susan answered immediately. "He's on his way home. Just get back here, okay?"

"As soon as I can." Hands shaking, Laura hung up the phone.

Pulling herself together with an enormous force of will, Laura approached David, and they rushed toward the crush at the gate as passengers jockeyed for position.

"What's wrong?"

She looked away. "Everything's fine," she lied.

David squeezed her hand one more time. His eyes were fixed on her as she passed through the gate. When she finally allowed herself to glance back she saw the expression of naked despair on his face, and she looked away.

CHAPTER FORTY-SIX

Laura arrived at Detroit Metropolitan Airport at 3:30 Saturday afternoon with an ashen face and puffy eyes. The trip had been a blur, and when the customs agent at O'Hare had questioned her more carefully than many of the other travelers, she realized she must look as bad as she felt, anxiety accompanying every thought as she boarded the plane for Detroit. What could have happened at home? Why was Susan there and not telling her anything? Could somebody know about last night with David? A desolate sadness combined with panic and guilt overwhelmed her as she headed for the taxi stand, relieved that she'd accepted the five $20 bills David had pressed into her hand without a word as they parted at the gate.

As the cab approached Puritan Avenue, Laura began to panic. The story of Steve's twin brother flashed before her eyes. Helen Nelson had been out, and when she had arrived home, Phillip was already dead. The vision seemed so real, Laura grabbed the seat with both hands, somehow knowing that whatever had happened, it was about one of the twins. Tossing two $20 at the cab driver before the car had fully stopped, Laura bolted toward her front door, noticing that its frame was cracked on one side.

Steve appeared from inside the house. He rushed forward and half-embraced her.

"What happened, Steve? What's with the door?" Without thinking, she pounded her fist against her husband's chest. "Where are the kids?"

Steve grabbed her wrists. "Hey, calm down now."

"What's happened?" she demanded. "Tell me for God's sake!"

"Laura, stop. It's important for the kids that you stay calm. Don't go inside unless you can promise that."

Laura pushed brusquely past her husband. Inside, she found Susan, sitting on the couch reading a story to the boys. Nicole was quietly playing with wooden blocks in the corner of the living room. Absently, Laura noticed that everything looked as she'd left it. She heard Steve come in and close the front door behind him. The sight of three of her children, safe and content, filled Laura with relief. But as she felt the welcome wave pass through her, she wondered about Natalie.

"Mommy!" Mikey and Kevin jumped up to greet her.

Taking a deep breath and hugging the boys, Laura tried to act normal. "Hi guys!"

"Mommy, Mommy!" Mikey began excitedly, "I had a gun. And the bad man ran away. And the policeman took away the gun. I was gonna shoot it, I really was."

Laura looked quickly from Steve to Susan. "Oh, honey," Laura responded, rumpling his hair. "Sounds like you've been watching too much TV, huh?"

"Mommy, up there." He pointed to the ceiling. "The police-mans were here and—"

"Hang on, baby, "Laura interrupted. "Where's Natalie?" She looked first at Steve, then at Susan. "Taking a nap?"

"C'mon, sit down," Steve said, going to her, taking her by the arm.

"Where's Natalie?" Laura repeated. She refused to sit down, looking again from Steve to Susan.

Susan exhaled sharply. "Laura, we've got lots to explain."

Laura ignored her and started for the stairs leading to the twins' bedroom. Steve tried to pull her back. Susan said nothing.

"Natalie's at the hospital, Mommy." Mikey ran over to Laura, tugging at her slacks for attention.

Laura reeled backward, every trace of color draining from her cheeks. Steve quietly reached for her once more and forcibly sat her down next to Susan. Mikey pushed himself against her knees, and was joined by Kevin and Nicole.

"What happened to my baby?" Laura managed in a voice fringed with panic.

"First of all, Natalie's going to be all right," he told her as all three kids tried to pile into her lap.

Laura looked to Susan for confirmation, who nodded. "Why don't I take the kids upstairs for a while so you two can talk. Come on, you guys, who can run up the steps the fastest?"

As Susan raced up after them, Laura stared at Steve. "Tell me," she demanded, not waiting for the children to disappear up the stairs. "Where is my daughter?"

"Nobody could reach you," he said. "When the cops came, they called Detective Reynolds. Apparently, he wanted to be notified about any 'unusual activity' about us, and I guess last night qualified. By the time he got here, the ambulance had taken Natalie and Stacy to City Hospital. He called Susan to come stay with the kids, which was lucky for us. Otherwise, they would have been packed off to some godforsaken temporary shelter."

"What are you talking about?" Laura sank into the couch, weak and lightheaded.

"They got me at the hotel," Steve went on. "I'd just come back from the first night's big dinner. I drove straight through to the hospital early this morning. Natalie's okay, I swear it. Then Reynolds showed up. He tried to call you himself," Steve hesitated, "but the hotel told him you'd checked out already."

Laura started to get up. "Steve, for God's sake, tell me what happened."

Laura grabbed Mikey's battered copy of *Green Eggs and Ham* and pressed it to her chest as Steve pieced together the story as best he could. There'd been an intruder. Signs of violence. Broken glass. Broken high chair. The baby-sitter was unconscious when the cops got here. Apparently shoved down the stairs. Laura tried to fight off panic as he explained that Natalie, her sweet-tempered, sensitive toddler, had been thrown out of her crib by the intruder. That she was in the hospital. That there'd been a gun. That there were so many awful questions remaining.

Laura suddenly bolted off the couch and grabbed her purse. "I have to see Natalie. Now."

"Laura, Natalie will be fine," Steve said, grabbing her shoulder, spinning her to face him. "I fed her lunch, and she fell asleep before I left a few hours ago. They're calling it a mild concussion and simple abrasions."

"She's really okay?" Laura hesitated. "What was that business about a gun? About Mikey?" she asked, her heart pounding with the assumption that it was the gun from their attic.

"The police took it from him. Thank God he didn't pull the trigger. You know how the boys are playing cops and robbers all the time."

"Where did he get the gun?" She held her breath. Certainly it hadn't been loaded. She'd seen to that and the weapon was locked away in the attic.

"The guy must have taken it out of his pocket and laid it down. Mikey said he saw it lying on the table. That he snuck down and took it so the bad man couldn't shoot it. The son-of-a-bitch must have chased him upstairs and gone into the girls' room first."

Laura struggled to fight the hysteria closing in on her. "Then it wasn't our gun?"

"No, of course not."

"Oh, my God, Steve, how could this be happening?" Laura's body slumped. She felt scared and ill and guilt-ridden.

"You going to be okay?"

"Yes," she forced herself to sit up straighter. "Who was this . . . intruder?"

"Don't know. Of course the detectives want to talk to us about it all. I said we'd call when you got back. I do know that when Stacy regained consciousness, she said she didn't know. Said he was young and black. Said she thought he was a friend of ours so she opened the door and he barged in, started trashing the place."

"Thank God it wasn't our gun?" Laura whispered. Why hadn't she gotten rid of it?

He stared at her. "How could it be? You said it was in the attic, locked up."

Laura was pale. "It is. I put it there when we moved."

"Reynolds said they have fingerprints, so maybe they'll get lucky. I don't like the thought of thugs running in this neighborhood."

Laura leapt from the couch. "I have got to go see Nattie."

"Okay. Why don't you stop in to see Stacy too? I was too much in a hurry to get back here. I feel responsible for what's happened."

"She's going to be okay?"

Steve frowned. "Physically, yes. Emotionally, who knows?"

CHAPTER FORTY-SEVEN

Saturday afternoon traffic was light, and Laura made it to the hospital in a half-hour. The student parking lot was nearly empty, and she parked the wagon and ran toward the hospital entrance. She headed directly for the pediatric ward on the seventh floor. Laura blinked when she saw the cartoon characters that covered the walls, the little red wagons and bright strollers scattered throughout the hallways. It was so cheerful here, so different from the drab gray med-surg wards where she'd trained so far.

Natalie Nelson was asleep in a large steel-railed crib. The child looked tiny and pathetically alone, her blonde curls tousled and partially obscured by the white bandage that covered the left side of her forehead.

"Dear God," Laura murmured as she inspected Natalie's head and peeked at her slumbering body under the loose toddler hospital gown. Respirations seemed normal, as did her daughter's heart rate. She grabbed the stethoscope from the night table and placed it over Natalie's chest. Everything sounded perfectly normal. Next, Laura pulled the chart from the holder at the foot of the bed. She scanned the doctor's orders and the nurses' notes, tears blurring her eyes and smearing the ink. Satisfied, she confirmed the diagnosis: mild concussion and superficial abrasions, just as Steve had reported.

"Thank you, God," she whispered.

*   *   *

"Excuse, me, are you Natalie's mother?" a small voice behind her interrupted.

Laura turned to face a young black girl of sixteen or seventeen. She wore a hospital gown and an oversized hospital issue bathrobe over her slight frame.

"Yes I am," Laura responded. The girl seemed familiar. Her gaze fell to the girl's arm that was heavily bandaged and supported by a sling. Her eyes then darted to a series of small butterfly closures running across her forehead.

"Do I know you?" Laura asked.

"I'm Stacy Jones, Mrs. Nelson," she said slowly, her eyes unnaturally bright. "I'm so sorry about what happened last night. I did everything I could to keep him away from the kids, I really did."

"I'm sure you did," Laura said, intending to reassure her that whatever happened had not been her fault."

"You know?" Stacy squinted, her eyes flashing recognition. "We have met before. You're the doctor who tried to help my brother, Anthony. After the riots. You probably don't remember?"

Laura stared at Stacy. Who? Anthony? Not her first patient, the Anthony who had died. "Anthony Diggs?"

Stacy nodded. "Yes. Diggs is my mama's maiden name. My mother's Lucy Jones."

Laura stiffened. Lucy Jones?

"She works for Mr. Nelson at social services, you know?"

The Lucy Jones who was Steve's assistant? That was Anthony's and Johnny's mother? Laura felt dizzy. She reached for the rails of the crib to steady herself.

"Are you okay?" the young girl asked. She seemed on the verge of tears herself.

"I'm okay now," Laura murmured, as much to Stacy as to herself. "Let's go across the hall and sit down."

Glancing carefully at Natalie, asleep in the metal crib, Laura led Stacy to the small waiting room. "Stacy, I don't know exactly what happened, but I want to thank you for everything. Detective Reynolds told my husband how you'd been hurt and taken to the hospital. I want to know anything you can tell me," Laura said softly.

"You don't remember me," Stacy tried to begin again, "but I know you tried to help my brother."

"Yes, I do remember now. You visited your brother all the time. And you've certainly grown up, haven't you?"

"I guess."

"I'm so sorry about what happened to you last night. Tell me about it."

"I'm not sure, Mrs . . . I mean, Dr. Nelson."

"Stacy, please, call me Laura."

"Uh, okay. You know, I used to hate you," Stacy said tentatively. "I thought you wanted my brother to die."

"Do you still hate me?" Laura looked directly into the young girl's moist eyes.

"No. You were kind to my mother. She told me so. I thought you wanted my brother to die."

Laura reached over and squeezed Stacy's hand. "I was only a freshman med student then. Anthony was my very first patient. I really did care, and I'll remember him every day of my life."

Stacy shook her head miserably. "Anthony was in a coma. Then my other brother, Johnny, got shot. He got killed. They never did find out who killed him."

Johnny Diggs.

Laura was speechless at how intricately her life intertwined with this family. Finally, she said, "Stacy, I had no idea that the Mrs. Jones who worked with my husband was Anthony's mother. This has really caught me by surprise. All of this is a surprise."

Stacy nodded. "For me too."

"Honey, can you tell me what happened at my house last night?"

Stacy held onto her bandaged arm and began to weep. She told Laura that the man had a gun. That's why she let him in. That he'd laid the gun on the table when he tried to force her onto the couch. That Mikey must have heard her struggling. That Mikey must have crept down and taken the gun. When there was pounding at the door, the man looked for the gun, but it was gone. She tried to stop him from going upstairs. That's all she remembered until she woke up in the hospital in the middle of the night, her mother beside her, and three detectives ready to ask her questions.

"Did he rape you?" Laura asked, assuming the worst.

"No."

"Thank God for that," Laura breathed. "I can't tell you how sorry I am."

Stacy's eyes filled. "I'm sorry about the children. I tried to protect them."

"Hey, listen to me. It's not your fault. I'll never be able to thank you enough for what you did for my children. I hope to see you again when everything's back to normal. You know, and just talk."

"Uh, okay. That'd be real nice," Stacy said, managing a slight smile. "I'd better go. My mama'll be here soon, and I'm pretty sure they'll let me go home. I just want to get back to school and forget all this."

They both stood, and Laura gave Stacy a hug before heading back to Natalie's room. The pediatrician showed up and assured her that Natalie should be just fine. Then Laura called her own mother. Just hearing Peg Whalen's soothing voice made her cry. Laura promised to call her from home to explain everything, knowing she never could. She returned to Natalie's bedside and sat silently for a while, her fingers gripping the steel bars of the crib.

Stacy Jones. Lucy Jones. Back in her life. Certainly there wasn't any connection between what had happened last night and that nightmare night in 1967.

CHAPTER FORTY-EIGHT

On Alexandrine Avenue, darkness was descending as Lucy settled Stacy on their worn living room sofa, propped her up with pillows and placed a cool washcloth on her forehead. She couldn't help a sigh of relief as her three younger girls adjusted hesitantly to their sister's bandages before plying her with questions. Lucy witnessed the girls trying to emulate their older sister in every way — her speech, the way she dressed, her mannerisms. Again, she mentally counted her savings. Soon she'd have enough to get all four girls out of this crime-ridden neighborhood to somewhere safe. As intensely as Lucy missed her eldest daughter, she was anxious to get her back to the safety of the academy.

There was a knock on the front door, and Lucy answered it.

It was Willie Allen, Snake's sidekick. "Stacy home?"

"Yes she is," Lucy said reluctantly, "but she's resting."

"Hey, girl?" Willie slid past Lucy and approached the sofa. "Heard you had a problem last night? Hanging out in the wrong honky neighborhood, huh? You should stick around here, where we take care of you, girl."

"Mama, I'm gonna go out and talk to Willie for a minute. I could use some fresh air. Just be a little bit."

Lucy frowned. "Thought you had a headache."

"Took two Tylenol. It's gone," Stacy rose, reached into the closet for her coat, draped it over her injured arm, and walked to the door with Willie.

Willie did not say another word until the door closed behind them. "Listen here, girl. My man Snake, needs to talk to you about something. Says it's important."

"Not to me it isn't."

"Hey now, my man says it's important, it's important." Willie smiled a thin, menacing smile. "He says you better come, you don't want more trouble. You know, your little sisters."

Stacy found Snake stretched out on a cot in the tiny back room of his mother's tenement apartment just down the block. There was a makeshift splint and bandage on his lower leg, which he had propped up on a pillow.

"Leave us alone, Willie," Snake ordered when he saw Stacy standing at the entrance to the shabby room.

As her eyes adjusted to the dim light, Stacy skipped a few breaths. The room was filled with small portraits of her. Snake had made her look beautiful, surrounded by reds and browns and swirling colors. All she could do was stare as the previous night came back to her. How he'd promised not to hurt her. Then he'd pushed her down those stairs. But deep down, she knew he hadn't meant to hurt her.

"Like my pictures?" She felt his eyes bore into her.

She said nothing.

"You okay, Stacy?"

"Yes."

He shifted his leg. "Damn this hurts. Fuckin' leg's busted. What'd you tell those fuckin' pigs?"

"That I opened the door, thinking it must be a friend of the Nelsons, but it was a stranger. That you, I mean the stranger, had a gun." Stacy hesitated. "Then I said I must have fallen down the stairs and hit my head."

"That all?" Snake's filmy eyes bore into hers. She looked away.

"That's all, Snake, I swear."

Snake smiled. "You got it all figured out, huh?"

"I don't want any trouble. I can't believe you hurt that innocent baby."

"Yeah right. Look at my fuckin' leg. What about that? Won't kill me, but it sure gonna make me think 'bout how white you are now."

"I am not!"

"Yeah, you're turnin', turnin' away from me and the rest of the brothers and the sisters 'round here. Everybody say so, too good for us or somethin'. It's that fuckin' school, I say. No time for me, no way. I wanna show you my paintin' last night, and you stand me up for that honky, that yellow-hair doctor fucked up Anthony. And her man, the one fuckin' up my mama's benefits all the time."

"You're wrong about the lady doctor, she's really nice. She didn't hurt Anthony. She tried to help him. Just ask Mama."

"Just ask Mama," he mimicked. "So that's what she told you, huh? So, you don't believe your own flesh and blood? Johnny was there. In that emergency room. Don't you forget it."

"Snake, I gotta go."

"Last night, you loved it, didn't you, girl?" Snake managed a grin. "Wanted more, am I right?" Next time he'd go all the way. He'd felt her heart beating so fast, proof that she'd been turned on when she felt his stiff cock pressing against her. "You gonna be beggin' for it once I'm a famous artist with lots of money."

"I just want you to leave me alone, Snake. I swear I'll never tell anybody about last night because you could get in real trouble, but," Stacy continued slowly, "if you do anything like that again, I'll tell them you did it. You could be in trouble already. I mean, I didn't tell them who you were, but what about fingerprints? Can't they find you from your fingerprints?"

"You been watchin' too much TV, girl. They ain't never gonna find me cause I ain't got no fingerprints on file cause I never been arrested. I'm clean." Snake struggled to sit up. "But we ain't finished here. I'm gonna get that motherfuckin' yellow-hair doctor, for your brother, you hear me? No white bitch is getting away with that shit. And you stay away from that black-ass detective cop! That's right, I circled round and seen 'em last night. That's the cop breakin' everybody's balls after Lonnie got his dick shot off!" He shook his head slowly. "Another brother, man, acting like Mr. Important Whitey. And now you, at your fucking white school. Your mama and her fucking job. Got no use for us brothers at all. Fucking white doctors killed your brother, and you don't even give a shit."

"That's not true! You're wrong!" Stacy grimaced, grabbing her sore arm. "I gotta go. I gotta get out of here."

"Yeah, girl, you go. But this ain't settled yet."

Without another word, Stacy backed slowly out the door.

When Laura arrived home, an exhausted looking Steve was waiting for her in the living room. Susan had gone home, and Mikey and the other two children were napping.

"Oh my God, Steve, how did any of this happen?" Laura asked, sinking into the rocking chair.

"I don't know, babe, I don't know. I feel bad about getting Lucy's daughter involved in all this."

"I met Stacy Jones in the hospital," Laura said. "And you know what?"

"What?" Steve said absently.

"Remember the first patient that I had in my physical diagnosis class? Well I found out that Stacy is his sister. And Lucy, your assistant, is his mother. I never would have expected it with their last names being different. And there are so many Jones."

"That's quite a coincidence," Steve said as Laura headed toward the stairs. "Laura, why don't you just come on over here?" He patted the couch beside him. "Sit down for a while. Just let me hold you. Just you and me, babe. Maybe we could listen to some music? It's been a long time."

She hesitated. "Not right now. I promised my mother I'd call her back. And Susan. And didn't you say Detective Reynolds wants to talk to us?"

"Those calls can wait. Come on, Laura. I need you."

"I need you too," Laura stammered as the previous night intruded into her reality. "But, I don't feel well at all."

Upstairs, Laura shut her bedroom door and collapsed on the bed as she tried to focus. She needed to organize the swirl of competing emotions. Too much had happened. Too fast. She called her mother back. She explained what had happened the night before at home, but not what had happened in Montreal. She couldn't think about that right now.

Finally, Laura took a deep breath and dialed Detective Reynolds' number.

John Reynolds arrived promptly at eight accompanied by Morris Willard. When Steve held out his hand for him to shake, Reynolds refused, explaining that he had a cold and didn't want to pass along germs. At the detectives' request they spoke first with Mikey.

"What did you see the strange man do?"

"He did bad things to my baby-sitter," Mikey began. "He was hurting Stacy. Stacy told him to stop."

Laura cringed. "What was he doing?"

"He laid down on top of her, Mommy. She couldn't get up."

"Then what happened, Mikey?" Reynolds softly prodded.

"I snuck down and got his gun. Then I called the police. I dialed the big 'O' like you told me if ever there was a 'mergency."

"The gun was just lying there?" Detective Willard asked.

"Yup, and I took it. Then the bad man came upstairs. In Nattie and Nickie's room first. I was watching. They were both crying and he took Nattie out of her crib and said a swear word. Then he came into my room." Mikey turned to Steve. "I was gonna shoot him, Daddy, I was."

Laura sucked in her breath. The thought of Mikey with a loaded gun made her physically ill. She forced herself to appear calm as Steve reached over and patted Mikey's head.

The detectives took this all in silently. Then Reynolds asked, "So tell me, Mikey, where'd you learn about guns?"

"My friend, Keith, has lots of guns," Mikey beamed. "We practice shooting the bad guys, just like the real cops."

Willard laughed. "Using toy guns, yeah?"

Mikey shrugged. "They're Keith's guns. Mommy doesn't like me to play with guns." He hesitated. "Is the bad man gonna come back?"

"No, son, he won't be back," Steve said.

"That's why the nice detectives are here, honey," Laura added quickly. "They're going to make sure that everything's okay. Now why don't you go ask Mrs. Starke to read you a story?"

Reynolds stood up. "Mikey, you're a brave young man, but you can leave it to us to take care of everything from here, okay?"

Laura offered the detectives some pop and disappeared into the kitchen for glasses and ice while Steve took Mikey upstairs.

"Mrs. Starke?" Detective Reynolds asked when they returned.

"Our live-in baby-sitter," Steve said. "She was away for the weekend."

"So she wasn't here," Willard said, rifling in his notebook.

"What kind of gun was it?" Steve asked.

"Twenty-two," Reynolds said. "Serial number filed off. Saturday night special."

"What does that mean?" Laura asked, hoping to sound innocent.

"Untraceable. There's a test we do, swabbing with some hydrochloric acid that sometimes brings the numbers up, so we're not nearly done yet. You've got to go over it and over it."

Neither Laura nor Steve spoke. Then Laura said, "And so you track the serial number to the owner of the gun, is that it?"

"If we're lucky," said Reynolds. "So let's clarify. You do not own a twenty-two, is that correct?"

"Correct," Steve said.

"So for the time being," Reynolds summarized, "we'll assume Mikey's story. Your unwelcome visitor set his piece down. Unseen, Mikey picks it up, takes it upstairs."

Willard interrupted. "Your kid's lucky he came out alive. Scared the shit out me, waving that piece around like it was a toy."

"Let's hope we find this guy," Reynolds said. "Meantime, Mrs. Nelson, any more trouble with your car, your car tires, anything like that?"

"No," she answered, "not at all. That was a year ago."

It was at that moment that Laura felt her stomach tighten. She suddenly had a feeling that things, instead of getting better, were already much worse.

That uneasy feeling intensified each day as Laura merged back into her medical rotations at City Hospital. On the wards by 6:30 A.M. to draw blood; rounds with the house staff at 8:00; radiology conferences; patient rounds and chart notes; new patient admissions; a sandwich on the run; special procedures; mandatory lectures at 4:00 P.M.; then back to the wards until 6:00 or 7:00. Finally, home to the kids; throw together dinner if they hadn't eaten yet; bathe the kids; read to them; put them to bed; then homework. Except for every third night when she was on call and couldn't come home at all. Those nights she was lucky to get an hour or two of sleep in the women's quarters. No wonder she was anxious and queasy. Or was it that night with David that so unsettled her? She didn't know. By the third week of January, she only knew that she couldn't shake the panicky feeling.

That's when it happened. After a busy day in the delivery room, she'd had to scrub in on one last C-section, and there'd been complications when the young mother almost hemorrhaged to death on the table. It was already nine when Laura changed out of the blue OR scrubs and left the hospital, too impatient to wait for an escort. Shivering, she pulled her collar up, but as she did she sensed movement among the shadows. Telling herself to ignore her paranoia, she suddenly felt something hard pressed between her shoulder blades.

"It's a gun. Just keep your mouth shut so I don't gotta use it. Get the fuck inside the car."

With his free hand, the man opened the door of a rusty old Mustang parked next to her Falcon. Using the barrel of the gun, he shoved her inside the passenger door of his car. It wasn't until Laura dared turn toward him that she saw the smoothly shaved head of a black man. The man who had raped her had had a shaved head, but with lighter skin. Oh God, was it happening again? That knife flashed before her eyes, and she felt her heart pound. She pulled her purse against her, feeling the tangible void. There was nothing inside this time.

"What do you want?" she stammered. "Here, take my purse."

The man slammed the door shut. In the dimly lit lot, she stopped breathing as he kept the gun trained on her as he circled the front of the car to reach the driver's side. Was he limping?

He slid into the car, closed and locked the door. "I wanna talk to you, Mrs. Doctor. Fact is, I been wantin' to talk to you for a long time. Shoulda done it sooner."

"This is a mistake. I'm just a med student." Laura could barely breathe as she stared at the gun pointing at her chest. The car smelled sour, like beer and cigarettes, and her stomach rebelled.

"No mistake, lady. I know who you are. I know where you live: the social worker, the doctor and the fucking brats."

"I'm sure there is some mistake." Laura tried to sound confident, but her voice shook. What had he said about her kids? Her husband? He knew Steve?

"Matter of fact, I seen you that night." He stopped abruptly, expectantly.

"What night? I don't understand?"

"Seen you with Anthony. You 'member him, dontcha? Innocent black boy, dead of some kinda malpractice screw-up after the motherfuckin' riots. Remember now?"

"There were so many casualties from the riots."

"Shut up, bitch! Anthony Diggs. Ring a bell now?"

Laura stammered something unintelligible. She could feel her pupils dilate and her pulse accelerate. She thought she might faint. What did this man want from her? Why did he have his head shaved like Johnny Diggs?

"Yeah that's right. Heard 'bout you first though, from Anthony's bro. Told me all about the doctor lady fuckin' up Anthony in that 'mergency room. Had hair just like you. So it was you."

"It wasn't me, I'm only a student."

"Shut up, bitch." He tilted the gun to touch her breast.

Laura cringed, her hands clutching her purse. She'd heard Johnny Diggs yell at his mother about a yellow-hair doctor. They had mixed her up with somebody else. "It wasn't me, it couldn't have been me!"

"Course it was. I seen you for sure. Drivin' in your little black wagon."

Laura stared at him.

He nodded. "That's right, it was me shot out your tires. Wanted to scare you. Remind you, you ain't safe. Somebody seen you."

"Saw me?"

"Seen you that night, like I said, when I was visitin' Anthony. I even seen your little wagon takin' off that night after my man, Johnny, was shot. You just about run right into me."

Laura made a strangled sound before the words spilled out and her whole body slumped. "He was going to kill me. He had a knife. I didn't mean to kill him!"

He slumped back against the door and stared at her. "It was you," he finally said. "It was you that night. You killed Johnny, my best bro."

Laura sobbed, unable to think. So someone had seen her. She'd always known it deep down.

"I get it now. He was gonna get you, bitch, but you was packin'. Who woulda thought? A white bitch like you? You off'd him and walked outta there, free as a bird. Till I come along."

"He was going to kill me. He had a knife." Laura was sobbing now, her head throbbing. Her whole life destroyed as deep down she always knew it would be.

"You stupid bitch," he said. "I was meanin' Anthony before. I seen you fuckin' with Anthony the time I come with Stacy and her mama. But now I get the rest. You fuckin' iced Johnny. My best bro. Well guess what, bitch, you gonna pay for that, you gonna pay me."

Laura sat stunned, face obscured in hot tears. Incredulous at the stupidity of her blunder, that she had finally blurted out the truth.

"You listen to Snake, lady, or you'll do time for what you did to my bro. Man, I can see it now, 'Snake Rogers solves Diggs murder. Lady doctor ices black youth'. I been in the paper before, I can be there again. Get your hands up now. Do it!"

As Laura complied, Snake rummaged through her purse and her bookbag. "Not carryin' tonight I see."

Next, he patted her down. "Okay, you listen, bitch. I'll tell you what I want. You're Doctor Whitey now, so you can get drugs, pain killer drugs. You know what I mean, narcotics. I need 'em for my fuckin' leg. My mama needs 'em for her back. This way, nobody's gotta pay for 'em."

"But I can't do that. I'm only a student," Laura gasped. Elated that he was not going to kill her, desperate at his demand.

"That so? Well, you're inside that hospital all the time. They got morphine for pain, they got Demerol, other stuff. You so smart, you figure it out."

"But I can't. They keep them locked."

Snake laughed. "Doctor Whitey, don't give me shit unless you want me to turn you in. You got that?"

Laura froze. Her whole world was coming to an end. What should she do? Just get out and turn yourself in, a voice within her screamed.

"You'll figure out a way," he said.

"I'll figure out a way," Laura echoed. She remembered the penicillin she had stolen from the hospital once. How she had simply lifted it from the open cabinet drawer. But narcotics were locked up.

"Now get out. I know where you live out in Highland Park. Next week. Right here in this parking lot. Wait inside your car. I'll be here. You stupid enough to tell anyone, like your asshole husband or the fuckin' cops, you ain't gonna be seein' much of your precious little brats. And it would be my pleasure to fuck up your kid." The hand without the gun rubbed the side of his left lower leg. "Now get the fuck out. And remember what I said about me bein' famous."

Laura lunged for the passenger door, scrambling as fast as she could. Her whole body shook as she fumbled to open her car door and lock herself inside.

At first she just stared, afraid to move. Afraid, just like that night when she'd driven out of this very place. Not unseen, as she had so desperately hoped. Her heart slamming and her whole body shaking, she finally drove out of the lot. Very slowly, not carelessly, like she had that night.

Fear for her children blinded any sense of reason as she drove home, plotting how she could keep Snake Rogers supplied with drugs. She thought of calling the police, only to reject that option. She should have done that two years ago. It was too late now. But should she tell Steve? No, she decided. He would never forgive her for the deception that had become her life.

CHAPTER FORTY-NINE

Steve was not sure he really knew Laura anymore. Except for those occasional nightmares, she used to be a calm, serene woman, but recently she'd become jumpy, nervous, unable to sleep. The nightmares were worse, waking him up out of a dead sleep. Steve knew what was wrong with her. She needed to lighten her load. Hadn't she had enough of this idealized medical career shit? First she damn near dies when a lunatic plows into her. Then she gets stuck in Canada and the house gets broken into, her daughter injured. And what about that Reynolds still tracking her down? Why can't he leave Laura alone?

She must have sensed him staring at her because she looked up from her book. "Some good news, Steve. Next month I'll be able to spend more time at home."

"Why's that?" Steve asked. Don't tell me she's dropping out? Not Laura, giving up her dream? A selfish dream, Steve thought.

"Tomorrow I'm starting a new rotation. Internal medicine at Sinai Hospital. Just think of the time I'll save."

"That's good, babe," Steve said, "only ten minutes away. Maybe we'll have some time for each other?"

"Yes, maybe."

What did she mean by that? Ever since returning from Montreal, Laura had been aloof and evasive, particularly when it came to intimacy. Not that they hadn't had sex, they had. But it was different. She seemed distracted, definitely not enjoying it like the old Laura. He supposed that she worried about getting pregnant. She'd been so upset the last time. He'd suggested that she take the pill, but she'd countered that a medical warning just came out. And being Catholic, she argued that the Pope opposed all birth control except rhythm.

"So let's go to bed early tonight," he said with a hopeful wink.

"I have to study." The usual response, thought Steve with a familiar twinge of bitterness. He flipped on the television, searching for the Pistons game.

The next morning, Laura kissed each of her children on the top of their heads as she got ready to leave. They were settled at the kitchen table as Mrs. Starke poured milk on the boys' Rice Krispies. Kevin liked his drenched — Mikey, just a few drops. The twins ate oatmeal. Mrs. Starke had it all down. A godsend, thought Laura, even though she was expensive, as Steve continued to point out.

Laura drove slowly to her first day at Sinai Hospital, ironically wishing that the commute was longer to give her more time alone to think. She needed to think about how to handle her blackmailer. He'd given her a deadline. Would she have the guts to get him the drugs he demanded? And how to handle Detective Reynolds? Just one day after Snake had shaken her very foundation, Reynolds appeared at City Hospital, standing in the hallway as she left a Pulmonology conference.

"Laura, I've been waiting for you."

"Detective Reynolds, this is a surprise. Do you have some news?"

"Questions, really. I've been over all the transcripts. Let's go somewhere and sit down."

Laura glanced down at her watch. "Uh, okay."

"Don't worry, I won't keep you long. How about a coffee?"

"Okay."

"I'll buy."

Once they settled in the cafeteria, Reynolds came right to the point. "Laura, I'm worried about you. I'm concerned that the incident at your house was directed at you. Some kind of retaliation maybe. That the babysitter may not have been the target. The whole Stacy Jones thing seems too much of a coincidence."

"What do you mean?"

"Johnny Diggs gets killed near the hospital. His brother is your first patient. Now the sister gets assaulted in your house. Why don't you tell me?"

Laura stiffened. "Stacy's mother works for my husband, Detective. She was at my house on an emergency basis. You know all that."

"And?"

"Well, after meeting Stacy following the incident at my house, I realized I had seen her and her mother when they were visiting Anthony Diggs. But the other brother, I just don't know him." She paused. "Never seen him."

"No?"

"No. I'm quite sure."

"What if someone else saw something and put it all together and means to do you harm?"

"I don't know what you mean." She could hear the tremble in her voice.

"Laura, it's no secret I think you saw something that night. No question you were in the vicinity of the Johnny Diggs shooting right after you saw Anthony Diggs at the hospital. My thought is you were too afraid to talk about what you saw, and someone else saw you, and all this trouble is not random, it's targeted. Think about it."

"No," she stammered, vividly remembering the parking lot where Snake had grabbed her, when blackmail took on a human face.

"Then listen to me. I'll tell you what we know. We know that your connection to the Jones family goes beyond coincidence. We know you were at Anthony's bedside the day his brother was killed. In fact, we found a hair, similar to yours, on Johnny Diggs. We have to ask: how did it get there? Another coincidence? You tell me. Then there's the gun. It's not conclusive, but the .22 your son handed to Detective Willard and the .22 used to shoot out your tires is probably the same one. You're a cop as long as me, you don't believe in coincidence. Somebody's out to do you harm. You have to think of the safety of your family."

Laura sucked in her breath. "Detective, I don't know what to say. I guess it is all a coincidence because there's no other explanation. That thing with my tires happened two years ago. What you told me about the gun must be just a fluke."

Reynolds nodded. "Laura, you're a remarkable woman. I just hope to God you're not making a mistake you'll regret forever."

That remark continued to haunt Laura. Detective Reynolds was so close. If only she could just tell him everything. But it was too late. She could not tell him what had happened with Johnny Diggs any more than she could tell him that she was now planning to steal a bottle of Dilaudid, one hundred count if she could, from a hospital medicine cart and parcel it out to Snake Rogers. She had to keep him away from her and her family. If supplying him with drugs would accomplish that, she would take the risk until she figured out some other way. Whether it was a federal crime, whether the FBI would get involved, she just had to take the risk.

When Laura arrived at the hospital, her hands were shaking, and despite the frigid temperature outside, she was drenched in sweat. She had to pull herself together. Think about something else. Something that did not terrify her so. She thought of Steve. Then felt guilty. She knew he was becoming more and more frustrated with her panicky moods and her indifferent responses to his sexual advances. She wanted to blame it on four active kids and a tough class and hospital schedule, not on the real reason, that she was in love with David. Hopeless as that love was. For the last three weeks she had not seen him, and she would not for the next three that she was assigned to Sinai. Worse yet, she'd heard via the hospital grapevine that he'd resigned to become dean at Stanford. Just like he'd said he would do. She would never see him again. And that was that.

The same day that Detective Reynolds had driven off to see Laura Nelson at the end of January, Detective Willard hopped into his own car and drove the black Chevy to the old neighborhood on a hunch. It was just after five and getting dark, but he was sure he'd be able to recognize the kid if he saw him. After two cups of tepid coffee in the Chevy, Willard watched as the kid made his way, limping a bit, down Alexandrine. He got out of the car and started walking toward Snake Rogers. He'd do his own research into the Diggs — Jones — Nelson — 'coincidence.'

"Don't tell me you got the gout," Willard began.

Snake stopped. "Huh?" His eyes were glazed.

"Your leg. You got the gout, or somethin' else happen to you?"

"Come on, man, I don't want trouble."

"That right? So what happened to your leg? Why are you limpin'?"

"Had a little accident at work is all, no big deal."

"That so? Maybe I oughta take you down to the station to check it out."

"No sir," Snake said, trying to sound sincere as he berated himself for sucking up to the pigs. "No need for that, officer." Calling a pig "officer" almost made him puke, but he'd be fucked if the pig hauled him in for some bullshit. They'd print him for sure, and all his plans would turn to shit. Plus, he no longer had a job since he fucked up his leg jumping out that window. No matter, it gave him more time to work on his painting — or "mural" as the newspaper called it.

"You listen to me, punk. I know who you are, Mr. Rogers. My mama knows your mama. I've been busy puttin' two and two together. Stacy Jones lives here. Her brothers used to live here. Now tell me, any chance you made a little visit to Stacy at a babysittin' job recently?"

"I don' know what you're talkin' 'bout. Stacy's away at that big white school her mama sent her to. Ain't got nothin' to do with me."

"Someone left a .22. Ballistics matches the bullet hit somebody else you know. Lonnie Greenwood, right? You get my drift?"

Snake shook his head. "No way, man. I mean, sir."

"Right. And we found bullets by a certain automobile over by the medical school. Am I making sense yet?"

"Don' know what you talkin' about, officer." Snake dropped his eyes to the pavement. "That shit got nothin' to do with me."

"I'm workin' homicide now. Don't have time to mess with haulin' you in, but it don't mean I don't hear things. People seen you sellin' these days. Maybe a visit from the narcotic squad will jar your memory, Mr. Snake."

Just then a rusted Mustang slowed, then drove on. "Bingo," Willard whistled. How many rusted out Mustangs in Detroit? Probable lots, but this a coincidence? Willard smirked.

CHAPTER FIFTY

MARCH 1970

On the first Tuesday in March, David excused himself from surgical rounds and headed toward his Cadillac parked in the hospital lot. He'd spent the past week finalizing assignments on the surgical service and providing senior residents with the recommendations they needed to go out on their own. He had only one more thing to do before he and Cynthia climbed aboard the TWA flight to San Francisco, to the lovely campus of Stanford University in Palo Alto, California. Yes, Cynthia had chosen to go with him.

Despite his promise, he'd come to say good-bye to Laura. How could he not? The drive to Sinai Hospital in the northwest section of Detroit was a blur as David relived again their only night together. Every nerve in his body went numb as he pulled into the doctors' parking lot. For a long while he sat motionless as total hopelessness swept over him.

Finally, he climbed out of the car, denouncing himself for not having the strength to just drive away. That's what he'd promised. That's what she wanted. She did not want to see him. But he simply could not leave without saying good-bye. What if she had changed her mind? No, he cautioned himself as he strode toward the doctor's entrance. Laura would never jeopardize her family. With a surge of despair, he realized that he'd lived his life in one night, that snowy Friday in Montreal.

*   *   *

He strode through the doctors' entrance with a sense of disorientation. Sinai was so different from City Hospital. There were no overcrowded, multiple-bed wards, only private and semi-private rooms. The corridors were spacious, the equipment shiny and new. Hushed tones pervaded, and the staff was polite; they even called the students 'Doctor'. Yet David knew that even Sinai was changing as the more affluent of northwest Detroit switched their allegiance to Providence Hospital in Southfield and William Beaumont in Royal Oak. The fact was, downtown Detroit would never be the same after the riots. It was a watershed moment, a legacy of devastation. Would any Detroiter ever forget July 23, 1967, the night their city erupted in violence? He certainly would not.

The chatty clerk at the nursing station told David that Dr. Nelson was doing a procedure on a patient. Heading directly toward this patient's room, David watched silently as Laura deftly inserted a wide bore catheter into an elderly man's subclavian vein. She had readily located the course of the vein and had perfectly judged just the right angle to penetrate the large vein that lay protected under her patient's collarbone. David admired her natural skill; not many third-year students could master this procedure.

He did not interrupt until she had finished taping the IV lines to the man's frail arm. All the while she carried on a one-way conversation to reassure her ashen, anxious patient. The old man's mouth and nose were obscured by the plastic oxygen mask so he was unable to respond, and Laura, aware of that fact, murmured reassuring words.

"Laura."

She jerked, practically dropping the tray containing her used instruments. David's voice? Here at Sinai? Not possible.

"Laura, it's me," he said softly from the doorway to the private room.

Laura turned and stared in disbelief. He looked thinner. His hair shorter; a tinge more gray.

"C'mon," he said softly, taking the tray from her and setting it down on the patient's table. "Let's find a place to talk." He led her across the hall into a small empty visitor's lounge.

They sat side by side on a vinyl-covered sofa, bodies barely touching; Laura remained silent. David searched her face for as long as he dared.

Laura looked away. "You shouldn't be here," she said finally in a hoarse voice.

"I know, but I had to come."

"Why?"

"I remember my promise to you. I live with it every day. Every night. I'll never betray it."

Laura looked up slowly, avoiding his eyes.

"I'm leaving tomorrow for Stanford. I had to tell you myself." He paused. "Maybe you already know."

She nodded. "You're sure this is what you want?"

"You know it's not what I want, but I can't think of anything else to do."

Laura held her breath as she felt him inch closer. She breathed in his scent. She pressed closer, her heart aching.

She heard him say, "If I stay here, I won't be able to keep myself from trying to see you."

"I'll be leaving Detroit next year when I graduate," Laura whispered.

"It's too long, a whole year. I can hardly get through a whole day." David had slipped his hand against her thigh. "I just came to say good-bye."

Laura finally looked at him directly. When she did, she was blinded by tears.

"Please don't cry," David whispered.

A nurse appeared in the doorway.

"Dr. Nelson, are you finished with Mr. Korey's chart?"

"Just a moment, please," Laura answered shakily. The nurse left as Laura wiped tears from her eyes.

"Why is it like this?" she asked. Then, "You're doing the right thing."

"There is no right thing, Laura. I wish to God that we could be together."

"Don't, please don't. It can't happen."

"Laura, life can change anytime. The memory of you is all I've got."

"Dr. Nelson, we need you to complete Mr. Korey's procedure report." The nurse sounded impatient. "He's going down to radiology."

"Of course." Laura rose. With a shaking hand, she recorded the placement of the subclavian catheter and signed the report.

After the nurse left, Laura remained standing. "Maybe you should go now." She tried to keep her voice steady, keep the tears from gushing, keep her heart from exploding.

David rose from the sofa and turned toward her. "Good-bye, Laura. I love you."

He leaned forward and kissed her lightly on the cheek, grasping both of her hands in his. "I love you more than life."

Willing herself with all her might to just let him go, she whispered, "Good-bye, David."

CHAPTER FIFTY-ONE

"Blue Hawaii" played on the radio as Steve drove back downtown to handle an incident with one of his clients. Hawaii, so exotic compared to the dregs of Detroit. One day he'd like to take the kids there, but first he'd promised Laura he would take her to Las Vegas to see Elvis Presley live. That's how they'd met. He'd been working in a music store on campus when she came in, shopping for the sound track of *Viva Las Vegas*. Love at first sight, they'd always said, and it was true that from the moment he'd met Laura, he'd known that he would marry her. Now here they were five years later. Two careers. Four kids and she's pregnant again. That meant putting Elvis off indefinitely, or at least until she started to make money. Mrs. Starke was expensive, and he was sick of having someone living with them in their house.

And Laura was pregnant again. For the life of him, he couldn't figure her out. Last time she'd been so upset. This time she seemed okay, maybe even pleased. Over her objection, they'd agreed that she'd start birth control as soon as this baby was born.

Enough of personal problems, Steve thought as he flashed his county ID allowing him to park in the secure lot next to the Tenth Precinct. His promotion to supervisor hadn't taken him out of the field entirely. He still maintained a cadre of his own clients, and today he was fighting for Leona Rogers. He considered her a prototype of the "little people" pitted against the "system." She had been brought in with a crowd of people in a drug raid downtown.

Depending on how long the cops were going to hold her, he'd have to put her young kids in foster care since her oldest son was sitting in jail. Leona had no money to bail him out.

Steve took a deep breath before rapping sharply on the dirty sliding panel. The top of the worn oak counter was just below eye level and the entire desk was enclosed by protective Plexiglas, extending up from the floor to several feet above Steve's head. He could see his breath condense into a sudden white circle in front of him.

"I'm here about Leona Rogers," Steve said to the desk sergeant. "I just need a time frame so I can get her kids placed if need be."

"Lemme talk to my supervisor." The desk sergeant grunted and reached for the phone just as Steve felt a hand clamp a firm grip onto his left arm. Stiffening, he half expected to be tossed out.

"Mr. Nelson, what brings you into the station house?"

Steve wheeled around to face Detective Reynolds.

"Detective Reynolds," Steve said, sagging with relief. "I'm trying to get some information about one of my clients."

"Come with me," Reynolds nodded and escorted Steve upstairs to the bullpen where the detectives' desks were crammed together under harsh fluorescent lights. The room was crowded with file cabinets and vibrated with loud voices and ringing phones.

"Here, have a seat." Reynolds gestured to a straight-back metal chair next to a desk that was covered with piles of paper, a wide gray typewriter, and empty paper coffee cups. "I'll see what I can find out for you. What's the name?"

Steve sat down. "Leona Rogers. You guys hit a joint over by Lafayette Park."

Reynolds picked up his phone and dialed. "Reynolds here. Can you check the log, let me know on one Leona Rogers." He paused. "Uh huh. Uh huh. Okay, thanks." Reynolds hung up.

Reynolds leaned back in his chair, causing a drawn out squeak which filled the silence between them. When he spoke his voice was flat. "Here's the story. She's got a boy goin' down on drug charges. Claims she was there trying to get bail money from the homies. Doesn't matter now, he's gonna do time."

"That Leona doesn't need," Steve stopped as they both lifted their gaze to Morris Willard, who was walking into the room holding a box of donuts.

Steve's shoulders slumped. "One step forward, two steps back."

"It's people like you who make a difference." Pointing to the donuts, Reynolds said, "Want one?"

Steve shook his head.

After an awkward silence, Reynolds coughed. "Hey, you just keep up the good work, and say hello to your wife. Not much longer to graduation. Huh?"

"One more year," Steve replied.

"How's your son? He start school yet?"

"Finishing kindergarten."

"Great. So whattaya think of the Pistons?"

Before he could say anything, the phone on Reynolds' desk rang.

"Got it," the detective said into the mouthpiece. "Sounds good. Thanks."

Reynolds hung up and smiled. "Mr. Nelson, your client will be released in a few minutes. If you want you can meet her downstairs."

Steve stood up. "Thanks."

"No problem. You remember Detective Willard."

"Detective."

"Mr. Nelson. How's the family?"

"Fine. Excuse me, detectives. Thanks for your help."

"Small world, ain't it?" Willard said once Steve had left.

"Shrinkin' every damn day," Reynolds answered. "So how'd it go in court?"

Willard smiled. "Judge slapped Mr. Snake Rogers with two

years in Jackson. Possession and dealing. Narcs moved in after my call. Score one for cleaning up the old neighborhood. Interesting thing came up in court. Apparently, Mr. Snake fancies himself some kinda big-time artist. Tried to impress the judge. Didn't work."

"I feel bad for the kid. I saw that painting of his after it got written up somewhere. Wasn't half bad."

"Had no idea you was an art lover."

"A lover of life. I'm glad you got that Rogers kid off the street. Still think he had somethin' to do with that .22 we found at the Nelsons? You ever shake him down 'bout that limp you told me about? Or get anything on that car, a Mustang, if I recall?"

"Nope. Since he's goin' in the slammer, I'm putting it on the back burner." He opened the box and picked up a chocolate donut.

That night Laura lingered in the parking lot, waiting for Snake. So far she'd gotten away with stealing Dilaudid when she'd been at Sinai. Nobody had questioned her. She'd simply lifted a bottle of 100 Dilaudid tablets. She'd given Snake fifty the first time. She had the last fifty with her, which he was supposed to collect tonight. Snake had specified 7:00 P.M.

At 8:30, she was still waiting. She passed the time worrying about how she would get the next installment of narcotics. Just the thought burned a hole in her stomach.

At 9:30 Laura started up her station wagon and headed home. She hadn't even bothered to call Steve. She'd been late so many nights that he no longer bothered to worry. Since they had Mrs. Starke to watch the kids, he didn't even seem to care.

The following morning Laura crossed over the Chrysler Freeway to meet Stacy Jones for lunch in Greek Town. After their meeting in Natalie's hospital room, Laura had invited Stacy to tour the med school so she could get a feel for what it might be like to go into medicine. Stacy had been so excited that Laura started to feel like a big sister to this bright young lady, and they'd agreed to meet for lunch when Stacy was home on spring break. Now there was another more urgent reason Laura wanted to see Stacy. That Snake guy who was blackmailing her had said that he was best friends with Johnny Diggs. So wouldn't Stacy know him? Maybe she'd know why Snake hadn't shown up last night.

"Hey, are you pregnant?" Stacy met her on the sidewalk outside the Plaka Café.

"Yes, I am," she said, taking Stacy's arm to lead her inside. "Just over four months, and I can't believe I've started to show this early."

"Wow, five kids and med school." Stacy stopped short. "Oh, oh, what if you have twins? That'd make six, just like my mama."

"I sincerely hope it's not twins this time," Laura said, patting her abdomen.

Stacy kept prattling as Laura reflected that for the second time, while pregnant, she had good reason to be scared that she could leave all her children motherless. Suddenly, she jerked as she heard the word "Snake." Laura suddenly paid attention.

"Actually, my brother Johnny's best friend. He'll be in jail for two years. Drugs."

"Excuse me, Stacy, I've lost you." Laura tried to keep her voice steady. "Who are you talking about?"

"Sorry," she said. "His real name is Ray Rogers. Everybody calls him "Snake" except Mama. She hates that name."

"Rogers?" Laura repeated. Yes, he'd said his name was Snake Rogers.

"Know what?" Stacy asked, frowning at Laura. "Hey, are you okay?"

"I'm okay. What?"

"I used to have a crush on him. Then something happened." Stacy did not elaborate, but Laura was too distracted to notice.

Laura's life took a turn for the better once she confirmed that Snake Rogers was in jail. Surprisingly, Steve corroborated Stacy's story. One night at dinner he'd told her about his client, Leona Rogers, and Laura had innocently asked if Leona had a son. "Yes," Steve said before unloading his concerns about Leona now that her oldest son was in jail for possession of drugs. Could his arrest have anything to do with that Dilaudid she'd stolen for him? If so, why hadn't Snake already implicated her? She'd started to sweat, and Steve looked at her strangely asking if she was okay.

But the days went by without a visit from the FBI or the DEA or the Detroit Police. Drawing upon her considerable will and discipline, Laura fought harder and harder to keep her life compartmentalized. Safe compartments: the kids, Steve, medical school rotations, chit chat with the girls, Stacy.

The closed compartment, the horrible chamber in her mind that contained violence and darkness: killing Johnny Diggs, even though in self-defense; grabbing a bottle of Dilaudid off a pharmacy cart. Someday she'd be caught, wouldn't she? They kept such tight restrictions on narcotics. Someday there'd be an investigation, and she'd be found out. She'd end up in prison, or at the very least, barred forever from practicing medicine. She tried to keep this chamber tightly closed, and only when she was physically and mentally exhausted did her efforts fail and the nightmares break through her defenses. Each time, Laura ended up in jail, separated from her children and her bitter, horrified husband. Poor Steve. Her nightmares didn't even wake him up anymore.

A third compartment: David. She rarely allowed herself to open it, but when she did, she could actually hear his voice, feel his every sensuous touch. She found herself letting this compartment open up that one hour a week when Steve watched the kids so she could attend Mass at the Church of the Precious Blood. Sacrilegious, she supposed. But she could only hope that God would forgive her as she relived every detail of her night with David. At the closing hymn, Laura clamped shut that forbidden compartment and left the church to return to her family. It gave her comfort that David had once been a Catholic.

CHAPTER FIFTY-TWO

SEPTEMBER 1970

Patrick David Nelson arrived right on schedule at City Hospital. It was a relatively uneventful delivery in comparison to his twin sisters'. Laura was on a psychiatric rotation, meaning no night call, and she'd been uncommonly relaxed.

When her three best friends organized a catered dinner on her last night on the maternity ward, Laura was delighted. She'd just finished breastfeeding when Rosie arrived, followed by Susan, both with baby gifts galore. In spite of the stress in all their lives, tonight was a night for celebration. Would Laura's friends notice the hint of hazel flecks in her baby's eyes? Steve's eyes were a light blue and hers were green, but David's were brown with those same distinctive hazel flecks. It would be some time before she could tell if Patrick's eyes would lose the blueness common to newborns, and that was when those brown hues that seemed so obvious to her now might raise questions. Also, all the other children had had fuzzy blonde hair as infants. Patrick had lots of hair, too, but his was chestnut brown.

Vicky arrived last, just as trays laden with an array of scrumptious-looking food were wheeled into the narrow hospital room.

"You just missed little Patrick," Rosie announced as Vicky breezed into the room.

"He's so adorable," Susan added, shaking her head. "But how are you going to manage one more baby, Laura?"

Laura just laughed. "Vicky, I just want you to know, my baby has lots of hair."

"Alecia's hair is still in the fuzzy phase," Vicky said, reaching into her purse for a stack of pictures of her one-year-old daughter, "but she's madly adorable anyway."

"What do you do, hire a photographer to follow the baby around all day?" Rosie laughed.

"Very funny. I guess Raymond goes a little crazy with the camera," Vicky grinned. "Oh, speaking of Raymond, he unloaded a juicy tidbit of gossip at dinner last night."

"And?" Rosie encouraged. Vicky and Raymond were socially connected. Rosie liked to say that Vicky's news often predated the *Detroit Free Press*.

"Well, girls, it seems quite a scandal is developing out in California. You remember Ruth Davis, Raymond's law partner?" Vicky paused for effect. "Well, she's come out of the woods, or the closet, or whatever you call it. She's a lesbian."

"Really? That must have caused quite a stir in that conservative firm," Susan remarked.

"It did. But get this. Her lover is none other than Cynthia Monroe! Yes, Dr. Monroe's wife. Now Ruth has moved to California to be with Cynthia."

"Mama mia," Rosie interrupted, "that's unbelievable."

"Cripes," Susan said. "Where does that leave Dr. Monroe?"

Laura didn't say a word.

"On his own," Vicky continued. "Raymond had offered to take some paperwork for Ruth to sign since he was going to California. Anyway, he couldn't get her on the phone, so he went to the address she'd given the firm, and Cynthia Monroe actually answered the door."

"On his own?" Laura whispered so low that no one heard her.

"Well, Ruth told Raymond outright that she was living there with Cynthia. Things hadn't worked out in California for Cynthia with her husband. He moved out to some condo or apartment or something, and then Ruth moved in with her."

"How cozy," Rosie said, swallowing the last of her Vernor's ginger ale.

"I have to say my husband is not very perceptive." Vicky was enjoying herself. "He didn't think anything of it. He just left the paperwork for Ruth's signature and said good-bye. But by the time Raymond got back to his hotel, there was a message from Ruth saying that she had to talk to him."

"Get to the point, will you?" Rosie demanded between bites of smoked salmon.

"Hey, these little round black things, very tasty," Susan cut in.

"The little round black things are caviar," Vicky explained. "Have a little vodka with it."

Rosie's pager went off, interrupting the chatter. "Damn, gotta go to the delivery room," she announced, standing up. "I hate obstetrics. No offense, girls, but I'm never having kids, it's just not for me. Vick, finish the story so I can answer this page."

"Well, here's the bottom line, girls. They met for dinner, and Ruth told Raymond that she was a lesbian. That she and Cynthia were 'involved'. That was the word she used."

Rosie sat back down.

"It's hard to believe," Susan said. "Cynthia Monroe?"

"As you can imagine, Raymond's firm wants no hint of scandal. So girls, not a word of this outside this room. I'm only telling you since we all know Dr. Monroe so well."

"Whew!" Rosie got up. "Later, girls, I gotta go pop a baby out."

Laura arranged the cutlery on her tray, not looking up as three sets of eyes observed her with curiosity.

CHAPTER FIFTY-THREE

DECEMBER 1970

By December, Laura Nelson, the twenty-six-year-old senior med-ical student, and Stacy Jones, the seventeen-year-old high school senior, were quite close. The ominous cloud of Snake Rogers dark-ening their lives had dissipated. Laura would drive over to St. Mary-of-the-Woods Academy and pick up Stacy about once a month. They'd have dinner, usually at a nearby Chinese restaurant, or sometimes they'd go for pizza or pasta, but never once had Stacy returned to the Nelson home on Puritan. Occasionally Laura would bring Mikey and Kevin, and sometimes they'd include Sharon, Stacy's younger sister, who was now a freshman at the Academy. But usually it was just the two of them, enjoying each other's com-pany away from the stress of the hospital and kids for Laura, and the Academy's advanced placement classes for Stacy. Tonight, they were eating at Café Italiano.

Stacy had maintained a near perfect grade point average dur-ing her years at St. Mary's. There was little doubt she'd receive a college scholarship, and Stacy and Laura talked at length about the opportunities ahead. Much to Laura's delight, Stacy was still inter-ested in med school. They talked of college options, and they talked about racial issues, trying to come to grips with the preju-dices that were everywhere. Today, a Thursday in early December, they talked about the future.

"Laura, you know I'll really miss you after you graduate."

Laura smiled. "Hey, maybe you'll end up in Florida when I'm an intern there. We're going down this year for Christmas. Finally the kids will get to spend time with their grandparents."

Laura counted the days until she left for Florida. Snake would not be out of jail for 18 months, and every day she began to feel less scared that the Dilaudid that she'd given him would be traced to her. If only Stacy and her sisters could get out of Detroit too.

"That's great. I did include University of Miami on my list of applications," Stacy said.

"Well, I'm betting on University of Michigan for sure, with a good shot at Harvard and Georgetown. And what were the others we talked about?"

"Cornell, UCLA, and Case Western Reserve," Stacy said.

Laura took a bite of her primavera. "You'll have lots of choices, Stacy."

"I hope so. Mama will pressure me to go to Harvard or Cornell if I get in, but I'm leaning toward U of M so I can be close to home."

"C'mon now, we've talked about this before. You need to move on, get more experience, more exposure," Laura counseled. "I know it's uncomfortable, but you need to push yourself. Put Harvard, Georgetown, and Cornell as priority choices and the others as back-ups, okay?"

Stacy smiled. "Okay, Doctor Laura. You know, I feel that I have a real advantage over the other girls because of you. The counselors at the school are okay, but you know exactly what I need to do. Common sense stuff."

They laughed. "I don't know about that. But I do know that you're talented and that it's you, nobody else, who must set your course. You'll do so much for your family and yourself if you push yourself hard enough. Look at the impact you've already had on your sisters. They want to be just like you."

Stacy beamed. "I'm so proud of them. The nuns were telling me just yesterday how well Sharon was doing. It's tough to be one of only two black girls in a class of fifty."

"I'm sure that's true," Laura answered.

"How many black girls in your med school class?"

"Just one out of 150 students. She's my best friend. But you know what, Susan is tough."

"Not surprising if she comes from a neighborhood like mine, right?"

"At least Sharon's had you as a role model. By the way, Steve tells me your mom is planning to move."

"She is so excited about it! The girls are a little scared, especially Rachel. She's twelve, and our neighborhood is the only one she's ever known."

"But the violence is still there, it's dangerous to stay."

"I know. Mama told me that she's almost saved enough to put a down payment on a house out in the northwest, maybe somewhere around where you live. The sooner, the better. We all thought that things would get better after they cleaned up from the riots and put up some new buildings, but things only got worse and worse. Nobody I know from school goes downtown to shop or to concerts or anything."

"It's just so sad," Laura said slowly, "to see a city die. It's like those riots beat the life right out of it."

"And out of some people, too," Stacy added.

"It's Christmas Eve and eighty-five degrees. Doesn't that seem weird?" Laura said to Steve as they sat soaking in the Florida sun, wriggling their toes in the warm white sand of Anna Maria Island. The gulf was calm and the water reflected the glorious blue of the sky. "Palm trees and beaches instead of ice and snow."

The children played among the lapping waves as Mikey recruited help for his sand castle.

"Honey, are you really okay with moving down here?" Laura asked. "My interviews went well, and I think I'll get matched to my first internship choice. Matter of fact, Tampa was pushing me to commit right away."

"Whatever's best. You decide."

"But what about you? I feel so selfish. Moving to Florida, close to my parents. What are you going to do?"

"Find a job."

"You think it'll be that easy?"

"They need social workers everywhere, right? Besides, I can't wait to get out of Detroit, even though I actually think I did some good. Leona Rogers and a few others, was proof of that." He paused. "She was like my gauge. If I could help her navigate the system, I knew I was on the right track. And she's okay, even though that Snake kid of hers is in jail. Some of the others are more than okay, so I'm okay too. I'm not worried about work. Matter of fact I was thinking about going into something else, my old major, communications, maybe."

Laura cringed at the mention of Leona's son. She hadn't even heard Steve's last remark. She just had to get out of Detroit while he was still in jail. Once she was far away from that city, all her nightmares would surely cease.

"Do you mind that we'll be so far from your parents?"

"My parents?" Steve shot a sidewise look at his wife. "Are you kidding? How often do we see them anyway? It's your parents who'll help us out with the kids."

Steve pointed to the baby gurgling in the portable crib they'd taken to the beach. "Look at the little one. He's going to love growing up in Florida." Steve leaned over and kissed Laura again before pulling himself up and out of the beach chair. "Kevin, come on over here. Let's help your brother build a big sand castle!"

Once they moved to Florida everything would be different. She would make a point to spend more time with Steve. Go out with him without the kids on a regular basis. She marveled that something had happened to Steve after Patrick was born. Even though he had not been pleased with her last pregnancy, he ended up paying more attention to her youngest son than he had to any of the kids. It was like Patrick was a new lease on life.

Laura smiled as Kevin came running over to grab the red pail that Steve held out. Such a charming child that strangers would come up just to pat his curly head. He adored the attention so much he was on the verge of being quite spoiled, but Laura didn't mind. He was in that deprived middle child position. Trying to keep up with six-year-old Mikey was hopeless, and his younger twin sisters were also tough competition, and now there was Patrick. She watched contentedly as Kevin happily filled the pail with the powdery sand, and Nicole rushed to bully her way into the center of the boys. That left Natalie alone along the shore until she toddled over to the empty chair beside Laura, who scooped her into her arms. If only Steve could conquer his demons and allow himself to open his heart to Natalie and Nicole. As the months passed, Steve's detachment from them was getting more and more noticeable. All due to that fateful day when a pair of ten-year-old twin boys squabbled over their dog.

CHAPTER FIFTY-FOUR

SUNDAY, MAY 30, 1971

Graduation day. The culmination of four years of grueling effort. Laura Nelson, graduating with honors, was near the top of her class.

A perfect Michigan spring day, the sun bright, the air a gentle warm. The university garden would be resplendent with magnificent color, a haven of beauty within the tumultuous inner city; the garden a rare place of tranquility among the remains of the burnt-out, still ravaged surroundings. The ceremonies would take place outside under a big white tent with the usual pomp and circumstance: the doctoral robes with the traditional hoods that displayed the rich green school color, the recitation of the Hippocratic Oath, the students' friends and family congratulating them.

At the Nelson's everyone had finally arrived: Laura's parents; both siblings, Ted and Janet; and even Steve's parents. Thanks to her mother and sister, all five Nelson children were dressed and ready to go. This gave her a few moments alone. For Laura the impossible had been accomplished. Four years. Three babies. The internship of her choice. Her dream was coming true. By this afternoon she would be a physician. So why did she feel so unsettled? So horribly incomplete? In the midst of the gaiety in the Nelson household, Laura felt as if her world was falling apart.

She would see David today, that was it.

David would be the keynote speaker at graduation. He was also scheduled to receive an honorary doctoral degree. For the past two weeks, Laura had known she would see him, and she had tried to suppress the swirl of emotions, to bury them deep down somewhere. Until now, she'd succeeded. As she stood in her bedroom preparing to change into her graduation outfit, her feelings collided violently. She was deeply torn by a desire to see him alone, if only for a few minutes, and by an absolute dedication to her family on this special day.

Thankfully, there were enough relatives around to handle and dress the children. Everyone was bustling about trying to help. Laura overheard both her mother and her mother-in-law asking Steve if she was okay. They were concerned that she seemed so distant, and as her mother put it, so "un-Laura."

"Just exhausted," Steve answered. "What with final exams and parties and getting ready to move." The others murmured in agreement, though the concerned expression on Peg Whalen's face belied her mute acceptance.

Laura sat at the edge of her bed. Over the past year, she'd received a bulletin from Stanford in her mail slot each week. Tucked inside the back cover was always a single typed page: David's schedule. If he was to be away from Palo Alto, his itinerary was also included. Nothing more, except for his signature at the bottom. So Laura had always known just where David was and how to contact him. Sometimes the longing to do so had been so strong that her fingers started dialing.

She had never completed a call. They had not spoken since that day at Sinai Hospital, but Laura knew the silence must break between them today. It was only through Vicky that Laura knew of his separation from Cynthia. What would he say when they saw each other face-to-face? In public, she reminded herself, not in private.

Would his wife be there with him? She didn't know. She hoped not. She knew they were separated. Yet that was not public knowledge in Detroit, so she might come just to deter rumors. Detroit's socialites would expect her to appear beside her husband as he delivered the keynote graduation speech, wouldn't they? No,

Laura told herself. David would not allow her to be with him today. Not today.

"We're going to be late!" Steve called. With a slight start, she pushed her thoughts into the chasm inside her, rose from the bed, and ran a brush through her hair.

"I'll be ready in a minute," she called back, as much to herself as to Steve.

She wore a creamy white dress with a full skirt that came just above her knees. Her hair was combed with a simple part on the side with fluffy bangs covering most of her forehead. White sling-back heels accented her legs. Though she did not feel that way, she looked young and innocent as she walked into her crowded living room lined with folding chairs to accommodate her relatives.

"You look just lovely, honey," Carl Whalen appeared at his daughter's side, embracing her.

"Thanks, Daddy," she murmured, returning his embrace with a smile. Her father's gray hair had thinned, and his girth had thickened, but his ever-ready smile still came quick. "It wouldn't be the same if you and Mom weren't here."

Laura glanced around and noted with satisfaction that the children looked fresh and perfect, thanks to her mother and sister. The boys were dressed in short navy blue suits and white short-sleeved shirts with snap-on bow ties, while the girls wore matching white dresses, embroidered in lilac, and white patent leather shoes. The twins, as Laura had anticipated, hovered around her mother, especially Natalie, always her mother's favorite. From the moment of her parents' arrival, the twins had climbed all over Peg and Carl Whalen. It was also interesting, and sad, to watch them stay away from Steve's parents.

As for Steve, he looked tired, even haggard. Most of the work for their move to Florida had fallen to him. Steve had insisted that Laura join in the festivities with her classmates as he excused himself to pack. As the graduating class of 1971 celebrated on an evening cruise to Belle Isle on the Detroit River, Steve loaded furniture into the rented U-Haul. When the class president stepped up to make the toasts, Laura had wandered off to stand alone at the prow, where a cold, metal object slipped unnoticed from her hand into the deep waters. Tomorrow Steve planned to drive the U-Haul south with her brother. Carl and Peg would drive Mikey and Kevin in the Pontiac, while Laura, Janet, and the three younger kids would follow in the Falcon. After one overnight stop, they'd be in their new rented house on Davis Island in Tampa. Tonight would be their last night in this house.

She approached her mother, who stood by the door with waiting arms.

"Baby, I'm so proud of you," Peg Whalen managed to say before tears glistened on her tanned cheeks. Ted, taller than anyone in the room and quite handsome, began to clap. Janet, always his partner in crime, followed. Like Ted, she was tall and curly-haired. By the time Laura and her mother had embraced, the kids were all applauding too.

Overall, it was good to be leaving Detroit. So many memories: some lovely, some wonderful, some horrible and frightening. Her mind occasionally flooded with images of the rape, the murder, those awful moments with Snake Rogers, the narcotics she had stolen for him. It would all stop when she got to Florida. It just had to.

Today, of, course, she would encounter Susan's dad, Detective Reynolds. Well, she would try to avoid him in the crowd scene. She would see David. Would he seek her out?

Laura was silent during the ride into downtown Detroit with Steve and his parents. The senior Nelsons were tense and polite. Helen seemed sedated, as if she were in some kind of chemical straightjacket. Laura suspected she was on a neuroleptic, maybe Haldol, to control her emotions. Laura wished that Aunt Hazel had come, but she'd sent a postcard from Madrid, full of apologies.

Seated in the car, Laura could not help but think back over the past four years. The memory of Anthony Diggs, her very first patient, would be embedded in her consciousness forever, along with his brother Johnny, her assailant, and her victim. Now their lovely sister, Stacy, was her friend and had promised to be at graduation. Laura was relieved that Lucy's family would soon be moving to the outer city limits, away from the ghetto.

As Steve pulled the car into the parking lot surrounded by barbed wire, Laura shivered.

CHAPTER FIFTY-FIVE

The graduating class was scurrying to assemble in the proper order, which seemed an impossible goal. Laura and Vicky created a stir as they approached with their small children in tow. Vicky was gorgeous as usual. As valedictorian, she had to make a speech, and Laura wondered how she could be so nonchalant as she frolicked in line with her husband and daughter. Laura was tense. Maybe that was why Natalie had clung to her. All Laura had to do was to walk up and accept her diploma, but her knees were buckling and her stomach churning.

"Laura, what's wrong with you?" Susan slipped out of place and stood beside her. "You look like you've seen a ghost."

"I'm okay," Laura said. "Really, Susan, all I've got to do is walk up the aisle, right?"

"Right. Just take it easy," Susan took Laura's hand and gave it a little squeeze. "Guess who's lurking over there?"

"Where?"

Laura followed Susan's gaze to the tell-tale red hair. "Tim Robinson."

"Let's hope Rosie doesn't see him. She has never forgiven him for coming on to you in Montreal. Funny, isn't it? With her outrageous flirtations."

Laura groaned. "Maybe I shouldn't have mentioned it. It wasn't such a big deal."

"Well, it sure put him in the dog house. Oh, oh," Susan

pointed. "We're going to see Rosie in action. She's marching over there."

They both watched as Tim swung around and thrust an armload of long-stemmed red roses at Rosie.

"Would you look at that," Susan sighed. "They're kissing."

The graduates proceeded slowly toward the entrance to the white tent. Laura finally saw Stacy, who looked beautiful in a slim red skirt and matching silk blouse. Her hair hung long and loose in the style of the Supremes.

Stacy saw her and gestured excitedly. Laura waved back and pointed to the area where Steve and the rest of the family had headed. She didn't want Stacy to sit by herself in this crowd.

The procession moved slowly, deliberately. The traditional *Pomp and Circumstance* came blasting forth from the university orchestra, exciting the crowd. The faculty followed the graduating students. Will Cunningham was in their midst, having been named assistant professor. Then came the department chairmen, the board of directors, and the invited speakers. The last among them, flanked by the dean of the medical school and the president of the university, was Dr. David Monroe, the honorary degree recipient.

David looked regal in the long black robe with edges embroidered in the crimson and gold colors of Harvard, his alma mater, the doctoral hood with its slash of red draped dramatically over his broad shoulders. The traditional mortar cap obscured much of his face, but his expression was somber, even plaintive. Only a fringe of hair could be seen peeking through on either side. Laura allowed herself the briefest glance as he passed by her row of seats.

The ceremony proceeded with the welcome by Dean Burke and the invocation. Vicky delivered the valedictory speech as if she were a professional speaker, without a trace of nervousness. It was then time for the honorary degree recipient to speak. Laura held her breath as David mounted the podium.

He removed the black mortarboard cap and with a clear steady voice addressed the graduating class. Laura heard everything and nothing. She felt as if each word were spoken to her and for her, though she had no idea what he was actually saying. It was his tone, his inflection, as if he were talking directly to her in a secret language that she alone could interpret. Laura couldn't breathe. Tears welled in her eyes, and she could do nothing to stop them from flowing. She didn't have a handkerchief or a tissue. She didn't care. One contact slipped out of focus. It didn't matter.

Later, Laura heard that it had been an awe-inspiring speech. The entire class rose for a standing ovation as David concluded. As if in a trance, she rose, too. And then she sat back down with everyone. The Hippocratic Oath followed. Laura didn't recite with the rest of the class, she was too overwhelmed. Seeing David again, hearing him speak after all of these months, she'd had no idea how she would really react. She wondered how he felt. No, she knew.

The graduates proceeded one by one to receive their diplomas from the dean. Accept the diploma. Shake hands and leave the stage without tripping or falling down. Laura forced herself to move forward when her name was called.

David stood next to Dean Burke as she walked up onto the stage. Every cell in her body quivered. She prayed she could do this. Yes, she was doing it. As she stepped aside after the obligatory handshake with the dean, diploma in hand, David stepped forward slightly. He took her hand and pressed it between both of his. This slight movement was imperceptible to most of the congregation, but the dean noticed. Maybe whoever was behind her in line did, too. She didn't care.

David looked directly into Laura's eyes, a stab of anguish crossing his face. What happened after that Laura would never recall. Somehow she'd made it off the stage and into the jostling crowd.

"There she is!" shouted Ted over the din of the celebrants. At six foot three, he was tall enough to spot Laura. "Come on, Mikey. Let's be the first ones to give her a big hug!"

Her brother threw his arms around Laura as Mikey tugged at her long black gown. "Way to go, Sis!"

Laura reached down and patted her son's soft head.

"Everybody else is over there," Ted said. He pointed to the right of the stage. "I think we were the loudest clappers when you got your diploma. Right, Mikey?"

"Right, Uncle Ted."

Stacy came over and embraced Laura.

"Stacy, I'd like you to meet my brother, Ted Whalen. Ted, this is Stacy Jones, a really special friend."

Ted shook Stacy's hand and said, "Glad to meet you, Stacy. What's happened to the others?"

"I saw Mr. Nelson over there somewhere." Stacy pointed into the distance.

Laura turned to scan the crowd.

"Let's all get together. Follow me everybody." Ted grabbed Mikey by the hand and led the way over to the rest of the family. "Laura, or should I say 'Doctor', there's a surprise for you."

Laura followed blindly. She didn't even feel the persistent little tugs as Natalie clung tightly to her long black gown. Meanwhile, Nicole and Kevin played chase in the crowd despite the efforts of the adults to keep them in line. Who was playing with the kids? Aunt Hazel, Steve's aunt? Laura greeted her tearfully, chiding Hazel for lying to her about being in Madrid.

"But I was in Madrid, child," Hazel said, reaching up to cup Laura's cheek tenderly. "And I left just to be able to congratulate the family's first doctor in person! Now, listen, I do have this ache in one of my knees that just won't quit."

When Stacy crouched down to intercept Kevin before he crashed into some graduate's grandmother struggling through the crowd with a four-legged walker, she noticed a figure lurking at the edge of the crowd. Although partially obscured by spruce trees, she knew instantly. She scooped up Kevin, handing the squirming little boy to the nearest Nelson relative. Wasting no time with explanations, Stacy headed for the spruce trees.

*   *   *

"That's it, gentlemen. You should have more than enough." David had endured what seemed an unending round of photographers. Posing with the dean, with the faculty, with the President of the university. He thought it would never end. He had to find Laura.

"Andrew," he said to the dean, "it's been a real honor. Wonderful to be back in Detroit, but I need to excuse myself now."

"We'll see you at dinner tonight, David? After all, it's in your honor," Burke answered jovially.

"Of course, Andrew. Now if you will excuse me." Still in cap and gown, David hurried from the small group of lingering dignitaries. He harbored no illusions. He just needed to see Laura. Shake her hand. Hold it in his again, however briefly. She'd be surrounded by her husband and family, but that was okay. Her children would be with her too.

David had been stunned when he heard from Bill Clocker, the new chairman of surgery at University Medical School, that Laura had had another baby. A boy, Dr. Clocker thought he'd been told, but he wasn't really sure. All these months Laura had never communicated. He wondered whether rumors of his separation from Cynthia had reached her. He had found a modest apartment in Palo Alto, close to the hospital. No legal separation, no divorce talk, just separate lives. Cynthia and Ruth continued to involve themselves in their charity work. Ruth had become active in gay rights, even taking on legal work pro bono. He didn't care. The truth was, he was deeply relieved that he didn't have to live with Cynthia any longer. He had his work, and he had the memory of Laura.

Would it make a difference if Laura knew that Cynthia and he no longer lived together? David answered his own question again and again. The response was always no. Yet he still couldn't help but wonder if she knew that there would never be anybody else for him. That without her, how empty and hopeless his life always would be.

CHAPTER FIFTY-SIX

"Stacy's not here," Lucy Jones informed the young man standing in her doorway.

"Uh huh. And where might she be on such a fine day, Mrs. Jones?" Snake strained to sound polite. "I want to take her over to check out my mural."

Lucy hesitated. The last thing she had heard about Snake Rogers was that he had been in jail for drug dealing. Hadn't he gotten two years?

"I know what you're thinkin', Mrs. Jones, but I been rehabilitated. That's why I got out early. Did half my time 'cause of my successful rehabilitation. I've been workin' on myself real hard. With Stacy, I just want to pick up where we left off, you know? Man, did I miss the old neighborhood and everybody in it."

"Stacy's at the medical school graduation, Ray." Beyond the doorway, Lucy saw the shiny black car again, the one she'd been seeing off and on all day, parked down the street.

"That right?"

"She has a friend graduating," she said proudly. "Stacy plans to be a doctor, too, and Dr. Nelson, says she'll help get her into a good school," Lucy said and smiled. "Far away from here, I hope."

Snake's upper lip curled. "What you sayin', Mrs. Jones? Stacy's gonna be my lady, soon as she's outta of that fuckin' white prison you got her in." He looked beyond her into the apartment, stopping when he saw the piles of boxes scattered about.

"What's going down here?" he demanded.

"We're moving," Lucy said icily. "Just who do you think you're talking to, Ray Rogers? You just run along now. Remember how we all got along so well when Anthony and Johnny were alive, son, no need to spoil that now. Your mama is a friend of mine."

"Stacy's my woman," he insisted. "She's all I thought about when I was on the inside. I changed my life around because of her. Nobody, specially that fuckin' white doctor gonna take her away. Same one that fucked up Anthony and snuffed Johnny."

"Ray, she," Lucy began, but Snake had slammed the screen door and bolted out onto the street and into Lonnie's old Mustang. As she closed and locked the front door with a shaking hand, Lucy noticed the black car pull out and start out after Snake.

All those days in prison, thinkin' about Stacy. Plannin' to share his dreams to become a famous artist. In prison, even the art instructor said he had real talent. With pride he'd passed around the tattered copy of the newspaper articles about his murals. Someday he'd be rich and famous, and Stacy'd be his wife. He'd come to her house first thing to pick her up and together they'd go straight to look at his paintings. But she wasn't home. She was hangin' with that Nelson bitch, the one who off'd her own brother, and she didn't even know it.

He'd had plenty of time in the slammer to figure out what to do about Johnny. It was what they called a dilemma. If he told the pigs about the Nelson woman killin' Johnny, he'd be heading right back inside. Musta left fingerprints all over the Nelson house. They'd have him on assault. On the other hand, there was no proof that the bitch shot Johnny, and wasn't nobody gonna believe that she gave it up to him that night in the car. With no eyewitness and no evidence, she'd walk and he'd be the one fucked. Make her fuckin' pay some day, he decided, but for now, go back to usin' her to get those pain killers to sell again, just until he got back on his feet. Yeah, he felt guilty that he let the bitch get away with killin' his best friend, but he vowed someday he'd get true revenge. Retribution, they called it. He thought about it day and night.

Now his plans were crumbling. Rage coursed through his veins. Stacy should be with him, not with that killer bitch. All that vengeance he'd suppressed exploded to the surface. He decided to make a surprise appearance at this graduation, let the bitch know he was back, and get Stacy the hell out of there. Then he'd take her over to Theodore St. to look at his murals, and he'd explain his plans to take the project further east.

On the way over to the med school, Snake decided to drive by Theodore, take a quick glance at the mural. When he slowed Lonnie's Mustang to take a look, he couldn't see the building. He looked around, stunned. Had he taken a wrong turn? Other buildings were familiar. This was the right street. He got out of the car and stared. There had to be some mistake. He panicked and staggered forward. No, there was no building: it had been torn down. There were piles of rubble, busted walls, and bricks everywhere. His mural, his last chance, had been torn down. He teetered backward, and overcome with shock and rage, slumped against the car, his hand reaching into his pocket, touching the cold, hard gun. The fucking city deserved to die. Yes, somebody would die.

"Take it, man. I got no use for it," Lonnie had insisted as they'd sat at the kitchen table that morning admiring his new Glock. "Take it and take my wheels. Least you have a life. Lookit me sittin' here. No fuckin' dick. No Maya. You don' take this piece—" Lonnie poked the barrel of the gun into his ballooning Afro.

"Don' fuck 'round like that," Snake said, reaching for the weapon, afraid that one more brother's life would be wasted. "No way I'm goin' back into the joint, bro."

Lonnie shoved it into Snake's pocket. "First day out, no parole cop gonna jump you. Feel good to be carryin' again, man."

So it all came down to this. After all that thinkin' and all that plannin', hot rage, cold metal, and nowhere else to go.

In cap and gown, Laura stood in the midst of her family, struggling to appear interested in the fragmented tidbits of conversation while accepting congratulations and meeting her classmates' guests as the kids ran among them.

"Laura, will you take Patrick?" Steve asked with some exasperation. "I've got to corral Kevin, the little menace."

"I think this one belongs to you." David stepped up behind the Nelson clan, Kevin in tow.

Laura froze at the sound of David's voice behind her. Her heart pounded wildly, drumming into her ears. Certainly everyone could hear it.

"Dr. Monroe," Steve said, "good to see you. Thanks for catching this little guy." Steve reached for Kevin and whispered in his ear, "Go play with your Uncle Ted." Steve then offered his hand to David, saying, "I thought your speech was truly inspiring. Almost made me want to go to med school."

Laura finally turned around, holding Patrick over her left shoulder. She extended her hand to David, who held it for a long time. She managed to utter his name, yet she could not meet his eyes. Standing between Steve and David, she was completely unable to say anything else.

Mikey broke the silence as he approached with his sisters. "Dad, here're the girls. I lost Stacy."

"Mikey, this is Dr. Monroe?" Laura heard the tremble in her voice.

David reached out and shook Mikey's hand. "I remember you, Mikey. Your favorite color is green and you're an expert on cars."

Mikey beamed. "I like red now."

"He knows more about car models than I ever will," Steve said. "Now, son, Kevin's been looking for you. He's over with Uncle Ted."

Then Steve took each twin by the hand. "These are the babies you helped deliver," he said to David.

"And they're beautiful, absolutely beautiful." David looked from one twin to the other several times, crouching and patting each girl on the head. "Nicole and Natalie, as I recall."

Laura nodded.

"You don't know how lucky you are to have such a beautiful family," David looked quickly at Laura and then at Steve. "I'd give anything for this."

"You haven't met the newest member of the family," Steve said. "Here's Patrick. He's eight-and-a-half months old. Kind of tired right now, but usually a bundle of energy." To Laura, he said, "Listen, I'll take the girls over to see Aunt Hazel. She wants pictures. She's got some crazy idea about getting them into modeling."

Laura smiled. "Okay, Steve."

As Steve walked away, Laura turned so that David might see Patrick's face. Holding her breath, she watched David's expression change. At that instant, she knew. She could feel the outpouring of love for his son.

Without a word, David held out his arms. Patrick grabbed playfully for the colorful edge of David's cape, obviously intrigued by the gold and crimson embroidery. Laura released the baby. Holding Patrick close to his heart, David struggled to find the right words to say to Laura, any words at all.

CHAPTER FIFTY-SEVEN

The image of someone crouched in a clump of bushes at the edge of the crowd, grabbed Stacy's attention. She sped toward the spot where Snake was hiding, dodging graduates and their families, oblivious to startled looks as she rushed by. She almost knocked the camera from the hands of a balding black man in a trim sports coat busily snapping photos of a tall, thin graduate with short curly hair. Moving quickly, Detective Reynolds thrust the camera into the hands of his surprised daughter as he turned and followed the racing young woman.

At the rear entrance to the courtyard, the bushes parted.

"Snake, don't!" Stacy screamed.

With a steel gray pistol in hand, he took deliberate aim and fired into the crowd. Hearing Stacy's voice, Snake straightened up and turned toward the narrow path that led from one corner of the yard to an open gate. People nearby who'd heard the shot began to back away, but Stacy was blocking his path, her arms grabbing at his shirt.

"What are you doing?" she screamed.

"Done it for you," Snake snarled. Grabbing her, he pulled her forcefully through the fanning crowd. "Girl, you're coming with me. Let's go."

"No," she screamed. With a violent twist, Stacy lurched free of his grip.

In a flash, Snake thrust out his free arm to grab her, gun still smoking in his other hand.

Stacy lost her balance as she tried to evade Snake's grasp. Lurching forward, she hit the ground hard, biting her lip, tasting blood. As Snake bent to pick her up, she clutched his baggy pant leg, so that he too nearly fell. The crowd shrank back further as the gun flailed in the air.

"Get up, girl." Snake tugged at Stacy to pull her upright. "We gotta get the fuck outta here. Now!"

Behind them footsteps pounded the ground and John Reynolds arrived breathing hard, his weapon out and ready. "Police! Drop the gun," he shouted. "Drop it now. Out of the way, people!"

Snake let go of Stacy and stood up, pivoting as he did, such that the muzzle of Lonnie's Glock directly faced Reynold's chest.

For a fraction of a second Snake's and Reynold's weapons faced each, a stare of terror on each face.

Behind them, more heavy steps. Beneath them, Stacy too terrified to move. Surrounded by horrified onlookers, dropping to the ground.

Then the sharp "pop" of another gun being fired filled the air. Screams coming from everywhere.

Then Stacy heard a booming voice from behind, "John, you all right?"

"Holy shit! That you, Willard?"

The next instant, Stacy felt a crushing weight as Snake tumbled to the ground, clutching his chest, falling onto her. Frothy pink fluid bubbling from Snake's open mouth mingled with the blood flowing freely from Stacy's lip.

Terrified, Stacy struggled to get out from beneath Snake's weight. Was he dead? She didn't know, but her eyes widened in horror at the pool of blood expanding on the ground beneath them. From her position, she could see that Snake still clutched the gun.

"Help me!" Stacy tried to scream, but she had trouble catching her breath and it came out as a whimper. "Please, somebody get me out of here!"

Wriggling frantically, her heart pounding like it would burst,

Stacy was able to free her right arm and shoulder, but Snake's body still immobilized her. When she tried to push him off, she felt hot stickiness on her hand and retched, choking back the horrible vomit. Why wasn't anybody helping her?

Then she recognized Detective Reynolds as he stepped up, and with a single kick knocked the gun out of Snake's hand. Immediately he bent over and rolled Snake's body to the side, releasing Stacy.

From behind them, Stacy heard the static of a radio.

"Detective Willard here." The male voice was urgent and loud. "I need back up. There's been a shooting. Send an ambulance and a supervisor, pronto." He proceeded to give the address and exact location.

"Let's get you out of here," Detective Reynolds was saying, but Stacy was too scared to move. She stared at the gun the detective still held in one hand.

"Too many guns," she stammered.

"Too true," said Reynolds, glancing around before stuffing the gun under his belt and extending his hand. "Let me help you up."

Stacy's whole body shook with wracking sobs as she took the detective's hand and stumbled to her feet.

Screams rose from the area of the courtyard where the Nelsons had been standing. After the first shot had been fired, dozens of people had dropped to the ground as others ran — pushing and shoving. Steve Nelson had pulled his sons down into the grass, shielding them with his body. Hazel Nelson threw herself down, too, encircling the twins with her arms. Panicked men and women shouted and ran. Laura had just lifted Patrick from David's arms, her gaze locking with his.

David's eyes were huge. Patrick, this beautiful child, was his son. Still dazed by the realization that he'd been holding his own son, David hardly felt the bullet penetrate his chest but what was this searing sensation near his heart? Slowly, he slumped to his knees. He tried to speak. There were so many things he had to tell Laura. Would she reconsider? Could they raise their son together? Did she know how deeply he loved her?

Laura had ducked down, protectively covering Patrick as David fell backward onto the grass. The black embroidered robe initially obscured the dark red blood that spread rapidly, yet his eyes were still open, a small, contented smile on his face. It wasn't until David's blood-covered hand fell from his chest that Laura understood. Clutching the baby, she crawled toward him. "Get an ambulance!" she called out.

"No, David, please," she moaned as one hand reached to touch his face.

"Our son," David rasped. His eyes closed.

Laura could not see. Could not hear. She set Patrick down so she could hold David's motionless body against hers. Leaning forward, she caressed him, her hair cascading over his face. As she pulled him to her she felt the warm pool of his blood expanding. What should she do? Keep him breathing, keep the heart pumping, start an intravenous, order blood transfusions: the ABCs of trauma. But this was all different. There was too much blood. He was dying. Dying in front of her.

"Move aside, let us through," a firm voice commanded. Bystanders parted as Detective John Reynolds and a uniformed rescue squad pushed forward.

In front of the best surgeons in the world, many of whom David had trained and to whom he had dedicated his career, his life ebbed away. They found no pulse, faint and erratic respiratory efforts, massive blood loss.

He was lifted onto the gurney and moved toward the ambulance that would rush him to City Hospital Trauma Center, the center that he himself had developed. Laura, having picked up Patrick, stood back a few feet, soothing the squealing baby. Suddenly Steve was there, his arms around her, telling her everyone was safe. Sobs burst from her then, and Laura allowed Steve to comfort her, letting him believe that her tears were out of concern for her family.

"You all right?" Morris Willard asked Stacy. Wrapped in Reynolds' sport coat, she rocked from side to side, staring at the green ambulance that held Snake's dead body. Reynolds, a uniformed officer at his side, walked toward them just as Willard was about to offer Stacy a ride home.

"It's okay, young lady. The officers over there have gotten in touch with your mother to let her know you're okay. If you go with this officer, he'll make sure you get home safely," Reynolds said.

"Okay," Stacy whispered. She began to remove the jacket, now stained with her blood and Snake's blood, but Reynolds slipped it back up over her shoulders. "You keep it for now. I'll come see you and your mother later."

The detectives watched Stacy get into the patrol car in silence. Then Willard turned to Reynolds and pointed at his shirt. "Got no vest," he commented. "First night out with you, the vest lecture. Ring a bell?"

"My daughter's graduation. Is nothing sacred in this city?" Reynolds clapped Willard on the shoulder. "Think the vest woulda stopped that Glock?"

"Course it woulda stopped the bullet, that's why they call it bulletproof."

"If that's your way of askin' for my undyin' gratitude, Willard, I'll think about it. What the hell you doing here anyway?"

"Thought I'd keep tabs on Mr. Rogers, knowin' that he just got outta jail. He hangs out with that Lonnie Greenwood. Remember the Nam vet in City Hospital? Fool got his dick shot off? My first case. Never did figure where the girlfriend got the gun or where it disappeared to. Anyway, back to Rogers. It dawned on me to check prints."

"What prints?"

"Lookin' for a match. From the Nelson house and the Roger's kid's. Now he's got an arrest record."

"And?"

"Bingo — a match. Now I'm kickin' myself for not bringin' the kid to the station on suspicion of assault. Was on my way to tell you after your daughter's graduation. Drove by that Greenwood kid's place. I don't know why, hunch, maybe."

"Go on, Willard. You've got my attention."

"So comin' out of his house is Mr. Rogers, here. I follow him in Greenwood's car to the Jones house. He stays for a few minutes then I trail him over to Theodore. They tore down his paintings, by the way, the whole building. Then over here. Didn't want to collar him on the Nelson assault till I discussed it with you."

Reynolds nodded.

"Fuckin' shame I got here too late for the good doctor." Willard paused as a siren pierced the air. "Why do you think the punk wanted to kill Dr. Monroe?"

"We may never know," said Reynolds as he pointed to the Glock, now sequestered in an evidence bag. "Where'd he get the gun?"

"Don' know, probably from that Greenwood guy. I been watchin' the old Alexandrine gang. I ever told you? My mama lives down there."

Reynolds looked approvingly at Willard. "A cop who knows the streets is a better cop. You proved that today. Good work, Detective."

"The girl," Willard's eyes followed the patrol car that had pulled out with Stacy in the back seat. "She knows Rogers, that's obvious. Grew up in the 'hood. Poor kid."

"Meaning?"

"Meanin' he didn't need a gun that night. She let him in, remember?"

Reynolds shook his head and frowned. "I'm not sayin' you're right or wrong, just that we can't do a damn thing about it either way. The perp's in that ambulance, dead. Why drag a young kid like that into a dead case? You're gonna have beaucoup paperwork to fill out already. I suggest we tell it like it was here this afternoon, forget what might have happened that night at the Nelson house."

Willard nodded. "Simplify the paperwork and make life much more pleasant for that sweet Jones girl. She's been through enough."

CHAPTER FIFTY-EIGHT

Saint Paul's Catholic Church on Lake Shore Drive in Grosse Pointe was filled to overflowing the following Wednesday. Faculty from University Medical School and staff from City Hospital filed in through the huge doors and jammed the center aisle lined with floral sprays. Hushed tones expressed the shock that this could have happened to such a young, vibrant man at the peak of professional success.

Laura was there, settled into one of the back pews. Upon learning that David had died in the ambulance before even arriving at his beloved hospital, she had made two decisions. First, she would not go to Florida the next day as planned. Her family would, taking all the kids but Patrick; she would remain in Detroit with her son to attend David's funeral. There was so much distraction with all the relatives here that Laura's contrived excuse, finalizing some record-keeping details at the hospital, sounded plausible.

The truth was that Laura desperately needed time alone. Alone, except for David's child. Patrick would remember nothing, of course, but Laura would know that Patrick had been at his father's funeral.

That much she could do for David.

The second decision Laura made was to call Nick Monroe, David's brother. During their first dinner in Montreal, when Laura and David discussed what was important to them in life, he'd told her about being raised as a Catholic. Because of Cynthia, he'd had a Presbyterian wedding, thus ending his Catholicism. But he did tell Laura that he wanted to return to his religion.

Laura identified herself to Nick only as "Laura, a friend." No last name. She pleaded with Nick to prevail against Cynthia in making David's funeral arrangements.

"My sister-in-law can be a very difficult woman. Very used to getting her way," Nick bluntly replied. "Certainly Cynthia won't allow it. Maybe David did tell you he wanted to return to the church, I'm a devout Catholic myself, but there's nothing I can do about it. Final arrangements are Cynthia's responsibility. I'm sorry. It really is too bad."

Laura persisted. "Then threaten her with exposure." She apologized before continuing on, telling Nick about Cynthia's relationship with Ruth. "Blatant exposure would make her change her mind, if she is truly that socially conscious."

Nick Monroe hesitated. "David told me about Cynthia, but a threat like that. I don't know."

"Please think about it." The passion in Laura's voice was impossible to ignore. "I can only tell you how sincerely David wanted this. It's the only thing that you'll be able to do for your brother ever again." And the only thing I can ever do for him, she echoed silently.

Laura's words had prevailed. David's wish was honored.

The Sacred Heart Seminary Church, like nearly every other building in the neighborhood, had suffered damage during the riots. Located on Linwood and Chicago, the most obvious difference to this Catholic church from others was that its Jesus, lying in the manger outside, was now black, its ivory skin tone painted over during the riots. Inside the church, the sober congregation listened to the priest speak of forgiveness and healing. He bemoaned Ray Roger's lost innocence and the loss of an entire generation of young black men to the war, to the riots, and to rage.

Her eyes clear and dry, she was clean for good, Leona Rogers sat with her two young children in the first row, only a few feet away from the open casket where Snake lay. Nearby was a handmade poster displaying a photo of Snake's mural and copies of the newspaper article that had touted Snake as a promising young urban artist.

Several rows back, Stacy sat with her mama and younger sisters. Sister Mary Agnes and Sister Portia held rosary beads. Stacy had not said much since the graduation ceremony, not to Lucy, nor to John Reynolds or Morris Willard, both of whom had shown up on Alexandrine Avenue to check on Stacy later that day. What could she say? That she'd lost her last connection to her brothers? Snake had been so faithful to Johnny. Life had betrayed him. She had betrayed him.

As the priest led the small band of mourners in "Rock of Ages," tears started to trickle down Stacy's face, and she rose to leave. Lucy nodded an "okay" at her, seeming to agree that Stacy didn't belong here, not at this funeral, not in this neighborhood. Just a few more days and Lucy would have her family moved to their own little house just off Hamilton Avenue in Highland Park.

Stacy slowed her step only slightly when she noticed Detective Willard alone in the back row of the church. Nodding his head in rhythm with the hymn, he smiled sadly at her. Stepping out into the sunshine, Stacy squinted, looking around at the shiny piles of broken glass and concrete rubble that littered the curb where Lonnie and Willie stood smoking cigarettes. She ignored them both and began to walk back to Alexandrine. She had a few more things to pack and then she was leaving this place forever.

At the service at Saint Paul's, Laura positioned herself as inconspicuously as possible in the back of the imposing cathedral, cradling Patrick in her arms. She wondered why people were looking her way until she realized that hers was the only baby in the crowded church.

Cynthia arrived wearing a black sheath, which clung to her shapely figure. Her coiffed hair was pulled up into a fashionable bun with a few tendrils peeking out from around the black lace veil. She sat beside Nick Monroe's family.

Three monsignors presided over the solemn high funeral Mass. A full choir and the huge pipe organ filled the church with dolorous hymns. Laura never really heard the eulogy. She couldn't see or hear anything. She could only feel. Feel David's body with hers on that one night, their only night. She moved automatically through the sitting and standing routines of the mass. As rich baritones nearly shook the nave of the church with "How Great Thou Art," Laura carried Patrick up the long center aisle to receive Communion. Soon the exit procession began, led by the clergy and followed by David's casket, which was carried by six somber department chairmen. As altar boys swung incense canisters, the cortege slowly progressed up the center aisle. Cynthia Monroe was escorted by Nick. His family followed as vaguely familiar Latin hymns filled the air.

Patrick had woken up after dozing through the latter part of the service, and Laura rocked him as silent tears streamed down her face. When Nick passed by the last pew in the cavernous church, he caught Laura's eye. He hesitated, briefly holding up the procession, as his gaze locked on her and the child.

Later, he looked for Laura at the graveside, but she had not accompanied the mourners to the cemetery. Instead, Laura had held Patrick David tightly in her arms, watching the scores of people file out. She'd been the last person to leave the church.

John Reynolds stood by the rented Ford Fairlane as Laura, Patrick in her arms, approached in a blur of tears. He thought he understood her grief, and wondered if she thought, as he did, that the gunman had aimed at her rather than Monroe. Regardless, the official report stated that what had occurred that Sunday was a random shooting by a malcontent.

"Seems you always have a baby in your arms," he said pleasantly.

She shifted Patrick as his little fingers playfully tugged at the black crocheted shawl covering her shoulders and hiding the scooped neckline of the same dress she'd worn that first dinner with David. "Detective Reynolds, it must seem that way."

"I'd like to talk to you for a minute. Off the record. Agreed?"

"All right, Detective."

"Did he rape you that night?"

"What?" Stunned, Laura's whole body jerked forward. She felt she might stumble. So Detective Reynolds knew? She'd been on the verge of getting out of Detroit. Now, it was over. The police knew. She couldn't fight it any longer. Her children. Terror ripped through her at blinding speed.

"We found your blood type, B-negative, not the most common type, under his fingernails. And remember when I told you about the blonde hair?"

Laura steadied herself and looked at the detective for a long moment. "Yes," she said simply, unable to stem the tears flowing down her cheek.

Reynolds nodded. "My hunch was that someone had seen you. Too many coincidences."

"Snake Rogers," she said faintly.

"Well, he's no longer a problem."

Not daring to say anything more, she adjusted Patrick over her shoulder and groped in her bag for a tissue.

Reynolds removed his handkerchief from his suit pocket and handed it to her.

Laura took it and wiped at her tears. "Remember when you warned me not to make a mistake I would always regret?" she stammered.

Reynolds stepped forward and put his hands on her shoulders. "Laura, you're a good person. Leave Detroit behind and don't look back."

The detective leaned in to give her a quick hug and started to walk away before turning, "One more thing."

"Yes?"

"The gun. We know it was a .38. Get rid of the gun."

"Yes," she said. "I did. And thank you."

"Oh, and what I said about leaving Detroit, doesn't mean you can't come back for Susan's wedding." John Reynolds smiled as he waved good-bye.

Allowing her tears to fall, Laura placed Patrick in the car seat and drove slowly along the same streets ravaged by fire and desperation nearly four years earlier. So much had happened, so much lost, so much her fault. Feeling as torn and tentative as the damaged city she drove through, she wondered whether either would ever recover.

Tomorrow she'd be leaving. A new home. A new future. Simple, not complicated with fear. A resolve to make it up to Steve. She'd failed him in so many ways. And the eternal optimism of five children with their whole lives in front of them. And always, the memory of David.